Call Me By My Rightful Name

Isidore Okpewho

Africa World Press, Inc.

P.O. Box 1892
Trenton, NJ 08607

P.O. Box 48
Asmara, ERITREA

Africa World Press, Inc.

| P.O. Box 1892 | P.O. Box 48 |
| Trenton, NJ 08607 | Asmara, ERITREA |

Book and Cover Design: Roger Dormann

Library of Congress Cataloging-in-Publication Data

Okpewho, Isidore.
  Call me by my rightful name / by Isidore Okpewho.
    p. cm.
  ISBN 1-59221-190-9 -- ISBN 1-59221-191-7 (pbk.)
  1. African American men--Fiction. 2. Yoruba (African people)--Fiction. 3. Americans--Nigeria--Fiction. 4. Nigeria--Fiction. I. Title.

PR9387.9.O38C35 2004
823'.914--dc22

                2003023580

In treasured memory of my father

DAVID OMOJEMITE OKPEWHO

We may digress and ponder how a son of the descendants of Obi Ezechi ran all the way from Ejime to Igbuzo, a distance of about 25 kilometres. It is said that he did not know Igbuzo before. He was only told that his great grandparents migrated from that town. He was a farmer and it is said that on occasions an animal called atu would go to eat all the yams in his farm, even though his farm was in the middle of other people's farms. Nobody could understand why it was so until one day he left on a race—nonstop—through the 25 kilometres between Ejime and Igbuzo and after staying in the sacred bosom of Mother Oboshi, for several days, he came out of the stream carrying huge stones and shouting that Mother Oboshi had crowned him. After parading himself with the stones on his head, he went straight to Umuogwo and to the spot where Obi Ezechi lived when he was alive, and deposited the stones there.

—Oral testimony from Igbuzo, Nigeria. *Jos Oral History and Literature Texts: Western Igbo,* ed. D.C. Ohadike and R.N. Sham

Part One

TIGER

Hush, hush, somebody's calling my name
Hush, hush, somebody's calling my name
Hush, hush, somebody's calling my name:
Oh my Lord, oh my Lord, what shall I do?

—Traditional Spiritual

One

IN A LITTLE VILLAGE, DEEP IN THE HEART OF *Yorubaland, at the burnt end of a dusky harmattan afternoon, two aged twins indulge themselves in the meager comfort of their mud hut, biding their time for an all too routine supper. They are so old, these women, they can quite literally see time pacing about the house. So tender they have learnt to welcome the cruel art it continually works on their bodies. So resigned to fate they no longer feel thankful to be alive nor desirous to die.*

They have never married, these sisters, and have no children to outlive them. As far as the village knows, they are the only survivors of their old pedigree. But they are so old the village sees no need of any history beyond them. For they have played so many roles in the life of the community that each role has become a time marker, more highly valued, in the oral memory of the people, than the combined wisdom of successive rulers or the feats of the brave. Old men are often heard to say, "A long time ago, in the days when our two mothers bared their buttocks to the invaders, and drove them off our borders..." Or they may say, not knowing any better, "If our venerable mothers did not encourage the white man to come among us, would our sons have been the first to go to school in all of Yorubaland?" Older women may tell younger ones, "Look what you have done to the dance our two mothers taught us in our youth."

Although the public roles of the sisters live vividly in the oral history of the people, their private lives, even the details of their family history, have received far less attention. True, the community has recently fortified the mud walls of their hut and roofed it with corrugated iron sheets to save it from the ravages of rainfall. The people have done this in gratitude for that sense of history the sisters have bestowed upon them and to preserve these living monuments. Otherwise, they have been content to leave the twins very much to themselves and their modest effects on the outskirts of the village: a lean patch of yams, plantains, and greens, and a goat so old it sustains the women more with the warmth of its company than with any promise of meat.

1

Hence no one, in this grateful but negligent village, is in the least aware of the one incident that has continued to haunt the lives of these women, although it marks the dawn of that history the people have come to cherish. On this fateful harmattan afternoon, one of the women is sitting on the front porch of the house, watching the goat as it squats in the yard a few feet from her. The other woman is minding the fire in the backyard, where a pot of sliced yams is boiling. Suddenly the woman on the front porch is roused by an instinct and rises from her seat. She does not know what it is. But it agitates her whole body and causes her to feel a little warm. She adjusts the wrapper round her loins. Her breathing comes a little faster. A certain cheerfulness lights her face. Her limbs tremble lightly. She begins to feel like dancing.

Kehinde. Kehinde. She cannot help communicating the feeling to her sister, so she trots to the backyard. Kehinde. I don't know what has come over me.

Like what? asks her sister, surveying the other in mild astonishment.

A certain feeling...

Like...joy? For there is a dash of cheer on Taiwo's face.

Not joy. Compulsion.

Compulsion! To do what?

To...to dance. She begins to wiggle her frail body lightly, her arms swaying to a silent measure. Don't you feel anything?

Kehinde reflects for a moment. True, she is touched by a tolerable lightness of being. But this may be no more than a sympathy born of the bond that unites them as twins.

No, she says, returning to her cooking. But she cannot ignore her sister. So she asks, Are you all right, Taiwo?

I am, says the other. I am. Just...feel like...dancing. Do you think you might...want to join me in...dancing?

Are you serious? says Kehinde, turning again to the fire. Even the goat might laugh.

A little disappointed, but hardly dampened, Taiwo turns round and wiggles slowly back to the house. Once or twice Kehinde turns to look at her and shakes her head. Is something amiss? Could it be...might Taiwo be losing control? Or perhaps the time has....She refuses to entertain the thought, knowing well that whatever happens to her twin sister will happen to her too. At their age, strange sensations are the rule rather than the exception, almost daily. But, to feel like dancing! Hmmm....

Two

Boston, Massachusetts. A voice came one night to Otis Tiger Hampton as he slept. It spoke in a strange tongue, with words to this effect: *Ifa divination was done for Oyepolu, scion of those who performed cult rites at Ife. He was told it was because he had ignored the ancestral rites that his life was in disarray. He was told to visit his ancestral shrine and pay his respects. Once he did that, life would be good for him again. He did as he was told. Things became well for him.*

Rites. Ancestors. Shrine...Otis had not woken suddenly, as from a bad dream. There had been no dream. So he remembered nothing when he woke up in the morning. He had heard none of those words. They had not been spoken into his ears, but implanted into his instincts. From this point, he was conscious only of a burden of duty he could not grasp.

It is Otis's twenty-first birthday. His teammates have put a party together for him in a private residence in Cambridge. Popcorn. Some nuts. Kentucky Fried. Miller's. Bud. Some soda. Some grass, discreetly shared. Music so loud your ears want to scream. Couples snuggling as they dance. Or just talking and laughing.

Otis is not fond of alcohol but has had a few. He sits in a corner of the room, trying to cool off. Norma, Jamaica-born and Brooklyn-bred, is with him, her cheek against his hairy chest as they talk softly. Observing a mild vacancy in his eyes, she talks more, to get his attention. But his attention is divided. *Journeys. The longest journeys begin from your doorstep. The doorstep of your home. You must find it.* Otis makes an effort to stay composed.

Coach Gene Doherty is happy to celebrate the coming of age of his team's MVP—highest average in points and assists in the collegiate East. Doherty has had a couple of beers, with some nuts and popcorn. But this isn't his kind of music. He's also content to look the other way while the

3

grass passes between hands. It's just a party. Let them have their fun. They'll get over it before Monday.

Doherty is standing outside the room, talking basketball with Eddie "Stonewall" Goldberg who, having fallen out with his girlfriend, is wall-flowering. The coach looks at his watch in the dim light. It says nine fifty.

"Well, Stonewall," he says. "Think I'll leave you guys and turn in. Got the gift?"

"Sure, Coach."

"Okay. Let's go."

Doherty returns to a room drenched in music and smoke, and from the doorway he claps for attention. In a moment the music stops, the couples disengage. Norma lifts her head from Otis's chest, but leaves her hand there. Everyone turns to the coach.

"Uh," Doherty clears his throat. "I hate to break the party, but it's getting a little late for some of us who've already had our fling."

Grunts of "Aw, Coach!" A few laughs.

"I'll be gone in a minute. Before I do, I'd like to say how very pleased I am to be here with you all tonight. I should probably tell Otis how I felt on a night like this a hundred years ago. But I guess he feels that way already. If you haven't seen it on Norma's face and hands, that's your problem."

A chorus of laughs. Norma withdraws her hand, but hides her face in Otis's chest. Another round of laughs.

"You know what they say about turning twenty-one. For most people, that's the start of the race. And if you do a great race, why, it'd be great to breast the tape ahead of the pack. Except, the thing about *starting* the race of life is, you're already heading for the tape. Know what I mean?"

A few guffaws. Someone rubs Otis's head and mocks, "Yeah, old man!"

"I'd like to conclude by wishing Tiger a *very* happy birthday and a great race ahead. Stonewall, let's have the stuff."

Goldberg emerges from a corner of the room with a large gift in wraps and hands it to Otis. Otis unwraps it carefully, revealing a brass tiger lurching forward from a plaster base, a basketball between its paws. Hums of admiration. Otis kisses the figure and lifts it above his head for all to see. From the bar, Chip Benedetto comes forward with a bottle of champagne he's been quietly uncorking.

"Here's to Tiger!" The cork plops to the ceiling. Loud cheers. Benedetto raises the bottle over Otis's head, and lets the bubbles overflow on him.

"Hey, come on, man!" Otis protests mildly.

As the others look for their paper cups, Coop Williams shouts from the corner, "Hey, Norma, you gonna let all that juice go to waste?"

Norma turns Otis's face toward her, sucks up some of the champagne on it and kisses him full in the mouth. More cheers. The champagne is served out. Stonewall starts the team's battle song, *We'll dunk 'em good and dead...* They all give it two hearty choruses.

"Goodnight, everyone," says Coach Doherty. "Have fun, but don't forget: 5 p.m., Monday. You know where."

He sneaks out to a chorus of "Aw, Coach!" More music and dancing. More booze and grass. Everybody is having a great time.

"Whooh, what a night!"

Otis and Norma are cruising down Mass Avenue to Norma's off-campus apartment near Central Square. Between lights, Norma rests her sleepy head on Otis's shoulder. To control his distractions, Otis tries talking about the party. But Norma is hardly there. So he maneuvers himself into his private fantasies. The certainty that Bradley University will win the collegiate championship this year. The Celtics. Everybody seems to assume he'll join the Celtics next season. But why not the Lakers? Besides, he's lived all his life in Boston, the West Coast might be nice for a change.

Norma too. Smart. Pretty. Great company. Radcliffe radical. Black nationalist. Always talking about the great kingdoms of old Africa, and that we're all proud princes and princesses. That's cool. But would their affair survive a move to the West? And who cares about all that Africa stuff, anyway? *Ifa says of him who has forgotten his forefathers: If he does not take care of the departed ones, there will be no one on earth to take care of him. Whether your forebears are in heaven or on earth, care for them, or your affairs will come to grief. It may be tomorrow. It may be next year.*

The West Coast? Something suddenly stirs in Otis. A doubt grows. He wants to listen. But it is too deep inside. And he is at the wheel. With Norma asleep, the silence becomes too heavy. Otis turns on an FM station. The volume is loud. The pounding beats of a drum suddenly assail his ears. Norma lifts her head, surprise written all over her face.

"Sorry, baby," says Otis. He fumbles with the volume control to

5

reduce the noise.

"How long have I been out?" Norma asks, rubbing her eyes.

Otis does not reply. A strange sensation is creeping over him. Not of cold nor of warmth. Some kind of agitation. First it's mild, but soon it grows to a throb. His arms and legs begin to shake. The next lights are some ten yards ahead. Otis's hands are rattling on the wheel. Norma, whose question hasn't been answered, looks at him, confused, not sure what's going on. The drum music presses on.

"Hey," Otis shouts, looking helplessly at his shaking limbs.

"What's the matter, Otey?"

The car begins to veer to the left. The lights turn red. The car ahead of them slows to a halt. Otis fumbles for control, but his limbs are obeying a different order. Now his lips are shaking, rattling some incomprehensible sounds. The car is dangerously close to the one in front. On a sudden impulse, Norma screams, grabs the wheel, thrusts her left foot forward upon Otis's right, and presses on the brakes. Too late: she's jolted the other car.

The driver of that car storms out, shouting, "Hey, what's going on here?"

He walks to the back of his car, examines the point of impact, but finds his fender is only mildly bruised. He looks up at the offending car. Walks to its driver's window.

"What's the problem, buddy?"

The music is still on. Otis is ejaculating his strange speech with even greater agitation. Norma struggles to wind down Otis's window to offer an explanation.

"Sorry, but..."

The other driver cups his ear to indicate he can't hear what she's saying. Struggling to break through the babel of sounds, Norma turns off the engine. Suddenly, as one released from a spell, Otis shakes his head, looks first at Norma, then at the other man, and back again at Norma.

"What happened?"

"*You* tell me!" she says. "You nearly got us all killed."

Still baffled, Otis begins to climb out of his car. The lights have turned green again. The cars behind are honking cacophonously. Norma follows Otis out of the car, ignoring the build-up behind and the honking.

"We just hit this guy's car," she explains. They move to the point of impact. She ignores it, and instead stares at Otis's eyes, wondering what came over him. "Are you alright?"

"Yeah, I'm fine."

"Are you sure?"

"Yeah, I'm okay."

The drivers behind them have grown impatient and drive off on the next lane. Some scream curses as they pass. Luckily, all this has gone on without a police presence. Otis's eyes are truly apologetic as he surveys the damage, then looks up at the owner of the bruised car. Although he is still confused about the drift of things, he is about to offer an apology when the man holds up a hand.

"It's okay," the man says. "Just be careful, that's all."

"Thank you, sir."

As he and Norma walk back to their car, Otis turns to look at her. He is as confused about what may have happened as he is about her place in the scheme of things. The look in her eyes is no less quizzical, even a little frightened. She is the first to break the silence as they get in the car and belt up.

"What happened?"

Otis shakes his head, signifying innocence. He turns the ignition key and drives off. But the flourish of drum music is still on, because, in the confusion to turn off the engine, Norma forgot to turn off the radio too. So no sooner does Otis drive a few yards than he is beset by the same sensation as before. Again he is driven into a state of frenzy, his whole body shaking, his mouth ejaculating strange, unintelligible words, and his fingers now working free of the wheel as though being steadily pried by an invisible hand. The car veers off, threatening the car in the next lane. On a sudden and frightened impulse, Norma grabs the wheel with her left hand, then presses on the brakes, bringing the car to a screaming halt. Another chorus of horns. Cars behind quickly break, and curses fly.

"Quick," says Norma, opening her door. "Move over, Otey. I'm taking over from here."

"What are you doing?" asks a bewildered Otis. With the sudden cessation of the music, he has recovered from his trance-like state.

"I don't know," says Norma, taking control of the wheel. "We can talk about that later. Right now we're going to *your* place. So be steady, okay?"

Before turning the engine on again, she has enough presence of mind to turn off the radio. This time, they are not so lucky. For though the angry drivers have moved on, a police vehicle has drawn right up with a short warning sound of the siren, the arrest lights flashing. Great, thinks Norma: two blacks caught in an offending car by a cop, deep in the night! Keep a cool head! Put hands firmly on the wheel! Otis, too, can feel the danger. Moments later, with a calculated glance at the rear-view mirror, Norma sees a white cop adjusting his gun holster as he walks towards them. Very carefully, she winds down her window and just as carefully returns her hand to the wheel.

"Don't look at him, Otis," she warns, in a suppressed scream. "Just lay back on your seat and pretend you're sick as hell."

The policeman leans over Norma's window, one hand on the roof of the car, the other finger-hooking his hip just above the gun. His eyes quickly survey the two black youngsters. He is struck by the hulky male in the passenger seat.

"Hi," says Norma, with a brief and uncertain smile.

"What seems to be the problem?"

"My boyfriend was driving. But he complained about being ill. So I made him stop the car so I'd take over."

Hand on stomach and eyes shut, Otis tries to play the part assigned him.

"In the middle of the traffic?"

"I'm sorry," says Norma. "I guess I wasn't thinking. The way he was carrying on, he could have run us off the road."

The policeman continues to look them over, without changing his posture.

"Where you guys coming from?"

With what they have on, it would be foolish to lie.

"A party. It was his birthday, so his teammates put up a little something for him."

The policeman is reasonably certain that he recognizes the hunk sitting by the young woman. Yeah, the jock. Thinks that gives him a right to fuck up the traffic.

"Pull over to the side and step out of the car."

"What?" asks Norma.

"I believe my meaning is quite clear," says the cop. His voice has risen more than a little and comes through with calculated menace. "I said pull over to the side and step out of the fuckin' car!"

Norma pulls over. She and Otis step out quietly. Neither of them has any illusions about the risks they face. In no time, two other police cars have pulled up behind the arresting officer's, their flashing lights lending added attention to the scene. The arresting officer has walked over to Norma and Otis. Now he has company, he has less need to be extra careful dealing with the black youngsters. He is chewing a gum.

"Put your hands to the back of your head and turn around."

Otis and Norma comply, without compromising their dignity. In fact, they make sure not to appear threatened by the cop. Norma masks a smile poised between courtesy and disdain. Otis abandons his little act and, turning around to face the car, gives the cop a far from friendly look.

"You got a problem with me, man?"

"No, I don't have a problem with you," Otis answers from the side of his face.

"Course you don't." The officer gives him a hard push. "Lean over, asshole."

A scowl flashes across Otis' brow. *Ogun kills on the right and destroys on the left. He kills on the left and destroys on the right. He kills swiftly in the house and swiftly in the fields. He kills the child with the iron toy in its hands. He kills the thief and the owner of the goods. He kills the master of the house, then smears his blood on the hearth. But the other gods hated Ogun for his anger. He was asked to make sacrifice, so they would welcome him among them. Ogun made sacrifice....*

Otis blinks hard, clenches his teeth, and swallows. But Norma does not disguise her outrage.

"Is this really necessary? He's done everything you asked."

"Look, are you questioning my authority?"

"No, but you're just throwing it around. If you're charging us with something, go right ahead. But you've got no right to treat us like animals."

The policeman gives her a hard look, restrained from doing more only by the approach of two other officers from the backup cars. One of them turns out to be black.

"Where they coming from?" asks the white one.

"A party. So they tell me."

He kicks Otis's feet apart and begins to paw him over. The other officers get into Otis's car and check through the inside for narcotics.

"May I see your licenses?" says the arresting officer.

"If I can have my handbag," says Norma, curtly.

The black officer hands her a handbag from between the two front seats. Otis pulls out his wallet. Both licenses in hand, the arresting officer walks over to his car to check them out. When he returns he is told by his colleagues that Otis's car is clean. Motherfuckers, he thinks.

"So what makes you think you have a right to hold up traffic?" he asks, handing back the licenses. Norma and Otis do not respond. "I asked you a question."

"Why don't you go ahead and make your report," says Norma. "I bet you'd love that."

The remark stops the officer's gum-chewing. "Look," he says, "you nearly caused a string of accidents out there, and you have the nerve to stand here and sass me? I can book you for holding up traffic, endangering lives, obstructing an officer of the law in the performance of his duty, and a whole bunch of other offenses I won't even bother to mention. Now, am I making myself clear enough?"

Norma looks away. Otis still has a faint smile on his face. The officer, uneasy in the presence of his black colleague, writes out a ticket, throws it into Otis's car, and walks away with the others.

Norma returns to the driver's seat. Although she was heading for Otis's dorm, it makes more sense to change plans now.

"I'm taking you to Quincy," she says. "I don't know what came over you back there, but it's nothing we can handle by ourselves."

"Wait a minute, girl. Wait. Let's talk about this first."

"In the middle of the traffic? Otey, *please*."

"Yea, but, we just can't go back to my folks this time of night. What do we tell them—have you thought about that?"

"No, but do we have a choice? You did some scary stuff back there, Otey. I'm not sure I'd know what to do if you got into that state again tonight."

Otis is too tired to argue further. He's not happy with the decision and for a moment thinks of making a point about the time of night. *The sparrow builds its nest, then curves its entrance downward. The nest is neither on water nor on dry land. It just curves downward...*

"Okay," Otis says, vacantly.

Four eighty-six Cabot Drive, Quincy. Quiet, middle-class neighborhood. Spain, the white labrador, barks so insistently Otis Hampton Sr. is forced out of his sleep. He sits up and squints out at the driveway. Who might this be...at this time of night? He reaches for his glasses and looks again.

"Who is it?" His wife Melba turns with some irritation.

"Oh, God," Hampton says, shaking his head. "It's Junior and Norma." He looks up the wall. "It's two o'clock in the morning! What on earth..."

Norma tries to put Otis's arm around her neck and support him into the house. Otis declines the offer and walks determinedly towards the front porch. Norma runs back to the car. She turns off the lights and ignition, then locks the doors.

"Hm," grunts Hampton "Maybe a problem out there."

"What?" asks his wife.

"I don't know. I'll go down and look."

He puts on his robe and goes out of the room, switching on the lights above the stairway. Otis has made it up the steps to the front porch and fishes for the front door key. Spain, pacified, whimpers and wags its tail as Norma hurries up the steps to the porch. The door swings open as Otis tries to insert his key.

"Hi, dad," he says. His face is heavy.

"Hey, Junior, what...?"

Otis simply waves apologetically and walks on up the stairs to his bedroom. On the way he meets his mother, who is even more surprised at the return of the pair. No one expected to see them after the birthday luncheon earlier in the afternoon.

"What's the matter, baby?" Melba clutches her robe, looking closely into her son's eyes.

"Nothing, mom, I just want to go and sleep. I'll see you in the morning, okay?"

As Otis goes into his room, his parents turn to Norma. She can see the question in their eyes, but she is just as baffled as they are. She simply looks aside, shakes her head, and tosses up her hands.

"Well, what's with him?" Hampton settles into a chair. He sighs in a way to suggest there might have been a quarrel between the two. As Norma paces about uneasily, Melba tries to get to the point.

"I don't recall ever seeing you two carry on like this. What happened, or don't you want to talk about it?"

"Oh, we didn't have a fight, Mrs. Hampton, if that's what you mean," says Norma. "He just started...raving in the car, saying things even *he* didn't understand. He lost control of the wheel, and got us into trouble a couple of times. Mrs. Hampton, I don't *know* what's happening to Otis. I-I-I..."

Her eyes are misty. She cups her mouth, to fight back the tears. Melba Hampton comes closer and embraces her.

"All right," she says. "You all try to get some sleep. We'll talk about it in the morning. Go on now."

Husband and wife look at each other as Norma climbs upstairs. They're at a loss for words. Raving and jabbering are not things they can associate with their son. Saying things even he doesn't understand: but what are they? After a brief speechless moment, Hampton merely raises his brow, shakes his head, sighs, and rises from the chair.

"Maybe they can tell us more in the morning," he says. "Let's go back to sleep."

Two twenty-five in the morning. Hampton slowly walks up to the room. His wife doesn't immediately follow. She has questions but not the courage to ask them. Please, Lord, not my only child, she says under her breath. She walks timidly up the stairs.

Otis has been staring up at the ceiling from the bed. Norma has given up asking questions for which she receives no clear answers. Drifting off to sleep, she throws an arm across Otis' body, partly for support, partly to be sure he will be there when she wakes up.

Hampton and Melba finally settle back to sleep, but only for a short time. As though straight out of a nightmare, they hear screaming from their son's room. Norma's voice is struggling to subdue Otis. One moment he's wailing, the next he's silent His parents are startled as Norma rushes from Otis's room and bangs on their door.

"Mr. Hampton, Mrs. Hampton! Come quick and look at Otis. Please wake up and see for yourselves!"

Ignoring his robe, Hampton jumps out of bed and dashes toward his son's room, his wife following close behind. Norma is gripped between tears and bewilderment. Sitting up and eyes wide open, Otis is spiritedly chanting a sequence of clipped phrases that are entirely outside anyone's frame of reference. Hampton is baffled to see his son in a state nearly as comical as it is terrifying. But he recovers quickly, bending over him and trying to steady him.

"Junior! Junior!" he shouts, trying hard to check his rising emotion. "Junior! Pull yourself together, man. Hey, Junior! Stop it."

Otis continues his chanting, obviously recognizing nothing or no one. His mother turns aside from the fearful spectacle, sobbing heavily and intoning again and again: You only gave me but one child, Lord. Please, don't take him away from me. Hampton, momentarily distracted by his wife's condition, wishes he could be left alone with the boy. He tries to ignore her, holding on to his son in hopes the strange paroxysm will wear itself out. Otis continues his agitated gibberish. Finally, in a climatic outburst, his arms flail wildly, his head swings from side to side, and the mysterious performance comes to a close in phrases that register themselves more as sound than as sense: *Barmy yo, yea! yea! Barmy yo, yea! yea!*

When it is all over, Otis heaves a deep sigh and opens his eyes. Realizing he has been through this before, he lowers his head in embarrassment. He soon recovers himself, raising his head to ask, "It got to me again, didn't it?"

His father pats him on the shoulder. "It's alright, son. It's alright," he says. He clenches his teeth to steady himself as much as his son. "Just...let it go. Try to sleep. Put it all behind you, and...just go to sleep."

Melba Hampton leads Norma quietly downstairs to the living room. She wants to find out what the girl may know about the root of Otis' strange behavior. But Norma can hardly go beyond the familiar sequence of events: the convulsive ejaculation of strange words, the loss of wheel control, the slight accident, the encounter with the policeman. Suddenly, however, she remembers something else: Otis's behavior seems to have some connection with some music that was playing on the car radio. Norma recalls that the first seizure subsided when the car stopped, and that Otis's second seizure began when she restarted the car...and the music was still on.

"Music?" asks Hampton, who has left Otis and rejoined the women. "What kind of music?"

"I don't know," says Norma. "Some kind of drum music. More like African drum music, or maybe jazz. I really couldn't tell. It didn't ring a bell with me. I don't think I ever heard it before."

Hampton can make no sense of any of it. He doesn't bother to look again at the women. He simply sighs and lowers his head as he tells Norma, "He's asking for you. You be sure to keep him cool. And you two try to get some sleep, okay?"

But no one in the house can catch anything like sleep. All too soon, daylight comes pouring through the blinds. The sounds of the stirrng neighborhood can be heard from the house.

Three

HAMPTON AND HIS WIFE SPOKE VERY LITTLE IN those few hours before dawn. The burden of explanation, what little of it there was, seemed to weigh on them. Mostly, each made a private journey as much into the past as their fears would allow. Otis Jr. was their only child. But he had grown up normal, to a robust and commanding six foot seven. He was doing all right in grades, had made a name for himself as an athlete. So what could the matter be? Whatever could have brought him to a state where he spoke in foreign tongues, like one possessed of a demon? Was he into drugs? Some alcohol, maybe, but nothing out of the ordinary. When he and Norma walked through the door, they carried no strange smells with them. Perhaps when he woke up in the morning it would make sense, with the experience of the night before safely behind, to ask them a few carefully considered questions.

Yet now and then Melba strayed beyond the night before. Suppose their son's condition could not be accounted for by anything from the recent past: was there anything in *their* own pasts that could be called into account? Anything in the family history of either or both of them?

For Melba Abigail Warfield, the past was another country she hoped never to revisit. Her childhood was not a happy one. Growing up in Jacksonville, Florida with an aunt who took care of her like the child she never had, Melba had what little the old woman could provide but the one thing she was reminded of by other kids in school whenever their parents showed up: "How come you ain't got no ma or pa?"

Melba remembered giving the one answer her aunt, Miz Sarah, equipped her with for such occasions, "They done went up to live with sweet Jesus."

But that wasn't good enough. Soon some wise kid came back at her with a rejoinder she could never have expected.

"Oh yeah, how come Jesus took them away? Maybe they was too

bad to stay down here 'mong decent folk. I bet Jesus couldn't stand for all them bad things they was doing, so he took 'em up there with him, jes' to keep an eye on 'em."

"No, he didn'."

"Yes, he did."

"No, he didn'."

"He did too!"

Usually, a fight, and Melba went home with a bloody nose and torn dress. Miz Sarah would scold her for getting in a fight. But at ten the child was judged old enough to hear the truth. Abel and Olive Warfield, her parents, had passed away in unhappy circumstances. Abel, who had worked as a house servant for a white family in New Orleans, had been accused of lusting after their daughter. One night he was strung up to a stake by a rowdy pack of men and set ablaze. As the story went, even the white men were shaken by the sounds that issued from the mouth of the burning negro.

His wife Olive, Sarah's younger sister, was uncontrollable in her mourning but had sense enough to know there was no future for her and her three children in that county. The next day, she took them with her on a train to live for a time with a friend in Baton Rouge. But friend should never be a burden to friend. Olive knew she had to find a place of her own soon enough. She tried to make a living for herself and her kids, but times were hard. Besides, the world was never a kind place for a woman and her children unprotected by a man, and Olive was a pretty woman who tempted the lustful will in men. One night, two men who competed for her favors had a messy fist-fight. The one who lost stayed to be nursed by Olive, who though disturbed by the unhappy event seemed nevertheless to favor him. Enraged, the one who prevailed went home, fetched a shotgun, turned it first on his rival, then on Olive.

"So, child," Miz Sarah ended her story, "I done told you once and I'm a-tell you again. Your folks done went to live up there with the Lawd Jesus. And if any o them know-nothin' kids you got in yo' school ask you why, you better tell 'em don't nobody merits to live with Jesus but them folks what's too good to carry on in this ol' sinful worl'. An' I don't wan' hear no mo' o' this foolishness, 'cause you got sense enough to speak up for yo'self."

Melba was four years old when she parted from her brother and sister, both older than she. While she was taken away by Miz Sarah, Simon and Esther went to live first in a children's home in New Orleans, then with a childless black couple who later moved to Atlanta. The couple were kind enough to trace Melba out. For a time the three children were linked up with one another in periodic visits by Simon and Esther to Jacksonville. Indeed, the couple offered to take Melba too, so the three children would be reunited and their loss minimized. But Miz Sarah, who never married nor bore a child of her own, would not give up a child that gave her a sense of fulfilment she had come to guard so jealously. The visits from Atlanta became less frequent, until the children lost contact with one another for good. As her siblings departed for Atlanta after their last visit, Melba stood staring after them far into the dim distance, tears in her eyes.

Miz Sarah died of a heart attack when Melba was in her first year of community college. With scholarships and work-study programs, she struggled to complete her two years of study and leave the South for good. Fate landed her a receptionist's job in a Boston construction firm, where she met a handsome young engineer who took her out only twice, surprised her on the second date with an engagement ring, and in all their life together had helped her outlive the traumas of the past. Deliverance, she remembered calling him once, though not to his hearing...

As she surveyed her past, Melba might have felt free of any responsibility for her son's predicament. But somewhere in the recesses of her mind, she could not help wondering: What was it her father was said to have cried out in that awful moment, as the flames consumed his body?

Otis Jeremiah Hampton was always proud enough of his background to believe he deserved his place in the white man's world. The son of an Augusta sharecropper and grandson of a slave, he learnt early in life to know his place but also to believe in his innate worth. His family were decent, God-fearing Baptists who earned the respect of both the black folk and the white aristocracy. His mother had worked as a maid for the Barclays of Augusta, Georgia scions of old Southern stock who had no regrets about their confederate service, embraced reconstruction with honest zeal, and treated their Negroes as decently as the times allowed. So, unlike most households of their race and class, the Barclays—father, mother, and children—chose to call their maid Miz Odetta and rewarded her service beyond the terms of employment.

Miz Odetta was the lead voice of her congregation's choir, a strong, vibrant alto of solid African timbre, which lent every song a touch of dignified mirthfulness, whatever its content. Miz Odetta brought her two children, Ella Pearl and Otis Jeremiah, into the choir, where they were able to give a good account of themselves. So deeply did Ella take to the music that, with the active encouragement of her mother, she learnt how to play the piano while keeping her role as the choir's lead sporano. When the congregation's pianist, Atticus "Fats" Johnson, died of heart failure in the course of a Sunday service, Ella Pearl accepted the invitation to succeed him with a proud sense of continuity.

Brother and sister made such an impression on both the black and white communities of Augusta, they were frequently invited to make duet appearances at functions organized by either community. Truth be told, Otis was less enthusiastic about this musical business than his sister. But it was in it that he learnt his first real lesson in self-pride. When Priscilla, the first of the three Barclay daughters, wedded one of the Farmingdales—another of Augusta's aristocracy, ruined by emancipation but redeemed by a new venture in agro-industrial business—the Hampton duo was invited to share the musical bill with a white string quintet that played dance music at the wedding reception. Stationed close to the service entrance, at a convenient distance from the white orchestra, the Hampton children played only at appointed intervals. But they played with an unabashed sense of duty and became the preferred center of attention.

During one of the long intervals, when players as well as guests were being served refreshments, a younger member of the string quintet walked over to the Hampton children, with a smile more of amused curiosity than of polite interest. At this point Miz Odetta, one of a team of blacks assigned to serve refreshments, happened to be bringing a tray of drinks to Ella and Otis, bowing ever so pleasantly to the white man who seemed to take an interest in her children.

"I was beginning to compliment your son, Miz Odetta," said the white man, "on his superb voice. You niggers sure have the singing thing in your blood, wouldn't you say?"

"I reckon so, Mas Nuffield, sir," she said, "and thank you mos' kindly."

Otis regarded the young man, who was probably no more than a year or two older than he but seemed bent on stressing his superiority, with guarded civility.

"I think, though," said Nuffield, turning his eyes now at Otis, "that he needs a few lessons in chord control. But of course that's something we whites do so much better than you niggers. If he could, maybe, scrub some of that black off his skin, he could *conceivably* get closer to being a white man and, *maybe*, do better on his chord control. Don't you think?" he concluded, chuckling under his breath.

Otis's face glowered, his back straightened, and his fingers closed tightly. But his mother took control to prevent the impending awkwardness.

"Oh, I don' know, Mas Nuffield, sir," she said, ever so cheerfully, "but if yo' color is what lie 'neath that dark skin o' his, he might regret using that ol' soap till the day he die."

That said, Miz Odetta bowed, and withdrew to the service room. Nuffield turned red in the face, drew up his chin, wheeled round instantly, and walked back to his ensemble. Otis followed him for a while with the mean look in his eyes, then shook his head as he turned toward Ella. She was no less hurt, but she bore her feelings with ladylike grace. From the service room Miz Odetta could see the gloom on her son's face. In no time she had returned with a fresh tray of drinks. Headed for another group, she stopped by her children long enough to whisper to Otis, "Think no more on it, boy. You got a job to do, now do it like a man." Then she quickly put on a cheery smile as she took the tray to the guests.

Otis Jeremiah never forgot this sobering encounterer and the resolve it inspired in him: to be proud of his black self, and, in his dealings with the white man, to cultivate a style that struck the right balance between firmness and discretion.

He had much else to be grateful to his mother for. But he remembered his father too. The son of an ex-slave, Daley Hampton was a man of few words who only said as much as he needed to anyone, family or outsider. Never got into any quarrels. Otis Jeremiah cherished the company of his father. But he often worried about the long intervals of silence between them and the brevity of the old man's responses to his questions. As he grew older and the realities of race revealed themselves to his maturing mind, he came to appreciate the old man's circumstances: Growing up the son of an ex-slave, at a time when slavery was a fact of life if not exactly law, his father must have cultivated silence as a discreet strategy of self-preservation. When Otis Jeremiah ventured to ask about his grandfather, the former slave, all he ever got from his father was, "Good man. Stubborn Af'can. Didn' let no man give him no horse shit."

Otis Jeremiah also saw that his father was content to let Miz Odetta attend to their education while he played the role of provider. But Otis also wondered about his father's lack of fellowship.

"Pa," he once asked, "how come you never speak with ma? Don't you like her?"

"I loves yo' mama, boy. She purty as a frog's hair. Smart too."

"But all you ever do is work. You don't talk to us."

"We needs food on the table."

Then he drew the boy close to him, pressed his head to his chest, and patted it. Otis was cheered by the rare warmth. He grew to accept his father as simply a proud man who saw himself chiefly as his family's provider. A man who, when a boll weevil blight threatened that role, quickly took jobs at dockyards out in Savannah just so he wouldn't fail his family. But Otis Jeremiah never forgot the rare smile that lit his father's ebony face, much lined by time and travail, as he and Miz Odetta flanked their son one sunny afternoon in '29 when the young man graduated from Tuskegee as a civil engineer, and again three years later when he earned a masters at Penn.

Ella Pearl loved their father about as much as Otis Jeremiah did. She just never got used to the man's economy of speech. She preferred the more liberal style of their mother, in whose company she cultivated a sense of independence, toughness of mind, and irrepressible drive. "I'll take it from here, Mr. Johnson," she often pressed her piano tutor. Upon graduating from a teachers' college in Atlanta, she returned to teach elementary school in Augusta, resuming her role as pianist in the black Baptist congregation. She clearly relished the social visibility her education and musical skills conferred on her.

Otis Jeremiah also recalled the avid curiosity of his older sister. Ella Pearl was quite active in community affairs and was for a long time president of the local chapter of a group called the Daughters of Africa. The organization set itself the task of redeeming the "true" facts of Africa's history and culture from the "tarnishment" of white prejudice, giving firm support to the call by Marcus Garvey and the UNIA for a return of Negroes to Africa. Ella Pearl even made plans to join the exodus, but for the fierce opposition of Miz Odetta, for whom she had a special respect.

"Ain't no sense in goin' less'n you know yo' kinfolk over there," their mother had said. "We done lef' Af'ca too long to know the way back. You bes' leave Af'ca be. We Amer'cans now."

Ella Pearl remained firm in her curiosity. It was from her, for instance, that Otis Jeremiah heard—much later, as they reminisced about their deceased father shortly after his burial in 1948—an expanded version of the meager information their father had allowed Otis to learn about their slave ancestor: not only was the slave stubborn, he spoke so little, especially in his days of bondage, that he was often called "the dumb African" or, in the family's more cosmetic version of the story, "the quiet African."

Miz Odetta departed the world in 1953. Ella Pearl, who never married—too independent-minded, and much too busy anyhow—stayed on in Augusta to enjoy a social visibility enhanced both by time and by the cherished memory of her mother among blacks and whites alike.

As he ran this whole history through his mind on that troubled dawn, Hampton could find nothing in it to account for his son's strange behavior. How could the stubborn reticence of a slave ancestor, which was as far back in that family's history as could be traced, translate into the frenzied gibberish of his great-grandson?

In the balanced rhythm of their anxieties, neither Hampton nor Melba can see any further into the past than they dare look. Even when they probed what little they know of each other's ancestry, as often their fears brought them to do, their queries were tentative, even timorous. Neither of them wishes to be insinuative, let alone accusatory. Instead, they prefer to embrace the easier, though no more plausible, hunch that Otis's problem may have its roots in last night's party.

"Hm. I don't know, Melba. God alone knows what else he took out there besides alcohol. I'm beginning to have my fears."

"You know he doesn't do any substances." Melba says, looking at her husband with some alarm.

"I know," says Hampton. "Or at least I could have said so before last night. But," he sighs, "you never know. There's so much going around these days, especially with college kids. Pot. Free love. What have you. Rock music so wild your poor head's about to split. Sit-ins. Marches. And it's not just California. It's all over the country now—you see it every day in the newspapers. I don't know…"

"Not Otis. He's not into any of that."

"Get real, woman!" Hampton rises from the bed and walks to the window. "There's such a thing as peer pressure. I love him same as you do, but times have changed. Kids today think they've had just about enough control from everyone—government, school, even their parents.

One kid gets the feeling, and it goes around the group he's with, and there's nothing you or I can do about it. I know how you feel," he adds, turning from the window and anticipating his wife's objection. "We've never seen anything abnormal in him until now. But it only takes but once, and look what we've got on our hands. I still think we ought to find out what happened at that party."

"How come Norma didn't say anything about it last night?"

"Maybe she didn't want to. Who knows, she probably was part of the whole..."

He isn't trying to give Norma the benefit of the doubt. He just isn't sure where that trend of thought is leading him. There are a few moments of silence between them.

"So what do we do?" Melba finally asks.

"I don't know," Hampton says, sighing. "Maybe go back there and ask."

"*You* ask," Melba is quick to say. "You brought it up. So you ask."

But, even for him, it is not easy.

Four

FIRST THERE WAS A HILL. THEN THERE WAS A RIVER. *Between the hill and the river, but closer to the hill. Find it. It may not be today. It may not be tomorrow. The sparrow does not shirk its duty.*

Past the midcourt, Otis flicks his eyes left and right, plotting his path round Buddy Payne, bouncing the basketball tactfully. Fade to the right. Retreat as Payne blocks his path. Fade right again. Again Payne is in his way, arms and legs poised to make a steal. Kessler and Rivera circle Payne, throwing his moves into complete disarray. In the split second that Payne glances left and right behind him, Otis moves quickly towards the paint. Payne rushes to block his drive. They clash. Otis fakes a fall, groaning aloud to emphasize he's been bucked too hard. It's just outside the paint, but the ref awards a shooting foul. An unbelieving Payne whirls round and screams, "What!" Otis smiles, satisfied his trick has worked. He gets a supportive handslap from Kessler as he prepares for the two free throws.

First throw circles the inner ring of the net, but the ball skittles off. "Damn!" says Otis between clenched teeth, shaking his head to clear away whatever caused the miss. Rivera touches hands with him for reassurance. Otis closes his eyes briefly to regain composure, twirls the ball between his hands, posts it up on his right hand, screws his mouth, then makes the second throw. The ball circles the inner ring, then hurtles down the net for a point. Shouts of support from the bleachers. The players run backwards. *In an old bush...*

Princeton has a very strong team. For an Ivy League team it is just as notable for rough play and trash talking. Despite his nickname, "Tiger," Otis is really better known for his fast dashes than for brute menace on the boards. True, like most players, he does the usual backup thumps and occasional elbowing that may draw some blood. Otherwise, he's more skilled at evasive feints and slips that bring him to the opponent's hoops faster than the eye can see. If there's any menace in him, it's the slam-dunk with a roaring yell, for which he receives an uproarious acknowledgment from the crowd.

But this is to be a play-off game like never before. Otis has become unusually edgy. His free-throws are shot: two of eleven so far in the first half! He's lost the ball four times to steals and twice off-bounds. His passes and assists are amazingly ill-focused. Sometimes, when he gets a pass in the paint he runs past the net before realizing he should have pitched. Coach Doherty benches him a couple of times and, though off-days are nothing new even to the best of players, can hardly resist belting out words like, "What the fuck is the matter with you, my friend? Didn't you have any sleep last night or something? Now the next time you go out there, show me I was only having a bad dream, okay?" Otis nods, but even he knows things aren't the same with him.

Things come to a head in the second half. Third quarter, Otis is pissed off by something he hears a Princeton defender—a white hunk with a baritone voice—say: "Got ya, monkeyface!" Otis maneuvers a contact with the abuser, and there's a scuffle. He has practically ripped the vest from the Princetonian before other players wrest him from the man. The Princetonian opens his eyes and mouth and spreads his arms, faking innocence. The trick works: since nobody else heard what the defender said, the referee awards a flagrant foul against Otis. He is benched again.

Fourth quarter. Otis is racing toward the net with a pass from Coop Williams. Suddenly he slows to a stop. There's a visible squirm on his face. Holding the basketball to his stomach with one hand, he drops to his knees and cups an ear. Williams quickly signals a time-out; the ref blows the whistle. As Otis's teammates converge round him, the coach runs up and parts the circle.

"What's the matter? Otis!"

"I don't know, man." The ball rolls off his knees. "I just...heard this sound...Kind of rocked my ear-drums. I...I don't know." He shakes his head to clear the lingering dizziness.

Otis is led off to the locker room, and play continues with a replacement. Bradley has no more time-outs, thanks to its troubled star. Otis doesn't return to the game. When the last buzzer sounds to his team's 89-93 loss to Princeton, a mournful mood sweeps across the entire arena. A few boos are even heard, as the home team files through the exit into the locker room. This is Bradley's first loss to Princeton in *nine* years. What happened?

Ifa divination was performed for Eyeko, the wild pigeon, who was weeping for lack of children. The diviner advised that she offer two plantains, two rats, two fish, and two hen's eggs in sacrifice. Eyeko did as she was told. When she hatched her eggs, two chicks emerged. In gratitude she paid a handsome fee to the diviner, requesting that a net be built for her within his compound. That done, Eyeko sang a joyful song:
I have given birth to two children
And have become a domestic bird!
I have given birth to two children
Now I am a domestic bird!
The diviner agreed, and gave her a new name, Eyele [turtle-dove]. *When he demanded that Eyele offer in sacrifice the chick she liked the less, she said to him, I cannot sacrifice either of them. I am fond of both. Henceforth Ifa decreed that pigeons should always deliver in pairs...*

Strange things have been happening lately. Black people have become increasingly uneasy. Marches and riots throughout the country, even here in Boston. Police unleashing their wild dogs on marchers and swinging their truncheons freely on them, young and old alike. So much talk about Africa. Many brothers and sisters wearing dashiki prints. Necklaces and amulets strung with bones and shells. 'Fros bigger than heads wearing them. Otis wears one, but for him it is just the do of the day, with no cultural or racial significance. The closest he gets to this kind of feeling is his girlfriend. Norma is all about Africa. Crazy stuff coming out of the radical chic at Radcliffe, more so than at Harvard.

Even his own university is now caught in a frenzy not unrelated to the politics of the day. Student union elections are on. An African student, as politically visible as he is academically respected, has contested the post of president with a white student who has little going for him besides a well-advertised brush with campus security in a recent student protest. When the votes are counted, the white candidate is declared to have nicked the African by *two* votes. The entire African student population at Bradley is up in arms, with a few other foreign students and some Americans on their side. The commotion is so strong and so widespread the university has to summon the campus police to maintain order and ensure classes are not disrupted.

Emerging from one of the beleaguered classrooms, Otis makes his way quietly through the menacing crowd. He needs to have lunch in a quiet atmosphere. The campus commons doesn't seem right under the circumstances. *Hurray for things that come in pairs...*On an instinct, Otis decides on one of the neighborhood pizza joints close to his university.

Tucci's, on Beacon Street, is particularly favored by students from BU, because it offers them many incentives: heavily discounted delivery rates, vouchers for lunch and dinner, work opportunities, even free large-size platters at numerous student receptions and outdoor barbecues throughout the year. Despite the often uneasy racial climate in Boston, Tucci's is known to be openly hospitable to minority clients and especially black students. Foreign students are given the most favored treatment. According to the folklore of the place, its founder came from Italy as a penniless immigrant and worked his way up in the Boston dockyards until he built up enough capital to start a joint. Any time his eyes fall on a foreigner, especially a young "helpless" student, his heart bleeds. He assumes that every immigrant is in America to stay and needs all the help he can get.

Boston is cold even on a spring afternoon. Upon entering the joint, Otis surveys the seated tables for familiar faces. He sees none, not even at the counter. There is not much company around, either. The political excitement on the campus...maybe. One table has a couple of blacks. They're probably students, he doesn't know. He moves to a table a little closer to theirs. Not exactly out of racial empathy: it just happens to be available. The blacks are having a conversation, periodically raising their voices and gesticulating. Although from their English accents Otis can tell they are foreign students, he does not pay much attention to their talk. He is looking at the menu, waiting to be served. *Ifa says: Twigs of the iroko are best pruned in their prime. Why wait too long? As they age, they demand greater sacrifice of us...*

Otis suddenly takes an interest in the conversation between the two blacks. One of them speaks excitedly in a foreign language Otis cannot place, but which has the dramatic flair often associated with African students. Otis turns his eyes to the men. Are they having a fight? More seriously, there is a growing sensation within him that seems connected to the speaker's level of excitement. Initially, one of the Africans speaks English in answer to whatever the other says in the native language. At such moments, Otis feels a seesaw of emotions, from uneasiness to calm. But soon their conversation grows more heated. Now they are speaking in their African language. Otis becomes more excitable, so much so that he has to take off his jacket. When one of the Africans realizes Otis is looking at them, he motions to the other to tone down his voice; they have become the object of an intrusive interest. But the other doesn't care. After a quick dismissive glance at Otis, he continues in his African tongue, as abrasively as ever.

Other eyes have turned towards the speakers. For Otis, the event has a more serious emotional effect. When his body can no longer bear the telepathy, he rises from his seat and moves towards the Africans. On his approach, they ease off from their argument. Ignoring him, the more intractable speaker raises his glass of soda to his lips. Otis fixes his attention on the one who has spoken more in English.

"Excuse me, I don't mean to bother you, but—"

"And what do you think you're doing?" says the militant one. "Two people are having a perfectly friendly conversation that has absolutely nothing to do with you. You suddenly jump in between them, and say you don't mean to bother them. So what do you call that?"

"I know. I'm sorry," says Otis. "But I have a reason for doing this. Could you tell me what language you guys are speaking?"

"What business of yours—" the militant one cannot contain himself. His friend tries to cool things by motioning him down. But he is clearly in no mood for conciliation. Picking up his coat, and leaving some money on the table, he makes one final statement in his African language to the conciliator, indicating that he's out of there. The conciliator is caught between loyalty to his friend and a polite regard for the African American. He simply says to Otis, "Look, man, let's just forget everything, okay?"

"I just asked a question. What's the matter with him?"

At the door the militant one hurls one last angry retort in his native language, followed by some English, "After all, they're all part of it. How did they ever help us in the whole business?"

"What's he talking about?" Otis asks.

"Didn't you see what happened in the elections?"

"Oh, that. But what's that got to do with me?"

The conciliator looks at him for a brief moment, shakes his head, and smiles.

"Like I said, man, forget it, okay. Sorry, but I have to go."

He, too, picks up his coat and leaves.

"Hey, wait a minute." Otis starts to dash after them. But he feeels awkward making such a spectacle of himself. So he resumes his seat. The Africans have gone, along with their language, and he feels no more troubling sensations. But somehow, he feels slightly relieved. Something...a connection is growing within him...those Africans...their words...their language...the music, *that* music. He can't link these things. What they are, or their sources...he hasn't the foggiest clue. He finds himself with a strangely vacuous feeling, of being poised between a gulf and an endless road. The waiter who has come to take his order finally shakes him out of his reverie. The attention he has drawn to himself suddenly comes home to him. He is no longer hungry. He declines the service, picks up his jacket, and leaves the place.

Damned Africans, Otis thinks, as he steps outside. I should have held them down. *In fury, Ogun builds roads. In fury, Ogun rights wrongs. It will not be long. Between the hill and the river.* Otis squeezes the jacket in his hand.

Norma answers the door. Nobody else rings the bell like that. When Otis walks in, there is a wan smile on his face. He kisses Norma's mouth, but only because she opened it to him. He's not exactly in the mood for romance. He holds her a little longer, rocks her body, even rubs her back and neck, just to keep the feelings warm. And she *is* warm. He throws his jacket aside and stretches out on the sofa. She senses his reserve, but says nothing as she runs back to finish the dishes. The TV is on. He watches only because it's there.

"Be right with you, Otis. *Ooo-wee*!" she lets out. "You don't know how *ecstatic* I am. I think I finally got the lead I needed on my project."

"Tell me about it." His tone is flat, unemotional. The faint smile hangs around his mouth. But she's too excited to notice.

"You know that Caribbean restaurant on Cutler and Dean, not far from the metro bus station? You know—Pleasure Island?"

"I...think I do. What about it?"

"You remember we passed by it some...six months ago or so. There was this guy with a huge afro and a long flowery gown reaching to his ankle, and he gave us leaflets advertising their menu, and we promised we—"

"Yea, yea. I know. What about it?" A crease flashes briefly across his brow.

"Well, I'm meeting a guy there tonight," Norma says. She turns her head momentarily toward him. "Are you coming with me? We could have dinner there."

"Oh, I don't know," he says, wearily. "I'm not that hungry. Maybe I'll skip it this time."

"Why?"

His poorly disguised detachment can no longer be ignored. A woman's body can cut through a full-mouthed kiss and hands coursing over her back and neck. The dishes done, she dries her hands on a towel and sits beside him.

"What's the matter, Otey?" she says, looking him full in the eye. "Want to talk about it?"

He tries to turn his face aside, but she takes it in her hand and turns it back towards her.

"Don't be like that, Otey." Her voice has lost some of its felicity. "What happened?"

He sighs deeply and lays his head on her lap, looking up at the ceiling.

"You know, Norm, there's been...I'm not exactly sure how to put this.

"What?"

He tries to collect his thoughts. She doesn't take her eyes off him for a second.

"Somehow, these days, I'm not so sure I know which way my mind seems to be working. It's like, you know..."

Again, he holds back.

"Get yourself together, Otey. What exactly is going on?"

"I wish I knew what *is* going on. It's like...I'm losing control of the power to decide I don't know what. That's just it—if you ask me *what*, I can't even begin to describe it."

"There's no way you can be...specific about how you feel?"

He shakes his head slowly. "I know I feel a pull inside, like some unknown power is there, and there's nothing I can do about it. Believe me, I *will* take back control. I've *got* to take back control. But...I've never dealt with anything like this."

"Something new's happened?"

"Yeah," he admits, faintly.

"Well, what? What happened?"

His legs begin to shake, which usually happens anytime he's uneasy about something he has to talk about. Knowing this, Norma holds his legs to steady him.

"Tell me. What happened?"

"I saw these two guys. Africans."

"Where?"

"I was over at Tucci's for lunch. They had a thing going on. An argument, or something. They were talking at the tops of their voices. And then I began to feel...funny. Got me all shook up inside. I..."

He gets off Norma's lap and rises from the sofa. She follows him with her eyes as he begins to pace the floor aimlessly. She gets up herself and moves towards him. She manages to hold his arm steady and to bring him back to the sofa.

"Otis, get a hold of yourself. Talk to me. What happened?"

"I don't know!" His voice rises one notch. "You think I'm trying to hide something from you? I can't explain it myself."

"Okay. So they were arguing. What were they talking about?"

"They were...they were speaking in some African language—at least that's what I thought it was. I couldn't tell for certain because they wouldn't tell me anything."

"How d'you mean?"

"When I got to feeling funny, I moved over to them. I was as polite as I could be. Asked them what language they were speaking. I guess it was the wrong time to ask the question, because they were having an argument and were mad about something. Well, I..."

He tries to get up again. This time Norma holds him down. Not too hard, but she doesn't want to lose him again.

"Go on, Otey."

"Well, one of them got hostile. I guess he didn't like me butting into their business. I let him understand I had a personal reason for asking. But he wouldn't let up. He flared up at me, took his coat and shot right out the door."

He shakes his head, looking down at nothing. Norma is no less baffled.

"Was that the first time you saw these guys?"

"Never met them before. But they must be students at BU."

"How d'you know that?"

"The other one, who wasn't so hard on me, asked me if I wasn't aware what happened at the student union elections. He took his coat as well and excused himself. His friend looked in one more time and said something about '*they* never helped us anyway.'"

"Who's 'they'?"

"Some stuff about African Americans not backing the African candidate for president of the union. Every time they spoke that African language, something tugged in me, like strings were being pulled inside. There's got to be a connection, and that's what I was trying to find out. We were beginning to cause a scene in that pizza joint, and I didn't want that. So I let them go. Now I wish I hadn't."

Norma looks now at him, now on the floor. She's having uneasy memories of the birthday party night, and of the basketball match he later told her about.

"If you saw those Africans again, you think you'd recognize them?"

"Maybe I will, maybe I won't. I never saw them before. Why?"

"Well, maybe after some time they'll cool down. And you can talk to them again, in a more friendly way. Maybe they'll cooperate."

"I *was* friendly to those motherfuckers—excuse me! I was apologizing all over the place." He gets up and starts pacing again.

"Okay, okay. I heard you."

Ifa says: If we do not bear suffering that fills a basket, how can we receive kindness that fills a cup?

For a while neither of them says a word. But the silence is as uneasy as a charged conversation. Norma gets up and goes over to Otis. Wrapping her arms around his waist, she rests her head on his back and sighs, "Otey, let's not get upset about this. Try to put it behind you. Sure, we'll do our best to figure out what it's all about. But let's give it a rest for the moment. Let's go to the Caribbean place tonight and take this thing off our minds for a little while. I've never met this guy, but I *know* it's gonna be good for me."

Otis feels suddenly relieved, having gotten the load off his chest. He obliges her cheerfulness.

"And how, might I ask, did you *get* to know him?" he says, turning to look in her face with mock suspicion.

Her arms still wrapped around him, she fixes his eyes with a warm, seductive smile.

"Wha's mattah, lovah bwai?" she cooed. "You no trus' yo' gyal no more?"

"I ain't said nothing," he beams, throwing up his hands.

"Then don't ask nothing," she says, the glow still in her eye. "Whatever's between me and me islan' maan is nothing you can't handle, okay?"

Her hands slide roguishly, ever so teasingly, down the back of his pants. When he makes the same move, his hands find nothing but a smooth, naked butt. Pleasantly alarmed, he looks down her legs and sees a little pile of silk on the ground.

"When did you—"

"Sshh!" she gently chides, one hand against his lips, the other busy with his belt and his bulging fly. He kisses her waiting mouth rabidly, sliding his right hand into the wet angle of her parted legs, collapsing readily when she pushes him onto the sofa...A half hour later, they have regained enough awareness to smile again into each other's eyes.

"Seducer," she whispers.

"What!" he draws back, mildly scandalized. "Girl, as I *re*call, you were all *over* me before I even took one look at you."

They kiss again. She looks deep into his eyes.

"Hungry now?"

"More than ever!" he growls.

"*All right!*"

They rise, clean up, and get ready. Norma has already packed a portable reel-to-reel recorder in a bag.

"Tell me some more about the project," says Otis. Norma is driving. "What's this guy supposed to do in it?"

"On its way to Oyo, it faces Oyo. On its way from Oyo, it still faces Oyo."
All praise to the drummer, who coaxes sweetness and truth from the taut skins
of the duiker. The path to our fathers can never be erased.

Pleasure Island is located in a "safe" ethnic neighborhood. By day, it is hardly distinguishable from the rest of its row of Georgian architecture. The name of the place is splashed in orange against a backdrop of tropical ecology: A smiling sun. Blue waves lashing a light brown beach. A thatched hut beside a line of coconut trees bending to a sea-breeze. The sign draws little attention in the daytime. But by night the whole scene comes alive when tiny electric bulbs ringing the sign illuminate it with blinking lights, revealing a subtext, in green scrawl, that makes more sense to the prospective client: Caribbean Cuisine.

Weekend nights often draw a sizeable company of blacks as well as whites for whom the Caribbean might be just around the corner for the rest of the year. On such nights, the front door of Pleasure Island opens, as early as 6 p.m., to a blast of calypso music and an equally loud aroma of spices. On a midweek night like this, however, the traffic is light. It might be 7 p.m. before anyone shows up to eat. Service takes a while to come. For music, you are just as likely to hear the Andrews Sisters as Lord Kitchener.

Norma's sociology project is a paper on the family in maroon culture. The growing literature on the maroon societies of the Guyanas and the islands presents a wide enough field of choices so that Norma need not overexert herself. But she is not only bright, she is also adventurous. Inquiries have revealed there is a Jamaican entrepreneur of tropical foods in Boston who shuttles regularly between the island and the city. A "wild man," he has big sleepy eyes and sports long, untended dreadlocks reaching beyond his shoulders. Otherwise he is soft spoken, even likeable. He hails from the heartland of Jamaica, where maroons waged a stubborn redoubt against the British in the past and still keep their traditions alive. On the anniversary of Jamaica's independence two years earlier, he put on an impressive show of Jamaican "bush music" (as it was called in the program of events) with the most bizarre troupe of performers Boston had ever seen, something even more exotic than the usual African fare on television.

Everyone calls him "Guinea Man." When Norma rang him up with the number she was given, his voice was deep and imposing. He listened quietly to her outline of the subject of her interest. Only then did he begin to speak at any length.

"Who give you my number?" he asked.

"I'm sorry," said Norma. "I'd asked everyone I could. I can't even remember who gave it to me. But I was assured you'd help me. Well...I'm Jamaican myself..."

"I know."

"You do?" she said, feeling encouraged.

"I can tell."

"Is it really obvious?"

"A lickle. When you wan' come meet me an' talk 'bout dis?"

"Any time you want me to, Mr...?"

"Barrett. Where you know in Boston?"

A few more one-liners later, Pleasure Island was decided as the meeting place. In the three years she has been in the area, Norma has only been inside the place once—in her first year as a Radcliffe student, when an older Caribbean female student offered to introduce her to the favored ethnic haunts of most "West Indians." Norma had few ethnic or

Isidore Okpewho

nationalistic empathies at the time, and fewer still when, early in her sophomore year, her affair with Otis drew her much closer to African American culture. Later that year, she was swept by the growing fervor of black nationalism among student groups in the Boston area. The decision to research maroon culture is her effort to return to sources she has innocently disavowed, growing up in an America that sees the world outside, especially the black world, as primitive. She's looking forward to her meeting with Barrett. It would help her new consciousness.

Barrett is already settled when Norma and Otis walk through the door. Past a little booth to the right, there is a counter to the left that caters drinks and take-aways. A young man with a flared Afro and a black and orange dashiki is cleaning the counter. He gives the couple a quick nod as they move to a table at one end of the restaurant. Other than a white couple seated with drinks immediately opposite the counter, there is no one else here but the man who looks every bit the description Norma was given. He casts an aura that further dims the already controlled lighting of the restaurant. His left hand strokes a heavy black beard. The right is hidden under the flower-patterned cloth draped over the square table. His eyes, neither friendly nor hostile, fix the approaching pair with unblinking steadiness. Never having met them before, he gives them the benefit of their intent but seems to guard his personal circumstances with careful reserve. When they come closer to him, he bows lightly, dropping his left hand to show them to their seats opposite him. He does not rise, for were he to he would be much shorter than the hulky Otis. He doesn't want that.

Norma smiles warmly as she introduces Otis and herself. Guinea Man's lips, generously thick and chapped, and with a toothpick sticking out from between them, draw lightly thin as he allows a faint smile. In the seconds that follow, he observes the penetration of Otis' eyes. He ignores this and turns to the alert looking young woman by his side.

"So." Guinea Man's voice is deep and husky.

"I'm so grateful you could come, Mr Barrett," Norma says. "Frankly, I had no clue how far I could go without the help of someone like you, directly connected to the culture. I know so little about this subject."

She laughs, a little embarrassed at saying that. Barrett himself smiles. Her honesty impresses him.

"When you laas' been to Jamaica?"

"Promise me you won't laugh."

33

He shakes his head. Norma positions her hands to indicate a new-born child held to its mother's bosom. Barrett breaks his promise and laughs with her. Otis laughs as well. The atmosphere is warming up delightfully. Barrett withdraws his right hand from under the table cloth, placing both hands on the table.

"Ya 'ave family dere, no?"

"My grandmother used to visit us in New York. But she passed away three years ago. I have uncles and aunts in Jamaica. My mum always promised to take us home, me and my sisters. Well, I guess working hard to raise us never allowed her to live up to that promise."

Nothing was said about a father. Barrett understands. He's had his share of relationships.

"I definitely plan to go there sometime in the near future. Meeting you is my first step. By the way, Mr. Barrett, we'd like to have dinner. Would you please join us?"

"G'wan. Me already 'ad som'n."

"Sure?"

"Yeh, mon." He holds up a hand and snaps his fingers to the young man at the counter. The steward comes with a menu. "Take cyar' me friends, Seeco."

While Norma and Otis look through the items on the menu, Barrett works the toothpick in his mouth. He takes a good look at the young woman's companion. He might have seen him somewhere, but isn't very sure. Otis looks up at the same time, and their eyes meet. Both men smile, but the guardedness returns between them. Each has a sensation of something sinister about the other, but tries his best to avoid being awkward. Otis finally allows Norma to order whatever she thinks fit for them to eat.

"How much you know 'bout maroon people dem?" asks Barrett.

"Not very much, really," Norma says. "I've read a few things in books written by white people. And they are not very good."

"Wha' dem say?"

"Always about maroons being African savages. You know, that kind of thing. But they always say such things about all black people."

She looks at Guinea Man's face, thinking maybe he would say something in response. All she finds is a calm, steady stare, with a thin smile around his mouth. She continues talking.

"Two things in particular troubled me, which I thought I should ask you about." She looks at his face again. This time he nods slightly. "I read in one place, that during one of the wars maroons fought against the British, the people were so starved they ate the bodies of their own men—the ones who died in the fighting. Is that true?"

Guinea Man chuckles, letting his body rock a little in amusement. Otis shifts uneasily in his seat, his eyes riveted on Guinea Man. This face, he thinks. I've never met him before. But I could swear...*Ifa says: You will see me in an abundance of blessings.*

Guinea Man still doesn't say anything. But Norma feels encouraged by his laughter to go on.

"I also read that when the maroons finally made peace, they were so happy the war was over they did everything they could to show the white man they did not want any more trouble. Like, anytime a British official visited a maroon chief, the chief would offer him one of his daughters to take to bed for the night. You know what I'm saying? I also read the chiefs treated their own wives almost like slaves. I'm not saying I believe all these stories. But, how did the people live in those difficult times? What kind of family structure did they have? How did the women live with the men, or raise their children, and so on? You know what I'm saying?"

The smile turns wry on Guinea Man's mouth. But he hasn't lost his patience. His hanging locks show he might have made a guerilla warrior. And like a seasoned guerilla, he might have seen enough not to be rattled by these weak shots of the enemy's propaganda, even from the mouth of this "countrywoman" from the university. The things they teach them!

"Me heah you, sistah," he says. "But, you know, is good you no believe de white man dem. Because dem tings you read ina dem book coulda put wrong ideas 'bout you own people ina yo' head. Me no say no read book, seen? But you ha' fe tink say, wha' me a-go trus', wha' de white man say or wha' me people say. Me no say no read book. But book is white man tool fe take poison we people mind, make dem forget say we ha' we own culture. Seen, lang lang time we people a-know 'bout culture and civilization. We ancestahs from Africa, dem be civilize people lang time 'fore white man dem go dere and learn how fe govern demself. Hear wha' me a-tell you now?"

"Yes, yes," says Norma. "There were great kingdoms and empires. Benin, Ashanti, Zulu, Dahomey. I know."

"Good. An' we people dem come from Africa. Is a pity dem white man bring us heah in slave ship. Dat be trick dem white man make fe ketch we fe come from Africa and work in dem plantation. But dat no mean say we forget we culture. If we people so primitive and savage, like dem white man say, why you tink the maroon war laas so lang? Tell me dat."

"I know. They must have been well organized and disciplined people, to be able to fight back the British for so long."

"You right 'bout dat. An' let me tell you someting 'bout we people. Remember, we no call weself maroon. No, no. Dat de name de white man dem call we. We call weself Kramanti."

"What?"

"Kramanti. Dat we African name. De white man dem a-call we primitive an' all. But me a-go tell you a lickle someting 'bout we culture. How we govern weself. How we run we family life. How we treat we women an' children. We religion and ev'ryting."

"Mr. Barrett," says Norma, holding up one hand and reaching into her bag with the other, "if you don't mind, I'd like to record this conversation."

"Wha' you wan' do da' for?"

Guinea Man's brow tightens. A problem of trust has suddenly arisen. His mouth hangs open, as he watches her pull out a portable recorder from her bag. He looks at Otis, and finds the young man is still studying him.

"Trust me, Mr. Barrett," Norma says, with a smile. "You have nothing at all to worry about. I simply want to record our conversation so I'll have information I need for writing up my research paper. This is what we students usually do."

The word "information" doesn't sit well with the man. In his many years of living in Boston, he's been subjected to interrogation by various government agents, uniformed and plain-clothed alike, whenever there's any activist trouble in the area. His looks clearly mark him as a likely troublemaker. On one occasion, he spent a whole day "downtown" answering questions from policemen about some radical group whose name he'd never heard before and wouldn't remember thereafter. He never succumbed to their harassment, however long it took, which drove the cops mad, so much so they would have gladly locked him up for the night. But they realized it would be a waste of their time. The man was a nationalist with a clear conscience and a deep interest in black culture, oral and material; he merely identified himself as a *kaltchaman*. Otherwise, he had almost nothing to do with anything that did not help his trade in tropical foods.

Guinea Man looks deeply into Norma's eyes, just to be satisfied her intentions are genuine.

"In fact, Mr. Barrett," she says, "I'm prepared to make a copy of this recording for you to keep. I just want you to be satisfied I'm not using it for anything but my research. Trust me."

"A'right," he says, nodding, "dat do for me." Norma hits the record button. Otis closes his eyes, to shut out the images from Guinea Man that seem to continually assail his senses. "Now, I tink me tell you say we name be Kramanti. Dat be we ol' name from Africa, from Gol' Coas.'"

"Ghana?" asked Norma.

"Yeh, mon. Dat de new name now. Great people. Fight plenty wah wid dem white man ina Africa. Jus' like we Kramanti people ina Jamaica. Because we no wan no man, white man, yellow man, blue man, no man atal, fe hol' we ina dem subjugation. Black man ha' fe hol' tight to 'im belief and entitlement, I say."

The images are becoming harder for Otis to deal with. He tries, but cannot fix them with the power of his will. They are demanding more and more of his concentration, drawing him to a region he can hardly recognize. His mind tells him to get up and leave, but all his instincts press him to confront the inevitable. How long can he continue to run? *Not for nothing does a runner race across a field of sharp spear-grass: if he is not after something, something is after him. Not for nothing does the young bride walk stiff-necked into the bride-groom's home: either she is already with child for another man, or there is common knowledge of her secret affairs, though she bear her breast up ever so arrogantly. It will not be long...* Otis cannot take it any longer. He excuses himself and makes straight for the bathroom.

Norma, fearing the conversation is not much to his liking, hopes Otis is only taking a needed break. She nods to Guinea Man to continue.

"Black man ha fe hol' im own. We say it ina word a mouth an' we say it ina music. Ever hear we Kramanti music?"

"No," says Norma. "I'd love to."

"Well, when you do, you ha fi understan' why we people tan' up an' fight lang time 'til bukra man kneel down an' beg fe peace. Seeco, I say," he motions to the steward. "Gi' me some a dat ridim."

A few more people have straggled into Pleasure Island, in singles and pairs. But they have made little difference to the life of the place. Except for the occasional eruption of black laughter, they speak with one another in hushed tones. Suddenly, from nowhere, a loudspeaker crackles to life, first with the grates of rusty needle on vinyl, then with a spirited outburst of drum beats and voices in contrapuntal but measured drives of polyrhythms. Although Pleasure Island appeals to its clients as much with its music as with its food, the sounds from the loudspeaker come with such sudden report that some of the guests are startled to attention. Guinea Man looks at Norma to see the effect of the music on her. He likes what he sees. A smile spreads across his face. Norma is smiling too. Her head and torso sway to the music. Her hands held above the recorder, she snaps thumb and middle finger in syncopation with the throbbing rhythms. She seems transported to some half-remembered homeland, to be having an idyllic reunion with a life she knows mostly through tales told by the old folk. Seldom has she known such joy.

Then things get out of hand. Otis bursts open the bathroom door with a frightful display. His body jerks in powerful movements, somewhere between boogie-woogie and St. Vitus' dance. For a very tall man the scene is better imagined than witnessed. Now and then he rears in a menacing leap. From his mouth sounds of an unintelligible language issue forth. He has a grin on his face, yet he hardly seems to be enjoying his exertions.

There is immediate turmoil in the restaurant. Seeco, who is coming through the swing-door of the kitchen with Norma and Otis's orders, loses his balance as he struggles to steady the swaying tray. The dishes collapse on the floor. Norma is beside herself as she runs towards Otis and tries to steady him.

"Otis!" she screams, gripping his possessed torso.

Some of the guests, including a couple who are halfway through the door, have second thoughts about their presence in the place and leave. Others rise from their seats, either to satisfy their shocked curiosity or to see what they might do to help.

"Stop it, please stop that music!" Norma pleads, looking to Guinea Man for help. Already approaching the pair, he runs past the transfixed steward and stops the music. By this time, Otis has ended his wild gibberish in a spirited coda, something that sounds like *Bamiyo, yeh yeh! Bamiyo, yeh yeh!* His body slumps into calm, and he lowers his eyes on a sobbing Norma. The tape in the recorder continues to whirr in the charged silence. She runs back and hits the stop button, then returns to Otis.

"Otey, are you all right?"

"Yeah, yeah. I'm okay."

"Would you like some...water?"

"No, I'm fine. I'll be okay."

He moves to his seat. A quick survey gives him some sense of the stir he must have caused. Embarrassed and angry, he lowers his head, fighting the urge to pound the table with his fist. Norma draws closer to him, rubbing his back gently with her hand, whispering a few words.

"Cheer up, mon," says Guinea Man, amid the dread silence, trying his best to bring comfort to the pair.

"Mr. Barrett," says Norma, "I'm sorry for the trouble. But we really must be going."

"No, mon, no trouble atal." Even he is a little disconcerted. "Anyting I can do—"

"Oh, you've done a lot already. I'm very grateful. I'll be in touch."

"Yeh, mon. Any time atal."

Seeing the confused look on Seeco's face, Norma moves towards him and says, "Sorry for the orders. I'll settle the bill."

"No, mon," offers Guinea Man. "No worry yo'self. We know wha' fe do."

"Thank you."

Otis has stood up. He shakes Guinea Man's hand in uncertain courtesy. Neither has received the other warmly from the start. The man's music has only complicated the relationship. Not that Otis hates him. He is simply conscious of a power emanating from Guinea Man that pulls at his instincts, however much he tries to resist. On his part, Guinea Man has become increasingly conscious of an empathy between them. A gut feeling, not of blood ties, but of vaguely cognized paths of convergence. Neither says a word as they disengage their hands. Otis walks ahead of Norma towards the door.

Putting the recorder in her bag, she smiles goodbye to Guinea Man. As she walks past the others, she holds her head up and even manages a smile. There is nothing to be ashamed of.

Five

TOWERING IROKO AND AN OVERGROWN BUSH. *Iron in the trunk, a giant's design. A ditch for a watering hole... Ifa says of him who has forgotten his forebears: If he does not take care of the departed, who will take care of him when his time comes?*

His encounter with Guinea Man deepened Otis' dilemma. He had begun making a connection between the Africans he met at Tucci's and the music that caused his spasms on the night of his birthday: if their speech had the same effect as the music, then it must have been African music. So where did Guinea Man and his Jamaican music fit into the equation between African speech and African music? Although the conventional wisdom of the growing black nationalism saw Africa as the common denominator to all black culture, those like Otis who hadn't embraced the revolution saw this African essence as little more than a pious myth. At this point, however, Otis could no longer take anything that happened for granted. Instinct was steadily getting the better of reason.

Even Orunmila was forced to make sacrifice. On the day he was to go on a divining tour, he was told to offer a goat so his ori [protective spirit] *would speed his mission. Orunmila refused to make the sacrifice. When he arrived at his destination, no one came to consult him. He began to starve. He returned home and sacrificed a goat to his* ori, *sharing it among the town's elders. That was the day Orunmila came into wealth.*

Decisions had to be taken, some of them not so pleasant. First, Otis excused himself from the rest of the basketball season. Not only for his own sake, but for the team's as well; he had done enough harm as it was. The decision was as hard for Coach Doherty as for his star. He had asked Otis to think it over, even suggested benching in case he felt like going onto the court at any time. But the young man knew how much he loved the game, how much it would hurt to sit and watch the team go on without him.

It was no easier deciding whether to raise the matter of Pleasure Island with his parents. Norma insisted this wasn't something Otis could handle by himself. His family needed to be brought urgently into the picture: who knew what harm Otis faced from these seizures?

"No, Norm," Otis had said. "Let's not tell them just yet. I *know* my mother. She'd just break down and cry. I don't want to do this to her. I'm willing to hold out and figure this out first."

"Figure *what* out, Otey? Man, you don't even know what it is you're dealing with."

"I know, I know. You're right. But I know too what...you remember the first time this stuff happened, and you took me home?"

"Uh-huh."

"Now, you probably didn't see the shape my mom was in the morning after, but I did."

"Then let's not tell your mother."

"So, I tell my old man, and she doesn't hear about it? You know they're not like that. But you know what?"

"What?"

"You asked me the other day if I'd recognize those Africans if I saw them again, remember? And said I should try talking to them, maybe they'd cooperate?"

"Yeah?"

"Well, that might be the best thing I could do now. If they could just tell me what language they were speaking...I don't know, but it might be connected in some way to whatever I've been saying in my spasms."

On that compromise, Otis set about scouring the BU campus on the off chance he'd find the two Africans, even one of them alone. He missed a few classes; he was having trouble concentrating on anything his teachers said. So preoccupied was he with his problem, he looked every bit like a stalker, pacing about slowly and looking closely at every unfamiliar black face he came across. He didn't linger too long with African Americans. But you could reasonably tell an African. Something about the way they walked. It was said that, while African Americans walked with a cocky swagger, Africans picked their every step because they had trouble adjusting from swinging on branches to walking on paved ground. More than once, Otis stopped a black student he thought was an African. But a few such mistakes made him wiser about these silly prejudices, for certain accents he heard from them suggested that Southern brothers might well fit the description generally claimed for Africans. *You will find me in an abundance of blessings...*

There was hardly any place on campus Otis didn't go looking at faces. He went to the cafeterias more frequently than he was accustomed to. He stood outside the library, pretending to be waiting for someone. He walked through reading rooms, library and bookstore stalls. He attended chapel services—he hadn't done this for God knows how long—and took a back row seat, just to have the chance to watch the faces that filed past at the end. He even audited classes that had nothing to do with his major. A professor once asked him what he wanted, and he lied, saying he must have gotten the wrong room. He got up and left.

Once he really got close. He'd seen a poster for a meeting of African students at the Fassbinder Lecture Hall. A few minutes before the meeting started, Otis stood by the door to see who might show up. But after a while he felt odd just standing there looking at faces. The way some of them looked back at him, he might have seemed like a spook or something. So he ambled into the room and sat through the proceedings.

The meeting was his first real education about Africa. Some political leader, named Mandelay, or something like it, had been jailed by the South African government. The group was meeting to draw up a resolution calling on the U.S. to demand the leader's release from jail and to punish South Africa for its human rights record in Africa. There were a few white men at the meeting, though they were not nearly so loud as the blacks in denouncing South Africa. Two things struck Otis. First it became clear, as one speaker after another identified himself before speaking, that there was some variety in speech styles and physical features between the Africans—a revelation that stirred within him an interest he'd never had before.

There was something else. This was a modest crowd. But because he sat in the back row where he thought he had a good chance of spotting the likely quarry, he felt lost any time the meeting degenerated to rowdy exchanges between random groups, sometimes in their respective African tongues. At one such point, he started to feel the old troubling sensations. He was uncomfortable, so uncomfortable he started to stand up in the chance he might discover where exactly the sounds that troubled him emanated from. But when the chair of the meeting called for order, he had to sit down again.

By the end of the meeting, there were furrows and sweat on his brow as he watched every face file out of the room. He had come so close to his quarry, or so he thought. But what could he have done: stop every one of those people to ask where in Africa they came from, what language they spoke? He had done it once before, to his own cost. He might seem to have narrowed his search to a convenient body of Africans on the campus. But suppose the Africans he was looking for never came to such meetings?

Norma kept the spirit of the compromise between her and Otis, but ultimately had to find a way out of its bond. Back in her apartment, she had proceeded to play the tape recorded at Pleasure Island. The aim was to start transcribing Guinea Man's intriguing information and designing a scheme for her paper. She needed a break from the disturbing thoughts about Otis' troubled condition, what it might mean for them. She also had work to do. So, snacking on a veggie sandwich and glass of milk, she had reclined comfortably on her sofa to listen to her recording. Now and then, a smile came across her mouth as she heard the homespun grammar and rhythms of Guinea Man's speech, or recalled her reaction at the time.

She gave the entire recording its full run. Suddenly, as though hit by a bolt, she was jolted from the sofa by the garbled chant of Otis coming out of the tape. It was faint, for Otis was coming from the bathroom at the end of the restaurant when the spasms hit him. Rather than move closer to the recorder to catch the sounds more clearly, Norma backed away from it. It was as if some monstrous object had been trapped in the box and was threatening to emerge and harrow their lives. And here she was, alone in the prison of her apartment, wondering what to do if the monster actually materialized and flew at her face. When the chant ended and the tape rolled to a stop, Norma sighed in relief. Still, she waited a little before stepping forward to stuff the recorder into her bag.

It was late afternoon. She reached for a coat, threw it round her shoulders, grabbed the bag with the recorder in it, and dashed out of her apartment.

Before the secretary has finished announcing her name, Norma rushes into Hampton's office at Revere Plaza. He is so shocked by the disoriented look on Norma's face that he rises quickly.

"What's wrong, Norma?" he asks, showing her to a seat.

"Please sit down, Mr. Hampton." She is nervous. "There's something here I think you should hear."

Hampton sits down hesitantly, holding on to the arms of his chair. Norma pulls out the recorder from the bag. Before pressing any button, she holds up a hand to steady herself and catch her breath.

"I wasn't really supposed to do this. Otis warned me not to tell you any more problems he's been having. You see..."

"Wait a minute, lady," says Hampton. He goes to sit closer to her. "I understand what you two must be going through. But remember we're his parents. If you don't tell us what happens to him, who else will you tell?"

"I know. You're right." Norma closes her eyes and takes a deep breath. "It's not you we're worried about. It's Mrs. Hampton. Otis is afraid she'd be extremely worried to know he's been going through those terrible moments again. You understand?"

"Yeah. Yeah. Good kid," he nods. "I see his point. Okay. Okay. Let's keep this from her for a while. But...what's this all about?"

Taking another deep breath, Norma gently places a finger on the play button of the recorder, only to discover she has not rewound the tape.

"Excuse me," she says. She runs the tape backwards to the very beginning, then sits back to listen. When Guinea Man's voice comes on, Norma again presses the stop button.

"Sorry again. By the way, this is about a project I'm doing in school on Jamaica's maroon culture. I found some guy here in Boston who knows about the stuff, and he invited me to meet him at the Caribbean Restaurant—you know, Pleasure Island, on Cutler Street, not very far from the Attucks monument on Dean?"

Hampton nods.

"Okay. That's where we went to meet this guy. His name's Barrett, but people call him Guinea Man. Okay. What you'll hear now is my conversation with him. He speaks Jamaican patois, so you may not understand a lot of this."

She presses the play button and sits back again. Despite the dialect, Hampton listens with rapt attention. Partly, he is intrigued by a speech style he has often heard but never heeded. Besides random affairs like the one between Otis and Norma, there isn't much bonding between African Americans and "West Indians" here. But Hampton now listens, rather intently, for whatever in the tape has caused Norma so much trouble she is reluctant to disclose it to Otis's parents. Now and again their eyes meet instinctively, as the tape approaches its critical moment.

And then the drum sounds emerge. Norma braces herself for the inevitable. Suddenly, Otis's voice erupts in the background. Though faint, it is clearly recognizable to Hampton. He is baffled not only by the foreignness of the language but by the aura that seems to define both text and music. At the end of it all, Hampton asks Norma to rewind back to the point where Otis's voice came on. She does. He draws closer to the recorder to catch the sounds more clearly.

"Were these not the same things he was saying the other night?"

"I think so."

"Have you figured out what they might mean?"

She shakes her head.

"Again, I wasn't supposed to tell you any of this." She sighs. "Some days ago he went to a pizza joint, close to his campus, and heard two African students speaking their language. He said he began to feel uncomfortable. So he went up to them and tried to get them to tell him what language it was. But they got angry with him and walked out of the place."

"African language," Hampton says, half to himself, his head moving from side to side as he tries to figure it all out. His face looks decidedly troubled. "African language..."

"You know, before I came here, I had a mind to take this tape to an African student..."

There is a knock on the door. Hampton's white secretary shows her face through.

"Oh, dear. What time..." He looks at his watch: 5:25. "I'm sorry, Jane. Go right on home. I'll see you tomorrow, okay?"

"Night, Mr. Hampton."

"Good night. African language..."

No sooner have they taken their minds off the departing secretary than they hear her talking to someone. Norma is hurriedly trying to put the recorder in the bag, when Hampton's door opens and Otis walks in.

"Hi, dad. Hey, girl..." A vague question flashes across his mind. "I was over at your place and..." There is an uneasy silence. Norma, who has risen on hearing the door open, is transfixed. "What's up? Something wrong?"

The dreaded monster has materialized from the box! Norma dashes forward and hugs Otis tightly, suppressing a tear. Otis looks at his father. Hampton responds with a clenched-teeth smile, trying hard to contain

45

an uncomfortable moment. Otis sees the recorder by Norma's bag. Oh God, he sighs.

"What's this?" he asks, backing her up lightly to look in her eyes.

"Sit down, Otis." Norma clears her choked throat. "Let me explain."

"Explain what, Norma?"

They both sit.

Taking a deep breath, she says, "After I left you, I went home and tried to begin working on my project. I turned on the recorder to listen to the information I got from Mr Barrett at the restaurant. I had no idea the tape had captured the things you said when you fell into your spasm. Believe me, Otis, I just couldn't deal with it alone. I'm sorry—I just couldn't."

"Oh, man!" says Otis, standing up. "So you came—I thought we agreed to keep it all from my parents?"

"I know. But what was I supposed to do? You weren't there with me, and even if you were I don't think you'd have wanted to hear it. I did the best thing that came to my mind."

Hampton moves in to intervene.

"Look, son, I don't think Norma should be blamed for doing what she did."

"Dad, I'm a grown man, okay? I believe I can handle my problems myself. I don't have to drag you and mom into everything I get involved in."

"All right, so you're a grown man. But how do you know what you're up against? You don't even know what language you speak when that stuff hits you. So how do you plan on handling *that* problem?"

"I'm working on it."

"You're working on it. How're you working on it?"

Otis walks slowly back to his seat. The discussion has already drained him emotionally. *Ifa says: Two by two do I help people. I do not help them singly.* He sighs, and holds his hands against his chin, thinking how best to tell them what had happened on the campus. Norma puts her hand to his back, rubbing it gently to help him compose his mind. For a while nobody says anything.

"Dad," Otis begins, "some days ago I was in this pizza joint, close to the campus." Norma and Hampton eye each other quickly. "There were these two Africans, arguing over something. It didn't matter to me, until they started talking in their own language. Then," he sighed, "that feeling came over me again, and...Well, I went up to them. Friendly as I could, I asked what language they were speaking. They got angry, one of them anyway. Thought I was butting into their business. He started fretting. I kept my cool, but he wouldn't oblige. He stormed right out of the place. I've been trying ever since to figure out what possible language they could have been speaking. Something they said about the student elections made me believe they were BU students. So I've been going every place I know on the campus, hoping to find them. All day today I was on that beat. Nothing. I got into one meeting of African students and was looking all over for those guys. Nothing. They weren't there. I don't know. This stuff...I mean, why *me*?" More silence.

If you are wise, your ori *has made you so. If you are not wise, your* ori *must have made you more stupid than a tuber of yam. We chose our heads from the same place, but our destinies are not the same. No god blesses a man without the consent of his* ori. *Make sacrifice to your* ori, *that you may realize the blessings of the choice it made on your behalf!*

"Son," Hampton breaks the silence. "Suppose...suppose you don't find those fellows. And, even if you did, suppose they still won't cooperate. Have you figured out what to do next?"

"Not yet. But I've got to find them first. There's nothing anyone can do unless we deal with the language problem. Everything hangs on it."

"You may be right. But there just might be another way." Hampton looks carefully at his son before continuing. "Don't you think we should consider seeing...a psychiatrist?"

Otis is alarmed. He sits straight up. His eyes move from his father to Norma. She too looks at Hampton with some surprise.

"I can't believe you said that, dad. So I'm crazy now, is that what you think?"

"No, no, no, no, no. I don't imply that for one moment. Please don't get me wrong."

"So why do I have to see a shrink?"

"Because, however you cut this, it's a personality problem."

"Jesus Christ!" Otis rises from his seat, moving some distance away to take a good look at his father. "Yeah? A personality problem. So now I need to be...*opened* up...*analyzed* by a shrink. Is that it?"

"Don't make it sound like that. They don't *open* you up. They just ask questions, have a little talk with you, friendly like, just so they can get to the root of the problem. That's all they do." Otis is still looking at him intently. "Look, I'm your father. You think for one moment I'd suggest anything that wasn't in your best interest?"

Otis is still looking at his father when Norma, rising from the sofa, breaks the awkward silence, "You'll be fine, Otey. People see psychiatrists all the time. It doesn't mean they're crazy or anything. Your dad means well."

Otis moves to the sofa and sits down again.

"Believe me, son, we've got to start somewhere. Seeing a psychiatrist may be our best way to begin dealing with this problem."

Resigned, Otis slowly begins to concede the possibilities. It just doesn't feel right to be judged a nut case. But this whole thing has put some brakes already on the normal run of his life. Things could get worse.

"Well, who do you have in mind?"

The room suddenly appears brighter.

"Frankly, I have no idea just yet." Hampton paces for a while, thinking. "I've never had anything to do with a psychiatrist. The only one I know, and even then only casually, is one Dr. Fishbein. Friend of Bob Hutchins. Remember Reverend Hutchins, Roxbury Ebenezer AME?"

"Yeah, I think so."

"Well, I met Dr. Fishbein in a fundraiser Bob did in his church premises about a year ago. He and I got into a conversation. Somehow we got to talking about his line of work. He sounded a little interesting. I haven't seen him ever since, but if he's still in the area, I believe Bob can hook us up with him."

Still making his own calculations, Otis asks, "This Dr. Fishbein, is he...black or white?"

"He's...white. But, hey, it doesn't matter."

Otis looks up at his father. There is a quirky smile on his face.

"It doesn't? You want to send me to a *white* shrink? How's he going to deal with *my* kind of problem?"

"Son, he's a *psychiatrist*—"

"Yeah, I know. But how's he going to deal with the *African* stuff? What does he know about...does he understand any African language?"

"What we have here may be more than just language. And we're not even sure yet that what we've heard you speak is an *African* language. You ever thought about that?"

"Then how come I feel funny when I hear Africans talking? Doesn't that say something? And African style drumming?"

"Well, you may have a point there. But...then who do we get—an African psychiatrist? I don't know there's any such person here in Boston. Do you?"

Hampton looks towards Norma, who may have a wider international network. She shrugs her shoulders, shaking her head slowly in wide-eyed reflection.

"Think about it, son. An African psychiatrist may be good for an *African*. But, you're not...What I'm trying to say is, all your life you've grown up...an African American, yes, but still an *American*. Anyway, whether we get an American psychiatrist or an...*African* psychiatrist, these doctors have their ways around the job. They've got skills for getting round personality problems, anything troubling the mind. Get my point?" Otis is listening. But he neither looks at his father nor says anything. "At least let's give it a shot. Mind you, I'm not saying it's got to be Fishbein—like I said, I don't know if he's available. But whoever it turns out to be, let's try a psychiatrist first, okay? Okay, son?"

Slowly, Otis rises from his seat, shaking his head.

"Let me think about this, dad, okay? I've got to deal with this for a while. Let me...let me deal with this for a while. So many things have happened to me lately, I have to figure it all out and come to terms with myself first. Let's...leave it at that for the meantime." *One hand alone cannot lift a water gourd to the head. One foot alone is unstable on a bridge.*

In the days that followed, Otis continued to study every unfamiliar black face he met on campus. He also looked out for posters announcing coming African events. He even sought out Africans known to friends of his, hoping to start a relationship that might provide viable clues. Nothing in what they said or the way they spoke English moved his body in any way. Even when he persuaded them to say something in their native tongues, nothing they offered succeeded in stirring any sensations in him. Still, he didn't stop trying.

Norma found a way of making her approach to the African student at Radcliffe. On another tape, she transferred that slice of her recording that contained Otis' chant against the drum sounds, and took it to the student. Her name was Ann Mqabayi.

"Do you mind my asking, what part of Africa you come from?"

Ann's head, small and ovoid, was topped by a low Afro cut. With high cheek bones and generously thick lips, she was always ready with a smile that revealed a wide gap in her exquisitely white teeth. Her breasts were full and hung heavily within her blouse. Her hips were disproportionately broader than her torso. She was solid black in skin tone, which was partly why her teeth shone so white.

"I am from South Africa."

The smile was immediate. Norma returned the compliment. In her limited knowledge of Africa, South Africa was as much the language as the topography of the country.

"If I play you some sounds from Africa, can you tell me where in Africa they come from?"

"I will try," Ann giggled.

Norma pulled out the recorder, pressed the play button, and looked steadily at Ann as the tape rolled. The South African listened with a smile. But the smile faded as she screwed her brow and drew closer to the machine. When the tape stopped, Ann shook her head and looked at Norma.

"The words are rather faint," she said. "But...I can't make out the language. It is certainly not my language."

"Really? What's your language?"

"Sesotho."

"I see. Oh, well," sighed Norma.

No point trying to figure out the difference, Norma thought. She put the recorder back in the bag.

"You could try someone from West Africa," suggested Ann. "I know a Sierra Leonean at Northeastern. He will probably help you better than I can."

Norma took Ann up on her offer. But when they finally played the tape to the Sierra Leonean, he too confessed he didn't know the language of the sounds. He suggested they talk to a Dahomean he'd recently met, a fire-eater in a traveling circus that was in Boston for another week. At this point, Norma decided to look elsewhere. Recent experience had taught her to beware the path of cultural melodrama.

Six

HAMPTON KNOWS HOW RIGHT OTIS AND HIS girlfriend are about not bringing news of his latest experiences home to his mother. The specter of the birthday night is still fresh in her memory. A caring mother, she, more than anyone else, would wish he never had those horrible attacks. She feels secure enough in the ease and comfort guaranteed her family by their berth in Boston's black middle-class circles. The past, which they have worked hard to erase, has no right to haunt them—certainly not any past they cannot account for even within an uncomfortable memory. For her, such a past does not exist. Hence, when her husband cuts to the chase and tells her of his decision to consult a psychiatrist, her response comes as no surprise.

"Not my boy! He's not crazy. He may act a little strange. But he's not crazy."

Hampton is a good husband. He also knows where to draw the line between love and duty.

"I know how you feel," he says, with a sigh that signifies more resolve than resignation. "But you'd be glad to have your son back again, cured and clean."

He does not discuss their son's problem with his wife for some time thereafter.

Yet the remedy he seeks proves no easier. At times he wonders if there isn't something to be said for his wife's misgivings. Boston, as it turns out, hasn't a single black psychiatrist, let alone an African one. Of the various contacts he has made, Dr. Fishbein seems the most promising: He is the only one known for going out of his way to cultivate the black community. He gives generously in their fund-raisers. He empathizes with the economic situation of blacks who seek his care and, to his staff's discomfort, adjusts his charges accordingly.

Fishbein is not doing this to enhance his practice with Boston's growing black population. A third-generation scion of a wealthy Philadelphia Jewish family and a director in not a few financial institutions in the northeast, he has no need of anyone's money. He is simply a decent man. Protected by his good fortune, he takes social liberties in Boston's touchy racial climate that many in his circle would never even contemplate.

But this liberal openness often comes at a price that some in the appreciative black community find a little high. Although he has never before consulted a psychiatrist, Hampton knows deep inside that he has survived a life that could have broken many of his kind. He is also aware that psychiatrists seek to know the sources of problems brought to their attention. But, in an exploratory visit with Fishbein, little does he know how far the doctor is inclined to go: Any history of murders in the family? Any dark deeds hidden in the collective amnesia of ancient plantation folk? How often in the past, as he built his way up the professional ladder, did Hampton crave to kill a white boss or set his place on fire? Any instability in his marital life? What effect could it possibly have on their son?

The visit survives its inherent stresses because each man addresses the other with guarded civility. Fishbein is experienced enough to know that sessions of this kind always have a chance of going seriously amiss. But he has also invested enough in terms of human relations to know he can get away with his daring probes: he always manages to remain nice doing them. For his part, Hampton has been obliging white people so long, he answeres each question Fishbein asks with the appropriate grin. With so much riding on the session, what does it matter to him now, any more than it did to his family and his people so many ages gone, how poorly one white man thinks of him? On top of it all, Fishbein concludes the session with profuse apologies for discomfort his questions, raised purely in search of the best possible remedy for Otis's condition, may have caused Hampton.

Coffee is served. In the more cheerful conversation that follows, the stresses of a moment ago are soon laid to rest. The doctor suggests a date for a separate session with the troubled young man. A tentative one is set. On his way home, Hampton begins to feel an anxiety that has been dormant during his conversation with the doctor: How would Otis possibly deal with the sort of questions he has just survived?

Ifa says: However tall the palm tree, it will yield its juice to the tapper's knife. However deep the well, it will yield its water to the drawing pail.

How wrong Hampton was! Otis had his first session, then another. After the first, he was indeed looking forward to the next. A bond had grown between doctor and patient nearly as strong as between father and son. Now he is here for his third session with the doctor.

With Otis, Fishbein carefully avoids raising issues of family and social history. Their sessions last long at each meeting, because Fishbein takes a purely personal approach: He pretends to be swapping stories with Otis as though they've known each other for a while and could share confidences.

They talk about sports. Fishbein had played competitively at high school in Philly though very little at college (Brown). Nevertheless, he knows a thing or two about basketball, for though Brown never distinguished itself in collegiate competition during his time, sports-minded students gave their team every possible support, even at road games. He could have gotten on Brown's tennis team, but the coach didn't like him. So upset, in fact, was he about the whole business that he had a shouting match with the coach that nearly ended in a fight. Does Otis, he asks, have a happier experience at Bradley? Any racial encounters?

Otis admits he's been treated pretty well. But the white man has broached such serious matters, the black youth is led to dig beneath the veneer of comfort he thinks he's enjoyed. Is it by accident or by design that he's the only black on BU's regular basketball team? Well, there's Shavers, and earlier on Rentrope. But both of these guys have been benchers. And has he forgotten how his white teammates behaved toward him when he first got on the team? And what about that occasion when.... Has he ever been so angry with anyone, coach or player, that he's gotten physical?....Yes, indeed, there was this particular incident....

Each time Otis reminisces, the doctor maneuvers his recollections—carefully, very carefully—until he gets to a point precariously close to Hampton's narrative of an old family trauma. Then he guides the young man back from that brink. It is proving an uncomfortable walk.

They turn to more intimate matters. Fishbein manufactures a black girl in his all-white private school in Philly. He loved her so much he could hardly bear to be away from her. They shared many lunches in school. She was frequently at their place for dinner and R&R. He doesn't mention going to *their* place. But he speaks glowingly about what a nice black family they were, how bereft he felt when the girl's family had to move to Texas. They never saw each other again. At Brown, he took an intense liking to an African female student he had met in a music history course. They went out together a few times, it looked liked their affair had a future. He'd suggested they pay a visit to her parents in Africa (Fishbein doesn't remember which country). But the girl confessed that her parents disapproved of their relationship. It broke his heart, but...life had to go on! Well, how is Otis' love life?

Norma, oh Norma....Heartfelt moments that crave to remain just what they are: a string of pearls, broken to be sure by gaps of imponderables that need not be filled, but nonetheless a sequence of happy moments that fate seems to have put together with no apparent design in view. Romance. Mutual support. Telephone calls when they miss each other...Supportive parents. Parties. Holidays. Days out in the sunlight. Swimming together in the pool....

How well do you swim, Otis? Pretty good...Yeah? Yeah. Me, I nearly blew it once when I dove into the waters in a beach up in Maine: I was struggling so hard to get back to the surface, but it seemed like I could never make it. Has that ever happened to you, Otis? Well, not in a beach. I dove into this pool, trying to make it from one side to the other under water. I made it all right, but moved so fast I hit my head on the concrete wall of the pool and just about passed out. I'd started going down when, luckily, someone saw me and came to my rescue. Man, I thought it was all over with me! My mind was spinning, seemed like I was seeing things, like I was in another place...Did you see anything familiar to you, in this other place? Not really, but all kinds of figures were just...

A recording machine is on somewhere, though Otis is not aware of it. At high points Fishbein, who periodically jots things down on a paper, scribbles a little faster and even draws some diagram or other.

They talk about music. I grew up in Philly, as you know. Great place for music. I love all kinds of music. classical, rhythm and blues, jazz. I *love* John Coltrane. Do you like jazz, Otis? Not really. I don't really care much for it. Rhythm and blues, yes. Jazz is too noisy, much too hot for me...Is it the horns, or is it the drums that you find too noisy?...Everything. They just go on and on with all kinds of instruments. Piano's good. Sometimes when the piano does a duet with a saxophone, that can be very soothing. Yeah, piano's good, it's soft...What about drums: do you like drums?...Not really, I don't like drums that much...*Otis shakes his head, rather forcefully. Fishbein scribbles, eyeing him. Silence*...Otis, I can see you don't like drums. Is there anything about drums that turns you off?...Well, I don't know. Maybe just the noise...Right, and as I recall, it was the sound of drums that upset you on two occasions, sent you into spasms. What is it about drums that does this to you? Try to think...I...I don't know. I've been trying to figure that out.... Think: something back in high school? In your church?...*Otis is deep in thought*...And when you go into those spasms, those things you say, are they things you hear deep in your mind—do you hear those sounds from somewhere?...*Otis is still deep in thought, his head rolling on the sofa, his eyes turned slowly toward the ceiling*...There's a man, or maybe a woman. Saying things. A man, yes, a man. But I haven't a clue who he is. Yes, he's dancing, and there's music. Many people. It's very confusing, I can't make out their faces. Men and women. But I can't figure out any of them. God, they look so weird. And, and they're all in a strange place...You've never been there before?... No, never. Never been here before...Think, Otis, you could have been there sometime but forgotten?...No—yes—no—no—no—*No!*...All right, Otis. That's okay now. Let's get out of that place. Come on, Otis. Relax now.

Fishbein draws him out of the brink once more. Otis, already startled into consciousness by his last denial, blinks a couple of times. He tries to re-cognize his surroundings. He is a little embarrassed. He buries his face in his hands, partly to clear the mist from his eyes. He is still so disoriented that, when Fishbein's pencil rolls off the table and drops on the floor, he turns briskly in the direction of the sound. Fishbein pats him on the shoulder.

"Coffee? Soda?"

"Soda's fine," says Otis with a sigh.

With Norma gone to New York for the Easter weekend, Otis spent much of the time by himself at his parents' home in Quincy. His mother checked frequently in his room to be sure he was okay. It became so frequent that Otis, even when he was awake, would shut his eyes and pretend to be asleep, just so she'd leave him alone. Melba Hampton would take that as a sign that nothing was wrong with him.

She needed the reassurance. Hampton, who for some time had suspended any discussion of their son's condition, had found it unavoidable to tell her the next step decided upon in the investigation of Otis' case. In reviewing the evidence gathered in separate sessions with father and son, Fishbein had detected certain strands that led to contiguous points in family history, but needed a clinching thread to link them up into a coherent picture. That last session with Otis took them precariously close to a credible terrain. But he had to pull the young man from the brink to save him from a regression that might complicate the task in hand. Still, he was sure he was on to something that might prove their surest bet for a solution: If they could capture the words Otis chanted during his spasms, a lot of the threads might converge into some meaningful picture.

Otis was not exactly thrilled by the idea. But, he thought, the doctor seemed to know where he was going with his probes. If there was one real good the last session did, it was to bring Otis closer to those buried sensations that had been impinging on his consciousness and yet eluded every effort at understanding. The picture was still not clear to him. But gradually his mind was getting adjusted to a fate his instincts had only hinted at. If Fishbein's efforts had a chance of bringing about the final convergence of instincts and understanding, why fight them? Hampton was only too glad his son was prepared to go along with the decision.

The original idea was to install a record player in a room adjacent to Otis's bedroom in the Hampton home. Otis would be made to lie on his bed, connected to a tape-recorder with a very long cord, while a recording of African drum music was playing next door. If the music set him off in a chanting spell, the cord was long enough to allow Otis whatever movement he was induced to make while his chant was being recorded. When Hampton informed Melba about the decision, she vehemently opposed it. She did not want to see her son tied to anything programmed that might cause her worst nightmare for him. So it was decided the recording session would take place in Fishbein's office, which already had some recording equipment.

The next problem was what music they would play. It made sense to borrow the record Guinea Man had played at Pleasure Island. Norma, who had chosen to terminate her contacts with the man to avoid any further embarrassment, had nonetheless agreed to seek his help again. But when she tried to reach him, she was told Guinea Man was off to Jamaica on his trade business; he might not be back for a while. Fishbein, who had his own way around problems, came up with a solution from his network in musical culture. The hottest drum artist of the day turned out to be a Nigerian by name Olatunji, a maestro whose drum suites fueled the romance of Africa in many an African American artist and cultural politician. It was not clear if his recordings would have the required effect on Otis. But, so far, the young man had reacted to at least two disparate strains of drum music: first the sounds (now lost to memory) from his car radio, and later the Jamaican maroon music played by Guinea Man. With luck, Olatunji's music might have a similar effect.

The session was fixed for the Friday after Easter. Once in a while, when his mother was not checking in on him, Otis would ask himself again and again: Why me? And why Africa? He had nothing against Africa. In fact, if there was anything his recent brushes with things and persons African had done to Otis, it was to make him increasingly aware of the current nationalist mantra: Africa as the proud homeland of all black people. But why should he be made to champion the cause of the race with neuroses no one seemed so far to have an answer for? Why not one of those activists who spoke on television and continually got into trouble with the police and their dogs? He had seen Malcolm X and the Black Muslims in the news now and again. He thought they made some sense. Good luck to *them*! But why was he burdened with these strange impulses, reacting to music he could never have chosen to play on his own time, chanting things nobody seemed to understand? What, on God's earth, was the source of those words? Could his family have done something wrong in the past he was being made to pay for today?

The more his reasoning mind questioned his fate, the more a hidden instinct stressed a charge he could still not grasp but that was steadily commanding the fabric of his will.

The recording session in Fishbein's clinic didn't take very long. Otis's reaction was more dramatic than ever. The drum music of the LP was particularly affecting, because it was accompanied by a song in a language described on the album's jacket as Yoruba, predominantly spoken in the Western Region of Nigeria. Through a shuttered glass window between Fishbein's consulting room and an adjoining office where they waited, Norma and Hampton watched—helplessly but with combined curiosity and horror—as Otis went through his motions. Fishbein had never seen the like in all his years of practice. Standing close by with folded arms, he did his best to stay cool as he watched his agonized patient. When Otis finally came to the end of his labors, the record was still playing. Slumping into a chair, he went into a fit of twitching, head bent and shoulders hunched. Fishbein ran at once to the player and stopped the music. Walking over to Otis, he placed a hand on his back and patted it a few times, warming him back to full consciousness.

The session over, Hampton drove Otis and Norma home to Quincy. Nobody said a word.

Fishbein set about trying to make sense of what he had captured on tape. Otis had been fitted with a microphone to which a muffler had been attached, the idea being to filter off ambient sound. Although Olatunji's music was fairly audible in the background, it did not much bother the doctor. Indeed he welcomed it as a context within which some sense might be made of the young man's predicament. Unfortunately, neither he nor his assistants had any clue how to begin transcribing the text of Otis' chant. Fishbein and his team were familiar with what in the profession went by the term "xenoglossy"—or, in the case of Otis's chant, what a more recent scholar had called "recitative xenoglossy." But how would they go about dealing with a language none of them could even identify as one?

The first step towards solving the conundrum led Fishbein to a linguistics professor at Harvard—a fellow Brown alumnus and member of Fishbein's old boy circle—versed in foreign languages. Although his interests were not exactly *African* (he was actually an Arabic specialist), he was willing to see what he might find as clues. He had in his office a miniature stereophonic machine, and proceeded to use it to isolate the text of Otis's chant from the ambient sounds of Olatunji's music. In the end, however, the professor confessed total bafflement with the resultant text. It didn't seem like anything remotely familiar to him. The professor recommended someone else he knew at Boston University.

The Boston University professor, an expert in southern African languages, was more discerning. Rather than play Otis's chant in isolation, he had Fishbein return with the music that had set off the young man's spasms. First, he played the sounds Fishbein had captured from Otis, including the faint sounds from Olatunji's album. Then he played the relevant cut from the album, listening very closely to every sound in each recording. He played the two pieces again and again in alternating sequence, bringing his ear very close to the player in each instance. He still did not know the language to which Otis's text could be linked with any certainty. But he was sensitive enough to African inflections to tell there was *some* affinity between Otis's words and the words of Olatunji's song.

"My feeling," said the professor, "is that the boy's words may be a corruption of the same language as in the music."

"You mean, Yo-ra—"

"Yes, Yoruba. It's a language spoken by millions of people in West Africa, mostly in Nigeria."

Fishbein nodded, wondering where on earth this could be leading.

"I'm really not sure who's the best qualified person to help you with this," continued the professor. "The only scholar I know who's worked on the Yoruba is an anthropologist at Berkeley. Name of Baldwin. Warren Baldwin. He's been collecting texts from Yoruba herbalists for years. He'd know better than I whether or not your boy's gibberish was in some form of the language."

Hampton was high enough in the executive ranks of his company that he could take off for days on a pressing private business. Fishbein had told him of his findings on his son's case, and suggested he make contact with Professor Baldwin at Berkeley. With so much at stake, Hampton simply had to make the time.

First he got Baldwin on the telephone. Hampton did not divulge everything the professor might need to know. Just enough details to excite the man's curiosity.

"Well," said the professor, "how can I get the material from you? Are you going to mail it, or are you going to send someone here with it?"

"I'll bring it myself," said Hampton.

Hampton had been out to the west coast only once before, many years ago, to interview for a job he never got. But the memory of that experience paled in comparison with what he felt on his flight to San Francisco. Prior to his son's problems, he had never given much thought to Africa. As a member of the growing cadre of middle-class blacks in Boston, he was satisfied with the privileges his position conferred on him. The increasingly charged climate of political activity among blacks should have qualified such feelings of security. But he did not feel compelled to participate in the growth of black awareness whether on a personal or a communal level. Whenever he was invited to contribute money to a black cause, he did so, but asked that neither he nor his contribution be publicized. He had worked too hard and come too far to be drawn back by anything that might link him to the past.

Yet here he was on a mission that forced him to grapple with a past that would not go away. Although there was little in his or his wife's family history, as far back as they could tell, that was linked to his son's problems, it was becoming increasingly clear there was some unresolved history lurking somewhere that needed to be dealt with. African drum music. An African language. Whatever else might there be?

The tapes he carried had a significance that went beyond this mission to Berkeley. While Otis was being recorded in Fishbein's consulting room, Hampton was so engrossed in his son's passion that he paid little attention to the drum music that seemed to activate such a response in his boy. The strains of that tune now came back to him, as his mind replayed the incident in the uneasy quiet of night before he finally drifted to sleep. Hampton had musical skills. He played the violin and piano and had performed at church and other occasions. So he could at least tell a good tune when he heard one. He had also followed the major trends in black music, including jazz. But he belonged to that sector of the black middle class who associated jazz with black low life and so kept their distance from it. For his son to be driven to spasms by such music was therefore a double tragedy. A question continually exercised his mind all through his flight: Why must the black man's dilemmas in America be forever referable to Africa: haven't we lived in this land long enough to find our own solutions here?

The door opens to Hampton's knock. A tall, silver-haired, bespectacled man with a green, short-sleeved dashiki and a toothy grin stands aside to welcome him.

"Come on in, sir. *E k'aabo.*"

"Excuse me?" says Hampton, stepping uncertainly into the office.

"That's Yoruba for, Welcome. Literally it means, Greetings for coming. The Yoruba are an extremely polite and cultivated people. They have greetings for a whole range of things people do."

"Oh." Hampton doesn't quite know how to respond to such a structured reception.

"*Ee-nii jokoo?*" To Hampton's continued bafflement, Professor Baldwin adds, "It means, Won't you please sit down?"

"Of course. Thanks."

While the professor closes the door, Hampton settles into an upholstered seat. He puts his briefcase on the floor. Running his eyes across the compass of the office, he finds so many artifacts placed here and there that he feels somewhat beleaguered by them. He tries to imagine his son

Otis sitting in the midst of so much devilry. His eyes are particularly fixed on a huge black mask hanging over the door. It has large, red-ringed holes where the eyes and mouth should be. Underneath the eye-holes are patterns of scarification, etched in white. There is a circle of white dots round each eye. Long leafy frills overhang the sides of the mask from the top of the head. Sweet Jesus! thinks Hampton.

"That's an *egungun* mask. Egungun is a masquerade. You should see what the whole thing looks like. I've taken off the long body piece so this place doesn't get all cluttered up. But you should see a fully dressed masquerade. Quite a sight!"

Hampton nods as though he understands. He knows Africans do all kinds of crazy, superstitious stuff, but this is the first time he's come into full gaze of their primitive artifacts.

"Why...what does the masquerade stand for?"

"Africans, you must understand, mark all kinds of occasions with celebration. There's music and dancing when a child is born, when someone is made a chief, when someone dies. All kinds of occasions. The mask you see up there is worn by a masquerade performing at new year rituals in the Yoruba town where I did my research."

Hampton nods again. This time his gaze is fixed on Baldwin's face. His mind is asking a lot of questions, all prefaced by "Why." So beleaguered is he that he is unable to formulate any of those questions.

"Coffee?" Baldwin asks. The offer relieves the awkward silence.

"Oh, no, thanks. I had a late breakfast. You can't imagine how long I slept last night."

"I know. The east. Any connectiing flights?"

"Yes, one. In Austin. And that took three hours. You know what it's like, sitting in an airport with nothing to do but read mindlessly."

"Isn't there something I can get you? Soda, water..."

"A glass of water would be perfect, thanks."

While Baldwin goes off for the water, Hampton ventures another look round the room. Carvings. A string of beads. A round wooden tray, with all kinds of figures etched in it. A beaded gourd. An iron staff with a knobbed end wrapped in cloth, or something like it; various things stuck around the cloth. A stuffed monkey, hanging with its left hand from a peg on a bookshelf. Sweet Jesus, what on earth...?

"Professor," says Hampton, receiving the glass of water with thanks, "may I ask you a question?"

"Sure. Anything."

"How long were you in the…Yoruba?"

"Among the Yoruba? Let's see: seven years, on the whole. I first went out there with a team of British anthropologists from Oxford University. That was in 1952. They'd been commissioned by the colonial government to study aspects of Yoruba life and culture. I was invited to join them as an expert on language systems. God, the first time I heard the Yoruba language spoken, I just flipped! *Ah, ede Yoruba n dun gan-ni!*' Seeing Hampton's raised brows, Baldwin adds in explanation, "Means, the Yoruba language is very delightful.' I stayed with the group four years. When our grant ran out, I returned to the States, first at Indiana University. Then two years later I received a Ford grant, so I returned to my Yoruba village for two more years, and another one as an extension. You know, I had such a great time with my hosts, when I was leaving, the *Baale*, that's like mayor of the town, made me a chief. You know what my title is?"

Hampton is too bemused to shake his head.

"I was appointed *Oluwe*. That means, King of Books or Master of Learning. They gave me so many gifts—some of them you see here—I couldn't take them all home. I've been here at Berkeley just over a year."

Late morning has become lunchtime. Baldwin invites Hampton for a bite out. Past Sprawl Plaza and across the street there is a row of restaurants, regular American and every variety of ethnic, serving the diverse Berkeley community. The two men chat cheerily about the college, and especially the west coast. Hampton tells Baldwin of his hapless job visit many years before. Baldwin admits the west has its problems, but all told he prefers California to the cold, cold midwest. All through lunch, their conversation stays at a polite, convivial level. By the time they return to Baldwin's office, Hampton has been much regaled by the walk and the occasional laughter.

As they resume their seats, however, he is still looking Baldwin straight in the eye. His mind has managed to put some weight to the questions that assailed it an hour ago. Why is it that a white man has "flipped" for a language that he, a black man whose ancestors obviously came from Africa, would sooner recoil from and that causes his son so much trouble? Granted, Otis has a peculiar problem, one that Hampton is here to resolve. But is his reaction to Africa common to all black men in America, or is it something that goes back specifically to his family's history?

Although he has done well in the white man's world and would sooner forget his past, every time he comes face to face with a white man who gives him cause, his mind goes back in a flash to that moment, so many years ago, when at a music performance a white man tried to hurt him with rude words about his race. Now, how could a white man, whose ancestors did untold havoc to Africa, bringing millions of Hampton's kind as slaves here, be treated so well by the same Africans the white man despoiled? Could they have lost their memory, or is there something wrong with black people like Hampton, here in America, who just won't forget the wrongs of the past?

"Now, Mr. Hampton," he hears Baldwin say, "let's get to your business. I believe you have something for me? What exactly is the matter with your son?"

Hampton takes a deep breath before giving Baldwin the history of Otis's predicament. He recounts the night of the birthday party, right up to the seizure in the family home. He mentions other instances of the seizure—at a ball game, in restaurants. He mentions efforts Fishbein has made, in his clinic and in consultation with language experts in the Boston area, to make some sense of his son's strange trauma. It was one of them, says Hampton, who finally recommended that he see Baldwin in hopes that he would determine what Otis has been saying during his seizures. More than once Hampton, on the verge of tears, reaches for the glass of water Baldwin gave him earlier on.

A man of bubbly spirits, Baldwin tries to revive Hampton's own by rising briskly, rubbing his hands cheerily, a wide grin on his face.

"Well," he says, "seems like our young man has been through quite a bit. You've got the recordings with you?"

Hampton reaches for his briefcase, and brings out the two items: Olatunji's LP, and Fishbein's recording of Otis. There is a language laboratory adjoining Baldwin's office. He takes Hampton in there. First he plays Fishbein's recorded tape. His brow is furrowed from start to finish. He shakes his head, turns to the LP. Hampton shows him the specific track Fishbein used for recording Otis. Baldwin plays the LP on a turntable, adjusting the volume controls so he can hear the words clearly. He's not familiar with the artist, but he occasionally smiles and nods his head as he listens to the words accompanying the drum music. Throughout the playing, Hampton stares at Baldwin in hopes the professor will tell him what it is that gives him such pleasure. Only at the end of the cut does Baldwin turn, still smiling, to Hampton.

"Well!" Baldwin sighs.

"Make any sense? I mean, what's the connection between the two?"

"Nothing *directly*, as far as I can tell."

"So what does the record say that set my son off? The music has obviously had a strong impact on him."

"Well, the words of the music simply salute all black people in the world. Wishes the blessings of the god Ogun on them. Pays special homage to...Coltrane?"

"Yes, John Coltrane. Jazz musician."

"Yes, whom he calls a true son of Africa. Something along those lines. Mostly a salute to black people. That's all."

"So what about the recorded tape—what's my son saying?"

"That's what I'm trying to figure out. It's an attempt at a Yoruba chant, possibly a salute to someone, which is probably why it bears *some* link, though I can't see what, to Olatunji's song. If I could only.... Here, let's do this."

Baldwin quickly moves across the lab to a large machine by a window, taking Fishbein's tape with him.

"This machine will transcribe the text of your son's words, and hopefully I can *try* to make sense of what he's said. It's a machine I use for reducing my taped recordings to print. The neat thing about it is, it will separate ambient sounds from recorded voice and at the same time print the text of the voice. Let's see if we'll get lucky."

Baldwin sets the tape in the machine, presses the play button and watches the machine do its job. He then pulls out the printed sheet, runs his eyes through it, and searches for a seat.

"I'll be goddammed!" he mutters under his breath. Hampton hears, so keen are his ears now.

"What?"

"This is *some* garbled Yoruba if I ever saw one!" The text has left Baldwin's brow steadily creased. "I can see some words here and there. But I can't string them together to make a coherent statement. Going by its structure, it seems to be a salute to someone whose name is Akindiji, or Akindeji. It goes on to say a few things about this man.... Tell you what, why don't you leave me with this stuff for now. I'll work on it and try to figure it out. Let's meet again tomorrow or so. How much time have you got on this trip?"

"I can spend another day, if you want me to," says Hampton. "Just tell me how much time you need, and I'll call my office and let them know when I'll be back."

"Okay. Frankly, I can work all night if I have to, just to crack this thing. Let's meet at ten tomorrow morning, and I'll let you know how far I've gotten. Fair enough?"

"Fair enough. And I'm much obliged to you, professor."

"Not at all. I'd be glad to help."

On seeing Hampton to the door, Baldwin regales him with a parting phrase, "*O d' ola.*"

"Now," responds Hampton, aptly amused, "you know I can't say anything to that!"

"Oh, it simply means, Until tomorrow. All you need say is, *Oshe*, meaning Thanks."

"*Oshe*, professor!"

"Well, how about that—you might get the better of me pretty soon!"

For now, as he leaves Baldwin's office, Hampton is in better spirits than he was not so long ago.

But when he returns to the professor's office the next morning, Hampton finds that Otis's text, though reduced to a readable script, has defied Baldwin's skills. Employing the latest trends in error analysis and transformational grammar, he has worked throughout the previous evening and the better part of the night, but has been unable to bring the script to good semantic health. When Hampton finally shows up in his office, Baldwin is so exhausted, he can hardly repeat the courtesies of the day before—wide grin, Yoruba speech, and all.

But he is unwilling to send the poor man home with nothing to show for his trouble.

"I think we may have another chance of cracking this thing," says Baldwin. "One of my old students, a Nigerian scholar whose work I directed at Indiana, happens to be in the U.S. right now. His name's Bolaji Alabi, postdoctoral fellow at Northwestern's program in African Studies. He's Yoruba. Believe me, this guy is a genius in everything that has to do with the Yoruba language and culture. At Indiana, why, he taught me more than I taught him! I took the liberty of calling him up last night and telling him about this problem. You know what? He's prepared to help."

Hampton nods weakly. What else can he do but hang on to yet another peg of hope?

"My advice is, take the recordings to him. Let him listen to them. I think you should take the transcript as well. I've made a photocopy in case he and I need to compare notes over the phone. Mr. Hampton, you stand a better chance of cracking this thing with Professor Alabi than with me. It's his language. It's his culture."

Returning to Boston, Hampton quickly calls Professor Alabi. But it's another week before he flies to Chicago and drives up to Evanston. Upon presenting himself to the Nigerian scholar, Hampton is struck by how much more at ease he is this time. Alabi is the very first African he's ever met face to face and is actually going to settle down to talk with. Two things, in particular, disarm Hampton about Alabi. First, he is so self-effacing, so polite and warm, it's as if the two men have known each other before and are reuniting after a long spell. Second, Alabi doesn't try to disorient Hampton with a foreign language, however well-intended this may be. In fairness to Baldwin, his Yoruba speech helped to introduce Hampton to the culture he needed to deal with. But, to a man already suffering some stress over his son's health, a communicational debit was clearly an added nuisance.

After the customary introductions, Alabi offers Hampton a seat. The office is so sparsely furnished, Hampton feels very much at ease. There's nothing strange here—none of those fetish objects that disconcerted his Christian soul in Baldwin's office.

"Professor Baldwin tells me that your son has been having a problem," Alabi says.

His English has a heavy foreign accent. Never having spoken with an African before, Hampton can understand what Alabi says only because it is enunciated slowly.

"Yes, indeed, he has."

"Well, let us see what we can do to help. Do you have the materials with you?"

Hampton opens his briefcase and fishes out the recordings and the transcript. Alabi gives more attention to the LP, smiling with some recognition. He then puts aside the recordings, and proceeds to read the transcript to see what sense it might make to him. This is the text of Otis's chant as reduced to print by Baldwin's dictagraph:

Kindijay, Kindijay, Kindijay oh
Mokiseo lermata motami
Coorin kosakitty famita losugun
Ballugoo bakimboly babiji
Laaya beinakky fibira osororun
Coorin koyan tankytank sibra outa
Kosaisili pelorin lero
Libby kitty reberun-par
Occashakey bakimboli babiji
Ookuroo yantapa
Marry cango eikimi yopeck wollorey
Motaimi shoo polobar
Ballugoo laaya nakky canty coorin arrow coorin oogun
Jagojago paranaloo rabaray
Abeyiye lurayere
Baamiyoh yeh yeh
Baamiyoh yeh yeh

Having read through the strange text, Alabi simply smiles at Hampton, shaking his head. Odd stuff, he seems to say. Next, he takes Fishbein's tape and listens carefully while the whole thing is playing. He rewinds the tape, and runs his eyes along every line of Baldwin's transcript as he listens again to Otis' chant. Once more he rewinds the tape, and with his eyes follows every line of text that matches the sounds from the tape. This time, when he gets to the end of the tape, he breaks into a low chuckle, makes a repeated guttural sound, and takes a deep breath.

"Mr. Hampton," he says, "do you think you can leave these things with me for some days?"

Hampton, fearing the Nigerian has come to the same dead end as Baldwin, is a little dismayed by the question.

"You mean, you can't make anything of the chant?"

"No, that's not what I am saying. I think I can guess what is going on here. I could hear a number of words a little better than they have been represented in the transcript. I also think I can guess what dialect of Yoruba I hear in the chant."

"Which means...?"

"Which means that, if my guess is right, I may have an idea what part of Yorubaland this text comes from." Hampton blinks a couple of times, and adjusts his sitting posture. "But I don't want to jump to any conclusions as yet. That is why I asked if you would leave the materials with me for a few days, so that I could study them more closely."

"Sure, professor, I..."

"Do you have another copy of this tape?"

"Yes, the psychiatrist attending to my son has another copy. But what about the LP?"

"Oh, I wouldn't worry about that. I heard the background words and music from it, but there is actually no relationship between them and your son's chant. Well, they are both songs of salute, but neither refers to the other. Besides, the dialects are different. At least I think so. Let me make a copy of the transcript, so that you can take the original and the LP away with you."

When Alabi leaves the room to make the photocopy, Hampton feels considerably lighter in spirit. And his mind says, Sweet Jesus, please! Make this good!

There was a basic problem with Baldwin's earlier attempt at deciphering. He had done his study of Yoruba divination from one base: the village of Fiditi in the Oyo area. Although like most good scholars he had cross-checked his findings with evidence from other parts of Yorubaland, his familiarity with the Yoruba language was rather limited to the Oyo dialect. Even if he could manage a conversation in Yoruba, there was little chance of his being sensitive to inflections in other Yoruba dialects. His analysis of Otis's chant ran into difficulties evidently because the chant was laced with speech habits alien to Oyo Yoruba. Alabi, on the other hand, is a homegrown indigene. Although a native of Apomu, an Oyo Yoruba village, he has both a native ear for dialectal differences and his training as a linguist to aid him in tackling even Otis's heavily corrupted text.

Before sending Hampton on his way, Alabi tries to reassure the troubled man by sharing with him something that occurred to him in the course of copying Baldwin's transcript.

"Take a look at this word in your son's chant." Although this is all strange stuff, Hampton moves closer. "It says *yantapa*. Now, when I listened to the tape, the sound I heard was slightly different from what I see in the transcript. I am not saying that Professor Baldwin's dictagraph is faulty. But my ear tells me to edit the transcript so as to bring it closer to what I think your son is saying there. This wouldn't be clear to someone unfamiliar with the dialect or the culture of this specific part of Yorubaland. There are a few such words scattered across the text. But I would not like to risk a guess at this point. In fact, I will go ahead and run this tape through a dictagraph here and see if my transcript will agree with Baldwin's. When I have done my own analysis, I will be in a position to make an informed guess as to what I think your son is saying. You understand me?"

"I understand you perfectly, professor."

"Good. This is not something that should be rushed. So, let me see.... Suppose I say, let's give it a week?"

"I'd appreciate whatever you could do. A week is fine."

"Okay. Leave me your number, and I will call you to tell you what I have come up with."

The session with Professor Alabi brought Hampton closer than ever before to a native African. With every statement the scholar made, Hampton became steadily attuned to speech habits he could hardly have given the time of day. And perhaps because so much seemed to depend on Alabi, it made that much sense for Hampton to listen closely not only to the intriguing music of his speech but to the likely wisdom of his counsel. As the plane takes him back to Boston, he wonders a little more about Africa than he ever did before. This time, it's his heart that says, Sweet Jesus, please...

Melba Hampton is sitting in a sofa in the living room, a hand against her head. Neither she nor Norma, sitting next to her, has slept much the night before. Otis has gone through one of his chanting spells, evidently prompted by a dream, but has since gone back to sleep. The two women in his life, who watched helplessly while he went through the gyrations, simply went downstairs afterwards to console each other in the living room. Hampton, who has borne his share of the burden for the past week and more, has retired to the bedroom.

Norma, resting her eyes on the grief-striken Mrs. Hampton, feels sorry for her. What a toll this whole thing must be taking on one so naturally weak. A mother too. If she, only romantically tied to Otis, can feel so troubled by his condition, how much greater torment it must bring to one who bore him in her womb so long and nurtured him to adult life. Norma wonders how her own mother would have dealt with the situation. How even she, Norma, would have fared to see her own child suffer so deeply with an ailment that defied all available wisdom. Reaching out an arm, she tries to comfort Mrs Hampton by rubbing her lightly on the shoulder.

"Norma," says Melba, turning slowly, "tell me about Africa. What do you know about it?"

The question arose because of the trend of events in the past four days. First, Alabi had called Hampton to report he had gone as far as he could with Otis' chant. He had run the tape through a dictagraph and had come up with a text essentially similar to Baldwin's, but for certain variations he had supplied from his own knowledge of Yoruba dialects. He had mailed everything—tape, transcript, and a cover note—to Hampton, praying that God would bring a happy end to the family's troubles. Hampton had asked how much Alabi wanted as fee for his work. But the Nigerian had responded that the work took so little time, it would be foolish of him to demand payment for it; the only satisfaction he sought was to see the young man regain his full health. Hampton had been rendered speechless by such rare fellow-feeling.

The first thing Hampton did after receiving Alabi's package was read through the contents. But, trusting neither his nerves nor his judgment, he quickly arranged to see Fishbein. The psychiatrist's interest in the strange case had steadily grown—partly because he had taken a personal liking to Otis, partly also because Otis's condition brought him an unprecedented challenge. Not merely a professional challenge; that came with the job. More than that, he was slowly beginning to realize, after so many years of wading through good relations with black people that cost him nothing, that it took not much more to commit himself to people *as* people without counting what he stood to gain. Once, while Hampton was away in Berkeley, he had called Mrs. Hampton to assure her not worry, everything would be fine. He hadn't known the Hamptons very long. But he felt good doing this.

The transcript Alabi constructed from the master drawn from the dictagraph, and which Hampton took over to Fishbein, read as follows:

Akindeji, Akindeji, Akindeji o!
Mo ke si o lere meta, [motami]
Okunrin [kosakitty famita] lo s'ogun
Balogun [bakinboli babiji]
Alaya bi aya inaki [fibira] o sororo irun

Okunrin ko yan tenkitenki [sibira outa]
Ko s'aya sile, pelu erin lerun
Libi [kitty] regberun apa
Oko Asake [bakinboli babiji]
Uku[roo] ian Tapa
Ma rin kangun [eikimi yopeck] uwoluwo re
[Motami] usu po l'ogba
Balogun alaya inaki kannti, okunrin ero, okunrin oogun
Jagunjagun [paranaloo rabaray]
Agbe ayiye luran eye re
[Bamiyoh yeh yeh]
[Bamiyoh yeh yeh.]

Fishbein had run as quickly as he could through the script, since it made no sense at all to him. He then moved on to the cover letter, written in a language he could at least follow:

Evanston, Illinois
5 May, 1964

Dear Mr Hampton,

I am glad to be able to report to you my findings on the problem that you brought to me last week. Enclosed you will find my transcript of your son's chant, as well as the one done by my former professor, Warren Baldwin. Equally enclosed is the tape containing the chant. I hope you don't mind that I have taken the liberty to send a copy of my own transcript to Professor Baldwin. Since he had sent me his own transcript, which I found helpful for comparison, I thought it was only proper that I should reciprocate. Also, as my former teacher and colleague, he and I have continued to share the results of our researches with one another, as much as possible.

Now to my transcript. While I think I have come very close to capturing the original Yoruba text of the chant, I am afraid there are still many words I could not decipher, so I have left them exactly as Professor Baldwin had them, and in brackets. I have my guesses as to what some of them could be. For instance, I suspect the two words I bracketed on the fourth line to the end, *paranaloo labaray*, might be reordered into something like *panranun luran aba re*, which says something about somebody

71

descending from the father's line, or something close to it.

However, if I am right, then that leads me to attempt another guess that may bring us closer to what I think is the source of this chant. The phrase that occurs on line four from the top, and also somewhere in the middle of the text, as *bakinboli babiji* might really be *aba Akinbola, aba 'beji* (father of Akinbola, father of twins).

What this would mean is that this chant originated from somewhere possibly among the Ekiti, an ethnic subgroup in northeastern Yoruba-land, who use the word *aba* instead of the more general Yoruba *baba* (father). There are other words and phrases in the text that cause me to identify it as hailing from the Ekiti area. Words like *sororo, libi, uwoluwo, usu, ayiye,* and one or two others are clearly Ekiti dialect for standard Yoruba variants—for instance, the standard Yoruba for Ekiti *usu* is *isu* (yam). *Mo ke si o lere meta* is the way an Ekiti person would express the act of saluting somebody three times.

A particularly interesting phrase is *ian Tapa,* roughly in the middle of the text. *Ian* is, again, peculiarly Ekiti, but the real point in that phrase is the word *Tapa.* This is the word generally used (especially by the Ekiti) to refer to the Igarra or Igbira, an ethnic neighbor north of the Ekiti, with whom they fought many wars in the past. If I am right, then the man being saluted in this chant must have been an Ekiti warrior who fought in those campaigns. His name may be Akindiji (which is what Prof. Baldwin suggests) or Akindeji, which is my guess. He is said to have a chest like a gorilla's, and to be in the habit of waging war with bare chest and so on. He is also identified by the names of some family members.

Let me add that the name of the person being saluted is very important. Among the Yoruba, poetry of this kind, which is called *oriki,* is used for saluting or describing the main attributes of persons (e.g., rulers, warriors, and hunters) or objects (e.g., wild animals which the hunters meet in the bush). The oriki used for one person or object can hardly be used for another person or object. This is why it would help to be sure whether the person named in this song is Akindiji or Akindeji. However, I should add that if you sang an oriki like this one in the area from which it came, the citizens of that area would be able to tell you the family that owned it even if you got the name slightly wrong. This is because a family's oriki (or *oriki orile,* as it is generally called) often carries attributes that belong to that family alone.

Incidentally, those last two lines gave me the greatest trouble.

Whether or not they are Yoruba, I have absolutely no idea why they should appear in a praise song of this kind.

I hope I have been of some help. If there is anything else I can do, please do not hesitate to get in touch with me. I will be in this country until the end of August, when I will return to Nigeria.

Best of luck, and may God solve this problem for you.

Yours sincerely
(Signed)
Bolaji Alabi

P.S. In case you want to find out about the Ekiti, they live in the Western Region of Nigeria. The capital of the region is Ibadan, but the administrative headquarters of the Ekiti area is Akure. All the best. B.A.

"Well!" said Fishbein with a deep sigh. "At least we're getting somewhere. But, you know what?"

"What?" said Hampton.

"If you *really* want to know what I think...I think," Fishbein sighed again, removing his glasses and looking Hampton straight in the eye, "I think the solution to your son's problem does not lie in this country."

Hampton had no illusions about the doctor's meaning. He had simply never thought things would get to this point.

"You mean...?"

"Mhm," said Fishbein, clenching his teeth and nodding. "That's exactly what I mean."

Melba Hampton has doubts about the wisdom of Fishbein's counsel. But Otis's last attack of spasms has rendered the prospect of his going to Africa increasingly inevitable. She only hopes that Norma, with her broad knowledge and her radical commitment to black culture, will answer one pressing question for her: Even if Dr. Fishbein is certain that the cure for her son's problem lies in Africa, what protection can anyone offer him against the horrors that American cinema has inscribed in everyone's mind?

But that's not how Norma reads the question Mrs. Hampton asked about Africa. Instead, she takes it as an opportunity to bring the poor woman round to accept something that cannot be avoided. Removing her hand from Mrs Hampton's shoulder for a moment, she rests her head on the sofa, allowing her eyes to contemplate the ceiling as she indulges in the familiar romance of Africa.

"You know, Mrs. Hampton," she says, "there was a program on television the other day. This brother—I think he was introduced as a professor at Columbia—he had just returned from Africa. He was speaking with Johnny Carson about his experiences there. He said he'd gone out there because he wanted to see things for himself and not spend his life believing what so many people have been saying about the place. He showed a few pictures of places he'd visited there, people he'd met and spoken with. Writers. Artists. Modern hospitals. Skyscrapers. All kinds of things you'd find here in Boston or New York. He also met some African kings. Even the president of one country, I believe it was Ghana. You know, all the time the professor was showing his pictures, I kept asking myself, 'Where are all those people we've always been told live on trees?' Believe me, Mrs. Hampton, I saw nothing but the most beautiful, beautiful people in the world. People who look just like you and me. Living normal lives on the most beautiful part of this world God ever created."

All through this song of black pride, Melba Hampton has regarded Norma with furrows in her brow, waiting for her to come down to earth. The young woman has simply not answered her question, and her fears are too real to be wished away. She, too, remembers seeing a few things on television lately.

"I hope you're right, girl," she says. "But what about...wasn't it in Africa they've been doing all that fighting—didn't they just kill somebody, their president, some fellow named Lo...bam..."

"Oh, you must be talking about the Congo, where they killed Lumumba. That's in Central Africa. And it was actually Europeans who started all that trouble. They didn't want to give up the Congo, which was a Belgian colony. I'm not saying there are no problems. But they are nothing at all compared with the beauty of the place."

Melba Hampton lets that sink in for a while. Still, something seems to be missing.

"You say there are problems. What kind of problems?"

"Well, in some places at least. There's poverty. Hunger. Just like here. You've been to Harlem, haven't you—right in the middle of the richest city in the richest country in the world?" Melba shrugs her shoulders. "Well, those African countries are becoming independent from European nations that held them down. They're just starting to put their houses in order bit by bit. There's bound to be a few problems, like they're having in the Congo. Maybe some more fighting between tribes."

The word *tribes* evokes the horrors of savagery once again in Melba's mind.

"This country they're taking Otis to," she says, "Nige..."

"Nigeria."

"They have tribes too, don't they?"

"Of course," says Norma, relieving the moment with a little laughter. "Don't we have our own tribes? What about Jews, blacks, Greeks, Anglos, Chinese, Japanese, Native Americans. They're our American tribes. And don't we fight each other *every* day?"

"I guess so."

Norma's hand returns to Mrs. Hampton's shoulder. There is a tender, quiescent glow in her eye as she tries to calm whatever concerns remain unspoken. She has her own worries about Otis's impending absence. But someone needs to be strong.

"Relax, Mrs. Hampton. It's not as bad as you think. To be honest with you, I think we'd be glad to have all this behind us. If the doctor thinks Africa will do it, well, I guess he must know what he's talking about. It's his field. And we *know* Otis can deal with this. Relax."

Hampton wonders what his wife is still doing sitting up late. On opening the bedroom door, he sees the two women holding to each other. He doesn't say a word. He just withdraws.

Part Two

SON OF ITAYEMI

This necessary chaos follows me.
Something to put in place,
new categories of the soul
of those I want to keep.
What I needed was to be thrown
Into this toneless school,
An arrogant rhythm to release
My buried style.

—Jay Wright, *The Homecoming Singer*

Seven

TAIWO RAISES HERSELF TO A SITTING POSITION. *The goat has been bleating ceaselessly at the door of the sisters' bedroom. It is not exactly the goat that bothers her, though it is too late in the night for a goat to be carrying on like that, disturbing the peace of old women. Rather, she has been roused by a complex dream. She tries to shake her sister awake, only to discover that Kehinde has herself been awake for a while.*

I saw the goat, if that is what bothers you., says Kehinde. But I had more serious things on my mind. I left it only because I thought it strange that it should be going on like this at this particular time. Still...

Kehinde, too, rises to a sitting position. Together the twins shoo the goat away from their door. Yet neither of them goes back to sleep. They exchange glances once or twice, each waiting for the other to be the first to lie down again or else wondering what exactly the other has in mind.

Did you notice how she hesitated before yielding to us? asks Taiwo.

Kehinde does not respond, does not even look at her sister. But she does not want to play the waiting game either.

Sister, she says, I believe you have something to say, if what my body tells me is true. Not without reason have I, old as I am and feel, found the strength to sit upright so long. No doubt the same is true of you, far stronger though you are than I.

It was a dream, Kehinde.

There, I knew it. But why wonder at a dream? How different is that, for us, than what passes for reality? Have we not long blurred the lines between them?

So I fear. Or rather, hope. This time, at least. For the air is thick with movement, drawn on the wings of an eagle. The eagle knows its way. And it will speak of things both strange and familiar. Things both bitter and sweet.

Kehinde turns again to look at her.

We will welcome both kinds, won't we? We have weathered all seasons, across so many ages. Too soon the breath of concurrence rises from within her, and she coughs. But this eagle, it is not alone, is it? For though my dream was of the frankolin, a k'omo ode pe k'o ba 'bon e n'nuje,[1] *not the eagle, it too had graced itself for its journey of peace with company not of its kind.*

Strange company, indeed. The one was firm in its purpose, the other doubtful of the wisdom of the mission but curious about the fancied destination.

So on they journeyed, joined only in the compact to restore their hosts to an honor long denied. But the path of such kindly mission has never been easy.

What could they stand to gain, these birds?

Does the prospect of gain always guide our undertakings?

Who said anything about us—I thought we were talking about eagles and frankolins?

Yes, but surely all creatures are kindred to us, as we to them. Has it not always been so?

Carry on, Kehinde chuckles. I only meant to be assured of your full wakefulness.

Still, your question is well within reason. For have we not the saying, 'As with the lizard, so with the mouse'? Sadly, I went no further in the dream, for that pesky goat soon bleated me awake, just when my birds had coasted close to their target.

Kehinde says nothing. She had been awakened by the goat's bleating before Taiwo. But she recalls now, with the same sense of foreboding that caused her to lie staring into space while Taiwo was already sitting up, that the birds in her dream had flown uncomfortably close to a spot in a bush where little children had been playing. The children were forced to abandon their play, because the playground had suddenly erupted in white heat, scalding the foliage of the surrounding trees and spreading their ashes out of sight. Far off where they stood, the children cried to see their cherished stomping grounds go up in flames. To soothe their hearts, the birds from afar were flying in to rebuild the spot, carrying in their beaks twigs of the palm and kindred vegetation. Their hope was that the children would be gracious enough to reward them with nesting privileges on the new trees. The children, seeing the birds coasting toward their old playground through the surrounding bush, were dancing with renewed joy. It was at this point that Kehinde was rudely jolted by the goat's bleating.

Dawn peeps roguishly through cracks in a wooden window, as though listening to their silent thoughts. Taiwo, turning to look at Kehinde, can almost feel the trend of her unspoken narrative. Time, an undeclared but trusted ally, has long equipped them with an instinct for deduction capable of penetrating the sturdiest armor of secrecy. Knowing she cannot keep her thoughts from her sister long, Kehinde is compelled to tell Taiwo the rest of her dream.

Does that tell you something? asks Taiwo. She has listened carefully and now nods as understanding slowly dawns on her.

It does. Was it not said, even by generations before us, that dreams of happy prospect too often bode a rueful reality?

Ah, and yet we abjured the line between dream and reality!

Well, says Kehinde, take it whichever way you will. Sad dream, happy reality; or happy dream, sad reality. Reality and dream remain happily bonded in the union of their crossed paths. I merely wondered: What if the good of the birds' mission bodes ill for the children? What if the prospect of new life bodes the reality of death—to what end is their joy at the birds' coming? Who will sing their songs, dance their dances, for them?

Taiwo has her own ways with analyzing things. As she ponders Kehinde's questions, she is at once drawn to translate them to their unique circumstances. She could respond that life and death are just as closely linked in their crossed paths. Have they not lived long enough in the land that their fortunes may be said to overarch, even superintend, those of their townspeople whom they have steadily seen coming into life and leaving it? Have they not vicariously experienced the fates of these people each time they have been born or have died, so that each birth is for them a death deferred and each death a prospect of vitality renewed? She could say all this and much more. But she knows her sister and her cerebral ways too well to embrace the temptation to read their dreams in the ominous terms of their lives, though even she can see the logic of the reduction.

Daylight grows brighter. The goat bleats once again, waiting for someone to unlatch the door so it can go outside. Taiwo rises to the job, abdicating the urgency of answering her sister's troubling questions.

Eight

ALTHOUGH MELBA HAMPTON WAS A LITTLE encouraged by Norma's portrait of Africa, her fears for her son's safety never quite left her. It was for that reason that Ella Pearl Hampton, her sister-in-law in Augusta, was now northbound to Boston.

"I don't know," Melba had said. "Everyone seems so sure Africa will do him a lot of good. But I don't know..."

"Don't know what?" replied Hampton. "Oh, come on, woman. I thought we'd all agreed on that. What are you worrying about now?" Melba didn't say a word. "*He* seems to have come round to the idea. Besides, Fishbein has been making contacts with his friends in Washington to link us up with the U.S. embassy out in Nigeria. Now, going over there seems to me the one thing that makes sense for the boy's condition. So why don't we give it a chance?"

"I don't *know* it's the only thing that makes sense."

"Well, what else have you got in mind?"

"I've been thinking." This time Melba turned full face toward Hampton. "Suppose, just suppose—I'm not saying I'm certain—but suppose this trouble he's having is the work of some evil spirit that's come into him from Heaven knows where. What sense does it make to send him out there into pagan country where the devil himself lives with all his angels? You thought about that?"

"There you go again, you and your notions about Africa, land of darkness and the devil. Has it ever crossed your mind that today, as you and I talk about this, that there are lots of young American men and women living in Africa?"

"You know any one of these Americans?"

"No, but that's a fact. Americans living *and* working among Africans like themselves, who are educated just like Americans. Where do you think Professor Alabi came from? Nigeria. And he's over there at Northwestern University teaching *Americans*. You think they'd let an African devil come over here and teach Americans?"

"I don't know..." was all Melba could say, turning away again.

"So what have you got in mind? What else *can* we do?"

"At least we can try a good old Christian solution first."

"Like what?"

"Like prayer."

"Prayer. Oh, God."

Hampton turned away in despair. He could envision the sort of scenario he had sought to avoid: the family's troubles exposed to a whole congregation who, however united they might feel as Christian brothers and sisters, would some time or other succumb to the temptation to confide a member's private problem to someone outside the fold.

"Melba, do us a favor. As much as possible, let's keep this problem within the family, okay? I *know* about those prayers."

"Fine. Let's keep it within the family." Melba felt mildly triumphant. "How about Sister Ella?"

"Ella Pearl?"

"Mhm. She's been known to heal members of her congregation in Augusta with prayer, hasn't she?"

"So?"

"So why can't she come over and help her own family? That way, we don't need to go to a congregation. Just a quiet family affair. Here in our house."

Hampton had nothing to say to that. Since no firm date had been set for the trip to Nigeria, there seemed no harm in buying time with the new option. If the prayer did its job here in America, why take the trouble of going on what might well be a wild goose chase in Africa?

When Hampton made his phone call to his sister in Augusta, he told her just enough about his son's troubled state. He said nothing about the various modes of analysis done, nor about the suggested trip to Africa.

For the liar: death, death in a forest fire. For the wicked: death, death in the sun-scorched wastes. For the righteous: a joyous, peaceful death beside a jar decked with jewels. Strait is the path of truth, wide the highway of evil.

Ella Pearl could not remember the last time she came up north, so wedded was she to her local community in Augusta. It had been over twenty years since she had traveled to Boston for her brother's wedding.

81

Three years later, there was a Baptist convention in Cincinnati. When the plane she took made a forced landing, she decided never to make another flight if she could avoid it.

Her function in her local community was, indeed, the only life she knew. She had never married and was perfectly happy that way. The only man who ever stood a chance of sharing her vows was a no-good, hard drinking, loud talking railroad engineer from whom the good Lord saved her just in time. What a pity that Ella Pearl Hampton, known otherwise for her strict adherence to a conservative moral code, fell prey to Licks Porter, who was in nearly every way a contradiction of her own life style. Truth be told, she did her best to bring him round to more decorous ways, hopeful the Lord would, in time, make him a deserving partner. It took just one event to bring home to her the mind of the Lord.

That was about twenty-five years ago. The First Baptist of Augusta had moved into its new chapel on Brownlow and Warmington. The congregation had organized a reception, which grew into a robust hootenanny because the younger members proceeded, unbeknownst to the elders, to raise a supplementary budget and mount a folk music concert. There was a prohibition against alcohol. But the youth had smuggled in, under the cover of darkness, some moonshine and spiked some of the soda to lend it a little snap.

In such situations, something often goes wrong. Amid the singing and the merrymaking, a few couples fell to dancing. Ella Pearl, who had no interest in such things, kept her distance and would not be persuaded, even by Licks, to join the dance circle. So he went over and grabbed one of the other ladies for a spin. The wine having gone to his head, he carried on as though he and his partner were the only pair on the floor. At one point he got carried away with the fun, drew his partner to his body, and squeezed her tightly on the butt. The lady got so upset she pushed him away hard, sending him crashing against another couple.

"What d'you do that for?"

"You keep your little prick away from me, you hear?"

"Me? Little prick?" At once he unzipped his fly and, in full gaze of everyone, flicked out his cudgel, it too obviously fired up by the drink. "How dare you call *me* a little prick?"

There was an instant uproar, some in outrage, some in undisguised respect. But Ella Pearl was not at all amused. Rising up from her seat, she walked straight to Licks, and fetched him a clean, hard slap on the face.

"Alexander Porter," she told him, "from this day on, I never want to see you at my door."

There was silence as Ella Pearl walked away from the scene. She had hardly left when another woman, who must have had a few to drink, wiggled up to Licks, a smile around her mouth, a gleam in her eye.

"Honey," she said, circling him with her arms and a leg, "you can come up to *my* door any time you want!"

Ella Pearl never saw Licks Porter, or any other man, for the rest of her nubile youth. Instead, she threw herself zealously into her duties as a teacher and committed herself to church and community. She participated fully in local drives for women's rights, but later withdrew rather than be drawn into a rift between those who sought total independence from men and others who saw marriage as the inevitable destiny of womanhood. For eight straight years the choir of the First Baptist of Augusta won first prize in statewide contests, thanks to the passion and energy of their pianist and leader, the much loved "Miz Hampton." When Marcus Garvey paid his first visit to Atlanta, Ella Pearl, as president of the Daughters of Africa, led the association's delegation of three to welcome him at the town hall, where he made a rousing speech; she still proudly displayed the commemorative photograph of her handshake with the great black leader. Discouraged by Miz Odetta from going to Africa, she diverted her energies into helping the association initiate a program for collecting African cultural artifacts, which in time grew so large that the city of Atlanta, where the association's local chapter was based, donated a historic residence downtown as a museum to house the collection.

A virtuous life and an active community profile, added to the cherished memory of Miz Odetta, had made Ella Pearl a legend in her time. But they had done nothing to check the onslaught of an illness now bringing her close to the grave. When she was diagnosed with uterine cancer some five years earlier, and given no more than three to live, she made a quiet commitment to herself: to devote whatever time she had left to promoting the lives of her fellow folk: *The Lord's glory is greater the longer we live to proclaim it,* she told herself. For her age, and her service to her church, she had attained the status of "sanctified," one of the chosen few sought after to pray over the sick and the troubled. She grew thinner as the cancer took its toll on her body. But because she had told no one, not even her family, of her condition, it was assumed she was growing thinner because she was growing older. The sick and the troubled got over because they *believed* in the power of their saint. She, too, prayed to the Lord on her own behalf. But she asked only that she die in the midst of good thoughts and deeds, and that she be laid safely in the bosom of His glory.

When her brother Otie Jay (as she had grown up calling him) telephoned to say his only child was troubled with an illness nobody could understand, she thought she might as well extend to her nuclear family the good she had done others in her Christian family. But she had no illusions about how much time she had left in this world; by the wise reckoning of the doctors, she was living on borrowed time. Putting together all she thought she needed until God saw fit to call her (her not so little brown book; an old crucifix given her by Atticus Johnson, her predecessor in the church's choir; a few items of clothing; a pair of shoes; a few sanitary items—all tucked into a modest bag), she had made her journey to Boston, flying, as she thought she never again would.

Hampton had not seen his sister more than once or twice after their mother died in 1953. Even when he spent about a week at a conference in Atlanta four years back, he could have taken time off to call on Ella Pearl. But he had bidden a long goodbye to the old homestead. Though he cherished the memory especially of Miz Odetta, there were things he didn't wish to be reminded of. No, his sister wasn't one of them; he still loved her very much. But when he saw her at the airport in Boston, he recoiled a little even when, in their embrace, he pretended to be happy to see her.

"You alright, Ella Pearl?" he asked, taking her bag from her hand.

"Of course I'm alright," she said, managing a smile. "Why?"

"Well, you look a little...tired?"

"*That* I am." She blinked, the smile waning from her face. She would not lie. But she would not tell the whole truth either. "These flying machines just aren't made for the likes of me. Take too long up there and don't know where they're going till they get there."

"There you go again about airplanes," laughed Hampton. "There *are* devices that guide them through the air. They seldom make mistakes."

"So they told *me* once."

"I know. I know. You just never forget, do you?"

He was leading her to baggage claims when she pulled him up,

"Where are you going?"

"Your luggage...?"

"You have it in your hand, little brother."

"Is this all you've got?"

"How much did you expect? I'm a little old lady and don't need too much stuff."

That seemed to settle the issue. For now, at least. As they drove towards Quincy, not much was said between them. Not having been to Boston in a long time, she turned her face every now and then and seemed to marvel at how much had changed since last. Hampton let her indulge her curiosity while he negotiated his way through the traffic. Only once did he bring up a topic for discussion.

"Well, how's the old place?"

"You still know anybody out there?" she asked, truly surprised. "Go ahead. Name one."

"Well," he said, smiling over his guilt, "how about, how about... Rev Burton?"

"Rev Burton!" she mimicked. "Rev Burton, I would have you know, died seven years ago in a plane crash. He was going to see his son out in California."

"Oh, no!"

"Oh, yeah! Plane crashed into some mountain out there in the canyons."

"Oh, no!"

"Chalk one up for machines that *guide* you through the air and don't make mistakes!"

Turning to look at her, he was hardly amused. The profile he saw within that brief moment caused him a little sadness. He couldn't conceal it.

"Are you *sure* you're alright, Ella Pearl?"

Rather than answer him, she heaved a sigh. "And how is your lovely wife?"

He took no offense. She might be tired, he thought, and didn't wish to answer the same question again and again.

"She's fine. She's been looking forward to your visit."

"Good. And your son?"

"Oh, you'll see him by and by. He's in school, you know. But he too is looking forward to seeing his aunt. He's a hunk of a man. A basketball player, you know."

"Well, the Lord be praised. Tall goes in the family, I might say. He'll be alright. I *know* he'll be alright."

The car pulled up at the Hampton residence.

Melba Hampton has taken special care over the dinner. Her guest is someone truly special to her. She hasn't had many opportunities to entertain an in-law as dear to her husband as Ella Pearl. On the few occasions Melba met her, she had been impressed by the woman's vivacity and drive, qualities she herself doesn't have in abundance. Ella Pearl is one of those who take charge of a situation and somehow make things work out. Melba thinks she has slowed down a little, due perhaps to advancing years. But Ella Pearl is especially welcome because she has come with the promise of closure to the family's present troubles. Melba looks forward to her prayers over Otis with earnest faith, like the sick and the lame who once drew close to Jesus to touch the hem of His robe.

"Melba, my dear," says Ella Pearl, relishing her last morsel with honest delight, "this, I do declare, is the best dinner I've had in a long time."

"Oh, I'm glad you liked it, Sister Ella," says Melba, beaming with appreciation. "You know, we've been away from the south so long, I didn't think I could fetch up anything remotely agreeable to your southern tastes."

"You did mighty fine, girl. You did mighty fine."

"And believe me," adds Hampton, leering roguishly sideways, "coming from *her*, that's quite a compliment! She's such a hard one to please."

"I'm not hard to please. I just expect things to be done right and proper. Like some people I know had a hard time doing in their growing up days."

"Uh-oh!" jeers Melba, looking at her husband. "Some old family secrets now!"

"Now, you know that's not true, Ella Pearl."

"M-hm."

Ella Pearl says no more, having had her little revenge. Hampton is mildly amused by his wife's laugh at his expense. Outside, it is growing dark.

"Dessert, coffee—anyone?" Melba rises to clear away the dishes.

"Nothing for me, thank you," says Ella Pearl. "I've had more than enough already. I'd do with a glass of water though."

"Think I'll just have coffee," says Hampton, rising to help his wife. "Ella Pearl, why don't you go relax in the living room? I'll bring up the water."

Rising with more than a little effort, Ella Pearl moves across to the living room. She takes time settling in one corner of a posh sofa. She is so comfortable she would be glad not to rise from there for the rest of the night. But she knows she is here for a purpose.

Declining further help in the kitchen, Melba encourages her husband to join his sister in the living room. He makes his coffee and takes it along with Ella Pearl's water. He heard her groan as she got up from the dining room. On handing her the water, he takes a good look at her.

"You alright?"

She nods once, as she takes one draw of the water. But she does not encourage further questioning. In fact, she is uncomfortable with the silence that follows. Now she's had a good dinner and is reasonably relaxed, she'd be happy just to have a light talk about anything. The physical attraction of the house and the harmony she sees between her brother and his wife assure her all is well with the family otherwise. She'd be happy to dwell on these and thank God for little mercies. But she can feel Hampton's eyes on her.

Looking on the tragic figure of his only sibling, Hampton is touched by emotions he has not felt in a long time. The past comes back to him, but only for a fleeting moment. For Melba has rejoined them, rescuing what is becoming an awkward moment.

"You know," says Ella Pearl, "it's funny how much has changed over time. I can't even recall where you two lived when I came for your wedding so long ago."

"Oh, yeah," chorus husband and wife.

"That was an apartment way over inside Boston. Beadle Street, I think—wasn't it, Otie Jay?"

"M-hm, in an old but well-kept building. We had a mean caretaker though. Drove me crazy. Kept looking into our apartment, pretending he was making sure his tenants were comfortable. But I never saw him once looking in anyone else's. We waited till we could buy a place of our own."

"Yes," adds Melba, "he *was* strange. Once when he came, and I was alone, I offered him coffee. He said, Yes, I'd love one. I went to the kitchen for it. On my way back, I observed he'd been out of his seat and was hurrying back so I wouldn't notice. Lord, was he sneaky! And you know what? At the end of his visit, when he stood up to leave, he hadn't even touched the coffee!"

"Weird!"

"M-hm. I was glad we moved."

"Nothing like a place of your own," says Ella Pearl.

"So right!"

The telephone rings. Hampton walks across and picks it up. He speaks in a low tone. The conversation is brief.

"That was my boy," he says, resuming his seat.

"And when am I going to see my dear nephew?"

"More like tomorrow. He said to tell you he was sorry. Has a paper that's due first thing in the morning, and plans to stay up all night working on it. He'll be over sometime tomorrow."

"That's fine. School comes first."

"You want a nightcap, Sister Ella?" asks Melba. "Cocoa, maybe?"

"No, my dear, I'm just fine with the water. Thank you." After a few seconds, she turns to her brother. "Otie Jay, I know this comes a little soon. But before your boy comes tomorrow, I'd like to know what exactly is the matter with him. You didn't say a whole lot on the phone about it. Maybe you should tell me some more. I'm kind of in the dark about things."

"Well," says Hampton, sighing, "I'm not sure you'll be any less in the dark when I'm through telling. It's nothing you or any one of us ever saw the likes of. But—you don't think this can wait till you've rested for today?"

"If your son shows up sooner than I expect, I just don't want to be staring up his face, looking to see I know not what. I'm better off having some idea what this is all about."

"Makes sense to me," he says with a shrug.

Melba draws herself together, ready for the unpleasant narrative. Hampton takes his time recalling as much as he can. Beginning with the night of the birthday party, he traces the progress of Otis's pathology and the various consultations held over it—sessions with Dr. Fishbein, attempts by scholars at Harvard and Boston Universities to decipher Otis' chant, and Hampton's visits to Berkeley and to Evanston.

All through the narration, Ella Pearl never once takes her eyes off him. When he has finished, she turns her eyes to the floor, for a good spell, as though trying to piece things together.

"The things he said during those seizures, you say you have them on tape?"

"Yes, right here in the house. I also have a printout of the text."

Melba's brow tightens at this.

"Yura—what did you call the language?"

"Yo-ru-ba."

"Ah yes, Yo-ru-ba." Ella Pearl nods. Her face seems to lighten up.

"A Nigerian language. From some little tribe in the western part of the country."

Ella Pearl nods again. "And you have those things here?"

"Yes."

"You want to bring them?"

"Aren't you a little tired, Sister Ella?" asks Melba.

"No, my dear, that's fine. I'm anxious to hear it for myself."

In a short while, Hampton has set up the tape. Melba didn't know the articles were in the house, so carefully did her husband keep them from her. He knew how poorly she would take to these matters. Now she tries to excuse herself from the living room. But he gets in her way.

"Wait a minute, Melba," he says. "I think it's time you got a little stronger in this. He's your son, same as mine. If he has problems, you and I should face up to them clean and square. If his own parents can't stand by him in bad times as in good, how do you expect him to go through this alone?"

With some effort, Melba returns to her seat. No sooner does Hampton press the play button than she draws close to him, grabbing his arm, hiding her face behind his shoulder, her eyes closed. Hampton pats her on the head to reassure her. Ella Pearl, calm, unshaken, and with only a mild scowl, listens through the entire recording. Her eyes look unblinkingly on the player. When the tape comes to an end, she raises them slowly towards her brother. There is a smile on her face.

"May I have that paper, Otie Jay?"

Hampton hands her Alabi's transcript. She takes a good look at it, presses it to her heart, holding it there for a spell. She presses it to her head, holding it there also for a spell. Still smiling, she raises her eyes upwards.

"The Lord has finally done it!" she intones.

"What?" asks Hampton in disbelief.

Ella Pearl turns her eyes to him.

"That there, little brother, is our people's voice." Hers shake as she speaks. "*That* is our people talking. Don't tell me you don't hear it, Otie Jay. *That* is our ancestors talking through your boy. The Lord finally brought it home to us."

"What are you talking about, Ella Pearl?"

With Hampton and his wife looking on, Ella Pearl stands up, crosses her chest, the paper in one hand, and walks about, her smiling face once again turned upwards. She is singing a song under her breath. Or so it seems to Hampton and Melba, as they look unbelieving at each other. When she is done, Ella Pearl sits down with a sigh.

"Your son is *not* sick, Otie Jay. Our ancestors are talking to us through him. It took a long time coming. But God's time comes never too soon nor too late."

Though the past few weeks have been dominated by images of Africa, Hampton is visibly subdued. He has none of Ella Pearl's passion for the subject of course. Who can compare with one who has lived with thoughts of Africa for so long? But in the past few weeks he has been led, by those who should know, to accept the inevitability of Africa in the fortunes of his family. Ella Pearl's inspired proclamation does not sound so farfetched after all. He simply fears it has dropped too heavily too soon. He invited his sister to broker the wisdom of the experts and the misgivings of his wife. Little was he prepared for the suddenness and finality of her verdict.

Its effect on Melba is much more devastating. As she watched Ella Pearl carry on like one possessed, her hold on Hampton's arm steadily loosened. She looks once more to her husband for support. But he is obviously capitulating.

"Would someone please tell me what's going on here?" she says, moving away from her husband and his sister. "Maybe I'm stupid or something, but there's no way my son suddenly wakes up one morning speaking in tongues, and all you two can do is pretend he's in his right mind."

"Calm down, Melba," says Hampton. "There's no need to get upset. We're trying to find out what's best for the boy."

"The hell you are! You've already made up your minds. You've decided to send him off to Africa where he doesn't know anyone and there's nobody out there to take care of him. How come suddenly...Didn't you and I decide we would bring Sister Ella to pray over him, like she's done for other people? How come we're talking about Africa all of a sudden, when no praying's been done?"

"Well sit down for a moment and let's handle this quietly and reasonably. Nothing is gained by getting excited. Let's reason this all out carefully. We're still trying to do the best for our son."

Breathing heavily, Melba is hardly appeased. She sits down, reluctantly, away from her husband. Ella Pearl is not entirely unruffled. But life as an elder in her church has equipped her to weather the passions of the aggrieved.

"You're not wrong, my dear," she tells Melba. "I know just how you feel. I may not have a child of my own, but I do know how you feel. Having your only child sent off to some place he has never been before, and in the condition he's in. I know. But what I hear from that machine isn't quite speaking in tongues like Christians do in prayer. The speech of possessed people is not open to our understanding, because it comes from the Holy Spirit. But your son is speaking in an *African* language, like the experts have said. I don't know how it could have come to us but from a source that's bound to our line. Now don't ask me why your son was chosen to bear the burden of our family. That's just the way it is. There's no point in fighting the voice of our ancestors manifesting in our family at this point in our history. If your son has been chosen by the spirits to go to Africa and lay down whatever burden our folks brought across the sea, I know, I *know* the same spirits will take care of him. Don't worry. I'll pray for him. But I'll be praying for our Lord to help the spirits guide him on the right path to where he'll lay our burden down. Somehow, I wish they had chosen *me* and made me well enough to make the journey."

She reaches for her water, takes another sip. She thinks she may have talked too much.

There is none whom Death cannot kill. There is none whose child Death cannot kill. Death kills the rich, and brings his wealth to nothing. Death kills the mighty, and spills his word to the winds...Whether going to earth or going to heaven, we'll meet each other by and by. Termites never scatter without joining together again, said Ifa, as we mourned the dead. Wherever mortals came from is where they return. Why the weeping? Why the wailing? Why the flailing? Why the fasting? He who sent us out has called us home again.

Not long after Ella Pearl has retired for the night, Hampton knocks on her door. There is a weight on his mind.

"Yes?"

"It's me, Ella Pearl. May I come in?"

"Yes." His face immediately gives him away. "Something wrong, Otie Jay?"

He keeps looking at her as he reaches for a seat.

"Ella Pearl, I've asked you twice or thrice now if you were alright. But you've been putting me off. Sister, what *is* wrong with you?"

She had just risen from prayer when he knocked. She turns around and sits on the edge of the bed.

"Oh, little brother, nothing you need worry about."

"Enough of that kind of talk, Ella Pearl. I've been watching you since you got off the plane, and I *know* there's something wrong. Now what is it?"

Embarrassed by guilt, she looks downward, fumbling at her nightie like a little girl. She is fighting to stay strong.

"You know I'm not so young any more, Otie Jay."

"So? Everybody gets old, so what?"

She swallows, but still cannot look up.

"It's a woman thing, little brother. They...they found cancer in my uterus."

"Cancer?" She nods. "*Cancer?*"

"Yes." This time she looks up. Now she has said it, the strength comes back to her. "Yes, they did. But it's nothing."

"What d'you mean it's... What else did they say? What'd they do?"

"Gave me drugs, gave me three years. That was *five* years ago, and I'm still here. How about that?"

"Are you taking your dru...Didn't they say anything about surgery?"

"No. And no."

"No what?"

"I'm not taking drugs, and wouldn't have surgery if they told me to. I'm just...fine."

"Fine? Ella Pearl, this is your health we're talking about. You can't just take things in your hands. You're no doctor. Now, I suggest—"

"Please, Otie Jay, please!" she says, firmly but quietly. "I'm not a child, and I'm not stupid. I know what I'm dealing with. If the good Lord had no use for me, I'd have been gone when the three years were up. Drugs do nothing but slow down the time God has fixed to call me up. Must be He still has use for me, or I couldn't have made this trip. You

92

thought about that?"

Hampton bends his head and shakes it as he sighs.

"You'll just up and die on me, Ella Pearl, because you won't lay religion aside for a moment and do what the doctors tell you to do."

She chooses not to say anything to that.

"Don't you feel any pain?"

"A little. Once in a while. Nothing I can't handle."

He thinks for a while.

"Suppose I arrange for you to see a doctor here. How about that, Ella Pearl?"

She shakes her head, slowly but determinedly.

"I've seen enough doctors. Right now, little brother, I'm living on God's time. I'm not getting any better, but I'm not getting any worse either. If the Lord can see me through *two* years beyond what the doctors decided, He will see me through till His time comes to call me up. So set your mind at ease. My time is not up. I *know* it's not."

When Hampton gives his wife the news of Ella Pearl's illness, she can hardly sleep for the rest of the night. Hampton stops her from going across to Ella Pearl only because he pleads that, given her condition and her long journey from Georgia, his sister needs all the rest she can get. Still, the news does something to Melba. She has no more wish to lose her sister-in-law than she has to lose her son.

Will you prepare to enter, again, the sacred grove of the god? The glare of his face is hard on the eye: Ogun, spare me the sight of your blood-shot eyes. Ogun is a mad god who still makes demands of us after a thousand years. And where do we find him? Where battle's joined. Where wrangling's done. Where torrents of blood flow till they choke the fields. Warrior god, who sharpens his sword on his teeth. Avenging god, who takes from the strong and gives to the weak. Ogun of the hunters feeds on the dog: to him, a dog for sacrifice. And will you, servant of Ogun, prepare to enter, again, the hallowed grove of your god?

His arms wrapped around her, Otis and Norma are resting on her bed. It is 10 p.m. He has been over to his parents' place, where he met his aunt for the first time. If he had any qualms about his trip to Africa, that meeting brought home to him the inevitability of it.

The finality of the decision is not lost on Norma either. Ideologically, she is more attached to the idea of Africa than Otis or his parents could be. But deep down, she was hoping Otis didn't have to make the trip. In trying to reconcile his mother to the necessity of it, she was only doing her humane best to lessen the trauma for her. And when Otis informed her of his aunt's impending visit, she was quite as hopeful as his mother that Mr. Hampton would be persuaded to give the Christian method the benefit of its proven record. Now, even this hope seems to have come to nothing. Although she does not share Mrs. Hampton's fears about Africa, she doesn't want Otis to go away. Is there, perhaps, a final chance of raising reasonable doubt over the inevitable?

"Otey." Her own folded arms are intended to add strength to her reasoning..

"Hm?"

"Suppose...I mean, what makes the Nigerian professor so sure about the part of the country your chant comes from?"

Otis chuckles.

"Norm, you're asking the wrong person. I never even saw the guy, let alone spoke with him. And if I did, I wouldn't know what questions to ask."

"As I understand, Nigeria has a thousand different languages and tribes. Isn't there a chance he has put his finger on the wrong tribe?"

"Maybe he has. I don't know."

"So what do you do if he turns out to be wrong—wander about trying to find the right place?"

Good point, thinks Otis. But he's no more certain what the alternative is to going to Africa.

"You know," he says, "I've never been great with church and all that Christian stuff. But when my daddy told me he was flying in my aunt to pray for me, I thought: Hey, why not, whatever works. Now what do you know? My aunt prays over me and says go to Africa, and may God and our ancestors protect you over there. What could I say?"

Norma is speechless.

"I thought she was crazy, talking about ancestors nobody knows. But then I said to myself, How long can I go on here, dancing all this jigaboo, singing stuff I know not where from, looking ridiculous to everyone, including myself. Is that the way you want to see me? Uhn?"

Norma is gradually becoming ashamed of her doubts. But she is human, too. Her personal sentiments prove just as hard to abdicate.

"I don't know, Otey. I just don't want anything to happen to you."

"Like what? Hey, hey, hey—you're talking like my mom now! And I thought..."

"No, I don't mean it like that. What I mean is, I don't want someone making a mistake. And then we're back where we started."

"Me too. But, you know what? The way I feel right now, I am so doggone tired, they could as soon take me to the moon as to darkest Africa. Any old place, so long as I don't have to go through this strange stuff any longer."

Another spell of silence.

"Otey."

"Yeah?"

"I wish I could come with you."

After a brief reflection, Otis says, "Me too. But...what would you do over there?"

"Well...you know... take care of you. You know."

She feels awkward making such a weak excuse.

"You *know* I'd love that. But let's face it. I don't have the foggiest clue where I'm going or what I'll be doing when I get there. So why do you have to be in the same situation? Besides, what about school?" She doesn't say anything. "Look, baby, this is *my* challenge. Let me deal with it the best I can. Maybe I was *meant* to do this anyway. All you have to do is be strong for me. Believe me, girl, I *will* be back."

It does not befit a masquerade to ask for help. It does not become a hunter to disclaim his charms. It does not befit a god to call for help. It does not befit a hunter to forgo the hunt. Servant of Ogun: hunter, hunter, and hunter again. A true son of his fathers!

Norma puts her arms around him and buries her face in his chest. She is fighting to stop the tears from falling.

Nine

Orunmila says, To enter a room, you should stoop at the entrance. *Ifa, my question is: What god would guide his devotee on a journey across the seas and not abandon him? Orunmila says, Ever since humans began to die, has anyone's head been severed before burial? It is* ori, *says Ifa,* ori *alone, that would guide his devotee on a journey across the seas and not abandon him. All the good fortune I've met on earth, I credit to my* ori. *To you, my* ori, *all praise! Above all divinities, you take care of your devotee.*

Late May is hardly summer. Being a single man, with no one to account for in his plans, Abel Fishbein decided to take his yearly vacation now rather than the usual mid-July. Going to Africa seemed like a good idea, for two reasons. First, he had always meant to go there. Kenya and its wildlife would have been his first choice. But one place was as good an entry into the fabled continent as another. He could do Kenya some other time. The second and perhaps more compelling reason was what seemed like a peculiar case of racial memory. Manifesting as family trauma three generations old, it teased his curiosity to the point where he somehow felt his professional pride challenged. Whatever the outcome of this trip, if he came out of it alive, his horizons—human or professional—would surely be enriched. Besides the instructions he routinely left his assistants whenever he went on vacation, he gave no indication of how long he would be away.

In the interest of himself and the Hamptons, Fishbein pulled a few strings with friends in Washington who had any influence at the State Department. Someone had to ensure there were American officials out there in Nigeria who would make themselves available to the visitors for the duration of their stay. Most Americans know, of course, that it is the duty of U.S. missions anywhere in the world to protect American lives and interests within their areas of operation. But Fishbein feared that some diplomats might query the national interest in the sort of private mission he and the Hamptons were undertaking—one, especially, about an aspect of native African life few government officials would care to meddle in.

It took some three weeks to make the necessary calls and clearances. The U.S. embassy in Lagos, capital of Nigeria, and the U.S. Information Service at Ibadan, capital of Nigeria's Western Region, were briefed on the peculiar nature of the visit and the needs of the visiting Americans. Everything seemed to be in place. Getting the necessary travel documents—flight tickets, visas, immunization papers, etc.—proved even less difficult.

Hampton also took his annual leave early, requesting no considerations beyond his usual entitlement. His colleagues wished him well. Besides his suitcase he had, as hand luggage, a leather briefcase containing a tape of Otis's chant and Dr. Alabi's transcript and letter, the most dependable guides to their quarry. Of books he had been consulting on Africa in recent weeks, he took special interest in a large color atlas of Nigeria he had bought from a bookstore in Harvard Square. Some of its pages showed the distribution of the country's ethnic groups. That, too, was in the briefcase.

Ever since his aunt prayed for him, Otis seemed quite free of his spasms. It probably helped, too, that he had chosen to spend most of his time at home with his parents or with his girlfriend, away from anything on campus and elsewhere that might trigger the dreaded impulses. He had now resigned himself to the uncertain promise of his trip. He had little in his suitcase besides his clothes. Indeed, had Norma not insisted on including a few items like towels and sheets, his luggage could have been tucked neatly into the bag he slung over his shoulder. That, itself, had little besides toilet items, a face towel, and a basketball.

Ella Pearl had accompanied Melba and Norma to see Otis and his father off at Boston's Logan airport. She especially wished to assure her brother that she was fine, he need not worry about her. When they embraced at the last boarding call, she pressed the point by slapping him on the back with her hands and smiling broadly as they disengaged. Ella Pearl also drew Otis to her with a remark that relieved the tense moment: "Down here, boy! How do you expect me to reach your head way up there?" Otis complied, a little circumspect. He'd thought she was about to do another round of praying! All Ella Pearl did was place her hands on his forehead, kiss it, and say to him, "All will be well, child. Don't you worry. All will be *just* fine."

The longest embraces were between Otis and his mother and his girlfriend. When these were over, he walked quickly past his father and Dr. Fishbein toward the plane, not looking backwards. He could not bear to see the two women's faces.

Pan-American Airlines flew a regular schedule from New York to West Africa, making a connection in London for a first stop in Lagos. The visitors favored it above Nigeria Airways (with its nonstop New York-Lagos route), partly for its transatlantic record but especially for concerns over Otis' condition. Early summer, Nigeria Airways often had a large crowd of Nigerians going home at slightly lower fares than other airlines offered. The Hamptons and Fishbein feared that, if thrown in the midst of such a crowd, Otis might encounter the sorts of sound that had triggered his seizures. The chances were judged to be much lower in Pan-Am.

Still, some steps had to be taken. For one thing, the three travelers flew first class, which was less crowded and therefore afforded closer monitoring of Otis. For another, Fishbein was well supplied with fast-action tranquilizers, to prevent repeated occurrences of the seizure. If it happened once, Otis would be given enough doses to sedate him for the rest of the journey. Lastly, none of the three would accept an earphone from the airline staff: Otis might hear the wrong kind of music!

The three travelers occupied consecutive seats in the first-class compartment. Hampton opted to sit near the window. Otis sat to his left, with an aisle between him and his doctor. Fishbein busied himself reading flight magazines, repeatedly stroking his Freudlike moustache and goatee. Now and again he looked in the Hamptons's direction. If his eyes met either one's, he flashed a smile or raised his eyebrows. Occasionally, he made short talk or shared a joke with Otis, to be sure the young man was in a stable disposition. But mostly, he read or surveyed the environment around him. He might have drowsed once or twice. But neither of the Hamptons ever caught him doing that, so alert was he to his determination to keep an eye on things.

Hampton chatted with his son for a short stretch after they left Boston and later New York. But he had become so attached to the map of Nigeria, it occupied most of his attention. He had developed a passion for the unfamiliar African names, quietly enunciating word after word on page after page, especially those devoted to Yoruba country. He had fallen for the music of a language now ineluctably tied to the fate of his family. Indeed he conceded he might get to like the place and the people. But the tedium of reading soon got to him. He fell asleep with the book open on the table in front of him, his head tilting to the side.

Beyond his occasional exchanges with Fishbein, Otis scarcely busied himself with anything. Though he tried not to show it to his solicitous doctor, he found the trip boring. The refreshments served now and then came as a welcome relief. If he wasn't eating or drinking something, or visiting the bathroom, he would thumb casually through the odd magazine or other. For one used to short trips in the company of teammates, an interminable journey to a strange land, for a dubious purpose, and amid company he could hardly share jokes with, was something of a torment. He slept and woke, slept and woke again, thought about Norma and his mother, wondered what he was doing here, and longed for company his own age. *Any*body.

The only one who seemed to arouse his interest was a little white boy sitting by the window on the row of seats in front of him, occasionally talking with a woman who might be his mother or aunt. Now and again the boy, possibly a junior high kid, would look back, then whisper something to the woman. She looked back once, and smiled at Otis when their eyes met. Otis took it they vaguely recalled his face from a picture they might have seen in the media. He was so used to such things, they never bothered him.

Waiting for the connecting flight in London took over an hour. Several passengers had gotten off and a few came aboard, some of them Africans evidently going home. There was a moment of concern in the departure lounge. One of the new passengers, a woman of ample body and colorful attire, shouted to her child in an African language, then spanked him hard on the butt. The boy drew everyone's attention with his loud cry. The woman's words roused a tingling sensation in Otis, causing him to screw up his eyebrows. Clearly uncomfortable, he tried to ward off any impending anxiety by getting up and walking a little ways from the scene. Fishbein, wondering how many more such incidents Otis might encounter, fished in his briefcase and walked up to him, asking if he was alright. Did he want a tranquillizer? Otis said, No, he'd be fine, he'd manage without the drugs. Soon after, the boarding call came for first-class passengers and those with little children. Boarding went on without event. Safe in his seat, Otis eyed the woman and her child as they filed past to the economy section.

Otis had also discovered, during the London connection, that the white boy seated in front of him was among a group of kids apparently on an excursion. Most of them were flying economy; a few were in first class. Many were accompanied by adults. Otis had seen the boy and the woman again at the London departure lounge. They had exchanged friendlier smiles. Resuming their seats, they even said, "Hi."

The London-Lagos leg of the flight went much like the first. Now it was past midnight, with the plane scheduled to arrive Lagos about 7 a.m. Nigerian time. Fishbein continued in his vigilance and occasional chat. Hampton decided it was time to turn in. Carefully putting away his atlas, he pulled a blanket over himself and bid the others good night.

The young boy in front could hold his curiosity no longer. At the London lounge, he had shared whispers with some of his excursion group. Otis had in fact seen some of them looking his way. When the plane got under way again, and his mother was safely asleep, the boy paid a visit to his friends in the economy section, who had grown noisier than on the first leg of the trip. Back to his seat, the boy leaned over to settle the issue once for all.

"Excuse me, sir. Are you Mr. Hampton?"

"Yes, I am," replied Otis, smiling.

The boy beamed triumphantly, even laughed a little. His belt unbuckled, he swung round fully and knelt on his seat, brimming with excitement.

"May I shake your hand, sir?"

Otis reached out his own. "You sure can. What's your name?"

"Wayne Jennings. I'm very delighted to meet you."

"So am I. Where are you going?"

"Nigeria. My mum and I wondered if it was you. We never expected to see you here. My friends too."

"Well, it's me alright. Are you in a group?"

"Yeah. We're on an excursion to Nigeria."

"Uh-huh," said Otis. The boy and his friends had dashiki shirts of various colors and prints.

"What kind of excursion?"

"We'll be visiting the palaces of Nigerian kings and a few other places. One of our teachers is leading us there. He's Nigerian himself. Teaches history. Our school thought we should learn more about Africa by going over there. We're all very excited. Our parents too."

Some of the kids in economy had noticed Wayne talking to Otis. Convinced they were right in their guess, a few had emerged from their seats and were making signs to Wayne, indicating they wanted to come over.

"Sir, d'you mind if my friends come to meet you? They'd be mad if I kept you to myself."

Otis looked back and saw the eager crowd. He smiled and said, "Sure, why not?"

At Wayne's signal, some seven or eight boys and girls ran up to first class. Each one shook Otis's hand and gave his or her name.

"So you're all going to learn about Nigerian culture?" he asked them.

"Yeh!" they shouted together.

"When is your next game?" one of them asked.

"Well...not for a while. I'm going to Nigeria too. May not be back so soon."

"How long will you be gone?"

"That depends what happens when I get there. Going to see some Nigerian family. We'll see what happens. What school are you all from?"

"Compton School."

"Where's that?"

"Compton, New Hampshire. It's a private school."

"They call us Geek Academy, sir!" said a bespectacled, cherub-faced Mickey Rooney with an easy grin and squeaky voice.

The remark raised a laugh amongst the Americans in first class. Embarrassed, the boy's friends jogged his head and tousled his hair. But it was an honest remark. Compton was one of those old New England schools with an established liberal arts curriculum that stressed proficiency in Latin and Greek even more than the natural sciences and served as a breeding ground for the cream of the American elite, especially in the northeast. More recently, thanks to pressures from its trustees, most especially Senator John F. Kennedy of Massachusetts, it had started designing a more progressive profile, a multicultural outlook in student enrollment and faculty hiring, as well as a radical range of offerings in athletics and culture.

"Sir," another child said, "when we get to Lagos, would you mind taking a group photo with us?"

"I don't see why not. So, are you all excited about your visit to Nigeria?"

"Yeh!"

"We already know a lot about the country and its peoples from our Nigerian teacher," said one of the girls. "D'you want to meet him?"

"In a while."

Otis wasn't so sure about that. His father was still asleep. But Fishbein, who had been awake when the kids invaded Otis, never stopped casting glances at them. When he heard the question about meeting their teacher, he looked squarely at Otis and was momentarily satisfied with the answer Otis had given. Wayne's mother had been awakened by the conversation between Otis and the kids. The boy seized the opportunity to introduce her to Otis. They exchanged courtesies and shook hands. Otis was really having the fun that had most assuredly been absent since the initial flight from Boston. He even signed autographs on books and hats.

Some of the kids had run back to share their excitement with the rest of the group. This time they thought it might be nice if their Nigerian teacher came along with them. The teacher had taught them that one way the Yoruba saluted a great man was to sing his praises with a drum. One of them had in fact brought a "talking drum" from a store of props used for teaching aspects of African culture, hoping to impress their Nigerian hosts with his knowledge of the local culture and to hone his skills in drumming. As others led their teacher up to Otis, the impressario brought up the rear, the drum swinging from his shoulder. While his friends introduced the teacher to the famous athlete, the impressario, too far behind to be seen by the circumspect Fishbein, beat out a few strains from the drum: crude, but enough to set Otis off. The kids shook when Otis rose to his full height to do his routine. But thinking he was enjoying the music, they began to dance with him.

There was instant commotion. Fishbein rose from his seat and dispersed the kids, bringing them to realize this wasn't funny. Otis's father was startled from sleep to find the confused scene: his agonized son, Fishbein, the kids, everyone.

"What the hell is going on? Hey!"

The alarm sank in. The drumming came to a sudden stop. Everyone hurried back to their seats. Otis finally came to and slumped to his seat, spots of sweat on his brow. His father looked to Fishbein for an explanation.

"It's alright," said Fishbein. "Just an accident. It's okay now."

"But, what...?"

"That's okay, dad," said Otis, sighing. "I'm okay now. I'll be fine."

He opened some of his shirt buttons for air. Fishbein waited a few seconds before drawing close to whisper to him. Some first-class passengers were still looking in their direction. Fishbein eyed them, trying to reclaim the privacy of *their* space. The intruders got the point.

"Otis," said the doctor, "don't you think you should take some of the pills?"

"No, no. I'll be fine. No need to."

"Would someone please tell me what happened?" Hampton leaned over to ask.

Fishbein did the best he could.

"Some school kids are here on an excursion to Nigeria. They recognized Otis and came over to say hello. One of them had a drum and started beating it for fun. It was just an accident."

Hampton shook his head and sighed. He looked at his son who, head bent and eyes closed, seemed to be trying to calm himself.

"Are you alright, son?"

His eyes closed, Otis simply nodded his head. Fishbein stooped beside Otis to whisper again. He wanted to make his point some other way.

"Otis, listen to me. This could happen again, maybe not with a drum. Maybe...look, we've got a few more Nigerian passengers on the plane. You never know what they might start next. What happens when we get to Nigeria? They get all excited about coming home, and some of them start singing and dancing. Then what? You tell me you'll be alright?"

"I don't exactly fancy getting to Lagos all drugged up," said Otis. "How can I walk?"

"Oh, we're not going through customs and immigration with everybody else. The embassy has arranged for a car to pick us up as soon as we get off the plane."

"Fine, but how do I get to the car—on a stretcher?"

Otis had, of course, been informed of these special arrangements well before they left the United States. He had thought it was all good. But something was beginning to happen to him. Despite the uncertainties that he faced, his inner strength was quietly growing. Strangely enough, this last bout of spasms had helped in consolidating it. If, he reflected, going to Nigeria and facing his demons was his fate, what was the point in backing away? Why not embrace it, spasms and all, learn to grapple with his sensations, and wear them down? At any rate, he was finally bound for Nigeria to confront those demons right where they lived. No, there was no turning back now.

"I'll be fine," he reassured his doctor. "Don't worry about me."

Fishbein shrugged his shoulders reluctantly, and returned to his seat. Hampton looked at his son and seemed to borrow some of the boy's strength. He had long adjusted himself to the risks of the trip, had even created a space in his system for a place—once strange, even unthinkable—that his recent reading had made a familiar, if not exactly cherished, figure in his mind. He only hoped Otis would rise to whatever challenge the coming days might bring.

He reclined in his chair. Shortly after, Otis closed his eyes and was soon asleep. Hampton switched off the overhead lights. But it was a long time before he would fall asleep. He was thinking about Ella Pearl.

As he and the others disembark from the plane at Lagos airport, Hampton is struck by how much the surrounding environment feels to him like Georgia. Lagos gets muggy, even as early as March. But the vegetation here seems rather familiar to Hampton. The surroundings of the airport look much like swampland, the air heavy with the smell of leaves and clay. This isn't such a bad beginning to things!

A navy blue Oldsmobile van, with a golden eagle circled by the words "Embassy of the United States of America" emblazoned on its side, is waiting behind the airport terminal. Standing beside it is a short, stocky white man in white short sleeves and light brown tie over dark brown pants. Besides a few other planes parked behind the terminal, there are many people—apparently, airport personnel—moving about doing one thing or the other. Hampton and his men, being first-time visitors to Nigeria, may have felt that the man standing near the U.S. embassy van is the only white man around. When they finally get closer to him, he isn't quite so short after all, certainly not much shorter than Fishbein. He has a placard which reads "Hamptons" and a smile on his face. As they walk towards him, he lowers the sign, exchanges handshakes and compliments with them, and ushers them into the van. The visitors are relieved to step into an airconditioned car, which has been kept running for their benefit.

The driver is a very dark man with scarifications on both sides of his face. When the visitors enter, he bows to them, then waits for his boss. The officer has introduced himself as Phil Bigelow, first secretary at the cultural division of the U.S. mission. Having ushered his guests into the van, he takes off into the airport terminal. Fifteen minutes later, he returns.

"Okay," he tells his men, "here's how it's gonna play. I, er, need one or two of you to come along with the travel documents, so they'll be cleared by the Nigerian officials. Then...we'll move on to baggage claims. You identify your bags, and Lamidi here"—he nods to the driver—"will bring the bags to the car. There'll be no customs clearance. It's all been taken care of," he concludes with a smile. The visitors take it as a polite assurance they have nothing to worry about.

"Let's go then," says Fishbein to Hampton.

Honor leaves the home, honor returns to the home. What matters how long it takes? You will find me in an abundance of blessings.

Otis remains in the car while the others go into the terminal. Wow, so this is Africa! He lets his eyes survey the terminal, noting that all around there are only black people. He never saw such a scene before. He's never been in a situation where there wasn't even a sprinkling of white people in a predominantly black community. He looks closely at every black person who passes near the van, wondering if these are really black people like himself. Some of them are dressed differently, yes. Though he has seen Africans dressed differently in the U.S., the ones he sees here seem to blend so well with the surrounding environment. The woman who beat her child at London airport had also seemed oddly dressed. But she was surrounded by a lot of white people, which put her in the same position as other Africans he'd seen in the U.S.

Wow, so this is Africa! He's never seen trees like these in his life. He remembers the story about Africans living on trees; he actually looks to see if he will find anything of the kind. He doesn't. Instead, he sees people walking around, talking, laughing heartily. Just like blacks in America, but with an unconstrained abandon he's never quite seen. In America, the idea that his ancestors came from Africa was little more than a romantic conceit. Here at the airport, if someone told him that any of the blacks he sees walking around was a distant relative, he would hardly dispute the idea. Wow, this is Africa?

The four men return to the van. The driver is lugging two heavy suitcases, one in each hand, laboring under their weight. Hampton and Fishbein had protested they could handle their own suitcases while the driver took on just Otis's. Bigelow brushed aside their concern, assuring them the man was equal to his labors. Picking up the third suitcase, he let his guests walk empty-handed back to the car.

"Lamidi," says Bigelow, after the trunks have been loaded into the van, "let's go. Embassy."

"Yes, sir," the driver bows, putting the car in motion.

The drive from the airport further gratifies the Hamptons' feelings about the demography of the place. Fishbein takes in the view with a calm, benign smile. Hampton and his son turn their heads from one side of the human traffic to the other, regarding the scenes with alternating curiosity and approval.

In time the curiosity grows to an astonishment that is a thinly veiled shock. The Hamptons are not unfamiliar with scenes of squalor and disorder: Boston and New York, which they both know, have their share of such embarrassments. But here, they are observing degrees of crudeness and disrepair they never saw anywhere in the U.S. The streets on which they are driving are pocked with potholes deep as craters, some of them with pools of water, forcing the driver to swerve this way and that. Quite often he nearly collides with cars in the opposite traffic whose lanes he has been forced to enter. An overhead bridge straddling a fast motor road below has lost several spans of railing. Pedestrians and cyclists continue moving on it, free of care, when all it would take to topple over the dizzying precipice is a random nudge or a misstep.

The visitors and their host are sheltered from the sweltering tropical heat by the cool air in the van. But even the Hamptons can see, despite their empathy with this land of black folk, that the packed closeness of so many human bodies, under these circumstances, is hardly something they would wish for themselves. Somehow they recoil from it with a subliminal sense of history. At moments like these, their feelings of accommodation tend to fray.

"None of you guys has ever been in Africa before, right?" asks Bigelow.

"I've always meant to come here." Fishbein is the only one sufficiently composed to speak. "But, you know, one thing or the other always got in the way. Still, better late than never!"

"Right," says Hampton. He feels awkward keeping silent.

"So how do you like what you've seen so far?" Bilegow asks Hampton directly.

"Well, it's...let's just say it's...*different.*"

They laugh. But even they know the laughter is a polite evasion.

Past the overhead bridge, they jostle their way round a chaotic traffic circle. A policeman is standing casually aside, unperturbed by the zigzagging of cars and the jarring discord of horns. No sooner have they survived the chaos than they are forced to stop suddenly, clear of the road. So have several other cars ahead, in the dual carriageway leading from the traffic circle. Bigelow and the driver sit calmly while the others wonder what's going on. The shrill sound of a siren whines. Soon two grim-faced motorcyclists are clearing the traffic for a convoy of cars behind them. They don't have to threaten anyone; everyone is supposed to stop in their movements to let the convoy pass. In the midst of this ritual, shouts of "Zeek! Zeek!" erupt from the crowd of bystanders, even from cars that have been forced to stop beside the road. A man in a pure white apparel, sitting in an open-top Mercedes Benz limousine in the middle of the convoy, acknowledges the cheers of the crowd with a flashing smile and a waving hand.

Bigelow regards his guests with a quizzical smile. Fishbein returns a raised brow and a noncommittal smile. Though mildly impressed by the white-robed, white-capped figure of the man in the Mercedes, Hampton wonders why all movement has to stop when there is no impediment or threat to the man's progress.

"He's the president of the country," says Bigelow. "Everyone has to stop whenever he passes by. Isn't that something?"

"They must like him a lot," says Fishbein.

The Hamptons don't see much harm done though. Traffic resumes. Further along, they are stopped yet again when the gates of a railroad crossing are closed to allow passage of a train into a nearby terminal. It takes so long for the train to pass that the Americans, who are close to the gates, have time to witness two incidents. Two young pedestrians, whether impatient with the pace of the train or sporting with danger, scale the gates and dash across the rails when the train is barely twenty yards away. They make it to the other side, laughing all the way, as though daring the train to catch up with them.

While this is going on, a cripple has quietly crawled up the embassy van. A begging bowl in one hand, he has drawn the attention of the passengers by rapping on the side of the van with his other hand. Then, holding on to the door handle in the midsection of the van, he levers himself up to a level where he can appeal directly to the Americans. Otis, who is seated close to the door, looks out to see the miserable figure in rags straining for attention. He recoils, partly because he has no local currency to give but more because he's never had such a figure so close up: squalid, but menacing even in his helplessness. He looks to the others. Lamidi, observing the scene from his sideview mirror, winds down his window glass, and shouts curses at the beggar in his native Yoruba language. The beggar soon loosens his grip and crawls away. Otis, hitherto secure in the relatively noise-free zone of the airconditioned van, is momentarily unsettled.

It is a mild discomfort, much milder than he's felt under such situations before. No one else has noticed it, though Fishbein has strained his neck from the rear. Everything has happened rather quietly. Besides, Hampton and Bigelow are still recovering from the menace of the pedestrians who dared the train. The driver winds up his window, and things return to normal. When the gates reopen, the embassy van resumes its progress to Lagos Island.

The U.S. embassy is at the south end of Broad Street, close to the hub of political power in Nigeria's capital city. Looking southwest across Broad Street, one can see the lagoon along Marina Drive. There stands State House, residence of the country's president, Dr Nnamdi ("Zik") Azikiwe, hailed a while back as "Zeek!" by an admiring crowd. Closer still to the embassy is the Lagos Lawn Tennis Club, where the elite of the city recreates itself or strikes some political or business deals. Across from the tennis club are the grounds of the Island Race Course, the favored haunts of the horse-riding brass of the army and the police as well as privileged civilians. A short drive from the south end of Broad Street, which separates the lawn tennis club from the race course, takes you to the grounds of the National Assembly and some offices of the federal government. East of the embassy are Independence Building (home of most federal offices) and, across Bamgbose Street, King's College, a colonial secondary school that is the breeding ground for many of the nation's elite. On the whole, then, the American embassy is situated on prime territory from which it can witness and, whenever necessary, influence events in Nigeria's political life.

When the van pulls into the embassy premises, the visitors are hurriedly ushered into the office of the Cultural Attache. He and his staff have been fully briefed on the purpose of the visit and especially on Otis's sensitive condition. So everything is being done to shield him from the sort of environment that may cause him discomfort.

The Cultural Attache, Virgil Carillo, is a tall, broad, swarthy man of Mediterranean stock whose build indicates he must have played college football. He receives the men warmly, with added civility toward Otis. The meeting is not long. Carillo is anxious that the visitors, who have been in the air quite a long time, have all the rest they need. He also has no wish to witness anything he has been told about in communications from Washington. So, coffee offered and served, he cuts straight to the chase. The visitors will be accommodated for one night and possibly another at an embassy guest lodge in an exclusive residential section of Ikoyi. The mission has provided for an extra night in case the visitors think they need more rest. If not, they may proceed the next day to Akure, the administrative headquarters of Ondo Division, which the visitors have been told is the source of their text.

The U.S. mission isn't sure what other help they can offer with respect to the young man's condition. Since the Hamptons are traveling with the family psychiatrist, it is thought unnecessary to lend them the embassy's medical attache, who is actually a general practitioner. Nonetheless, the embassy has made a few contingency arrangements in the Akure area. Specifically, they have contacted two American Peace Corps volunteers teaching in secondary schools around Akure (one of them an African American), who have a respectable knowledge of the area. The volunteers are to hire the services of a drum musician in the region who can advise on textual issues relating to the chant in question. They are to meet the visitors at the lobby of the Government Rest House in Akure, on a day and time to be decided after the visitors arrive in Lagos.

Time being of the essence, the visitors agree the arrangements made by the embassy are excellent. There's no point in staying an extra day in Lagos; they will leave for Akure the next day. They thank Carillo for his provisions, and he wishes them success in their mission. Bigelow and the driver take them to the appointed guest lodge in Ikoyi.

The brief meeting with Carillo was a welcome breather for the visitors, especially for Hampton and Otis. As the embassy van takes them through the streets of Lagos to the guest lodge, it strikes them that the embassy is somewhat of an island of white presence in an otherwise large sea of black life in the city. Besides Phil Bigelow who brought them from the airport, they hardly recall seeing a white face all along the route that led to the embassy. On their way to the lodge, they find themselves once again in the midst of an almost entirely black population. Here and there they see a few white people, and certain Asiatic types, driving or being driven in cars. But they are such a pitiful minority that they make little difference to the general demography.

All this has no doubt affected the black visitors' sense of themselves in this setting. For a brief moment they recall the visit with Carillo. It was cheering to be sitting in an American institution set up to ensure the safety of Americans in a foreign land, and to be made to feel that, should any dangers arise, there are forces guaranteed to protect them from it all. The power and authority of America was all too palpable in the figures of Virgil Carillo and Phil Bigelow sitting with the visitors in the cultural attache's office. By the same token, against the backdrop of an over-whelmingly African population, the two African Americans may have felt the uneven power relations between the races that they have grown up knowing all their lives. Although they are here in Nigeria on a mission that has little to do with American politics, they may have sat through their reception at the embassy on the horns of a dilemma, however mild: on the one hand, proud to be American and sure of protection by America's power; on the other hand, confronted, even in this land of black people, by the same unequal power relations that continue to hold black people down back in the United States. This, too, has possibly made a difference to the Hamptons in this setting.

Ten

THE VISITORS HAD A TROUBLE-FREE, EVEN pleasant night in the comfortable quarters of the one-storied Ikoyi guest lodge. Early the next morning, Otis is awakened by sounds of someone singing within the premises. The sounds give him a slight uneasiness. He gets up from his bed and decides to check the source of the singing from his bedroom window. It turns out to be a gardener, bare to his waist, who, machete in hand, is pruning hedges at the back of the lodge, a couple of windows away. He is singing in a language that is becoming familiar to Otis from previous encounters. Otis is a little disconcerted. But he is determined to begin the fight with his demons right here and now; there is no use in running away any longer. His body tingling with sensations, he throws the window of his room fully open, inviting the sounds of the singing, even training his eyes fully on the man. This is for him as good an opportunity to affirm himself as any. If I flinch from *this* challenge, he thinks, what will I do for the rest of my time here: become permanently drugged by Fishbein, so I don't suffer any spasms? No! In time, the gardener observes Otis looking at him. Fearing he is disturbing the guest's peace, he stops his singing. Even before he does, Otis has felt a sense of triumph over his discomfort. He heaves a sigh when the gardener stops singing. He has at least survived, if not exactly won, this round of his fight with the demons.

Not long after, he cleans himself up and joins the others for breakfast. They've been warned it's going to be a long trip to the interior of the country. Carillo has also made contact with the two Americans in the Akure area. They will meet Bigelow and the visitors about 2:00 p.m. at the Government Rest House in Akure.

At the embassy reception, the visitors were told that Bigelow would be their guide on the trip to Akure. Bigelow is a first secretary at the U.S.

Information Service in Ibadan, the western regional office of the mission's cultural division. Since Ekitiland, in Ondo Division, where the visitors are bound, is in the Western Region, it was decided that their case be taken up by the Ibadan office. The Hamptons and Fishbein feel comfortable knowing they will be traveling with someone they have at least known for a day.

"Welcome to tropical Africa!" says Bigelow to the visitors.

They are getting ready to dash into the van parked close to the front door of the lodge. At 9:00 a.m., in less than a half-hour after it darkened with rain clouds, the sky has burst into a serious downpour. The visitors have seen rain many times in their lives, but nothing quite like the cascading sheets that make it barely possible to see anything more than a few feet away. In this quiet neighborhood of privileged Nigerians and expatriate personnel, very little noise is heard, beyond the occasional bells and horns of cyclists hawking a variety of items and services, from ice cream and newspapers to shoe repair. The rain has silenced all that with its varitone symphony: the rattle of water on asbestos and zinc roofs, banana leaves, wooden boxes in the backyard, aluminum buckets under the shingles, plastic toys strewn over the lawn, even dogs barking at people racing to avoid being drenched. These are all part of the random music of the tropical rain.

The progress of the embassy van through the city of Lagos is no smoother than it was the day before. The city council has an uneven record in environmental sanitation, so that poorly drained roads are frequently flooded each time it rains heavily. Vehicles have to negotiate their detours through lanes and side streets crowded by cyclists and pedestrians trying to find their own way. If any structure has collapsed across the narrow passage, there is a tortuous reverse by everything and everyone from more than a block behind. The problem is usually solved. But by the time Bigelow and his men finally make it to Ikorodu Road, which will head them out of Lagos, an hour and a half has passed. It might have taken longer. But Lamidi, an old Lagos hand, knows where to cut the right switches across its maze of byways.

It is still raining heavily outside Lagos. A few miles towards Ikorodu, there is a security roadblock. The driver of a long commercial bus, stopped for inspection by two armed police officers, is taking some time negotiating its release. But the embassy van has no trouble going through: there is a sign on its side identifying it as an official vehicle. This is generally respected by security officers, more so if the vehicle contains any whites, who are thought unlikely to cause trouble!

"We'll be seeing quite a few of these on our way," Bigelow tells his puzzled guests.

"What was that all about?" asks Hampton.

"Oh, there's been some political crisis in the country, especially in the Western Region, where we're headed. Religious politics, ethnic politics, you name it. There's been a split in the main political party in the region. The splinter party formed an alliance with the big party in the north to assure the north a foothold in the south. Most westerners, the Yorubas, don't like it, so they've been making trouble for the alliance. There are rumors the westerners have planned an armed revolt, which the federal government is trying to stop. So they mount roadblocks, searching for guns and explosives. Crazy."

"Do they have to stop every vehicle along these roads?" asks Fishbein.

"Well, official vehicles usually get through. Which is strange, because they probably have the best chance of carrying weapons, since the drivers know they most likely won't be held up for a search. The unlucky ones are the private and commercial vehicles. The police aren't really searching for weapons, and the drivers know this. They just put something in the hands of the policemen, and they're let go."

"Cash?" asks Fishbein.

"You bet!" laughs Bigelow. "Isn't that something?"

Otis takes one look at Bigelow. There's something about the officer that's beginning to irritate him. Maybe it's Bigelow's tone. But Otis doesn't say anything. He just sighs. His father says nothing either. He merely smiles and blinks. He has sensed an uneasy reserve in Bigelow's language: there may be things he's trying not to say. But he gives the man the benefit of the doubt. He has more crucial issues to deal with than the sentiments of a foreign officer.

By the time the embassy van passes Shagamu, towards Ijebu Ode, the rain has thinned to a drizzle. Tropical rainfall has the tendency to allow itself a relief that could last some time. The rain doesn't stop, but it's slight enough for the sun to come peeping through. A few birds brave the drizzle, fleeting from tree to tree, seeking other company or a quick forage for their young.

"Tell me about the volunteers," says Fishbein, sensing the Hamptons's reservations. "You have many of them in this country?"

"Quite a few, yeah," says Bigelow. "But, a couple of years ago there were almost none in the south of this country. We've only recently been allowed to reassign volunteers here."

"How's that?"

"Oh, some silly stuff happened back in...1961, I think it was. We used to have a training program for volunteers at Ibadan University—Ibadan's where my office is. The training was a period of adjustment, so they can adjust to living with Nigerians. Well, someone on the university campus, I believe a Nigerian student, picked up a letter written home by one of the volunteers, a girl by name Margaret Mitchellmore. Apparently she wrote about Nigerians going to toilet on the streets, among other things. The letter was made public, there was a riot on the campus, and you know the rest: Americans go home! That kind of nonsense. Hell, I mean, you've seen their streets. But they'd make a big deal out of anything."

"So what happened?" asks Fishbein.

"Well, diplomatic problems. The president of Nigeria got involved, called our ambassador, and all that. In the end, the U.S. pulled back on the program. That was only here in the south, where all the radical stuff happens in this country. The north, which is Muslim, doesn't go for all that. They didn't mind our volunteers going over there, so volunteers have always been there. But, like I said, in the last couple of years our boys and girls have returned to parts of the south."

"The two volunteers who're supposed to be meeting us—"

"McAdoo and Dubitsky?"

"Yes. How long have they been here?"

"Oh, about a year. They're good guys. They get along pretty well with the natives."

Hampton guesses McAdoo must be the black one of the two. But he doesn't ask the question that comes to his mind. He likes Bigelow even less now, him and his superior ways. Otis has drifted off to sleep. Fishbein is himself becoming wary about the foreign officer. Only two years or so ago he saw the movie, *The Ugly American*. Bigelow is a little on the fat side, but he has a moustache that makes him look not so unlike Marlon Brando. Still, like Hampton, Fishbein is willing to give him the benefit of the doubt. These officers, he reasons, may often be forced, in their difficult circumstances, to adopt defensive attitudes.

Past Ijebu-Ode and towards Ondo, Hampton and Fishbein are

admiring the country scenes. The highway is not in the best condition. But the vegetation is wonderfully lush. They take special interest in kiosks displaying foodstuffs—mostly fruits and what look like smoked game—between villages and small towns. Sometimes the vendors come closer to the road, offering these items to passengers who show any interest in buying.

Shortly before Ondo, the van slows to a crawl behind two vehicles. There's a small crowd skirting the traffic. As the Americans get closer, it turns out to be a group of young boys accompanying a masquerade. Closer still, the Americans can see the group is playing percussion music, faintly audible, and singing a song to which the masquerade sways lightly. The pace of the van now greatly slowed, Otis awakes from sleep, and looks a little bemused. To avoid any awkward scenes, Fishbein at once raises an alert with Bigelow.

"Excuse me," he says, touching Bigelow's shoulder, "but this can't...we can't go through with this. They've got to let us move on. Please—hey, driver. Honk your horn, quick! Mr Bigelow, we've got to get out of here fast."

"Lamidi," says Bigelow, "blow your horn for these people. Pass them quickly. We don't want to hear the music. Quick!"

The driver goes into action. The young boys accompanying the masquerade have pressed close to the passing vehicles to solicit cash donations. Lamidi veers quickly from his lane and dashes out ahead of the vehicles in front, pressing his horn continually to discourage any obstruction. The youths scamper clear of his way. But the driver has taken his orders too zealously. Though he avoids hitting anyone, some of the youths surge against a cyclist with gourds of palmwine strapped to both sides of his carrier. Everyone in the collision falls to the ground. The gourds break, spilling all their wine. Lamidi has driven clear of the traffic but doesn't stop, nor does his boss order him to. The Americans look backwards at the mess and hear curses being hurled at them. They shake their heads in helpless remorse. Bigelow is heard to say "Jesus," one hand against his brow.

Everyone is silent for some time. Otis knows the measure has been taken in his interest. Though he is sorry, he wonders why they had to go that far, since he felt nothing! Bigelow, he regrets, is becoming more a liability than an asset to their agenda.

"That was close," Fishbein says, to ease the tension.

"Yeah!" Hampton and Bigelow chorus in relief.

As the journey continues, the windows of the van are lowered to let in some fresh air. The visitors have put the unfortunate incident behind them, concentrating on the novel scenes of the tropical ecology. Palm trees. Irokos and silk cottons huge and tall. Across Owena Bridge, they see their first river—fishermen trying their luck, women washing clothes on the banks, logs floating by. After the rain, and in the searing heat, the air smells of dampness and smoke. An awkward blend, but still an idyllic change from the toxic mix of gases from industrial and other wastes in some cities they know.

Soon after, Lamidi pulls up in front of the Akure Rest House. It's 2:30 p.m., a little beyond the appointed time. The travelers step down from their van. Fishbein worries about Otis coming into the house with them, but Otis lets him know he has no anxieties.

Dubitsky and McAdoo come out to meet them as Lamidi drives to park the van under a large shaded mango tree. Each of them wears a dashiki shirt. Bigelow introduces everyone, and due civilities are exchanged. They all walk in to have the late lunch Dubitsky and McAdoo have arranged and to meet the drum specialist the volunteers brought with them as agreed. The drummer has not brought a drum with him. There's nothing especially musical in his looks. But when he takes his turn to shake the man's hand, Otis feels a sudden rush of emotion. *All praise! Sweetness and truth from the taut skins of a duiker! Will you prepare to enter, again, the sacred grove of your god?* His handshake is so firm the drummer cringes. On taking their seats, the two men look at one another with some embarrassment, given the awkward start of their relations. Otis's height doesn't help much either.

First there was a hill. Then there was a river....

"Olu has assured us that he knows the oral histories of most of the—"

"Would somebody please show me the bathroom?" Otis interjects.

"Sure," offers Dubitsky. "Just round the corner to the left. Door with a green curtain."

Otis walks to a door with the word "TOILET" in red capitals above it. The bathroom is clean, but Otis has actually no use for it. He is uncomfortable where he's sitting and simply wants to figure out how to deal with the situation. What he feels is not the usual general tingling all over his body; rather, a kind of impulsive tug pointing him in a specific direction, no matter where he may be facing. He walks to the toilet bowl and goes through the motions of urinating. But he has difficulty targeting the bowl, causing his urine to splash all over the seat and on to the floor. He doesn't even bother to clean it up. Zipping his pants even becomes a problem. In the end, he decides there is no use in concealing his discomfort.

"Excuse me, everybody," he says on returning to the table. "I think I know where we're heading."

They all look at him in amazement.

"What are you talking about, son?" asks Hampton.

"Dad, I *know* what I'm talking about. We're going *that* way." He points across the window, in the direction of a thick bush.

"What? In that...How do you plan to get through that jungle?"

"There must be a road through it somewhere. Now let's all get up and get going. I *know* what I feel deep inside me right now."

"Now, wait a minute," says Bigelow. "We're all just about starved. Can't we have a little something before we start?"

"No, we can't!" Otis shouts him down. "I'm sorry, but this can't wait."

In the next frozen moments, everyone looks at someone else for an answer. Hampton is embarrassed and pained at the same time, fearing the fate of their mission. Fishbein is speechless. Bigelow is doing his unusual best to be civil. The drummer is baffled, uncertain what these people expect of him. He is equally convinced that the young man has a unique case of madness that a good herbalist should be sought out for. McAdoo tries to save the situation.

"Okay. We had them save some sandwiches. Let's pick them up, take along a few bottles of soda, and be on our way. How's that?"

Otis tries to raise an objection, but Dubitsky has already asked the stewards to bring the provisions. He hangs around to settle the bill, while the others file into the vehicles: Bigelow and his guests in their van, McAdoo and the drummer in a sky blue Beetle parked by the bush. The embassy van has taken off before Dubitsky can even get to the Beetle.

The two vehicles are in nothing less than a mad chase. Since he claims to know where they are heading, Otis maintains his place in the van, beside his father, in the row behind the driver. Fishbein and Bigelow settle for the back row. But Otis leans forward, on the edge of his seat, all the while urging Lamidi on to a faster speed even when the poor driver has no clue where he is going. From Akure the chase heads towards Ado-

Ekiti. Lamidi is not even allowed to stay focused. He is continually pressed to veer off the road into the ungraded bush, until Hampton joins him in protesting there is no road there. Otis tries to check himself, but now and again he erupts, shouting a command.

In an old bush. Closer to the hill.

"There, to the right!"

"But there is no road there," pleads his father.

"There's no other way, dad. I *know* this."

"What do you think you're trying to do, get us all killed?"

"Damn!" swears Otis. He sees his father's point. But he is being goaded to a predetermined spot. Now and then the driver looks backward to his boss, who has almost reached the limit of his patience.

Between the hill and the river. Closer to the hill.

Shortly before Ikere-Ekiti, a path presents itself, veering off the highway to the right. It looks like a farm track, but wider than usual, perhaps because it is often used by trucks carrying geologists and their field assistants from the Federal Office of Surveys. Otis frantically directs Lamidi onto the path. The driver swerves quickly, nearly crashing into a roadside bank. The chase continues unabated. The road is so uneven, the van frequently tosses the passengers up and down. Yet Otis keeps urging Lamidi to drive faster. Impatient with the driver's leaden speed, Otis darts from his seat and settles in the passenger seat to Lamidi's left, his hands held towards the steering wheel as though trying to usurp the driver's role. Bigelow finally loses his patience.

"Now, wait a minute!" he says. "You're not going to try and—"

"Here," Otis orders Lamidi, ignoring Bigelow. "Turn right— here! Come on!"

"There is no road there!" shouts Bigelow. "Christ, don't you get it?"

Closer to the hill!

Encouraged by his boss's words, Lamidi doesn't turn right. Suddenly, Otis dashes right and wrests the wheel from him, forcing him out of the driver's seat. Swerving the car off the road, Otis drives straight into the bush and begins to maneuver his way around trees.

"Hey! What the hell do you think you're doing?"

Bigelow, now truly upset, grips the seat in front of him. Otis ignores him, laboring frantically with the wheel. His father is so distressed he is almost at the point of tears.

"Look *here!* What the—Dr. Fishbein, you better talk to your friends.

I'm through with this shit. I have no part in their primitive, mumbo jumbo stuff. They can go ahead and kill themselves over some old slave history. That's none of my business. *Hey*, listen to me!"

Bigelow jumps from his seat, lands in the middle row where Hampton is seated, and thrusts his arm toward Otis to try to stop him. Hampton grabs Bigelow's arm fiercely, and looks furiously into the officer's eyes.

"Let go of me, damn it!"

Hampton yanks Bigelow down, pressing his other arm on the officer's shoulder and pinning him to the seat.

"You just don't understand, do you?" His voice is shaky.

"No, *you* don't understand," Bigelow storms back. "I've got nothing to do with this bullshit. So *you* tell your son—"

A towering iroko. Closer to the hill.

Suddenly the van jerks to a halt. It has just got over a land rise, and on its way down it hits a stump in a patch between two rubber trees. Otis, sweating and quaking, starts the engine again and again. But the van is stuck. With one quick look ahead of him, he throws open the door, and dashes out.

"Come over! We've got to the place."

All eyes follow him as he crashes through the thick growth. Hampton and Bigelow suddenly disengage. Hampton is the first to run after his son. Fishbein follows him. Bigelow unbuttons his collar, loosens his tie, pulls out a handkerchief, and cleans his sweaty face. He steps slowly out of the van and reluctantly follows the visitors.

Lamidi is confused. Pulling the keys from the ignition and locking up the disabled van, he walks nervously behind his boss. McAdoo and his men have not followed the mad dash into the bush. Instead, parking their car beside the spot where the van veered off the road, they have followed on foot, trotting guardedly, through the rough path cut by the van. They stop briefly beside the lagging Bigelow and Lamidi, then resume their trot toward the Hampton party.

The landscape dips into a valley. Otis moves briskly through the thick growth as though he knows the terrain. Panting and sweating, he is like one anxious to keep a tryst, totally oblivious of those trailing behind him. At last he stops, looks this way and that, then dashes furiously to a spot beside a massive iroko. He falls to his knees, uproots some of the growth, and falls flat on his stomach, clutching the earth with both hands. He yells, rests his head on the ground, and heaves a deep sigh. Fishbein and Hampton finally catch up with him. Father kneels beside son, placing a hand on his shoulder.

"Here, dad," Otis says, rasing his head. "It's here."

Hampton does not ask what he means. He simply holds his son's head to his chest, and closes his eyes as the tears fall on Otis's head.

The others have been witnessing this moment silently. All of a sudden, they turn their attention to look in the direction of the emerging figure of a man in a white, large-sleeved tunic and white calf-length trousers. He is holding a wicker fan in one hand and some objects in the other. Peering quizzically at the strange party not far from him, he turns round and begins to walk away. A few backward glances later, he quickens his pace to a discreet trot along a clear path that dips into the distance. McAdoo decides the man may be of help to them.

"Hey, *oga*[2]!" he shouts.

The man looks back but does not stop.

"*E joo,*" the drummer lends his voice, "*e duro na-o. A fe beere nkan l'owo yin.*"[3]

Hearing a familiar tongue and tone, the man halts. McAdoo, Dubitsky, and the drummer walk up to him. With the drummer as interpreter, the Americans want to know if there is a settlement anywhere near. The man replies, yes, his village is just a short distance away. And who might they be? They are Americans, they tell him, but they are here with someone whose family hails from these parts. They would be grateful if he could help them trace the family.

The others have gradually met up with them. On seeing the man, Otis feels a gentle flush of calm. It is as if a hidden bolt has been unlatched within him. His instincts slowly yield intimations of self-revelation. *You will feel. You will hear. You will learn. You will know. You will be strong.* It is no longer a troubling sensation. Two birds have just flown past.

The man greets the new arrivals with a bow, and they respond similarly. In their exchanges with the man, before Otis and the others can join them, McAdoo and his party are told the name of the nearby village: Ijoko-Odo. The man's name is Akinwunmi, and he is the chief *babalawo* (divination priest and healer) of the village. Fresh from performing rituals at a shrine nearby, he was on his way back to the village when he heard their sounds. If they have matters to settle in the village, he would be happy to take them to the *Baale* (village head).

McAdoo asks Akinwunmi if there is a motorable road leading from there to Ijoko-Odo. The babalawo says yes, and points in a direction where their cars can make a detour to the village. He even offers to ride with them to the place. Bigelow and his party return to the stalled van. There is no mechanical problem; the suspension has only been caught in a stump. Everyone gives a hand; the van is lifted clear and backs out to the road. Akinwunmi rides in the Beetle, leading the way to Ijoko-Odo village.

On their way he surprises them.

"What family do you wish to visit?"

"Ah, so you speak English!" Dubitsky, sitting beside driver McAdoo, turns round to ask.

"Yes, I think so. At least I can try."

"How did you...I thought you were a herbalist."

"Well, I used to be a primary school teacher. But I was also trained as a babalawo by my father. When he died, about...nineteen years ago, I stopped teaching to continue his work."

"Interesting."

"What family are you looking for in our town?"

"Frankly, I have no idea," says Dubitsky. "I'm not sure any of us knows either."

"So, how will you recognize the family?"

"Our friends in the other car have something they will show your chief. From it, the chief might be able to tell them what family they are looking for."

Akinwunmi says nothing, but thinks this is an odd way to go about looking for family relations. The road soon opens into a clearing, revealing a sprinkling of houses, some mud with thatch, others concrete with zinc roofing. A short distance from the clearing, to the right but clearly at the edge of the village, is a lone hut. It is mud, with zinc roofing. Had the Americans walked with Akinwunmi rather than drive, it would have been the first house they encountered.

The van freed from the stump, Bigelow and Hampton made peace with one another. This happened when Lamidi was backing the van out of the bush and onto the road. While everyone went back to their seats, Bigelow grabbed Hampton by the arm and held his right hand out to him.

"Mr Hampton, I'd like to say something. Please, listen to me." His eyes evaded Hampton's. "I've said some silly things to you, things I should never have said. Believe me, I am truly sorry, I didn't mean one word I said."

"That's alright," said Hampton, stepping into the van.

"No, really, I'm not like that," Bigelow insisted, holding on to Hampton's arm. "Anyone who knows me would tell you that. I've got friends—"

"I said alright," insisted Hampton, freeing his arm gently but determinedly from the officer. "Frankly, I've forgotten all about it. We've got work to do here. We can't afford to bear grudges. Now, let's...get on to the village."

Neither Fishbein nor Otis says anything all through the ride to Ijoko-Odo. A change has surely come upon the young man. He does not like Bigelow any better, and perhaps wishes never to have much to do with him. More importantly, his body has been making the needed adjustments to the environment. He felt no uneasiness whatsoever at the exchanges in Yoruba between the drummer and the babalawo. Fishbein was the first person to notice this, and continues to keep his eyes on Otis. He intends to make a note when he finds the time.

Entering Ijoko-Odo, Otis feels nothing special either. The place is as strange to him as it is to the others. But he is quietly accepting that this is an environment he has to get used to. It may take some effort. Here and there, he notes a few more of the scenes they encountered on the way from Lagos. Women bare to the waist, with loads on their heads. Scabby-looking dogs running around, with no visible owners. Little boys completely or half naked, no shoes on their feet; some are playing soccer with a makeshift ball and posts. Goats resting in groups under the shade of a tree. Life here is plainly dirt-poor, despite a few houses with zinc roofs. There's none of the frenetic pace he witnessed in Lagos. If his ancestors came from this place, have things always been like this? The embassy van finally comes to a stop in front of a large one-story house with metal roofing and trees ringing the compound.

"This is it," McAdoo comes round to announce. "The ruler's palace."

Bigelow and his men step down and stretch their limbs, surveying the scene briefly. While Lamidi drives off to find a suitable parking spot, the Americans follow the babalawo and the drummer into the chief's residence. A very old man, barefoot, is seated on a mud platform in the front porch. A wooden crutch lies near him. He has seen the party approaching the house. When they enter and stand near him, he does not turn to look at them. His eyes half-closed, he seems to be chewing something. Akinwunmi draws closer and speaks a few words to him. He simply grunts, which Akinwunmi takes as a signal for the party to proceed indoors.

It is late afternoon. A few men, old and not so old, are faintly visible in the dim daylight of the chamber. Akinwunmi makes an elaborate bow towards the most prominent of the figures.

"*Kabiyesi* [Your highness]," he greets the chief, continuing their conversation in Yoruba. "I have brought some guests to see you."

"Isn't this our esteemed babalawo?"

"It's me, your highness."

"E-hen. You have done well."

The drummer also greets the chief, "Kabiyesi." He is not from the village, but takes care to identify his community. The chief acknowledges the man's identity, noting the ties between their two peoples. He bids the drummer welcome. Nothing has been said to the Americans as yet.

"Enh..."

There are not enough seats to go around. The chief glances suggestively round the room. Two of the younger councilors stand up from their seats. The chief thanks them.

"Akinwunmi, please ask your friends to be seated."

Akinwunmi motions to Bigelow and his party. They all take their seats. There are a few moments of silence. These men being foreigners, the chief doesn't think he should offer the traditional refreshment of kolanuts to be blessed and shared. If the white men have brought nothing to him, as he can see from the look of things, perhaps no more need be said about the matter.

"Well," says the Baale to Akinwunmi, "as you can see, the dying day has claimed the kolanuts. Perhaps, you should tell us who your friends are and what they seek with us."

Akinwunmi consults quietly with McAdoo, who next consults with Hampton and Fishbein. The consultations over, Akinwunmi salutes the Baale once again and tries to state the purpose of the visitors' mission as best he can.

"Many, many years ago, when white people were coming to our land and capturing people, they took away a man who these men"—he motions to Hampton and Otis— "think may have come from these parts. They are not sure whether it was from our town, or what family the man came from. But they have brought something with them, something our big man"—he points to Otis—"has been saying at certain times. They think it contains the name of a certain family. I had just finished performing my annual rites at Oke and was on my way home, when I heard their voices not far from me. They came up to me and asked if I would kindly take them to our Baale. I said it would be my pleasure to bring them to you. That is what I have done. Kabiyesi."

The chief reflects for a while before responding.

"You have done well, Akinwunmi. May the god serve you well." There is some silence. The chief looks cautiously this way and that at his councilors. Reading the same caution in their eyes, he continues, "The thing you say the young man has been saying, what is it?"

Again, Akinwunmi consults with the Americans. Hampton rises, excuses himself, and goes to the van. Lamidi, who has been snoring in the driver's seat, wakes up quickly on hearing Hampton open the back door. Hampton takes out the briefcase containing the player and tape of Otis's chant and returns to the meeting. On receiving permission from the Baale to set up his tools, Hampton takes one look at his son before going further. Otis nods his assent and braces himself. Hampton presses the play button. The song of the ages, albeit warped by time and medium, comes thundering out in the loud report of Otis's voice and the drum flourishes of Michael Olatunji. Hampton looks across at his son. The young man is shaking visibly, spots of sweat on his brow and his nose, his teeth clenched. He is doing his best to hold himself together. Hampton goes to him and holds his arms firmly around him. He does not really need to.

The Baale has a worried look on his face. Now and again he looks furtively at his councilors. Once his eyes meet those of the babalawo, who is otherwise nodding in thought. The drummer has a faint smile on his face. Perhaps he understands what the text signifies. Or perhaps he is pondering the aesthetic counterpoint between drum music and verbal text. When the playing is over, Hampton returns to press the stop button. Everyone appears relieved. But the Baale is visibly uneasy. The old man at the front porch makes some noises.

"Ehn," says the Baale. "We have heard what they played for us. But we do not understand what it said. It has nothing to do with our people. So—"

"Tell them the truth, Osunkunle," the old man in the porch declares, with obvious effort. "Others may not understand what that thing said, but you and I do. Do you think the truth will lie hidden for ever? Osunkunle, tell these strangers the truth."

The Baale looks embarrassed. But the old man is not to be checked. With what little strength he has, he takes up his crutch, lowers himself from the dais, and ambles round to the door of the chamber.

"If you will not tell them, I will. Let them go and play that thing to our two mothers where they live. If what those women hear from it says nothing to them about Akindiji, warrior son of Itayemi, banish me for ever from your doorstep."

Having said that, the old man returns to his stoop with the same effort that brought him down from it. In the silence that follows, the drummer whispers to the Americans what the old man has said. The meaning of it sinks into them, with varying degrees of insight. Otis and his father, in particular, exchange glances.

Baale Osunkunle looks this way and that. Resigning himself to the inevitable, he asks his two younger councillors to lead the strangers to the home of two aged women on the outskirts, who have the history of the village buried deep in their memories. No sooner has the party gone than Baale Osunkunle calls the remaining councillors for a hushed consultation. Occasionally his voice rises above the whispers, betraying the anxiety that caused him to lie about the message of the tape. Perhaps, too, he is having difficulty bringing the councillors round to his point of view. But the subject of their consultation is hardly lost to the old man pretending to be asleep in the porch.

"Beware, Osunkunle, beware," he says, loud enough for the conspirators to hear. "Think carefully what schemes you weave in your mind. Have we not had enough trouble in our land?"

"Whatever do you think I am scheming, Pa Fadipe?" retorts the Baale. "Or have your ears started playing games with you?"

"I am not a child, Osunkunle. And my ears are alive to their functions, thank you. But think carefully. Attend to the counsel of our scars. Was it not scheming like this that led our enemies to our doorsteps in the company of the white man? Do you know who these white men are?

Why do you lie to them? Have we not suffered enough from not doing what is honest and best for us? Have we not lost enough of our sons and daughters?"

"Pa Fadipe, when we need your advice, we shall call for it!"

"The young man was only seeking his way home. Is that such a great crime, I ask you?"

"I warn you, Pa Fadipe. An old man does not rub his palm on the dirt floor!"

"I shall say no more. Even a blind man walks with his eyes wide open."

There is a little bush between the mud house and a clearing that marks the inhabited bounds of the village. Only a foot-beaten path joins the old women as citizens to the rest of the community. The two cars having parked at the clearing, the Americans, their companions, and their guides walk up the path into the premises of the old women. Lamidi waits in the van.

The sun has begun its descent behind the trees. Osunkunle's advisers form the vanguard of callers at the hut. Akinwunmi follows closely. The Americans and their companions bring the rear, Hampton holding on to the briefcase. The advisers and Akinwunmi announce their presence rather loud, for the women are hard of hearing. A goat squats under a pear tree at one corner of the clean swept compound.

As usual, it is Taiwo who rises to answer the callers. This time, however, Kehinde follows closely. Their eyes are dim but alert, as though they have been expecting this call. The three chief callers greet the women— often jointly addressed as *iya wa meji,* our two mothers—with their complement of appellations, adding that they have brought visitors to see them. Taiwo has come close enough to the chief callers to recognize them. But, although she mumbles a response to their greeting, she is looking past them to the others still outside the door.

"Won't they come in?" she asks.

Akinwunmi motions to the Americans and drummer to come on in. As Otis files in with the others, Taiwo fixes him steadily with her eyes, following him every step he takes. Her lower lip droops and shakes. Everyone, including Otis, is certain, and amused, that Otis's physique makes the woman ill at ease. While they stand looking at her, she moves closer to Otis, and places a weak bony hand on his chest. Otis is no longer quite so amused.

"Akin. Akin," she mumbles.

Otis lowers his head, wondering what the woman is saying. She looks up, into his eyes.

"Akin. Akin *niyii ko?*"[4]

Otis turns to Akinwunmi. The Babalawo responds with a laugh, "Maybe she is mistaking you for somebody else."

"What is the matter with you, Taiwo?" intervenes her sister Kehinde. "Won't you let our guests enter properly before you set upon them?"

There is a long wooden bench by a corner of what looks like a reception room. The councillors motion the visitors to sit on it. A mat woven from palm leaves has been rolled up and placed against the wall near the bench. Akinwunmi unrolls it on the floor for Dubitsky and McAdoo to sit on. The four Yoruba men offer to stand, declining the appeal of the Americans to join them on mat or bench. The old women settle into two wooden recliners near the door through which they emerged. It leads to their bedroom.

One of the councillors, a middle-aged man of perhaps fifty, steps forward to greet the women once again, briefly this time. Speaking in Yoruba, he tells them that he and his colleague have been sent by Baale Osunkunle to escort the visitors there. They are looking for a family in this town, with no clue as to how to proceed. But they have brought something with them containing the *oriki* of the family. The young man sitting over there is in the habit of chanting the oriki at certain times, without knowing what it means. The Baale has advised that the chant be played here, in hopes the women will help determine what family it belongs to.

The councillor motions to Hampton to play his tape. The American sets up his equipment on the floor. Taiwo has not taken her eyes off Otis. Gradually overcoming the embarrassment of her gaze, he now stares at her with equal penetration. As soon as Hampton presses the button, and the recorded chant resounds in the room, Otis braces himself, summoning all his will to resist the old urges. While all eyes turn towards him, Taiwo rises from her seat and approaches him, with slow, measured steps and outstretched arms, mumbling, "*Se mo wi baa? Akin ni. Akin ree.*"[5] She reaches Otis just when the sounds have tailed off to a stop. Placing her hands on Otis's shoulders, she says, more directly to Kehinde, "*Akin ni. Se mo wi baa? Akin ree!'*

Otis has recovered from his sensations. He looks at the old woman with her hands on his shoulders, and doesn't feel repelled by her. Indeed, he manages to smile. Kehinde, Taiwo's twin, has also risen from her seat and joined the two. The babalawo approaches to offer what help may be needed. For the women, visibly excited, begin to examine the young man further. They address their statements to the babalawo to translate for Otis.

"*K'o je n ri ejika osi re,*" says Taiwo.

"She says you should show her your left shoulder," Akinwunmi translates.

Otis takes off his shirt, revealing an impressive athletic torso, and bends over for the woman's benefit. Taiwo looks closely at the shoulder. Upon seeing a scar there, she exclaimes, "*Ah! Ya oo, Kehinde. Oun niyii!*"[6] Kehinde comes up to look, and exclaims the same recognition, adding, "*Egbon wa ti de le-o!*"[7] Taiwo goes on to explain to Akinwunmi, for him to translate, that their brother had accompanied their father on his last campaign against foreign invaders; though they had repelled the intruders, their brother had received a cut on his shoulder that tested the medicinal art of Awo Kujore, great-grandfather of Akinwunmi. Kehinde goes on to explore Otis's forehead. Running her fingers through the hair just above it, she finds a tender spot indicating another scar. Between them, the sisters recall that when the enslavers tried to catch their brother, he put up an enormous struggle, felling two of them with blows; he was subdued only after one of the white men whacked his head with a gun.

As Akinwunmi translates these revelations to Otis, the young man turns to look at his father. Hampton only shakes his head slowly from side to side, one hand against his chin. His eyes are glazed with tears he would rather not shed. He recalls the surprise he and his wife felt upon seeing those marks on their newborn baby; they dismissed them simply as birth marks they needed not fathom. Years later, as he grew older, Otis felt much the same.

The twins do a gentle song and dance to celebrate the moment. The others look at each other, and especially at Otis, with a variety of emotions. Bigelow greets the events with some relief. He has something concrete to record about his consular service to his guests. Even more, coming now to the end of a flawed human relations encounter, he will go home to quietly lick his wounds. A quiet smile on his face, Fishbein takes in the experience with a not untroubled reflection on ideas, disciplinary and otherwise, he has lived with all his life. At any rate, he has a few more things now to record in his diary in due time. The volunteers are not as surprised as the visitors, having lived more than a year among the Yoruba and encountered various aspects of their metaphysics. Looking at Otis, McAdoo cannot help feeling that the young man's experience has meanings for him, another black American, beyond the politically inspired program that has brought him to Africa.

The experience has a different set of effects on the Yoruba men at the scene. The drummer has never seen such an event before. True, as an oral artist he knows the uses of the oriki tradition. But he has never thought it had any power beyond the local universe of his people. He now comes to appreciate, with renewed pride, the value of an art that can facilitate the return of a lost progeny to the land of their fathers.

The envoys of Baale Osunkunle are rendered speechless. Of course, they appreciate the good fortune in a reunion of long lost kin. Being relatively young, they know little of the history of certain relationships in their village. They wonder quietly why the Baale tried to avoid disclosing the source of the chant. But they choose not to air their feelings. The babalawo, however, is not fooled about their silence. The Kujore family has been in the divination and healing business for a very long time, and he cannot recall any oral history of a client who got sold into slavery. But the testimony of the centenarian sisters draws him closer to the troubled young man. And because by his profession he is privy to relations between so many of the Ijoko-Odo folk, he is not as innocent as the two councillors of the link between Baale Osunkunle's perfidy and this reunion of separated kin. He therefore pledges himself to vigilance over a family with which his own has been linked by a solemn history.

Night is fast approaching. Bigelow and his guests doubt that a village like Ijoko-Odo can provide them adequate comfort for the night. The three visitors know their business is hardly over. They're sure they need time to resolve the crucial questions, cultural and psychological, raised by Otis's condition. They need a place to stay while they try to bring a reasonable closure to things. Bigelow will return to Ibadan, while the Peace Corps volunteers will help the visitors with their needs in the unfamiliar environment. Besides, the visitors seem to have a friend in the babalawo, who has enough English to intercede for them in case of dire social straits.

The Americans take their leave of the old women, promising to return the next day to spend more time with them. Along with the two councillors, they return to Baale Osunkunle to express their gratitude for his help in tracing the family they have come to find. Bigelow and the visitors return to Akure for the night.

The old twins reflect on their encounter with qualified joy. The day has ended well. But what promise does the night hold?

Government Rest Houses in rural towns like Akure usually have enough rooms for guests. These motels are hardly the most comfortable places to stay. But they are often cleaner than many in the big cities because they suffer less wear and tear. Being located in the most exclusive part of town, where British colonial officials used to live, they offer their guests a quiet retreat from the hazards of the general society.

Bigelow retires early to sleep, following dinner with the visitors and the volunteers. It was decided to return to Ijoko-Odo after breakfast the next day. McAdoo and Dubitsky will not join Bigelow and the visitors, since they have classes to teach in their schools: Dubitsky at the new Government College near Ikere-Ekiti, McAdoo at Anglican High School, Iludun, one mile down the road from Ijoko-Odo (Iludun and Ijoko-Odo share the same river, *odo*, their natural boundary on Ijoko-Odo's eastern flank).

Bigelow will leave for Ibadan after the return visit to Ijoko-Odo. Fishbein and the Hamptons have no illusions about leaving the village so soon: their mission may take a while to accomplish. But there's another problem just as urgent as Otis's condition. Between their visits to Baale Osunkunle and the old women, they observed some foul weather in the town's social relations. None of them can put a finger on the exact problem. But they fear that, if care is not taken, someone, perhaps Otis, may be in danger. McAdoo and Dubitsky, who know the rural folk a little better, emphatically caution the visitors to watch their steps.

Bigelow will therefore return to Ijoko-Odo with his guests mainly to impress upon Baale Osunkunle the need to ensure the safety of the visitors. Dubitsky and McAdoo will, on their part, provide what social support they can to put the visitors at ease while they carry out their mission. They may, indeed, be in better luck than they imagined. It turns out that Ijoko-Odo is not quite so underdeveloped after all. There's a Baptist Secondary School in the town, headed by a Tuskegee graduate from Ikorodu (closer to Lagos). The school had been assigned a Peace Corps teacher, a young woman. But she was so often ill in her first six months that she was recalled from the program and flown home to the U.S. Her quarters, a one-story building near the principal's lodge, is now vacant. Bigelow can use his consular powers to make a deal with the principal: If the school will accommodate the visitors in the vacant house, Bigelow may consider replacing the volunteer the school has lost.

After Bigelow has retired for the night, Fishbein and the Hamptons hold further discussion on their major concerns. First, now the family that owns Otis's chant has been traced, it remains to finalize the text so they will know the real nature of Otis's problem. Second, what is so significant about *this* chant it had to be the one Otis sang? There's an even deeper concern. Why does Otis continue to be troubled by the chant after he has ceased to be disturbed by the language (Yoruba) in which it came, and *especially* after he has been reunited with the family from which it originated? Could it be the real problem is in the text itself? There seem to be links between these issues that need to be established if Otis has any chance of regaining his health.

The night is far gone. Otis, who has borne the major emotional weight of the mission, is exhausted and wants to sleep. Hampton and Fishbein are also tired. They all rise, agreeing to reconvene the next day at breakfast.

Hampton walks Otis to the door of his chalet, an arm around his shoulder.

"So how do you feel, son?"

"Much better, dad. Much better. But it's not over yet, and you know it. You know, the sooner this is over with…Isn't it strange though that, just when we've gotten so close, some other stuff seems to be coming up. You know what I'm saying?

"You're talking about the chief, right?"

"Yes, that and other things. Like, can you believe this Bigelow guy? Seems like every time he opens his mouth, some bad news comes out. Maybe he's better off staying away, or he might mess things up."

"I know what you mean. Believe me, I don't like him any more than you do. Boy, he *really* got me going there in the van. But, you know, he's not all bad. Where'd we be now without him? Yea, every little bit helps. Now you go in there and get yourself a good sleep. You deserve it!"

"You too, dad. Good night."

"Good night, son."

On getting into his chalet, Hampton shuts the door and sits quietly in a chair. He has some private reckoning to do. The events of the past few hours—Otis regaining some calm in the bush, the chief, the old twins, in short, the whole rendezvous with his family's history—seem to demand nothing less than the total truth from everyone. But is he, or anyone for that matter, capable of the *total* truth? Take the trip down memory lane on the night of Otis' first seizure. Hampton didn't have the courage to recollect certain details of family history known to him, which might have amounted to a regress from the comfort of his present existence. Nor did he volunteer very much to Fishbein in their exploratory session back in Boston. For instance, Ella Pearl had told him, a very long time ago, that their father's first name, Daley, was really a Europeanized form of the actual African name his slave father had given him. When Hampton read the transcripts the two language professors had made of Otis' chant, the name on the first line (Akindeji, Akindiji) looked uncomfortably like what Ella Pearl had tried to remember of their father's African name. It may not help matters much to bring this issue, uncertain as it is, to anyone's attention now. Besides, they're now in Africa. Let Africa take care of its own. Still, he cannot help asking himself: Have I done all I honestly could to help my son find himself again?

Before going into bed, Hampton gets down on his knees. He wonders which God to pray to now. The Christian God he has always known? Or the pagan God of his ancestors? Which one of them inspired the mumbo jumbo of an African language that has finally brought his son to the home of their fathers, where he may at last lay their burden down? In the end, he settles for an indeterminate God Almighty of the entire human race. He thanks Him for what He has done thus far and for what He has yet to do. He prays Him to make this their real journey's end, and he especially prays for guidance and protection in what appears to be a turbulent climate of relations. Whatever needs to be done to bring closure to their mission, he commits to His hands. He also prays for his sister Ella Pearl, whom he has left in Boston with some heaviness of heart. With her long attachment to Africa and the readiness with which she blessed the decision to take Otis there, he wonders if the trip would not have been just as good for her. She did indeed wish their ancestors had chosen her to make this trip. Hampton did not think much of the idea: the mission seemed so uncertain at the time, and as far as he was concerned her condition was a purely physical one. Before Bigelow takes leave of them the next day, Hampton will ask him to call his wife Melba for two things: to report the progress of their mission and to enquire about the health of Ella Pearl.

The notes Fishbein makes before going to sleep are scantier than he intended. He records the essential facts of Otis's behavior. But he is too tired to add detailed comments of a contingent or theoretical kind. He's been wondering where to fit recent experiences into the old disciplinary paradigms. When he first took on Otis, he was convinced this was the usual case of regression, at one level or the other. There is growing literature on the subject of unconscious memory and remembered trauma, much of it built on testimonies of Jews who had survived the holocaust. Some psychologists have given qualified support to the idea of memories going back at least one generation prior to the life of the subject. Hence, when Otis's problem was brought to his attention, he proceeded to explore his background as far as possible.

He has often agreed with psychologists who dismiss these specters of ancestral and other memory—previous lives, their later reincarnations, memories passed on from one existence to the next—as irrational myths, encouraged by pseudoscientific forays into primitive religion, that have no place in the more serious science of neurological medicine. But now he finds himself faced with the question: Have we been wrong all along, applying Western rationalist paradigms to cases occurring in cultures or systems different from our own? Of recent works on the subject, he recalls especially Ian Stevenson's prize-winning essay of 1961.[8] Fishbein read it then with qualified faith, like most of his colleagues. Now, Stevenson's argument makes more sense to him than it once did. He still needs to apply tests of "paranormal cognition" to establish Otis's previous life in this community. But, he now thinks, there may well be more to human life than "science" has prepared him for.

Perhaps, when he wakes up tomorrow morning, he will come to find that the events of today have all been a dream. Perhaps...

Eleven

BEFORE HIS CLIENTS ARRIVE FOR THEIR EARLY consultations, Akinwunmi washes his face, cleans his teeth, and goes to see the centenarian twins. Kehinde, who has let the goat out and wedged the door to let in the dawning day, is not surprised to see him. The twins knew he would come calling before the visitors did. Kehinde and Akinwunmi exchange early morning greetings. The babalawo follows her in and takes his seat. Taiwo joins them from the bedchamber, a kolanut and saucer in her hand.

The kolanut blessed and shared, Akinwunmi does not waste time stating his mission.

"The strangers will be calling on you later this morning. I want to be here when they come. In fact, they will probably want to send for me, to help them as I did yesterday. Before they come, I want to know a few things, because I did not like certain things I saw yesterday. This much is clear: Your long lost brother was captured by white people many, many years ago. Now, who in this town stands to lose, should your brother return today?"

Taiwo has been chopping the twins' share of the kolanut into bits small enough for their scanty teeth to manage. Neither of the two says a word for a while after Akinwunmi has spoken. It is Kehinde who finally breaks the silence.

"Taiwo, I think you should tell him."

"Yes. But there is something he has not told us yet. What happened when the strangers called at Osunkunle's place?"

"Well," says Akinwunmi, "they played the machine with the young man's voice and asked to know the family that owned the oriki. At first Osunkunle hesitated. He didn't want to tell them."

"So, what happened?" Seeing the babalawo hedging and ducking, Taiwo says to him, "Akinwunmi, we are not asking for the secrets of Ifa that lie locked in coded responses. A man in your profession cannot afford to be covering up for criminals."

"I am doing no such thing, *iya*. On the contrary, I am being careful to give everyone his due. It was Pa Fadipe who stepped forward and challenged the Baale to tell the strangers the truth, or he would do so himself. Osunkunle had no choice but to send Atilade and Kupoluyi along with us to your place."

The two women look knowingly at each other and chuckle. Taiwo passes Kehinde her share of the kolanut bits, takes a few in one hand, and looks past the babalawo to the growing light of day. Her words are carefully chosen. Her speech is slow and measured.

"You come from a good family. A family that knows its work and tells the truth. Something we cannot say for many families here in Ijoko-Odo. You serve the great Ifa. So you know what Orunmila the great one says about those who persist in their evil ways."

"Yes, Iya: *Orunmila ni, bobapetiti, elesan nbo wa ayika gbirigbiri*."[9]

"Bless you, my son. When the strangers return this morning as they promised, we shall tell them the full story: how their ancestor, our brother, was delivered to white people. You will then understand why Olodumare has preserved us to this day. But you ask who stands to lose should our brother return today. Our father, Akindiji, had first been installed Balogun of our people, and later Baale when the previous one, Akiwowo, died from the swollen body disease. There were some who thought their family had better claims than ours. They argued that our roots here went back only one or two generations. So they bided their time for revenge.

"Everyone knew our father's power. His enemies knew there was nothing they could do while Akindiji was alive. But death had its own plans. One evening, our father had been receiving some friends, former comrades in war. He had risen to see them to the door and bid them goodbye. Returning to his reception room, where I was busy clearing away the vessels of his entertainment, he uttered a sharp cry, held his hands to his throat, and slumped to the floor. I screamed for help. People ran to the rescue. But our father never recovered."

Kehinde goes into a fit of coughing. Taiwo is about to get up and fetch some water, when Akinwunmi rises quickly to offer his hand. But Kehinde gets over her fit. Holding up her hand, she signals Akinwunmi not to bother.

"Shall I stop talking?" asks Taiwo.

Kehinde shakes her head. Taiwo watches her for a while, to be sure she is fully recovered. Then she resumes her story.

"Towards the end of the funeral rites for our father, his enemies chose to strike. Some people said it was the Tapa who raided our town. But we knew better. Our father had repelled the Tapa in three fierce campaigns. So for a long time they had taken their adventures to other places, like the Akoko regions that side of the Ekiti. No, the people who struck our town came from villages around us. Citizens of Oguro and Imefun had claimed our father frequently looted their houses after fighting off the Tapa, just to have something to show for his labors in our town's defense. Well, we were too young to know the truth. We knew our father to be a good man. But war has its ways, so who was to say?

"At any rate, whatever our father might have done was no excuse for the cruel revenge his enemies exacted from our town. It was not simply that they raided the town in the company of white people and carried away many of our young men and women, including our brother. But they went on to set fire to the whole town, burning every house they could find. When my sister and I finally ran back to our house, we found it burnt to the ground. The raiders must have started torching the town before they got to the scene of our funeral rites. Some people had seen smoke from far away, but thought it was from some other burning. It was when the raiders charged at us during our dance that it became clear what had happened. By then, it was too late to do anything but run."

Obviously tiring from the account, Taiwo rises to get some water in a cup. She drinks a little of it and then puts the cup down.

"A few people recognized those who came with the raiders," adds Kehinde.

"Yes," continues Taiwo. "People from this town, who had led in the invaders and the white men. When they were accused later, they denied it vehemently. But let me shorten the rest of my story, lest the strangers surprise us soon. Not long after our people resettled here, competition to succeed our father as Baale began in earnest. The grandfather of Osunkunle was one of the rivals. So was the father of Ibidapo Fadipe, who was only a baby at the time. That the Osunkunle family won the contest was not such a great surprise. The family had done its share of deeds, good and not so good, for our town. No, what is shocking is that they have held on to the position one generation after another. The title of Baale was never hereditary among us, hence it passed to our father after the death of Baale Akiwowo. But times changed. These men were the cause.

"You can now understand why Osunkunle was trying to deceive the strangers. His mind is heavy with his family's guilt. Every time he hears a sound, he thinks the seat is about to be pulled from under him. What has the young man done but seek his way to the home of his fathers?"

Taiwo takes another draw of the water.

"We know you have other business to attend to before you bring the strangers to us," says Kehinde. "But you tell Osunkunle this, from us. We do not have long to live. In the time that is left to us, we intend to do nothing but the good we have always done. That boy is our brother come back to us. He shall not suffer as he did the first time. Should Osunkunle touch even one hair of his body, he would learn, to his cost, that good and evil do not live so far apart."

The women rise one after the other. They are not asking Akinwunmi to leave. But the conversation has touched sensitive nerves in their frail bodies. It is only wise to terminate it at this point. He bids them good day, without waiting for their response.

When the Americans dropped Akinwunmi off after the meeting with the twins the day before, they asked to pick him up at midmorning for the return visit to the women. They finally arrive at his place about 10:30 a.m. He has had his breakfast of *akara* (bean cakes) and *ogi* (corn porridge), and has seen a client. While Bigelow and his guests wait in the van, Lamidi the driver knocks at Akinwunmi's door. He is received by one of the babalawo's apprentices, who conveys news of Lamidi's presence to the babalawo. Shortly after, Akinwunmi and Lamidi emerge from the house. Salutations exchanged with the Americans, the door is opened for the babalawo to sit near Lamidi in the van.

Rather than go straight to the old women's place, the driver heads for Baale Osunkunle's residence. Thinking that Lamidi has lost the way, Akinwunmi tries to redirect him. But Lamidi says he's only following orders. The babalawo wonders why, but does not ask. McAdoo sees the van from afar as he drives in from Iludun and follows it. The drummer is seated beside him.

"What happened?" asks Bigelow, as the two cars come to a stop. "No classes today?"

"I had an early one. Then I had someone cover me for the next at eleven. I was actually going to meet you guys at Akure, when I spotted the van up the road."

"Thanks for showing up."

"Tim been to see you?"

"No. Must be tied up."

McAdoo exchanges greetings with Hampton and Fishbein. With Otis it's "What's up?" and punched fists. The drummer shakes hands with everyone, bowing as he does.

This meeting with Osunkunle is shorter than the first. Pa Fadipe is on his stoop as usual. The Baale, who is in his reception room with one of the older councillors of the previous day, did not expect the Americans to return so soon. With Akinwunmi as interpreter once again, they put him at ease on the matter of refreshments: their time is short and their journey long. But the Baale can read their faces.

Bigelow goes straight to the point, sometimes moving too fast for Akinwunmi's modest command of English. The Baale, says Bigelow, must have noticed that some Americans have come to his town. The Americans have come on a very important mission, to reunite a family long divided. The family has been identified. The visitors will stay a while longer to resolve certain matters. While they are in the town, the Baale should consider them his guests, and do all in his power to ensure that no harm comes to them. He reminds the Baale that his guests are *Americans*, not ordinary foreigners. As such, he must treat them with special care. His government does not like leaders who look on while Americans among them are treated badly or perhaps even harmed. If any harm is done to the visitors, he cannot say what his government will do; but it will be something *very* serious. In due time, other officers will visit the Baale to remind him how seriously he must take the responsibility now placed in his hands.

Having made his point, Bigelow rises from his seat, indicating the meeting is over. Given no opportunity to respond, the Baale looks on with alarm while his guests file out of his chamber. Although he rises after them, he is too shocked to volunteer a goodbye. He just stands helplessly by the doorpost to watch the van go into motion. Pa Fadipe renews his warning of the day before: "Even a blind man walks with his eyes wide open." The Baale has scarcely heard a word of it.

There is absolute silence inside the embassy van, behind which follows McAdoo's Beetle. Otis has his eyes shut, having no wish to join in any discussion, with Bigelow or anyone. Hampton, sitting next to Bigelow, keeps a studied calm. Fishbein struggles to curb his rage. Teeth clenched, he taps his fingers on his thigh. Fearing for his village, Akinwunmi would like an opportunity to explain to the white man that they are really a peaceable people.

Though ignorant, Bigelow is not stupid. He can feel the stillness in the air. All he wants is for this whole visit to be over so he can go home, back to more familiar ground. When the convoy approaches the old women's residence, he calls his party to a halt for a briefing. The visitors, he says, should go on to the women and resolve whatever else remains. The drummer should go along with the visitors, to do whatever he's needed for. Bigelow will go to Baptist High School and explore the possibility of housing the visitors there for the duration of their stay. McAdoo, however, says he already stopped by to prepare the principal for Bigelow's visit; in fact, the principal is looking forward to it. All are agreed. Fishbein, Hampton, Akinwunmi, and the drummer proceed to the women's hut. Unwilling to suffer any more discomfort from the tape, Otis decides to join McAdoo in the Beetle. Bigelow and Lamidi follow in the van.

The second visit with the twins is purely a working session, aimed at achieving a final text. But it is not as easy as the visitors hoped it would be. After more than a century, the women's memory has frayed considerably. From time to time, first one then the other rises and paces about, racking their weary brains with phrases they have given no thought for such a long time. The chant brings them sadness as well as joy. Joy, because it renews their links with a glory that will not be erased by time or the ill-will of others. But sadness, because even they, from whom time has so little more to claim, have grown weary of the suspended animation of a task deferred.

The sisters begin, with the Babalawo as interpreter, by educating the visitors on the history of Otis's defective text. Briefly, upon the death of their father Akindiji, there were four-weeks of extensive funeral rites, befitting a Baale who had many times defended the village, then known as Ijoko-Oke (Settlement-on-the-Hill), against attacks by Tapa warriors from lands further to the north. Everything went smoothly until the final week. Their father's body was laid to the earth. The cult of hunters and warriors did their nocturnal rites of song and dance in the sacred grove. The last four days were devoted to entertainments by the family, on both paternal and maternal sides: food and drink in endless supply, salvoes of cannon shot, masquerade plays, instrumental music and song, wrestling matches, and so on. Even non-indigenes presented shows, in gratitude to a leader who had ensured protection for everyone, no matter their origin.

It was within this final week that tragedy struck. Someone had exclaimed that smoke was rising in one part of the town. Few people heard, for most were absorbed in the excitement. But soon a greater alarm was raised: homes were on fire! Cries and wailing could be heard from the direction of the fires.

This happened just when they, Taiwo and Kehinde and their brother Akin, were chanting their father's *oriki* to drum music. No one realized the fire had been set as a diversion from the culprits' real purpose. Undeterred by the commotion, the twins and Akin pressed on with their performance. Suddenly, a band of armed men issued from the surrounding bush. Mostly black men, armed with clubs and machetes, their faces made grimmer with charcoal. There were some three white men in their midst bearing guns. They fired in the air, and the black stooges surged into the crowd, rounding up young men and women, ordering them to lie face-down or be macheted. Some victims were actually disabled with clubs.

Two blacks and a white man made for Akin and the twins. Akin ordered his sisters to take to their heels at once, tried to shield the invaders from them. The sisters ran a short distance, then turned to watch in horror as the attackers grappled with their brother. One black man swung his club at Akin. Akin caught hold of it, drew the man towards him, and brought him down with a blow to the neck. A second lunged at Akin with his club. Akin shielded his face with his arm, and the club caught his elbow. He cringed under the pain and had too little time to recover. Fearing his time was up, Akin tore off his amulet and hurled it to his weeping sisters. He could not see the white man whacking his head with the butt of a gun. He screamed for help, but soon slumped to his knees. The blacks tied his hands behind his back, and dragged him to the edge of the bush where the other captives were huddled, frightened and disabled.

Kehinde, Taiwo, and the other bereaved wept from a safe distance. To frighten them off, the white men fired one more salvo. The raiders began hauling off their captives....

The two old women are visibly tired. There is a shocked silence all around. No one is more shocked than Hampton, listening with combined horror and anger to this grim family history. Fishbein can hardly think of anything suitable enough to say. The babalawo and the drummer are speechless too. The account Akinwunmi has struggled to translate is hard enough for his ears. But neither he nor the drummer can fully grasp its relevance to the Americans sitting among them. For one thing, the event occurred so far back in time that it has paled in comparison with more recent traumas in their country. For another, they have no way of appreciating the peculiar forces in the visitors' country that inspire rather different responses in them to the same story. True, Hampton's ancestor was enslaved by men who looked like Fishbein. But they see both men as friends who have come from America in search of the ancestral home of one of them. And they know little of either the history or the dynamics of power relations that qualify their outlooks on matters of the kind they have just heard.

When Hampton has recovered enough from his heaviness of heart, he asks the Babalawo, "Do the sisters, or anyone, know exactly when these things happened—I mean, the year, month, whatever, that those invaders raided the village and took the captives away?"

Convinced the old women can offer no such data, Akinwunmi decides to speak for them.

"Well...it was a long time ago. No one can remember anything again. So, even I myself, I cannot tell you the time when they came here."

"Are there no official records, anything written down?"

Akinwunmi looks up with a calculative grimace, one hand cupping his chin. At length he shakes his head.

"I don't...think so. At least, not in our town. But what I can remember some of the old people say is that when that raid happened, everybody was surprised because for a long time white people were not coming to capture slaves again. That is why they were able to take away some people. In fact, we were told that slave catchers usually found it hard to capture people from this area, because anybody who saw them raised an alarm, and—*gbidigidigidim!*—everybody ran to hide in the bush."

The ideophone is accompanied by vivid histrionics, drawing a laugh from the drummer. Mildly amused, the two Americans look at each other. The relaxed atmosphere encourages Fishbein to throw in a question.

"Would you ask them—does anyone remember where in the village the event happened?"

Again, the babalawo can answer this without consulting the women. They are now looking downward, calm, hands clasped between the knees, perhaps trying to regain their strength and their internal peace.

"Ah! That place is now a bush. But the town used to be there before before."

"Was that where we found you yesterday?"

"Ehen, that's right!"

"You know, before we met you, Otis—the tall young man whose voice is in that tape—had run to a spot in that bush, fell down, and clutched the ground there. Do you think that was the spot where the ceremony was taking place when the invaders attacked?"

"Well...it may be. I cannot tell you the exact spot because I was not there myself. But it is in that area. You see, it was after the incident that our people moved away from there. Their houses had been burnt, so they had no houses again. That is why they went away and settled in the place where we now live. Ehen. That former place was called Ijoko-Oke, because of the hill there. Our present town is called Ijoko-Odo, because of the river near it. I think you get what I am saying?"

"Yes, yes," Fishbein concurs. "It makes a lot of sense."

The psychiatrist says no more. In his mind, he is mulling over the relevance of the entire testimony to psychological concepts he has been wrestling with. Akinwunmi looks across at the old women and whispers to Hampton that he thinks the time has come to play the tape once more and tackle the text. When Hampton mentions that he also has a transcript of the chant in Yoruba, done by a Yoruba professor in America, Akinwunmi and the drummer are quite relieved. Things would certainly be more difficult if they had to start from scratch!

The tape is played through once, so the Yoruba audience may get the full effect of the performance before tackling its language. Then, the transcript held between Akinwunmi and the drummer—himself an Ekiti man, even weaker in English than the babalawo—Hampton plays the tape in controlled stages, to enable the two Yoruba men to reconcile the corrupted sounds Otis made with what makes sense to them and the women. Taking a pen and notepad from his briefcase, Hampton numbers the lines of the transcript to facilitate corrections that need to be made.

ISIDORE OKPEWHO

The bracketed word on line two (*motami*) makes no sense to Akinwunmi or the drummer. But Taiwo tells them, with a smile, she thinks it
refers to their grandfather Itayemi, making the word a patronymic
phrase: *omo Itayemi* (son of Itayemi). That also takes care of lines twelve
and sixteen. The twins also help them unravel the family references in
lines four and nine: Otis' *bakinboli babiji* is an obvious corruption of *aba
Akimbowale, aba 'beji* (father of Akimbowale, father of twins). Akimbowale was the twins' enslaved brother.

Beyond family references, the twins and the two Yoruba men have a
hard time deciphering the rest of the corrupted text. But it is here the
expertise of the two men, in the coded idioms of Yoruba oral poetry, come
in to prop the sagging memory of the twins. Whoever composed the original text had deftly exploited some formulas for celebrating heroism in
careers such as war, hunting, and farming. The drummer, who is carrying
on the same artistic tradition, listens again and again to some of the bra-
cheted phrases, to confirm his conjectures of the correct forms the American has corrupted. In this way, the emendators are able to determine the
correct versions of several bracketed words and phrases: *kosakitty famita*
becomes *ko so 'kiti ofa meta* (line three); *fibira* ends up as *o fe gbaara* (line
five); *sibira outa* is close enough to *sigberi ota* (line six); *Uku[roo]* becomes
Uku orun (lines ten and sixteen); *eikimi yopeck* is corrected as *aye ki mi yo
p'eku* (line eleven), part of a heroic boast uttered by the warrior Akindiji;
paranaloo rabaray (line fourteen), which causes much trouble, is in the end
resolved by the twins in relation to line fifteen—both referring to the
known occupations of Akindiji's paternal and maternal families—as *panranun luran aba re*.[10]

The last two lines of the text are entirely meaningless as they stand.
The labors of emendation have finally reached a point where everyone,
most of all the aged women, decide to call it a day. Suddenly, on an
impulse, Kehinde remembers that when their performance was broken
by the invaders' sudden attack, specifically when the white man gun-
butted Akimbowale's head, he yelled for help: *E gbami o! Yeh! E gbami
o!...*[11] With one last flush of inspiration, Kehinde also remembers that
the original performance was to have ended in a final repetition of the
phrase *Uku orun ian Tapa...*, followed by the song

Tapa Tapa, eji nana baabo
Taaapa, eji nana baabo

143

Tapa Tapa, eji nana baabo
Taaapa, eji nana baabo!

—mocking the Tapa (or Nupe) warriors who learned the severe lessons of war at the hands of Akindiji. The emendation finally comes to a spirited close, as together the old twins, the babalawo, and the drummer perform a song that is part of the people's cherished tradition of oral poetry.

For Hampton, the performance is a moment of boundless pride. For Fishbein, it is a lesson in cultural education that touches regions of his heart far beyond the impersonal terrain of science. The visitors, realizing how much they have imposed upon the convenience of their hosts, struggle to bring things to a close. But for the women, it is as if the visit has merely begun.

"But where is our elder brother?" Taiwo asks through the babalawo. "Why have we not seen him today?"

"Oh, he's alright," Hampton assures them. "He has gone to find out where we'll be staying for the next few days."

"He should stay with us!" says Kehinde.

The four men laugh. Even the babalawo and the drummer know how poorly Otis would fit into the scant comforts of the old women's hovel.

"You'll see him tomorrow," says Hampton. "We have one other thing to settle before our visit is over. He will be here to join us in discussing it."

"And how have you been eating? Who has been feeding you?"

Akinwunmi urges Kehinde not to worry about such things: The men are staying in a hotel at Akure, where they are provided with the white man's food and other comforts; they are in good hands. The women appear satisfied, especially by the thought of seeing their brother again.

Otis actually returned to the twins' home. But, finding that his father and the others were still working on the chant, he retraced his steps and rejoined McAdoo in the Beetle.

The visit with the principal of Baptist High School, Mr. Ige Fagbenro, was successful. He received Bigelow, McAdoo, and Otis very warmly. The white man had come dressed in a navy blue suit and maroon tie, knowing the effect an imposing presence had on these Nigerians. When he was introduced, Mr. Fagbenro smiled and bowed so low you'd think he was offering to be beheaded. With McAdoo, who was already known to him, Fagbenro carried on so familiarly the American felt a little over-whelmed. Fagbenro was more careful with Otis. They had never met, and Otis's physique imposed itself on the short, wiry man. Still, he made the newcomer feel at home.

Fagbenro took his guests on a tour of the school. They started from the staff room, where the teachers waited to be introduced to a "deputy" to the American ambassador. One by one the teachers, all Nigerians, shook hands with Bigelow and the others. At the sports room, Fagbenro showed his guests the trophies the school had won in competitions with local schools, including McAdoo's Anglican High. For the rest of the tour, Fagbenro spoke more as a man pleading for support than parading his triumphs. Several louvers of the classroom windows were missing; a few had been replaced with dirty wood slats. There were not enough tables and seats in many classrooms; here and there, crude wooden benches substituted for regular desk and seat sets. The science laboratory was pathetic: beakers with missing handles, tubes with half their lengths of neck, a rusty kerosine cooker or two in place of bunsen burners, a plastic bowl for a porcelain sink. The tally of needs was endless.

The tour ended in the principal's office. Fagbenro reported he'd had no luck in appeals to both the Ministry of Education and the Nigerian Baptist Convention. So he would dearly welcome whatever the Americans might do to help his school. On the matter of the Peace Corps volunteer who had returned to America because of illness, Fagbenro counted her departure a serious loss to the school's math program. Her replacement was barely qualified to teach elementary school!

Bigelow crossed his legs and adjusted his tie, bringing his official seriousness up to speed. He told Fagbenro he would write to the ambassador, as soon as he got back to Ibadan, to see what might be done to help. Regarding a replacement for the volunteer, there might be a chance of doing something in the next round of assignments; until the subject areas of volunteers were known, no assurances could be given. Since the school year ended in December, there was still time to make the necessary consultations. In the meantime, Bigelow advised the principal to make use of Otis the best way he could, especially in the school's sports program. Arrangements would be made to support him on the budget already allocated for the departed volunteer. On that basis, he requested that Otis be allowed the use of the quarters vacated by the volunteer.

For Otis, Bigelow might have the right intentions but was severely short on manners. The idea of his staying in the school for the period it took to settle his problems had been proposed the day before. But the consul had no right to commit him to duties, however much they suited him, without talking with him first. He did not make an issue of it, as that would make for an awkward beginning. Sensing some tension nonetheless, McAdoo intervened, saying he was sure Otis's presence would enhance the chemistry between their two schools. Fagbenro and Bigelow both laughed. However they took the point, it seemed to ease the tension. MacAdoo gave Otis a conciliatory pat on the back.

The principal then took the party on an inspection tour of the residence in question, right next to his own house. For Otis, this was the real truce: To live close to the bush, listen to the sound of birds singing in the trees, and breathe the free, fresh air of an African village. A zinc-roofed house, standing alone. Large front yard and copious lawn. A palm tree. Two other trees he couldn't identify: fair enough, there would be time. No garage: fair enough, he had no car anyway. But ample space for hoops. Did the school have a basketball program? The possibilities grew larger...

Inside, the residence looked simple enough. It was daytime, but— no electrical power? The principal offered his regrets: this was among the many items included in a budget soon to be presented to the Inspectorate of Schools. An enormous living room. Kerosine lamp on a table in the corner. A sofa. Three wooden single chairs, each with two foam cushions. A square, wooden center table. A low wooden barrier separated the living room from a dining area with its oblong wooden table, six chairs, and a sideboard. There was an interesting item on the sideboard: a pink plastic doll without a head; instead, a blue rubber ball was stuffed through the neck, with eyes, ears, nose, and mouth all drawn in black ink. The doll lay on its back. From its flexible hip the left leg pointed upward, as though it had just kicked a ball. When was the last time he felt so tender?

There were three bedrooms in the house, with beds of various sizes and mattresses on them. Above each bed was a bunched up mosquito net, tied to the bed's four posts. The house was fairly well kept. Only in the kitchen were there any real signs of untidiness. There was a large, cast-iron kerosine stove, which evidently had not been used for some time. But there was so much soot on the walls, it was clear the last occupant was never bothered by the sight of the filth. The principal, noticing the grimace on Otis's face, promptly assured him he would send students over to clean up the house and its premises.

There was an aluminum tank under the roof in the backyard. A bore-hole supplied water to the school's major blocks and residences through a network of pipes. The tank, explained the principal, was for storing rain water during periods when the sum-pump of the well broke down and awaited repair. In the dry season, however, students were regularly assigned to fetch water, for the staff quarters, from the river behind the school. Otis, who had never suffered these inadequacies, was nonetheless cheered by the idyllic setting of his new home. Looking beyond the tank to the rest of the backyard, he could see three tropical delights located close to one another: mango, papaya, and orange trees, their glowing fruits all there for the taking!

It was agreed. Otis, his father, and Fishbein would move into the house in a day or two, as soon as it was cleaned up and fitted with basic needs: linen, bathroom facilities, cooking and dining utensils, fuel for the lamps and stove—and a spotless kitchen. Dubitsky and McAdoo, each with his own car (Dubitsky's Beetle was under repair), would assist the visitors in purchasing and transporting these items. Once settled in, Otis would be presented to the school as a temporary member of staff.

When the party returns to the home of the women, work on the text is still going on. Bigelow decides not to disturb the process. He is returning to Ibadan, but will get in touch with the visitors the next day through the volunteers. Meanwhile, they are guaranteed continued stay at the Akure Rest House until the Baptist High School has prepared the house for occupation. While Bigelow takes off, McAdoo drives Otis back to the old women's place, remaining with him in the car because Otis wants nothing to do with the job of emendation going on in there.

McAdoo's day is nearly all spent in the visitors' interest. However, since he's been covered for his second class, not much harm will be done by his absence. But he has other duties in his school. One of them comes to light while he and Otis are chatting in the car.

"So what do you do for sports?" Otis asks.

"Not a whole lot. Regular stuff—track and field. In the time that I've been here, I think I've made a little difference to the school's record: We took quite a few trophies in the last meet. We also have a soccer team.

That's not my territory, but the school hasn't done badly there either. The thing, though—the thing I'd really *love* to get started here is basketball."

Otis gives him a good look.

"You're kidding me, right?"

"I'm dead serious. I shot hoops in college, though I was never in the team."

"Then let's do it!"

"Are you serious?"

"Serious? I'm here with a ball."

"Okay, then!" They high-five to that. "This area is all country. But we can shop for stuff at Ibadan. Then again," says McAdoo, less excitedly, "won't this depend on how long you'll stay?"

"I know," says Otis. "I've got my priorities. But—as long as I'm here..."

Hampton and his team finally emerge from the twins' house. Space being short in the Beetle, Akinwunmi offers to walk home, since distances are not that great in the village. Otis sits beside McAdoo in the front, Hampton and Fishbein cram into the back seat with the drummer. Before they head for Akure, McAdoo and Otis take the group to the Baptist High School.

Akinwunmi makes time, just before nightfall, to call on Baale Osunkunle and deliver the message from the old twins. He needs the right language for the message: a message, as he well knows, need not be given in the same words in which it was received. He finds the Baale alone with his first wife in his meeting chamber. Pa Fadipe is not on his usual stoop in the front porch. Akinwunmi pays his respects. The Baale's wife knows she has to leave the men to themselves.

"Kabiyesi," the babalawo begins, "I have a message for you from *iya wa meji*. Before I deliver it, allow me the privilege of my office to recall the wisdom of Ifa, although you are no stranger to what the great Oracle has counseled us:

Eni aiye kan,
E s'aiye ire.
Bi o je iwo l'aiye kan,
Ki o s'aiye ire o.[12]

"Baale Osunkunle, what happened here yesterday and today, during the visit of our friends from America, was a sad thing. It should never have happened. Did news of it reach the ears of *iya wa meji*? Of course it did. Please do not ask me how they got to know—you yourself know the extent of their powers. They have simply asked me to tell you this. The tall young man among the visitors is their long-lost brother come home to them. They do not wish to see him suffer as he did long ago, nor lose even one hair of his body. I need not repeat what else the women said, for I know you are guided by the wisdom of your years and your office. I will simply end by saying this: Whatever may have happened in the past, please let it not happen to our people again. That is all I have to say. Kabiyesi."

Osunkunle nods his head. For a while he gazes on the floor. Then he turns to the babalawo.

"Akinwunmi, son of Kujore."

"I'm the one."

"Ehn, I never thought I would see the day when you would tell me such sad words."

"Kabiyesi, our people say that a messenger is not accountable for his message."

"That is not what I have in mind, Akinwunmi. Have I been a bad ruler to my people?"

"I never said so!"

"Then why is it that first Pa Fadipe, then the white man, and now *iya wa meji*—I'm not sure yet where you stand in all this. But let's leave that aside. Why is it that everyone thinks I mean the young man any harm? Has this town forgotten so soon what I have done for his family? When heavy rains ravaged the home of *iya wa meji* some years ago, who was it promptly sent out men to repair it, replacing their thatched roof with corrugated sheets? Have I not continued the tradition of having our farmers take food to their home at regular intervals? Some people have forgotten that the women and I are related on my mother's side. Did I not assign my cousin, Toyosi Remilekun, to make her medicinal skills available to them whenever their health has failed them?"

"You have done well, Kabiyesi."

"Then how have I failed, so much so that you found it necessary to preface your message with words from Ifa?"

"Whatever role he plays, a babalawo is always guided by the wisdom of Orunmila."

"Far be it from me to question the ways of your office. But since your business is the truth of Ifa, you will appreciate better than most people what I am about to tell you now. It is true I did not tell our visitors the truth. But I had my reasons. Ehn, I had my reasons. These women have lived for over a hundred years with the loss of their cherished brother. Does it not strike you that the return of their brother, never mind in what form, may presage the end of their lives? If I have erred in misinforming our visitors, it is only because, like every other citizen of our land, I cherish our mothers' presence among us too dearly to remember that for every one here on earth, there is an appointed time for leaving it. I am prepared to admit that much error."

"To each his lot, Kabiyesi. Still, you may be right in your fears. The thought did cross my mind as I listened again to the machine in the home of *iya wa meji.*"

"Then go back to them, Akinwunmi, and tell them this from me. I welcome the return of their cherished kin among us. I shall do everything in my power to ensure they are safe and well for as long as they choose to stay here."

"Kabiyesi! You have spoken well. I will not fail you."

Though he had been away from the visitors the previous day, Dubitsky was actually working in their interest. He had classes to teach and other school work, which took all morning and up to early afternoon. When his day ended at 1 p.m., he hurried to the roadside mechanic fixing his Beetle at Ikere-Ekiti. At about 6 p.m. he finally got the car back and drove to Akure for dinner with the visitors. Delighted at hearing all they had accomplished, he promised to return the next morning to help them shop for their quarters at Baptist High. Early that morning, he went to inform the principal he would be away the whole day taking care of visiting Americans.

The students assigned to clean up the place did their work well. The new residence was supplied with the basic needs. Fuel was provided for the lamps and the stove. The residence would be ready for occupation the next day. About five o'clock, McAdoo rejoined Dubitsky and the visitors, bringing along the babalawo. Hampton and Fishbein had promised the old women they would return once more to clear up outstanding issues. McAdoo had parted with the drummer, compensating him agreeably for services of which there seemed no more need for the moment.

When the party enter the women's outer chamber, the twins are excited to see Otis again. They are, of course, warm towards Hampton, who is also family. But Otis is their brother reincarnate, their superordinate link with a destiny long interrupted and now reestablished. When the party has settled down, the women regret they have not found the opportunity to share a meal with Hampton and Otis, as is proper between reunited kin. They are glad the visitors are well looked after at Akure. They would be pleased, however, to share traditional Yoruba fare with them. So Kehinde, who has been relaying her address through Akinwunmi, hands him two kolanuts in a saucer to wash outside. That done, the babalawo returns the nuts to her for the traditional rites.

Kehinde's hands are old and shaky. But she manages to split each nut carefully into its constituent pieces, offering prayers over them in the process. She thanks Olodumare, who orders the universe: He made possible the events of the last few days. She thanks Ogun, who brings equity between contestants and restitution to the aggrieved: He cleared the road for the reunion of sundered kin. Then she blesses the ori of everyone present for guiding them to join in the happy event. As the visitors have come, so may they safely return in due time.

Kehinde takes one piece of kolanut from the plate and gives it to Otis, who for all practical purposes stands for their long-lost brother. She takes another piece for herself and gives a third piece to her sister, Taiwo. Then she passes the plate to Akinwunmi to distribute the rest as he sees fit. There is much laughter as the babalawo tries to decide the order of seniority among the group. It seems right to offer the next piece to Hampton, who is next of kin to the women and evidently older than the others. Fishbein comes next. Then Akinwunmi takes his own piece. Dubitsky looks a little older than McAdoo, so McAdoo takes his share last. The visitors watch the volunteers, who are no strangers to local hospitality rites, as they eat their pieces happily. Fishbein leads his men in taking a bite, followed by Hampton, then Otis. The twins applaud when Otis bites his piece: The reunion has been sealed! Everyone joins in the cheering, relieving an otherwise solemn moment.

"We have a few questions to ask them, if they don't mind," Hampton says to Akinwunmi. "First of all, how old were they when the invaders captured their brother?"

Speaking for the twins, Taiwo says she cannot easily remember. She and Kehinde go into a private dialogue on history, recalling natural phenomena like locust invasions and epidemics, and social calamities like interclan wars. In the end, the women decide they were some fourteen years old when the invaders struck.

"And how much older than they was their brother?"

"Seven years," Taiwo seems surer.

Hampton widens his eyes to look, first at his son, then at Fishbein: twenty-one years, exactly the same age as Otis! When Otis looks at Taiwo, he sees the woman has her eyes fixed on him. A pale but tender smile labors around her mouth. Amused, he turns to take another bite at his kolanut. Taiwo chuckles at the youthfulness of her reincarnated brother.

Fishbein discreetly draws Akinwunmi's attention.

"There is one more problem," he says. "Two days ago, when we got to that spot in the bush where, I assume, their brother was captured by the invaders, Otis lay on the ground and seemed to be at peace with himself. And yet, when we played the tape here, he was still uncomfortable. Would you please ask them: Why does he continue to have this problem with the song?"

When Akinwunmi puts the question to the women, Taiwo looks to her sister. Kehinde clears her throat, and takes her time answering the question. Her eyes are fixed downward.

"Yes, there is a reason for it. Tell them, there is a reason for it. Have they not seen that, when they played that thing, the song was not completed? At the end, it was saying *E gbami o! E gbami o! E gbami o!* The song was not finished, because the people beat our brother on the head, and he could no longer speak. Then they carried him away. Now he is back, he should finish the song. The song is not yet finished. His ori is strong. It wants him to finish the song, and do it well."

"How can he do that," asks Hampton, "when he cannot speak the language?"

The old woman hesitates before responding.

"He will have to remain here, and learn our language. When he has learnt it, and can speak it well, we will arrange to repeat the ceremony. Then he will sing the full song with us. That is the only way he can be himself again."

Much later that day, the visitors return to the house that will be Otis's new home. Standing in the front yard, he breathes the air deeply through a distended chest. What use is there in fighting his fate? He walks over to take another look at the spot where he will post his hoops. Then he walks around the front yard, touching this tree, smelling that leaf, surveying the lawn. There is full proprietary air in his movement.

Hampton senses his spirit and feels much encouraged. But one small thought hovers naggingly on his mind. How will he face Melba's alarm at his leaving their only son to his own devices, alone in darkest Africa? As a father, he is not entirely without fears. But he has hopes to match, for the old horrors are gradually dissolving. In time, things will fall into place. This, after all, is the home of their fathers. In time, even Melba will understand.

Leaving Otis outside, Hampton walks quietly into the house. Fishbein and the others are already putting things in place.

Part Three

AKIMBOWALE

From flesh into phantom on the horizontal stone
I was the sole witness to my homecoming...

Serene lights on the other balcony:
redolent fountains bristling with signs—

But what does my divine rejoicing hold?
A bowl of incense, a nest of fireflies?

I was the sole witness to my homecoming...

—Christopher Okigbo, *Distances*

Ijoko-Odo
June 15, 1964

Dear Mom and Dad,

I'm truly delighted to be writing you. I needed to do this early, for mom's sake at least. I've never forgotten the state you were in, mom, when it was finally decided I should go to Africa. I hope this letter helps to set your mind at ease. Since I am new here, many things are still very strange to me. But I am learning. I'll be fine, mom. Trust me.

Coming here, in fact, was the best thing that could have happened to me. I have come to accept the logic of my existence: I have been chosen by the spirits of our ancestors to set our interrupted destiny in order. I am not exactly sure how I can do this. But I know I am not alone. Something inside me wants to be angry with whoever was responsible for what happened to our family way back when. The scene at the Baale's palace told me someone did some dirty business that caused our ancestor to be taken away. But I'll suspend my judgment about all this so I don't get mixed up in stuff that won't do me any good.

Fishbein has done his best—I must give him his due. Without him, it's difficult to see how we could have gotten this far. Now it's my turn to take charge of myself. I will no longer be a miserable patient waiting to be put right. I will learn this language and speak it well and do whatever it takes to make me the person I ought to be. If I don't, then this whole trip is wasted, and I'm a failure both to my family (that is, my now expanded family) and to myself.

Everybody here has been pitching in to help me settle down. The principal (Mr. Fagbenro) never stops asking anytime he peeps in here, Everything alright? Need anything? I tell him I'm fine. His children and I are great friends.. Two kids, a boy and a girl, ages 8 and 11. The boy, Deji, who is 11, is a junior in the elementary school close to the high school. Very likeable, very intelligent. So is the girl, Sumbo. She's a real delight. They asked their mom if they could be sleeping overnight at my place, and prepare for school from here in the morning. They say they're sorry I'm lonely! So I have company every night. Sumbo gets up in the morning, and first thing she does, she gets a broom from their house and sweeps my living room and kitchen! Deji boils water for me to have a bath. At first I didn't want it to look like I was using them. But their mom said it was alright, it would make them grow up to be responsible people.

People here have character!

A few days ago, Mr. Fagbenro formally introduced me to the school. First in the staff room, to all the teachers. Then at the morning assembly, to all the students. The kids are fun. Many of them still giggle every time they pass me, especially the girls. I suppose they've never seen anyone so tall. I'm sure they'll get used to my height soon enough.

The teachers are okay too. But I believe one of them has a problem with me, name of Mr. Dipeolu. He teaches art and doubles as sports coach—soccer, track, etc. I suspect he thinks I've been hired to take his job, because I've been asked to handle track and whatever else I want to do with the students in sports. Every other teacher smiled and said hello when the principal introduced me. He just shook my hand quickly and never said a word. Like I need another problem in this town!

Talking about sports, McAdoo and I mean to take our plans for basketball seriously. My principal likes it, his principal likes it. All that remains is for us to show them just what we can do. Next week, we're going to Ibadan to shop for hoops and things. I really look forward to it. That's something that could help me keep my sanity in this place. For the meantime, I bounce the ball around the front yard and over the branches of one of the trees—I believe it's almond. Students who have been around the house seem to love seeing me do this. Deji and Sumbo have also taken to bouncing the ball with me. This makes their friends jealous.

Awo Akinwunmi (diviners are called Awo here, short for Babalawo), has become a really close friend. I'm getting to like him a lot. He has taken me to see the twins twice now. And he is taking it upon himself to teach me things. I guess he knows I need to do this fast, considering the women don't have too long to live. I'm becoming fond of the women too. Awo advised me to address them as *iya*, but when I did so they said I should call them *aburo* (which means younger sibling). I am their lost older brother returned, they said, and they are supposed to be younger than I am. At first I was uneasy. But this culture must have its logic. I doubt I'll ever call them *aburo* though. They'll have to get used to me calling them *iya*.

I will write as often as I can. I'm not one for keeping diaries. So these letters are the best way I know of making a record of everything that happens to me during my time here. I never want to forget what's happened to me in the last few weeks and how everything will turn out.

My love to Aunt Ella. I hope she'll be alright. For her own sake, she

156

really should have been here with me. But maybe it was never in the stars for her. I love you both, you know that. I hope you write soon.

Otis.

P.S. Just got Norma's letter. Tell her to expect mine next. Love again.

June 22, 1964

Dear Norma,

Olufe mi. Se alafia ni? Se daa-daa l'o wa? I give you ten guesses! It means, Darling, how are you? Are you doing alright? Your answer would be, *Adupe l'owo Olorun*: We thank God. That's the Yoruba way of exchanging greetings. Nice, isn't it?

If you're wondering how I've learned all this so fast, well, I have a tutor here. I don't know how much my dad has told you, but we had the good luck of running into a babalawo the first day we came to this village. A babalawo is a herbal doctor, priest, soothsayer, philosopher—you name it! What makes it even better is that this man—his name is Akinwunmi, but I call him Awo, short for babalawo—Awo Akinwunmi was once an elementary school teacher. But he was also trained as a babalawo under his father. When his father died, he took over his job, following tradition. So I have the good luck of having someone who can teach me the tradition and still communicate with me in English. But Awo has warned me he'll do very little talking in English with me. That way, I can learn Yoruba fast. Which is fine with me, especially because few people here are interested in teaching me Yoruba. When I try to speak a few words with Yoruba colleagues in my school, they laugh at me and say I'm murdering their language! Left to them, I could never learn enough Yoruba no matter how long I stayed here.

Language is a strange thing. I haven't been here very long, but I'm beginning to understand there's a lot more to language than words. It's the whole culture of the people, with a lot of history and tradition locked into it. I'm beginning to understand that one reason my colleagues laugh at me is that though the words I say are not wrong, they don't quite fit in the contexts I use them. Other words would do better in those contexts. Like saying *march* in English, when you need to say *walk*. Though the two words suggest movement, you don't use *march* when you're talking about moving around your living room. You understand what I'm saying? Yoruba, like English I guess, has these fine distinctions. There are words you don't say, for instance, to elderly people even though they are acceptable when you say them to younger people. Believe me, Norma, I've been laughed at so often, I'm being pretty careful what words I use and in what situations!

You ask how comfortable I am. Well, there's a lot of things I'm missing. I miss you, most of all. I miss having you with me every chance we get. You bring so much sanity and pleasure to my life, there's nobody I'd rather be with than you. I guess you know that too. And I miss other things everyone learns to live with in American culture: TV, pizza, McDonald's, movies, James Brown, Smokey Robinson.... There's no electricity here, which means you can't do most things you're used to. Water runs, but not all the time, and that gets messy around the house.

And can you imagine me not shooting hoops? Luckily, I have some company here. My dad must have told you about Chip McAdoo, a Peace Corps teacher in a nearby school. Black, nice, and friendly. He and I are trying to do something about basketball in our schools. So, very soon that will be taken care of. But I'm learning you can't always have the things you're used to, so you appreciate the things you have around you.

How about your sweet self? Thanks for staying so close to my mom, she really needs that. Especially being near someone like you, who appreciates Africa. I'll do my best in these letters to give you the true picture of things as I see them. Though I haven't been here long, it's becoming quite clear to me I've never really taken control of my education. So far, the things I know are mostly the things other people taught me. About Africa, for instance. I'm glad of the opportunity to get a real education about Africa and Africans. In the short time I've been here, it's already clear to me how amazingly ignorant I (like most Americans, I suppose) was about the place. If I take my program here as seriously as I should, I expect to be much better informed even if I don't know everything there is to know about Africa.

It was also good for me to have been left all alone here to grapple with the world in my own terms. Get to know myself, *understand* myself better. Right now, I feel a little out of my zone. But I expect the time will come when I'll come as close as I can to the person I ought to be.

I love you and always will. *O d'abo* (Bye-bye)!

Otis.

June 30, 1964

Dear Mom and Dad,

Approval finally came for me to be paid from the Peace Corps account. The principal, Mr. Fagbenro, got a letter from Bigelow about that a week ago. So everything is fine on that score. McAdoo and I have been to Ibadan to shop for basketball stuff. Things are falling into place.

Everybody here seems pleased with the idea of learning a new game. Everybody, except the other coach, Mr. Goke Dipeolu (I call him Crabs). This school has only one sports field where everything is done. Mr Fagbenro got workmen to draw lines on the field with lime and post up the baskets at different ends of the field than the goal posts for soccer. Crabs tried to stop the workmen, but they told him they had orders from the principal. So he stormed across to the principal, and they had an argument: Crabs telling the principal he was ruining the school's sports program and the principal saying the more activities the better for the school. I'm told Crabs is threatening the boys I've picked for the game. Does that man have a problem! I don't much blame him though. I wonder if I'd do the same if I was in his place?

I spent much of yesterday with the Fagbenros. First, I accompanied the family to Sunday morning service. Not being much of a churchgoer, I felt funny. But I survived. Then I had lunch with them. Lunch here is not something light, like we have in the States. It's a full-blown meal. We had stewed rice (they call it *jollof* rice) and fried strips of ripe plantains (that's large bananas). Strips of it are fried in vegetable oil and called *dodo*. Then there was a bowl of stew with large helpings of fish and meat. They wouldn't let me make do with a small helping. Mrs. Fagbenro, who calls me *Tisha wa* (meaning our teacher), kept asking if I didn't like her cooking. I said I did, but that I just wasn't used to eating so much in the afternoon. She said that was because we didn't have much food in America. So now that I'm here, I should eat as much as I can!

Little Sumbo is simply adorable. She insisted on sitting next to me and bringing me everything I needed. When her brother Deji tried to get me a spoon she protested, saying that was her job! Deji let her, as always when she pulls stuff like that. He says he's too old to be arguing with her! I'm having a great deal of fun with these kids. This morning Sumbo asked if I could please accompany her to her school before going to mine. I did, and she seemed to enjoy the attention she got from the other kids.

She's terrific—makes me feel like a parent well before my time!

Nigerians tend to cook with a lot of oil. Otherwise I think the food here is quite good. I suggested to Mrs. Fagbenro I'd like to learn how to cook some of their food. She said though she understood, they wouldn't have their Tisha do any cooking. So the principal is arranging for one of the students to come to my place every day and prepare my meals. I think I'll just watch the student carefully and take over after a while. I'd be embarrassed to exploit my own students.

Give my love to Aunt Ella. And my best to Dr. Fishbein. I have no news yet for him on stuff he asked me to look out for—like, does anything in this place look familiar to me! I know everyone thinks I'm someone else come back to life. So far, I still feel like the same old me. When I begin to feel differently, nobody would need to tell me!

Love,

Otis

July 11, 1964

Dear Mom and Dad,

Thanks for sharing my letter to you with Norma. I imagine she'll share hers with you too. This way, I can split the news between all of you and won't need to write an awful lot of letters!

Good to hear Dr. Fishbein asks about me constantly. I rather like him, but I still don't have news for him. Right now I feel fine. In fact, I'm beginning to feel more and more like one of the natives, and most people here are very friendly.

But I had a rotten time part of yesterday. One of my players got hurt on the field during practice. He was given first aid at the school's dispensary, then taken to a nearby clinic in Ikere-Ekiti for further attention. Crabs, the other coach, quickly raised hell with the principal. How many more kids, he said, are going to get hurt before everyone realizes "this American fellow" is bad news for the school. Mr. Fagbenro told him anybody could get hurt anytime; it was just an accident. Then Mr. Fagbenro asked, haven't his soccer players been hurt before? I can't seem to do right by Crabs! For some reason, he's the only person here who keeps reminding me I'm not one of them. Everyone else treats me like a native, especially since my Yoruba is getting better day by day.

I did my best to stay cool. But it wasn't long before I was ticked off again. In the staff room, I sit next to a female teacher, a rather nice lady. She never stops telling me she thinks I'm twice her height! She's one of the few people in this school who don't mind conversing with me in Yoruba, to help me with the language. She had seen how upset I was with Crabs and tried to make me feel good. All of a sudden, Tim Dubitsky showed up beside me. I was glad to see him, so I said hi. I tried to find him a seat, but he said no, that's okay: some people are here to see you. So I go out with him, and what do I see? Two young white men, fully dressed as marines, standing beside a U.S. embassy car. I asked Tim, What's this, man? He said, Well, these guys have been sent by Phil Bigelow. They're to be taken to the Baale, so he would see Bigelow meant every word he said, that the Baale must make sure I'm safe.

I couldn't believe this. Bringing American military power to scare a little village, just for my sake? I'd quite forgotten how much I disliked Bigelow for the way he threatened the Baale, in that last meeting we had with him. But this visit brought it all back. I could barely restrain myself. I didn't even go with Tim to meet the marines, I just stopped at the steps of the staff room. Tell them, I said, I appreciate their coming all this way, but really they needn't have come. I turned round and was going back inside. I know that was rude, but it wasn't any worse than them coming to flex their muscle before a little community. But guess what? Tim said, Hey, come on man. Look, this is all for your protection. And I said, Protection from what? He said, Look, you don't seem to realize you might be in a heap of trouble. These people could be...but I didn't let him finish. I said, *These* people are my people. Now if you'll excuse me, I've got work to do. I left him and returned to my seat.

I was sorry I did that to Tim. He's really a nice fellow. I may be naive, but so far everyone—except Crabs, and I can handle that—everyone has bent over backwards to make me feel at home. If America has nothing better to do than call out the marines over one little fellow who hasn't even lifted a finger against them or me, then it needs help. I didn't tell him that. I just went back inside. I'll make up with him later. I'm sure he'll understand.

So Aunt Ella suggests we should build a house on the grounds where the twins live? How interesting. Maybe sometime in the future, when what needs to be done has been done. But give her my love, anyway. And love to you both. *O d'igba* (So long).

Otis.

July 26, 1964

Dear Mom and Dad,

The school calendar here is divided into two semesters: mid-January to mid-July, late August to early December, with breaks here and there for Christian and Muslim holidays. The two religions have an undeclared war between them, which affects the political, social, and cultural aspects of life in this country. Since the British gave Nigeria its independence a few years ago, the Muslims from the north have been in control of the government. So they've been busy changing things to reflect their interests. This means more holidays in schools, to balance the long-established Christian holidays with some Muslim ones. The kids love it!

Just before the midyear vacation, at the end of the midyear exams, there was a sports meet in our school. Incidentally, the school year is continuous: many subjects are taught from January to December, with a break in between to measure the progress of the students in these subjects. Well, at the sports meet, the school had an opportunity to see the hard work I've done in the few weeks I've been here as coach. Despite very poor facilities, three new track records were set: high jump, hurdles, 400 yards. But basketball drew the most attention. I found a good number of tall boys to make two teams. Their moves need some refining—their rejections alone are *brutal!* But the crowd had a lot of fun in the match we played on the last day of school. Many more boys want to join, so we need to do more work to find the very best when school reconvenes in August. I've agreed with Chip McAdoo (BB coach for his school, Anglican) to have a competition between our teams at the end of the year, in December. Guess what? Girls in my school are asking for a girls team! I don't know if I or the school can handle that.

I could have written just after we closed for the midyear holidays. But I've been getting around with friends. Sunday, the Fagbenros took me to a wedding in Ado-Ekiti, not far from here. This was my first opportunity to see how colorful Nigerians can get. The bride's friends and relations dressed in one set of color designs, the bridegroom's in another set of color designs. The uniform dresses are called *asho ebi*, meaning family wear, and each group sees itself as a family, whether or not they are related by blood. Patterns of blue, yellow, red, green, all kinds of colors everywhere. When the congregation came outside, the colors all blended beautifully together.

What happened outside was also interesting. Everybody moved down to the reception hall, and there was a lot of music from drum players. You'll be pleased to know that my troubles with drum music are finally over. I started hearing the sounds as we were filing out of the church, and I thought, Oh my God! But there was no tingling sensation whatsoever. I guess the demon of drum sounds (to use mom's word!) finally decided to let go of me now that I've settled here!

I learned something interesting about drummers. Many of them play a type of drum called *dundun*, a talking drum that is played to imitate human speech. In this case, the player moves close to a wedding guest and plays phrases that are supposed to be praises of the guest. He does this to guest after guest. The guest is supposed to paste some coins or currency notes on the drummer's brow, in gratitude for the praises. I asked Mr. Fagbenro how much a drummer could have known about all the guests he was praising. He said the drummer didn't have to know a whole lot about each and every guest. He only has to recycle the same phrases—like being good-looking or well-built, maybe a few about coming from a good family. Most guests are so pleased with these compliments they paste some money on the drummer's brow. Then I asked, What happens if the guest doesn't place any money on the player's brow (as I sometimes noticed)? Mr Fagbenro said, That's alright—the drummer will simply turn around and play you what a terrible looking person you are!

I believe the point of this is, if you're rich enough to be so beautifully dressed, you should be "beautiful" enough to share some of the wealth with struggling fellow human beings—like the drummer, of course! The Yoruba take this whole idea of sharing things seriously, which for them is the only way the world can get along. I've been to weddings in the U.S. and seen how the guests are mostly restricted to close family and friends. Frankly, I'd never seen so many guests attending a wedding as I saw at this one. The reception was in an open hall, which meant you didn't have to have been invited to be served. So long as you were inside the hall, you could count on being welcome to the food and drinks! This reminded me of something my mentor, Awo Akinwunmi, said about sharing your good fortune with others. He quoted a verse to me from the philosophy of Ifa (the Yoruba Bible) that says, Anyone who keeps goodness to himself at home, will never meet it outside his home. Can you imagine a free-for-all wedding reception back in America?

Love to Aunt Ella. Write soon.

Otis

August 14, 1964

Dear Norma,

Your letter was wonderful, as always. By the way, you should have been at that wedding I wrote about. The dresses I saw the women wear, the *asho ebi*, were terrific. I'd never seen such gorgeous dresses on black women before. They'd look smashing on you and my mom. I intend to find out how to get you two ladies that kind of outfit. You'd look like the princesses you might possibly be.

I had some fun reading that line of yours, that I should not get too close to the female teacher who gives me Yoruba lessons. Come on!

Still, let me tickle your jealousy a little further with some things that happened lately. The first happened a few weeks ago, when Awo Akinwunmi took me to see the old twins. When we got there, I was surprised to find they'd prepared supper and wanted me to share it with them. They said it was a shame I'd been in this town so long and never eaten one meal with my own family. If I hadn't gone with Awo Akinwunmi, I'd have been way out on a limb! To cut it short, I ate as much as I could, though the stew burned like hell, and they seemed amused at seeing me blow air through my lips to cool the burning. The visit helped to give my growing Yoruba skills some practice. I managed a conversation with them in Yoruba, with occasional help from Awo Akinwunmi. The women were pleased to see I was living up to the promise of my homecoming.

During our conversation, Kehinde, the older of the twins...in Yoruba culture, the second of the twins to be born is the elder, since she made the first go and see what the world is like! Well, Kehinde asked me if I had a wife. I said I didn't have any. She said they thought it was time I had one. I said I wasn't ready to get married yet, and they said I was old enough and big enough to get married. They said they knew just the right girl for me, who would take good care of me. They said she was a good girl, from a good family in this town, and they would personally recommend her to me since as a son of the place I should marry a girl from here. Well! We brought the matter to a close only when I told them I would think about it and let them know when to show me the girl they had in mind.

I'd quite forgotten about the whole affair, until about two weeks ago. You remember me saying in a recent letter that Mr. Fagbenro, the principal, was planning to assign a student as my cook? He finally did.

Her name is Tosin, a senior at the school. Not bad looking, if you ask me, and she had something in mind. Our school is now on midyear break, so she took to coming in the morning and being here the whole day, cooking breakfast, lunch, and supper! And that's not all. She would come here all cutely dressed and made up—eye shadows, lips and nails polished red as cherries, and some powder round her neck. All this on someone who was here to *cook*?

Of course I knew I was being seduced, but I laughed it off as a tolerable joke. Until she started making distinct moves. One morning, after she had made my breakfast and I was still taking a bath, she quietly made my bed and placed a red rose on it! When I came in from the bathroom and saw the stuff on my bed, I was speechless. I didn't get angry or anything. I just threw the stuff away. I went over to have my breakfast, thanked her for making the bed, and told her not to bother doing it anymore, I'd do it by myself. I said that in English, so she would get my meaning perfectly clear.

That might have dampened her spirits. But she wasn't discouraged, because she didn't stop trying. One day, after supper (incidentally, she never sat at table to have dinner with me, despite my asking her a few times to do so), I was in the living room reading a book, when I noticed her sitting quietly at the dining table. She didn't say a word. I felt awkward, because usually, after tidying up the kitchen, she would bid me goodnight and promise to return the next morning. On this particular night, she just sat there, probably expecting me to say something to her. I did. I said to her in Yoruba, It's getting dark: don't you think your father will be worried that you've not yet returned? She said to me, Are you driving me away? Don't you want me to stay the night? *Stay the night!*

Now, guess who helped me solve the problem? Little Sumbo. Oh, she's quite a prima donna around here, and I've come to love her for it. She never liked Tosin and never passed up the chance to let her know it. She and her brother Deji frequently have supper with me, and though she lets Deji make his own table, she never lets anyone besides herself make my table. She makes it not at the head of the table, but along the side, so she and no one else would sit next to me! One evening, I saw her struggling to snatch a plate from Tosin as Tosin was setting my table. They almost had a fight, until I pleaded with Tosin to let her do the setting! Well, she and Deji were sitting with me in the living room, flipping through picture books. They were there when Tosin was asking to stay for the night, and before I said anything in reply, Sumbo told Tosin, No you can't sleep here tonight. Uncle (that's what she and Deji call me)— Uncle sleeps in one room, and I sleep in one room, and Deji sleeps in one room. So there is no place for you to sleep. There was silence after she said that. When Tosin noticed I didn't say anything to the little girl, she got the message. She got up and left: put on her slippers (she usually left them by the kitchen door), said a quick goodnight and walked out the door into the darkness.

Frankly, I felt a little sorry for her. I told Sumbo that wasn't nice, she should show Tosin a little more respect because she's an older person. She nodded, but I could tell she was quietly pleased with her victory. Deji, who hadn't said a word all this time, gave her a big evil eye. But even he knew better than to mess with our little prima donna!

The first day Tosin came here, it was Mrs. Fagbenro who brought her. I assumed she was delivering on her husband's promise to find me a cook. But the grand design became clear to me last week when I visited the twins, as I've begun doing by myself. Mrs. Fagbenro had asked me once how I liked my student cook, and I'd said I thought she was good, I liked her a lot. But when the twins asked me the same question, *then* it struck me this must be the girl they planned for me to marry. I told them the same thing I told Mrs. Fagbenro. But that's when I made the decision to terminate the whole relationship before it got out of hand. On Sunday, after I had supper, I told her as nicely as I could she needn't come any longer, I could now prepare my own meals. She appeared saddened, and I was too. But, she knew it was all over. We said goodnight, and she went home.

I haven't been back to see my aunts, although I'm gradually building up my response to questions I know they'll ask me. I did find out a little more about their relationship to Tosin. She is the daughter of Madam Remilekun, a woman who tends to the health of the twins whenever any one of them is ill. The lady is said to have had Tosin for a man from the town of Abeokuta, elsewhere in Yorubaland. So Tosin is the young woman of good family I'd been promised. Mrs. Fagbenro didn't take my parting with Tosin too badly—even she might have noticed the girl was trying too hard. When I told her I had to let Tosin go because I could do my own cooking, she knew that wasn't exactly true. She might have heard a few things from her two kids. But she said it was okay. Wow!

I'm glad you did well in the maroon paper and hope the project has given you ideas about possible future study. If the study happens to be about Africa, I hope my letters will be of practical use to you someday.

Give my love to your mom on your New York trip. Tell her I hope to treat myself to her callaloo and curry goat someday!

Love, always,
Otis

August 22, 1964

Dear Mom and Dad,

Our midyear break is practically over. So far I've spent most of it in the company of helpful people. The Fagbenros have been totally hospitable. Mrs. Fagbenro, in particular, has taken my acculturation program nearly as seriously as myself. A couple of times, for instance, I've accompanied her to the market to shop for groceries and other household stuff. Little Sumbo went hand in hand with me: Deji says going to market is women's work! In the market I drew a lot of attention with my physique. One woman, whose stall we walked into for black-eyed beans, amused me: while Mrs Fagbenro was asking her the price of the beans, she continuously stared at me with a smile on her face. When she didn't respond to the question, Mrs Fagbenro asked her why she was staring at me. She said, *O wa bembe bayii!* meaning, He's so robust (or muscular)! I've been in such situations so many times. In fact, I'm getting to like it because I've made quite a few friends from it.

Market is fun. I'm excited learning the names of various items, their uses, techniques of bargaining, etc. Here in the traditional market, prices are not fixed. They are supposed to be negotiated. The idea of give and take, fair exchange, what's good for me should be good for you, and so on, is something the Yoruba take very seriously. That doesn't mean you shouldn't make a profit. It simply means that the profit you make should not destroy your client.

Why do I take all this trouble? I was advised by Awo Akinwunmi, my chief mentor, that it's alright for me to want to learn the language of this place. But I should remember that language does not exist by itself. Language is nourished by life, and in turn nourishes that life. So, to understand a language in all its dimensions and be able to speak it well, you must interact intimately with the life and the culture around it. I'm finding it a most useful policy. And I'm beginning to ask many questions: Why this is that, and what's the relation between this and that. And most of the people here are very helpful. They seldom feel I'm bothering them or imposing on their time. Could I take such liberties with anyone in the States? I don't think so. In less than three months I'm getting fairly comfortable speaking Yoruba!

I spend a lot of my time with Chip McAdoo and Tim Dubitsky. I made up with Tim. I just told him, Sorry man, I'd had a bad morning. He laughed it off and said, That's okay. He too had come to feel the embassy didn't have to go so far. Like I said before, Tim is a fine guy. Every day that passes, I'm getting to be more in control of my responses. I don't think I'd handle the situation the same way today as I did then. There are too few of us here to be at daggers drawn.

I spend more time with Chip than anyone though. In the past few weeks, he's *forced* the issue of black identity on me—what it means to be a black person in American society. For him, it's a mission. I don't recall what set him off, though I suspect it all started the first time I visited him at his place in Iludun, on the Anglican School campus. His house is loaded with artifacts: carvings of animals and people, cowrie beads, wooden combs of many designs, handmade mats for floors and walls, bronze figurines, and several other things, some of them items I've found only in the home of Awo Akinwunmi. Chip *always* wears a dashiki over his pants. You'd never see him in a European shirt. Then, he has bundles of books and periodicals from the States on the black struggle, and other books on African history, literature, and culture. He recently lent me one of the much talked about books of modern African literature, Chinua Achebe's *Things Fall Apart*. I haven't gotten round to reading it yet.

We had an interesting discussion one afternoon in his living room. He'd been looking at me for a while. Then he sighed and said to me, You don't know how lucky you are, man. I said, What do you mean by that? At least you've found your roots, he said, you know who you are. Well, I said, I'm still battling with it. At least you have your feet on the ground, he said. He was obviously leading up to something I could only imagine. He went on about how good he thought it was that he'd made the decision to come out here on the Peace Corps program: it gave him the opportunity to see the black American's situation from a distant perspective. The way he sees it, the black struggle in the U.S. is a futile struggle, because the black man is never going to win the respect and the status he's fighting for in American society.

Why, he said, the only man who looked like he was willing to give the black man a chance, President Kennedy, was gunned down in cold blood.

Though I haven't followed these issues as much as I should, I remember saying, Well, it may be true about Kennedy, but I think leaders like Martin Luther King and Malcolm X have scored some successes. Like what? he asked. Before I could respond, he said to me, How long do you think they're going to last, these leaders you talk about? He said he was around when Malcolm X visited Nigeria sometime recently. He was up at Ibadan University where Malcolm gave a public lecture. You'd have had a great time with Malcolm, he said. I asked why. He told me that after the lecture some of the black Americans in the audience went over to Malcolm to empathize with him. He'd ask each of them where they came from, and they'd tell him their native city and state in the U.S. Malcolm would answer, No, I mean, where you *really* come from?—meaning, where in Africa? Malcolm, he said, would have been extremely pleased to find someone who knew where he really came from. But the way he's been talking, he said, you mark my words: *They'll* get him soon.

I found all this strange, coming from someone who was here on a mission for the American government. Thinking about my particular position, I wondered how many black Americans would have gone through the experiences I've had to discover who they were. So I said to Chip, What if you don't find where you come from, what difference would it make? And he said, It's a matter of the choices you want to make. We'll never be who we want to be in America, he said, because the society won't let us, no matter what promises it makes to our leaders. I don't know what your plans are, he said, but this is it for me. This is where I'm going to stay. Here, in Nigeria? I asked. Yes, he said, and very likely here in Iludun, strange as it may seem. When I'm done with this Peace Corps charade next year, I'm staying on as regular staff in my school.

That's only half the story about Chip. He's deeply into music: Nigerian music and Afro-American music, especially jazz. Incidentally, his school has a private electric generator which is turned on twelve hours each day, 8 am to 8 pm or thereabouts. So he's fine. He has a stereo system with a turn table, so he's able to play his LPs. From his stack of records I've become familiar with names like Duke Ellington, Miles Davis, John Coltrane, Billie Holliday, Sonny Rollins, and so on. He talks of hot new talents like Archie Shepp who have done far-out things in sessions with John Coltrane and are part of the revolution. It's a matter of choices, he said. Know who you are, or at least dig deep, he said. Like the jazz guys. They don't exactly know what they're searching for. *I* don't even know what I'm hoping to find. The challenge is in the looking, and that's what I'm doing.

You must have read what I told Norma about my student cook, Tosin? Chip has firmly settled in with one of his students he's planning to marry—he has none of the qualms I had with my student. He also has a local palmwine tapper bring him a fresh supply of the drink every morning. Before he takes a draught, he does the ritual of breaking a kolanut and blessing "the ancestors," as he puts it. Chip *has* gone native!

I have no problem with Chip. I know why I'm here and what my program is. I haven't, until now, given much attention to black politics in the U.S. The good thing about meeting guys like Chip is, you begin to realize how you can live in America for so long in some sleepwalking state. You think things are the way they are supposed to be, even when you're hurting, all because you won't take the time to ask yourself the necessary questions. Mind you, I'm not so innocent about these things as I may seem. I may not be politically *radical*, as such. But if what I've seen recently with Bigelow and the marines tells me anything, it's that there are aspects of my life I should never shut my mind to, whatever my preoccupations happen to be at any point in time.

That's what I meant when I counted Chip among the helpful people I've been spending my time with. He's got his agenda and I've got mine, and in some respects I might even think he's weird. But he clearly encourages me to ask myself, What will you do with what you're hoping to find? For the moment I guess my answer will be, I'll find out when I get there.

It hurt to read from your letter that Aunt Ella's health isn't getting any better. I suppose that means it's getting worse? Maybe you can tell me something more specific.

Love,
Otis

September 13, 1964

Dear Mom and Dad,

We've been back to school about three weeks. I'm getting better adjusted to school and the village as a whole. Everybody seems to know me now. That's not surprising, since I'm the tallest person here! I even have a new name: Tokunbo. The full form of it is *Oun ti o lati okun bo* (the one who came from overseas: *okun* is Yoruba for sea). At first I didn't know I was being called that. I'd heard the name used several times to my hearing, but I never thought I was the one being referred to. It got to me when some kid came looking for me in the staff room during recess (lunch break). The student, a girl, walked into the staff room and asked to see Tokunbo. I was drawing water from a water jar nearby. When she said that, my colleagues in the room burst out laughing. Returning with the cup of water in my hand, I wondered what the joke was about. I'd heard the girl, but didn't think she meant me. Mrs. Fafunso (my Yoruba teacher) told me the girl was asking for me!

The poor girl was embarrassed, I could tell from the way her face dropped. But I laughed at the joke, and that put her at ease. Since then, I've gotten used to everyone calling me Tokunbo. I even like the name myself. Why not? If everyone takes me as a son of the place, I might as well have a Yoruba name. What does it matter that I was born abroad? Tokunbo! I guess I got the name mainly because people feel more comfortable with it than with Otis, or Mr. Hampton, which I've never gotten used to.

They've played other games on me. Last week, I accompanied three students to fetch water for my tank from the river behind the school. Our water system has been shut for repairs, and we haven't had much rain since the August break. So the students were assigned to fetch six rounds of water each. I accompanied them on five rounds, using a plastic container I'd picked up from the Fagbenro backyard. On the final round, I told the students (all males) to go on back to their dorms, I wanted to swim in the river. While I was pulling off my shirt, I heard them murmuring and giggling. I believe they were seeing the hairs on my chest for the first time. I enjoyed the swim: cool water, peaceful surroundings, birds singing, trees and grass along the banks swaying in the wind. I had a great time. As I went up the river bank to pick up my shirt, I heard a stampede. The boys were running away from the nearby bush! They'd been watching me swim, so they'd have stories to tell their friends. Again I smiled, amused by the prank. Yesterday, as I was leaving one of the classrooms, I overheard a student telling another, *Won ni Tokunbo yaa we l'odo* (They say Tokunbo went to swim in the river). They hadn't seen me coming. When I cut in with, *Ooto ni* (That's true), they broke up their conversation and ran!

Are you ready for some history? Yesterday I paid a visit to *iya wa meji*, the twins. This time, Awo Akinwunmi came along with me, because though I can speak Yoruba reasonably well, I didn't feel my Yoruba was good enough for the purpose. The visit was a follow-up to a previous one, where I told them I'd like to know more about our past. They agreed, and set the history session for yesterday. It went *very* well, in fact much better than I'd feared. I found I got along with little help from Awo Akinwunmi. And because I didn't want to miss anything, I took careful notes.

Before we settled down to business, Taiwo (the younger twin) treated us to a meal she had specially prepared for my benefit: *eko* (a cornstarch paste boiled in leaves until it becomes a white jelly) and *moinmoin* (pudding made from black-eyed beans ground with pepper, crayfish, and oil and boiled in leaves). It was an absolutely delicious meal—what *you* Americans would call finger-licking good! I intend to try making those things myself someday soon.

Now back to history. I'll make it short, though it's a fascinating account. The farthest back the women could go (mind you, no dates) was a man by name Ifaturoti, a staff bearer in the palace of the Ooni of Ife (the Yoruba say Ife is the beginning not only of their race but of the whole world; the world was created in Ife!). This Ifaturoti, the women said, was fired from his job because he'd been caught fooling around with the wife of another palace official. He was not only driven from the palace, he was exiled from the town because the woman's husband was a very senior official in the court.

The twins had no name for Ifaturoti's wife or wives, but they remembered the name of the son he had for our line: Ikotun. When Ikotun was a young boy, his family left Ife and moved to Ondo, east of Ife. He grew up to become a great hunter and farmer, and he had two wives. Only his second wife, by the name of Bayonle, bore him a son, whom they named Aderoja. Aderoja grew up with quite a different interest. He moved to Benin and became an ivory worker in the service of the Oba of Benin. He lived in Benin many years with his Benin wife, Olohigbe, who bore him two sons. Little is said about daughters in these histories. I gather that in most Yoruba societies family descent is traced through the male line, not the female. The first of Aderoja's two sons died fighting in one of the Benin wars. The family prevailed upon the second to leave Benin, fearing he might be drafted into the Oba's forces. They sent the boy, Itayemi, to

Ondo, the place his father Aderoja remembered as home. There he matured and distinguished himself as hunter and warrior.

The story about Itayemi is that he was highly honored and even feared as warrior, in spite of the fact that he was a little short. Part of his power, according to the twins, came from the strength of his voice. He scared the living daylights out of the enemy by simply shouting out loud in the front lines. He being so short and the shout so loud, the enemy would run away, thinking they were surrounded on all sides! Itayemi finally fled Ondo for the same reason Ifaturoti left Ife—caught in the act with the wife not just of an ordinary official but of the king of Ondo himself, the Oshemawe. He would have lost his life but for his clout in the town.

That was how Itayemi ended up in this village. He had two wives, both natives of Ondo. The second bore him no children, and refused to accompany the family on exile. No one has heard a word about her since. His first wife, Ebunola, whose father was a notable farmer, bore him a daughter and a son Akindiji. Akindiji distinguished himself as farmer and warrior. He was known especially for his success in fighting off Tapa (Nupe) tribesmen who often raided this area for slaves and other trophies. He married a woman of this town, Ashake, and with her fathered the twins and our direct ancestor, Akimbowale.

So there you have it—the history of our line since way back when. You should at least be familiar with the latter part of it, which bears the names of persons contained in the text of you know what (I still haven't looked at the copy dad left me).

I got curious about Akimbowale, so I asked the women to tell me a little more about him. I did this because *iya* Taiwo never stops looking at me whenever I'm over at their place. She always wears this smile on her face and goes on about how much I look like Akimbowale. So I said to her, Please tell me about Akimbowale, I really want to know about him. Akimbowale was tall, she said, not tall like me but of a good height, and he had a broad chest like his father Akindiji. She said he had a permanent scowl on his brow, like me (I hadn't noticed!), and was a good hunter and warrior. He accompanied his father to war even before he was considered old enough to go.

You know the rest about Akimbowale's wounds, whose scars show up on my body. I asked if Akimbowale was a nice person—was he kind to people? The question drew a laugh from both women, and Kehinde asked Taiwo to answer the question. Taiwo was Akimbowale's favorite. She was a real tomboy in her early youth, accompanying her brother to bird hunting while Kehinde helped their mother in the house. Taiwo recalled an occasion when she asked Akimbowale to lift her up so she could climb a mango tree and pluck ripe mangoes. She had thrown a few pieces of fruit down, when she suddenly saw a snake coiled round a nearby branch, its head raised as if to strike. She screamed and lost her grip and would have had a tragic fall if Akimbowale had not rushed in from wherever he was and caught her in his arms, just in time! On the day Akinbowale was captured by slave raiders, it was Taiwo who caught the amulet her brother hurled at the twins as the raiders overpowered him and took him away.

When I asked to see the amulet, Kehinde replied they would show me at another time. The day had darkened. The women looked tired. I was tired myself. There really isn't much more to tell. And if you're as tired of reading this as I've been of writing it, then you'll understand why I must now retire for the night.

In your last letter you said nothing about Aunt Ella, so I'll assume you either have nothing to report or you don't want to upset me. All the same, please give her my love. The same to you both.

Otis

September 30, 1964

Dear Norma,

A Caribbean festival in New York City, wow! The way you described it, you must have had a great time. I'm especially thrilled about your finding evidence of African survivals in the West Indies, especially in the costumes and songs. Did you record any of the songs in Nigerian languages? I'd love to listen to them sometime.

Now don't go thinking, I dont know! Why, I hear Yoruba every day here. I speak it too, not like a native, but I'm getting there. *And*, I sing Yoruba songs too. Some evenings after supper, I join the Fagbenro family for cultural entertainment in their front yard. Mrs. Fagbenro is a homegrown person and makes a point of raising her kids according to traditional Yoruba culture. Mr. Fagbenro doesn't participate at all. He lives a rather Westernized kind of lifestyle. So I sit with Mrs. Fagbenro, her kids Deji and Sumbo (who always nestles in my arms), and a few other kids from the neighborhood. They were holding these sessions long before I came here. When I started joining the group, Mrs. Fagbenro (she's the session leader) would tell some of her tales in English for my benefit. That slowed things down for everyone else and took the fun out of the sessions. But in the last few weeks, I've become comfortable enough with Yoruba. So now everything's done in Yoruba, and I participate as much as I can. It's a lot of fun.

Usually, we start with a few riddles and songs. Riddles like this one: What is it that passes before the Oba's palace but does not stop to pay respects? An oba is a Yoruba king, and everyone is supposed to bow before him as they walk by. The answer to the riddle: rain flood. Because the water just flows quietly past his compound. Another riddle goes: On my way to Oyo my face is turned towards Oyo, on my way from Oyo my face is still turned towards Oyo. What am I? Oyo is a Yoruba town. The answer: a *dundun* drum. That's a drum with leather sheets on opposite ends, which the drummer carries with a strap on his shoulder. Whether the drummer is going to or coming from Oyo, the leather faces Oyo! There's always a lot of excitement and laughter in these riddle sessions. Most of the time none of us knows the answer, but when Mrs. Fagbenro tells it to us it comes as an eye-opener. As you know, Yoruba kids go to school nowadays. But in traditional Yoruba society, telling and solving riddles was one way of sharpening the minds of the young.

After the riddles come the stories—mostly animal stories, and they're just as exciting. Some of them are about hunters and their encounters with animals and spirits in the bush. These stories are usually weird. Others are more lighthearted. My favorite ones are about Ijapa the turtle, who is the principal figure in most of the tales. He's a trickster, always getting into trouble one way or another. Sometimes he wins, but sometimes he loses. The important point is, he never stops using his imagination to play tricks on others. These tales are frequently accompanied by songs, which makes them even more wonderful. One of my favorite stories has a song we all sing that goes, *Babalawo, mo wa beebe,* and then there's the chorus to every line that goes *Alugbere!* It's one of those stories in which Ijapa plays a game that lands him in trouble. He eats a delicious dish prepared by a babalawo so his wife can get pregnant, and he ends up getting pregnant himself. So he goes back to the babalawo and begs to be released from his predicament!

These stories are not just fun and games, they really have an educational value. In fact, in most stories I've heard, there is some moral lesson at the end that tells you why you shouldn't do this or that or why things are the way they are today. For instance: Why do women carry their babies on their backs, like women here do all the time? Why doesn't it rain in the dry season? Why does the sun appear by day and the moon by night? And so on. These are all ways of teaching kids to observe the world around them and simply *ask* questions.

When I started hearing these Yoruba stories, I remembered some of those we read in elementary school—you know, Brer Rabbit and other animals. I used to think they were American stories. Then we were told they were stories that slaves brought over from Africa, but we didn't give much thought to them. Norma, *now I know!* The interesting thing about these morals and the answers at the end of the tales and riddles is that quite often they don't make a lot of sense—that is, if you judge them from the Western way of looking at things. I've been thinking about it, and it seems to me the people who made up those stories couldn't have been so stupid as to think people would take their statements at face value. Part of the value of the riddles and stories is in their indirect way of getting us to use our imagination to figure out the *actual* relations between things we see around us. Otherwise I doubt that anyone would go through life accepting such simplistic answers and explanations.

I've been trying to see the effect of these games on a child like Sumbo. She's eight years old, even a little kid like her tries to answer the questions her mother asks in these riddle games. Quite often she's off the mark, but close enough to it, so that her mother explains to her how close she is to the right answer and why the right answer is different from hers. That way, she learns to relate one thing to another. Even though she gets on other people's nerves when she fights to claim me all to herself, she's nonetheless a smart girl. Her mind is constantly alert about things around her, she's always asking questions.

About those African survivals you mention in your letter. I've visited a few places, traveling with Chip McAdoo. Just before the end of our midyear break, Chip took me to Ado-Ekiti to see some friends of his at a high school there—Christ School, one of the best high schools in the country, I'm told. One of Chip's friends there is a lady from Trinidad named Maureen Warner. She teaches English at the upper levels but she's really out here on a research trip, studying the Yoruba language for a book she's writing on Yoruba survivals in Trinidad culture. Yoruba in Trinidad? I asked her. Yes, she said, Yoruba *is* spoken by some black people in Trinidad, especially in religious ceremonies and songs. I thought, Wow!

That reminds me—how's our man in Boston, I mean our friend Guinea Man? Have you seen him lately? Isn't he from Jamaica, or is it Trinidad? For a moment during our discussion in Ado-Ekiti with Miss Warner I thought about Guinea Man, and he didn't appear as strange as he did in Boston. Frankly, here in Africa those slogans about black culture and black consciousness that you find all over the place in the U.S. these days—believe me, Norma, it had to take the kind of crisis I experienced for me to begin seeing things in a different light.

It wasn't just the lady from Trinidad who led me into the wider world of black culture. Chip and I also visited the city of Ibadan, and here we met even more blacks from the U.S. Remember, I told you we were there once to buy sports things. We didn't have much time for anything else, because we had to rush back to the village before it got dark. Well, on this trip, we were on a more socializing mission, spending the night with a Peace Corps volunteer who's teaching there. In the evening he took us to a cultural center called Mbari, in the heart of the city. There we met other Americans, black and white, with various kinds of agenda. I even learnt that black Americans have been living in this country since the 1940s and 50s. In fact, there's a black family—man, woman, and children—who have been settled in Ibadan for nearly ten years. They speak Yoruba fluently and have gone thoroughly native. I figured Chip took me to Ibadan so I could see that other blacks had made their "return" to Africa before me. Fine! He has his agenda, they have their agenda, and I have mine. During the trip, I was careful not to let Chip's angle on things influence me.

I met two interesting black Americans at Mbari that evening. One was Jim Meredith. He made news in the U.S. some years ago, when he was refused admission into the University of Mississippi, until the President sent the National Guard to open the university's doors to him. He has graduated, and is doing research at the University of Ibadan. The other guy—I don't believe I was ever told his real name. Everybody just called him Giant because he's tall, though not as tall as I am. He's from Alabama. Remember the KKK bombing of the Baptist Church in Alabama where those four little girls were killed? Giant's father was a minister in that church. Later that night, he was part of a jazz group that played at the center. He played tenor saxophone. Jazz is Chip's thing, of course. I must confess that, though I was never hot on jazz, I was impressed by Giant's sax playing that night—it was simply *dominant*. I kept turning to look at Chip, and he did the same to me, and I could tell he was asking me something like, What do you think, man? I didn't say anything to him, but I was really impressed.

I found these trips very enlightening, and I'll tell you why. When we were with Miss Warner in Ado-Ekiti, she used the word "diaspora" quite often, referring to Africans in the U.S. and the West Indies as part of a larger culture that spread from Africa during the time of slavery. Now, there were lots of Nigerians at the Mbari Center that night in Ibadan listening to Giant and his friends. There were three others in the band, one white and two black, all Americans, and these Nigerians seemed to really enjoy the music. I thought to myself, Did they enjoy it because it was black music and struck some native African chords in them? If so, was this a case of the diaspora returning home to make itself felt at its sources? I say so because in this little village where I live, where I have come to find my roots, there is little doubt in my mind that African *tradition*, whatever this may have been in the past, has had to trade a few things here and there and make an adjustment. I see it in the educational system. I see it in men like Mr. Fagbenro, who lives here in our village but thinks he belongs elsewhere, just because he was educated in America. I even hear it in some of the stories Mrs. Fagbenro tells us, like the one about the turtle and his friends eating with forks and knives, not with their bare hands like most villagers here do! So, when Chip tells me he's here to "find himself," I'm not quite sure what he's hoping to find.

I love you, Norma. I know my mom and dad will read this, so I love you too, mom and dad. Aunt Ella too. I'm fine, and I'll write again soon.

Otis

October 21, 1964

Dear Mom and Dad,

When you congratulate me on how quickly I seem to have learnt Yoruba, I feel both encouraged and confused. It's good to know I've made so much progress. But then I'm reminded of a question Dr. Fishbein asked me: Does anything here strike me as being familiar? I must be honest to myself and say I still don't feel like I've been here before. But how do I explain the fact that, in barely four months of being here, I am communicating in Yoruba with an ease I never imagined possible—is Yoruba such an easy language to learn? Could it be I have a greater capacity for learning languages than I ever knew I had? Or is there some hidden force making things so easy for me? Up till now, I've been content to think the ridicule I've been subjected to by several people here has forced me to take my education seriously. But is this enough of an explanation?

Perhaps the twins have something to do with it? Since I was told my problem would end only when I had learned the language well enough to join them in singing the song that's been bothering me, I must have felt I had to go on a crash program in order to get it over with. These ladies have lived an awfully long time, and I'm not sure how much longer they're going to be around. In the past month or so, they've had bouts of illness that made it necessary for Madam Remilekun, their herbal doctor, to visit them. I was on hand for one of these visits about two weeks ago. I'd gone to their place on a routine call, but found only Kehinde, the elder of the two, in their reception room. After greeting her, I was going to ask about Taiwo when I heard her groaning from the bedroom. I asked what was wrong with her. Kehinde told me Taiwo had been ill and was being treated by Madam Remilekun. Out of curiosity I looked towards the bedroom, which hadn't been screened off, and found Madam Remilekun with a gourd-pipe in her mouth, held against Taiwo's back! I knew better than to start asking questions in what seemed like a serious situation.

I said I hoped Taiwo would be well soon, but I didn't stay very long after that. As you know, Taiwo has shown a fondness for me that goes back to relations between her and her brother Akimbowale. I too have become fond of her, though I've done my best not to let Kehinde know it. Seeing Taiwo in such condition upset me quite deeply. I later asked Awo Akinwunmi what kind of treatment Madam Remilekun was giving her with a gourd-pipe in her mouth. He said it was a way of sucking out the bad blood caused the illness. This is a traditional form of treatment. First tiny cuts are made with a razor blade on some part of the body, so the blood will run. Then certain medicinal herbs and leaves are chopped to pieces and held between the body part and the pipe. The blood is drawn, and the herbs and leaves stanching the cuts inject medicines into the sick body. The treatment must have done some good, for Iya Taiwo is back on her feet.

Awo Akinwunmi has been generous in sharing matters with me relating to his profession and to aspects of Yoruba culture he thinks will help me get the education I need for my task. A seasoned babalawo usually has a group of students that he instructs in the different aspects of the profession—philosohper, traditional doctor, fortune teller, etc. I've counted about eight of these students in Akinwunmi's household. They range in age from about seven to fifteen, though there's a young man among them who seems to be in his late twenties or early thirties. Awo has a large house that holds his two wives and seven children as well as these trainees.

The first time I found Awo teaching the students, I tried to leave quietly, thinking I was intruding into his private affairs. But he said, No, sit down. You might learn a thing or two. I found that session so interesting I asked him if he'd mind my coming at other times. He said no, he didn't mind. So, these days I have a notebook and pencil in my pocket anytime I stop by his place or visit the twins in his company. Almost anything he says carries so much wisdom, I never want to miss a word of it.

Being in Awo Akinwunmi's company has helped me to appreciate how rich and deep Yoruba culture is. Remember what he told me, that learning a language involves learning as much about the life around the language as possible? That's essentially what goes on between him and his students. The main focus of training to be a babalawo is the body of Yoruba traditional knowledge known as Ifa. This is often understood as divination, but divination is only part of the profession of the babalawo. It involves a lot of other skills; from the body of knowledge in Ifa, the student gets to learn practically every aspect of Yoruba life. And because there is so much to know, a babalawo's training could take over a dozen years, depending on the student's speed of learning.

Most of the boys who train with Awo Akinwunmi are so young, you wonder how much kids that age *can* pick up. The truth is, they learn by a combination of direct and indirect methods, like simply sitting around and observing. For instance, when Awo Akinwunmi has guests, some of the boys are assigned to wait on them and serve kolanuts and other kinds of entertainment. They hang around and listen to what is said when these items are blessed, and even observe the ways they are served. For instance, there are things you don't hold in your left hand and ways of holding a bottle, etc. The students also listen to conversation, gossip, facts about social relations, among other things. They commit these to memory, because they'll need to be knowledgeable about social and political history, local industry, etc. when they become a babalawo themselves. The students also accompany Awo Akinwunmi to tend his farm in the bush somewhere outside the village. I'll tell you what happened on one of those trips to the farm that I joined at the end of August.

I remember referring to Ifa in one of my letters as the Yoruba Bible. That's exactly what it is. It's made up of a central body of 256 texts (called *Odu*), and even these consist of subdivisions taht expand on the ideas contained in the central texts. As if that's not enough, each of these Odu contains an extensive number of stories (called *Ese*) that provide explanations to the texts within the Odu relating to any of the problems a client seeks solution for. This is essentially what the babalawo is supposed to do—solve the problems that trouble people. If it's a marital problem, Ifa has verses dealing with aspects of relations between husband and wife. If it's a health problem, perhaps of a psychological kind, the babalawo will ask lots of questions so he can find the right verses that will pinpoint the source of the mental problem. If you want to get involved in a money-making project, there are verses dealing with how to conduct yourself in such a situation. In each case, after the babalawo finds the solution, you are told what sacrifice to make—that is, which articles to offer so that all goes well with you.

Ifa has several verses offering moral lessons on individual conduct, justice and fairplay, interpersonal relations, etc. One of the most persistent teachings of Ifa is on the need to build character, *iwa*, or what is often called gentle manners, *iwa pele*. One verse goes, *Iwa nikan l'o soro* (character is all we need). One of my favorite lines goes, *Iwa pele fi okun aiye ro peti l'owo eni* (gentle manners is what enables the strings of life to stay long with us). On the whole the Yoruba are decent and self-controlled in their dealings with one another and with strangers in their midst—unless specific problems of human relations arise at some point. Other verses of Ifa have to do with the responsibilities of leadership. One of them, for instance, reminds us that every human being in this world is entitled to happiness and a good life. And this includes women. If you think women are subsidiary to men, Ifa has news for you. It recommends that men and women live together in a balanced relationship, and that the only way the world can exist in proper order is for men to show respect to women: *O ni ti won bati nfi iba fun obinrin, ile aiye yio maa tooro*. And how about this for the need to keep our environments clean: *Omi ti ko san siwaju ti ko pada sehin a d'ogodo omi ibaje, ogodo omi arun* (water that moves neither forwards nor backwards will become an evil pond causing illness). There are even verses dealing with air and space travel. You have no idea how many notebooks I've filled already!

We had an interesting discussion when I accompanied Awo and his students to his farm. But I'll save it for another letter. Sumbo has a cold and wasn't able to come to school at all today. Before I left for class this morning, she made me promise to come see her at home, and I did. My day ended early, so I moved her over to my place to make sure she took her aspirin and had plenty of rest. That hasn't stopped her from coming over to nestle in my arms, especially since supper. (By the way, I have a new student cook, male this time!)

It's about midnight, and I have to stop now. I'm relieved to read in your letter that Aunt Ella looks much better. Has she come round to the idea of seeing doctors, or is her recovery just a temporary thing? If it is, I fear the same about her condition as I do about the twins—touch and go. I hope I'm wrong.

Love to everyone,
Otis

November 16, 1964

Dear Mom and Dad,

There's a problem stirring in this town. I haven't been unaware of it until recently, but it may have some effect on my staying here. Dad, you remember the old man who forced Baale Osunkunle to send us over to the twins the first day we got here? His name is Pa Fadipe. Since then, according to Awo Akinwunmi, things haven't been good between him and the Baale, who was embarrassed by the stand Pa Fadipe took. Things had gotten so bad the Baale stopped him from coming to his place to relax on the front porch, something the old man has done since God knows when. Apparently, the problem has been resolved, for Pa Fadipe is back to his usual place on the porch. I didn't like news like this, so I asked Awo what he thought it meant for me. He said I shouldn't worry about a thing; the Baale wouldn't have the nerve to cross the twins, because he knew what the consequences would be. At any rate, Awo said, he'd consulted Ifa on the matter and the signs were good. Still, he said, be very careful where you go, and who you go with.

I just thought you should know. I'm taking Awo's advice seriously. But I'm not scared, just a little disgusted.

Speaking of Ifa consultation: that's one aspect of Awo's profession I can't tell you very much about. It's very complex, and I only know the basic facts about it. I've met him about twice in these divination sessions, and he's allowed me to sit and watch what goes on. First, a client brings a problem to the diviner. The client does not have to tell the diviner *exactly* what the problem is. He (or she) may simply present it in the form of two propositions—one positive, one negative. The diviner brings out a bunch of sixteen palm nuts that he shuffles between his cupped hands. He throws them onto a divining tray to decide which of the 256 texts (the Odu) will form the basis of inquiry on the problem. A divining chain (*opele*) may be used instead of the nuts. The diviner throws again, twice I think, to find out which of the alternative questions (positive or negative) the nuts favor by the faces they show when they fall. Whether the answer is positive or negative, there are five kinds of good or bad fortune attached to a positive or a negative throw. The diviner throws the nuts five times, to find out which of the five the client will win. Then the diviner makes a few final throws to determine which objects the client should offer as sacrifice to the gods, including Eshu, messenger of the gods, and especially the god of divination, Ifa (also called Orunmila).

This is by no means the full story. Like I said, it's a very complex system. Thank God, I don't have to be a diviner! Even if I did, I'd need at least a dozen years to understand what's involved in the system. Nonetheless I'm particularly interested in the body of texts the system is based on, the 256 Odu. These Odu form the heart of Yoruba belief and culture, and they codify the entire Yoruba outlook on life. When Awo said I needed to know the life around the language, this must be part of what he had in mind. I'm putting as much effort as possible into learning the texts every opportunity I get.

Now let me tell you what happened just before the end of our midyear vacation, when I accompanied Awo Akinwunmi and his pupils to his farm. Awo had invited me to join in harvesting the crops on the farm, somewhere outside the village. We all went together on foot very early one Saturday morning. On our way he explained the farming system to me. The process begins at the end of each year's harvest. The farm returns to its usual condition as a bush, overgrown with weeds, for a period of about five months, say from September to the end of January. Sometime in February (or March), fire is set to the farm so the weeds burn. Then the first rains of March (sometimes April) fall. Awo says that's one way to help the earth breathe: like all living things the earth needs to breathe, or it would be ill! March or April, crops are planted for the new farming year. The farmer returns for the next four months to clear weeds that have grown between the crops, so they don't choke the crops. Some crops grow fast and are harvested during the four months. Either they are replanted, or other fast-growing ones are planted in their place. Then there's more weeding, more tending, until the final harvesting.

When we got to Awo's farm, there were three men waiting for him: friends of his, themselves farmers, who were there to help in the harvesting. I asked Awo if this was the practise, farmers helping one another on these occasions. He said yes, it helps the work go faster. Then I asked, Why couldn't the men harvest their own farms? He quoted verses from Ifa to support the concept of combined effort: *Asuwa da aiye, asuwa da orun* (it was by collective effort that heaven and earth were created). And again: *Ire gbogbo d'asuwa* (all good things come from collective effort). So today his friends help him harvest his farm; later, he would do the same for them.

Fair enough, I thought. But I wondered if there was any room in Ifa philosophy for people helping themselves, instead of expecting other people to help them out. Awo Akinwunmi said, Yes, of course, there is. Ifa recommends that people help themselves and constantly work hard to improve their lives. According to Awo, Ifa advises that we all do our best to accomplish something day after day (*k'a jeki ojo bori ojo*). Not only that, Ifa says emphatically that we should not be satisfied with the condition we find ourselves in. We should use our initiative to make ourselves better than we are: *Tite l'a te mi, ng oo tunra mi te* (as I was created, so must I re-create myself).

I found this idea of re-creating interesting. So I asked about the Yoruba concept of the supernatural and the place of human beings in it. Get ready for this! It's true, says Awo, that God creates people. But he does not do it all by himself, he does it in cooperation with the persons who are created. All human beings have an *ori*, a spiritual guardian, who helps them bargain with God about the kind of destiny they will have in the world. Ori can also be translated as destiny, since it is the guardian of the individual's fortunes throughout life. So I asked, Once you get your destiny, is that it—you're stuck with it? Not at all, said Awo. If it turns out later that the destiny does not serve you well, you may consult a babalawo, and he'll find out where the problem lies and what you can do to fix it so you have a better destiny!

Then I asked, If human beings are partners with God in creation, can they be said to be on the same level as the creator himself, or at least as some of the gods of the religion? He said he wasn't exactly implying that human beings were equal to divinities, but that the kind of separation we find between humans and God in Christianity does not exactly exist in their faith. He then cited me two parts of Ifa to show that even gods are subject to the same moral laws as human beings. One of them says that the house of Ogun, the war god, was once deserted because his character was found unacceptable to people. *Iwa Ogun ko sun won, nje bi a bi wi pe k'ile Ogun kun somusomu?* (Since they did not like Ogun's character, how could we expect Ogun's house to be full of company?). The other verse is even more revealing. Ifa, the god of divination, is often called Orunmila, usually taken as equivalent to the god of heaven (Olorun), the supreme god. One of the verses says that Orunmila must offer sacrifice if he expects human beings in the world to consult him and be at peace with him. Orunmila does exactly as he is told!

I said I thought it was interesting that Yoruba gods are seen in the same light as human beings, with the same faults that we find in human beings. And I asked, How can a god be shown to have a bad character? Well, he said, we don't have gods who are so different from ourselves. After all, they were human beings just like us before they became gods. For instance, Ogun was one of the sons of Oduduwa, the ancestor of the Yoruba, and he was a famous warrior. Some people say he came from Ila, others say it was Ire, while others still believe he was from Saki (these are all Yoruba towns). Many other towns claim him too, like Iwonran where he held the chieftaincy title of Ejemu: hence the hunters refer to him in his *oriki* (praises) as Ejemu Oluwonran. Wherever he came from, everybody knows he was a fierce warrior who had little regard for human life. Once, when he went to war to defend his people, he was so drunk with fighting power that he ended up killing both the enemy and the people he was defending.

You may wonder, said Awo, why we recognize this kind of person as a god. But only a god who lived this kind of life can appreciate the value of human life and the evil in shedding blood. As Ifa tells us, people deserted Ogun's company because they feared he might do them harm. Another verse tells us that he was asked to offer sacrifice so that in his fight with Obara, one of his enemies, Obara did not get killed, since both were such good warriors that neither of them deserved to lose his life: *Won ni adie kii ba adie ja k'oku* (Bird should never fight bird to the death). In these ways, said Awo, Ogun learnt his lessons which have been passed down to us. Hence, when a soldier is going to war he offers a sacrifice to Ogun and prays that, like Ogun, he does not fight a war without honor. If there's anything having to do with shedding blood, it's to Ogun that we pray so that it turns out well for us. So you see, Awo said, our gods were human beings like us. That is why we pray to them. They once went through the problems we now have and can understand them.

Most of this instruction came while we were doing the harvesting. Awo has an interesting farm. Later, I found out that this is the pattern of traditional Yoruba farms. They contain a combination of crops in the same plot, not like farms I've seen along highways in the States, where there's a whole stretch for one kind of crop and nothing else. Once in a while Awo would stop and ask a pupil the name of this or that plant or crop, or ask him to pull a yam from the ground without breaking it, or to cite an Ifa verse concerning a particular crop on the farm. He's such a great teacher, he never gets angry with a student who's slow in learning. He believes every student will learn in his own good time, according to his strength. There's no harm in going wrong, he says: after all, as Ifa tells us, *Ona sisi nii mu 'ni mo ona* (it's from losing our way that we know our way).

Some of our discussion also happened during our break in the long day of harvesting. Large Yoruba farms have a farm house equipped with enough things so you could spend the night there. Hence they are called *oko ayunsun*—they're good enough to sleep in (*sun*). Awo's friends who came to help with the harvesting were often amused by the questions I asked him. I guess they weren't used to someone asking Awo so many questions as I did. But they were sympathetic, and often helped in answering some of the questions themselves.

While we were out harvesting, some of Awo's pupils were sent over to the farm house to prepare our lunch. Great dish! Spicier than food prepared in the village. But in many ways richer and more delicious, because we were eating straight off the land. A trap set in the farm had caught a deer. It was skinned and barbecued over an open-air log fire.

Some cuts from the meat were used for the sauce, which was prepared without oil—thank God. Far too much food is cooked in palm oil here! Yams from the barn stock were boiled and pounded into a meal called *iyan*: you roll a ball of this in the sauce, and swallow it. I loved it, but I didn't eat a whole lot. Though I'm getting used to Yoruba spices, *this* was extra spicy! Awo said the added spice was meant to give the body the right spark for the hard farm work. One of Awo's friends made everyone laugh when he suggested I eat more food, to support my size of body!

We harvested a lot of crops: yams (especially), tomatoes, okra, cocoyams. Yams are considered the main crop. They're like big, hairy potatoes—unlike American yams—and very tasty when cooked. Our work ended about 6 p.m. Awo shared out some yams and other farm produce and some of the meat from the deer to his three friends. Then we stored up most of the yams in a barn at the farm house. Yams are usually stored there. From that stock the farmer or his wives can take whatever amount they need for home cooking.

We were all very tired as we walked home, so I didn't ask any more questions. Some days afterwards though, we discussed other related matters, some of them even more revealing. But my fingers are hurting now. I'll take up those issues in my next letter. I must spend a little time with Sumbo and Deji. It's nearly time for them to go to bed. A short while ago I heard Sumbo calling, Uncle, won't you ever come out again? So—more next time!

Love to everyone,
Otis.

November 27, 1964

Dear Mom and Dad,

Iya Kehinde amused me when I visited the twins yesterday. Why, she asked, didn't I call her and her sister *aburo* (younger sibling) as they had asked me to? I said I didn't think I should address people much older than myself as my aburo. She then asked, In that country where you come from, how would you have addressed us? I said I'd have called them Auntie or maybe Grandma. She asked me what the words meant, and I told her. She said, Well, we are none of those things to you: you are our older brother returned to us. If you won't call us aburo, how would you address someone as your sister, whether they are younger or older? I said I'd say Sis. Taiwo quickly jumped at that. Yes, she said, that is better. Call us *Sisi*. I could hardly contain myself!

Incidentally, the question of age is one of the things I took up with Awo Akinwunmi not so long ago. In this society, there's a great deal of respect for old age and seniority that someone brought up in a different culture like the U.S. would find quite confining. I asked Awo if he didn't think that too much respect for age restrained the youth from fully realizing their potential. He first smiled and shook his head. Then, taking his time, he said to me, You know, this world is very old. He went on to tell me a story from one of the Ifa verses about a young man who wanted to pluck a fruit from a tree called *ishin*. He tried everything he could, including waiting the tree out in hopes the fruit would fall into his hand. But nothing happened. Suddenly a group of elders appeared and asked him to prostrate himself before them (that's what younger Yoruba men and women do before older people). As soon as he did this, a fruit fell from the tree into his open hand.

I told Awo, This is precisely what I'm talking about. Why must everyone look up to the elders for everything: Are they the only ones who have answers to life's problems? I reminded him of something he'd said during our discussion at the farm, that we should use our initiative to help or re-create ourselves: *Tite l'a te mi, ng oo tunra mi te.* He smiled and nodded, impressed that I was learning my lessons. If that's the case, I said, why did the fruit wait for the elders before it fell? It would be a mistake, he said, for you to take the words of Ifa at surface level. Those elders who suddenly appeared, he said, are simply a deeper way of saying that the young man should find out how people experienced in plucking fruits from the *ishin* would have gotten round the task, rather than wait forever on luck. Everything we do has a method to it, said Awo, perfected by people who have done it before. It is our duty to subject ourselves to the wisdom built up over the ages, if we hope to succeed in anything we do. That, he said, is the meaning of those elders in the story.

That made sense, I thought. But I told him it seemed to me as if some verses in the Odu contradicted other verses. I wondered how the whole body of wisdom was put together and handed down. He referred me to the books of the Christian Bible. The Old Testament, he said, is a collection of the words of ancient prophets passed down from one generation to the next, but first in the oral tradition. The New Testament contains the teachings of Jesus Christ written down by his followers. In the same way, Ifa is the wisdom of our fathers handed over to Orunmila in the early days of mankind at Ife and passed on by word of mouth from generation to generation. There is no contradiction between verses in the Odu, he said. Each text is intended to answer one question or address one problem, and they may arise in different situations or use different individuals to make their points. For instance, he said, in the Ofun Di (one of the main headings of Odu) we are taught that anyone who does not share his good things will never benefit from the kindness of others. Yet in the Okanran Meji (another Odu heading) we are told, *B'elebo o p'eni, asefin o y'eni* (if a celebrant doesn't invite us to his feast, it is not right for us to join in it). There is nothing at all contradictory in the two pieces of advice, Awo said. Of course, if the celebrant finds you enjoying his feast he should not send you away—that is not our culture. But everyone should respect himself and not face the risk of being asked embarrassing questions. If we wait patiently enough, he said, we will get our chance to enjoy all the feasts we may desire. *Eni ti o ni suuru ohun gbogbo l'o ni* (all things belong to those who are patient)!

I'd been saving up what I thought might be a sensitive issue until I was sure the time was right. When I finally asked the question, I was relieved to find how calmly Awo addressed it. Tell me, Awo, I said, and please don't be offended if what I'm going to say does not sound very right to your ears: If our people have had this great wisdom for so long, and it contains all we need to know to survive in this world, why didn't it help us fight against the white people when they came to take our land from us and put us in bondage?

He understood the seriousness of the question, in light of my background. So he took some time before responding. Yes, he said, you are right. All these months that we have been discussing these matters, it should be clear to you that our culture does not encourage us to dominate other people. Ifa teaches us first and foremost to lead a decent and virtuous life, a life based on good character; to respect our fellow human beings as much as ourselves. This does not mean that we don't go to war, nor do we run away from war when it comes to us. But Ifa encourages us only to fight the war that brings us honor, not one that brings us shame. When we defend ourselves against those who attack us, like your ancestor Akindiji used to do against the Tapa, that is an honorable war. But, he said, Ifa does not look kindly on those who make a profession of fighting recklessly against others. Did I not tell you recently of the god Ogun, that his house was always empty, and that people avoided him, because his character was not good? That is what Ifa thinks about those who are in the habit of making war.

Now, he said, about white people who came here and fought us and dominated us. Perhaps it was our fault that we lost the fight. We must have done something wrong somewhere. If we had followed the teachings of Ifa properly, we should not have found ourselves in a situation where we surrendered ourselves and even our culture to other people. Perhaps we didn't listen to what Ifa said about togetherness being the only source of strength. Our people must have become so involved in protecting their private interests that they fell apart before the white people. Ifa says, *Asuwa l'esu nfi j'oko* (it is only as a group that locusts can devour a farm). When we fight wars of shame, or wars that we use only for promoting our private interests, we lose the power that comes from building a united community. And we will be unable to stand up to foreigners who come to strip us of the things we have held most dear since the beginning of time.

Talking about the Tapa: I have found out that one of Awo Akinwunmi's pupils comes from that northern tribe. They call him Audu. Though I've never raised the matter with Awo, I find it interesting that Audu is welcome here, given the history of relations between the two peoples. It must be that time has healed the old wounds. Still, the fact that anyone would come from so far away, or that any parent would find the profession of babalawo so attractive as to send their kids at such a tender age to study it, led me to ask Awo: Why do these little boys want to be babalawo? Why not go to school and learn to be a doctor or lawyer, especially since education is free for all children here at the elementary school level, and they have a chance of going further? The question must have touched Awo's pride. But he was too nice to show it. In fact he didn't answer it himself, he simply turned it over to one of his older pupils, Akinlabi, who was just passing before us. As if he'd been prompted to do a recitation, Akinlabi quoted a verse from Ifa on the subject: *Agba kan ko Ifa, ko j'obi gbo* (If an adult learns Ifa, he won't have to eat old kolanuts). Having said this, Akinlabi walked away with a smile on his face. Awo Akinwunmi said to me, with an equally proud smile, There you are. Ifa looks out for its own!

Incidentally, Mrs. Fafunso told me that there are books on Ifa in bookstores—not in this village, but in places like Ibadan and Lagos. They are mostly in Yoruba. But if I come across anything in English that you can read, I'll buy it so you too might learn something of this fascinating culture.

I must stop, so I can go to the sports field. My kids are gearing up to defend their honor in sports. McAdoo and I persuaded our schools to include basketball in the sports competition at the end of the school year, which is only a few weeks away. The deal has been accepted—Chip and I are pleased about it. We have our honor as coaches to defend—though I'm happy to say it's not a private honor or interest!

Great news! Chip has made arrangements to marry his student, the girl he's been living with, by the name of Ireti. Her family, who are from the same town, Iludun, has given its blessing. The ceremony comes up just before Xmas. Neither Tim nor I was surprised when he broke the news to us. I'll tell you more about it later.

Love to everyone. Tell Aunt Ella I *must* see her again!

Otis

January 8, 1965

Dear Norma,

Thanks for keeping me up to date on political developments in the U.S. of A. Chip McAdoo gets copies of *Newsweek* that his brother sends him from time to time. So we get to read some of the things happening at home, though two or three weeks late. Since no one has a TV set here in the backwoods, we don't get any fresh news beyond what appears in the Nigerian newspapers. They talk about confrontations between civil rights activists and the police in the South and boycotts and sit-ins in various cities. But your letter has given me the kind of detailed account I need to get the full picture. And I find your commentary superior to the ones by professional journalists!

Your report on Malcolm X and the Black Muslims was very disturbing. Chip has spoken about him a few times, and he's very much on the side of Malcolm against Elijah Muhammad. He fears Malcolm may not live very long because someone will get him real soon—if it's not the CIA, then maybe the Muslims. God, we certainly don't need this.

Yes, Chip got married in December. Not only was I there, but I was central to the whole event. First of all, Ireti's family wanted someone from Chip's family to represent him. In this culture, marriage is not simply an affair between a man and a woman, it's between their families too. Since Chip doesn't have any of his family around here, he asked me to take their place. This was a little awkward, because people here now see me as a citizen of Ijoko-Odo. But we made the point that, since a section of my family was American, Chip and I might arguably be related. Ireti's family "took the point," as they say here, so I stood beside Chip during the negotiations. When it was all over, I warned Chip to be careful not to mess with me from now on: I'm his uncle!

Negotiations: Yes, that's what happens here when you ask for a woman's hand in marriage. There are two stages. First, the man goes to the woman's family to announce his intentions of marrying their daughter. For this occasion, he must bring a few bottles of wine, both local and foreign, with him. I accompanied Chip on this visit. Some of the drinks were used to entertain Ireti's family members who were present. At the second stage, representatives from Ireti's family informed Chip and me that Chip's plans to marry their daughter were acceptable to them. They told us the articles we should provide as bridewealth for Ireti, some of them to be used for entertainment on the wedding day. The list included four bundles of a type of cloth called *asho oke*, four pods of kolanuts, a dozen fruits of something called bitter kola, a dozen pods of alligator pepper, three bottles of Gordon's Dry Gin and four bottles of Schnapps, six cartons of beer (the preferred ones being Star and Gulder, both made in Nigeria), two kegs of palm wine, and a sum of ten pounds (about $20). The money is a token symbol, not the price of a purchase: the fact that the sum is so small suggests she's much more than money can buy. That's what Mrs. Fagbenro said, when I asked why there was any money at all on the list.

The wedding took place in the assembly hall of Chip's school, Anglican Grammar School. Ireti looked truly beautiful in the Yoruba outfit she wore: White silk with gold trimmings for her *buba* (blouse). Calf-length wrapper and large head-tie (both of wine-colored calico). Brilliant gold necklaces, earrings, and bracelets. And wine-colored shoes. Her broad smile blended very well with her white *buba*. She was just adorable! She was accompanied by a large number of her kin—men, women and children all in *asho ebi* (uniform material) that complemented the colors of Ireti's beautiful outfit.

Chip didn't do too badly. Ireti had told him the groom's party needed its own uniform outfit. So we went shopping for our own *asho ebi* in
Akure. Tim went with us. The bill for the entire wedding expenditure
was shared among the three of us—we did this to help Chip, who is only
a poor school teacher. You should have seen us Americans—rather, one
Yoruba man and his American friends—all dressed up like full-blown
Yoruba men in everything from headwear to footwear! The biggest surprise was seeing Phil Bigelow, the U.S. consul from Ibadan, dressed up
just like Tim and me (Chip's outfit was a little richer). This was all Tim's
idea, to impress Ireti's people with the size of Chip's American family!
Tim had kept the secret to himself until the wedding day. I was really
glad to see Bigelow. I'd been hoping to put that unfortunate incident
with the marines behind us. We smiled and shook hands, even embraced
each other, and conversed with each other now and then. Besides, I was
grateful that he had arranged for me to be put under a regular Peace
Corps budget.

I forgot to mention that I made the Fagbenros part of my extended
family at the wedding. I fitted their children, Sumbo and Deji, out in the
same *asho ebi* that Tim, Phil Bigelow, and I had on. Sumbo was a real
princess in that outfit. She made sure she was at my side all the time, her
little hand in mine. Deji tried to distinguish himself as a classy gentleman, keeping his hands joined behind his back and walking in measured
steps. I have lots of fun watching the kids in their little rivalry!

The ceremony began with the oldest man from the bride's family
blessing the couple. He was Ireti's uncle—her father's oldest brother, an
old man who must be around eighty. He's lost most of his teeth, but his
frequent smiles would seem to indicate that he felt no embarrassment at
all. He blessed some kolanuts and poured some gin on the floor in honor
of the ancestors. And he prayed for the health and happiness of everyone
present, especially the bride and bridegroom. All this took place with
Chip and Ireti kneeling on the floor, side by side. Chip was flanked by
me, Ireti by her classmate and best friend Toun. When he finished praying, the old man offered a small glass of gin to Chip and Ireti to share
betweem them. Chip took some of the gin and held the glass to Ireti's
lips. She squirmed as some of the gin touched her tongue, refusing to
take any more. Everyone laughed and told Chip to help his wife out. No
problem for old Chip! Then it was time for the exchange of wedding
rings. Here the Western and Yoruba traditions blended well: The rings

were exchanged, and everyone clapped and rejoiced. No one asked the groom to kiss the bride when they finally got up from their knees, however. It's not a Yoruba custom. But Chip held Ireti tight anyway, and kissed her full in the mouth. She blushed, but her family didn't seem to mind at all—in fact, many of them laughed and clapped even louder than before.

The rest of the afternoon was spent in eating, drinking, and merrymaking. Women sang wedding songs. Drummers who attended the event played their drums, especially when we all joined the bride and groom in dancing. Chip's drummer friend, the one who helped decipher my chant, was one of those drummers. Chip told me the guy had asked him what special qualities he wanted featured in his drum signatures, but he never asked for mine. After he'd played for Chip and Ireti, he moved across to me and worked those skins for my benefit.

I happened to be dancing with Sumbo at the time, and having a good deal of fun. As his music went on, I felt a sensation course through my body. I straightened up for a spell. The strains he was playing had touched a chord in me, and I looked at him with surprise. Then it struck me that, since he had heard the tape of my chant the day we got here, he must have done his homework without anyone's help. The sensation lasted only for a brief moment—it didn't trouble me more than that spell. In fact, I did what most people did to drummers who played their praises: I dipped my hand in the pocket of my *agbada* (robe) and pulled out some coins, which I pasted on his forehead. After that, I continued dancing with Sumbo as if nothing had happened. The drummer moved on to celebrate other people. After the wedding I asked him what else he'd said in the drum praises he'd played for me. He said something about me wearing the sky for a hat and the earth for sandals. I hadn't realized I was that tall!

About the sports finals between my school and Chip's: My teams did very well in track and field—in fact we set new records in triple jump and the mile. The girls, especially, made us very proud. As for basketball, the less said about it, the better! Chip's boys gave mine a sound kick in the butt. Honestly, I don't want to talk about it because I had problems with Crabs that messed up our preparations. Things aren't going any better between us. I hope I can continue to keep my cool with him.

I love you, Norma. I'll send the wedding pictures as soon as they're ready. And please send me any recent shots of yourself you may have. I

want to keep my thoughts of you up to speed!
Always yours,
Chip.

January 18, 1965

Dear Mom and Dad,
The new school year has kicked off. The Fagbenros had gone to Ikorodu (their home town) for the Xmas break shortly after Chip's wedding. I missed their kids a lot while they were away. My house felt lifeless without Sumbo's possessive ways and her brother's priggish manners. They returned shortly before school resumed. It was such a pleasant surprise to feel Sumbo's little body bounce on me as I lay snoozing on the sofa the afternoon they arrived.

But the last few days have been heavy on me. I'm not talking about school work and school worries. Those I can take in stride. I'm talking about the twins. Looks like time is closing in on the dear old women. Last week I visited them on the usual routine call, but instead of a warm welcome I met a somber atmosphere. When I didn't find anyone in the outer room, I went into their sleeping chamber. Kehinde, the older one, was sitting beside Taiwo, who lay still on the bed. When I greeted Kehinde, she only turned her head toward me, but didn't say a word. She looked tired, like someone who had been up all night and all day too. What is the matter, I asked her in Yoruba. She took her time before she cleared her throat, and said, Taiwo. It's Taiwo. I don't know what more I can do. For two days now she has hardly opened her eyes or eaten anything. I know she is still alive because she still breathes. Once in a while she opens her mouth as if she wants to tell me something. Toyosi Remilekun has done everything she can for her. But for Toyosi, I would have lost my sister by now. I just wish she could open her mouth and tell me what she has in mind. Does she want to die? Has her time come? I wish she would let me know, so I too may prepare myself to follow her. Of course she does not want to die, I told Kehinde, and she is not going to die. She is just ill. Some illnesses take longer than others.

Near the head of the bed was a plate containing some cream paste with grains of black seed sprinkled over it: perhaps some alligator pepper, or something like it, put into Taiwo's food. Or perhaps the whole paste was medicine for her. I knelt on the floor close to the bed. I hoped Taiwo would feel my presence and be cheered. The room was so hot, I couldn't imagine anyone feeling comfortable there, especially if the person were sick. I asked Kehinde if she couldn't try giving Taiwo a little water. Didn't you hear what I said, she asked me, that she hasn't opened her mouth one bit? I said I was going to try myself. So I walked across to the cool water pot with a cup on top of it. I opened it, dipped the cup in, and drew some water. These clay pots are usually scrubbed clean inside and rinsed, then held upside down over fire to dry. They come out smelling fresh-baked, and the water they hold is very cool. I drew a cup, then returned to my kneeling position near the bed. First, I used an end of Taiwo's own cloth to clean her brow. To my surprise she seemed to open her eyes a little. I placed my right hand in hers. She gave me a weak squeeze.

My heart beat a little faster with hope. I called her, *Iya*. Slowly, she moved her head, and looked at me. I could feel the smile in her opening eyes. *Egbon mi* (Big brother), she said to me. I answered, Yes, it's me. How about a little water, I said. She nodded her head, very slowly. Quickly, I looked across to Kehinde. She brought the cup from the floor where I'd placed it and held it out to me. There was a brightness now in Kehinde that wasn't there when I came in. It made me glad. I disengaged my hand from Taiwo's to receive the cup from Kehinde. With my left hand I raised Taiwo's head up from the bed, while I brought the cup close to her mouth. It took some effort, but she drank a little water. Then she sighed, and I lowered her head on the bed again. She was breathing more easily then. Her eyes opened wider. Kehinde moved nearer, with obvious joy, and called her sister, Taiwo. Taiwo looked at her and said, Yes, my sister. Then Kehinde laughed, with relief. I rose from the floor, filled with joy and satisfaction. Whoever Taiwo took me to be, I was glad to have touched her life with some good.

When I visited them again the next day, she was on her feet once more and received me with the usual cheerfulness. I'd been over at the school for basketball practice and decided to stop by briefly before retiring for the day. But they wouldn't let me leave so fast. Madam Remilekun was with them. She never stopped marveling at the miracle, as she called it, I had worked on Taiwo. I said maybe all Taiwo needed was a little water. But they wouldn't accept such a simple explanation. Kehinde had prepared my favorite dish of *eko* and *moinmoin*. So I stayed and devoured it with relish and chased it down with cool water from the fresh-baked pot.

There is a new development. Two days ago, Awo Akinwunmi visited me at my place. He had a message for me from the twins. When I asked him what it was, he said, They think it's time for you to ready yourself. I said, For what? For the ceremony, he said. The dance you've come to complete. I took a deep breath and thought, Oh my God, is it really? Awo waited for the message to sink in. When I looked up at him, he knew I was ready to hear the rest of his message.

There is something that must be done, he told me, before plans can be made for the dance. I asked, What is it? He took a good long look at me, which made me wonder even more. Then he sighed and said to me, You have to be initiated into the cult of strong men. What? I said. There is a club in this town, he said, which young men like you must belong to. In the old days, he said, only people who had done powerful things like fighting wars or hunting wild beasts could belong to such a club. If you had grown up in this town, you would have qualified automatically. Mind you, he said, it is no longer compulsory for our young men to join the club. These days, most of them who live in big cities like Lagos or Ibadan, or even overseas, do not care about such things. But what you have come to do is no ordinary ritual. So I agree totally with *iya wa meji*. It is necessary to go through the initiation ceremony, so that you may be fully recognized as a son of the land who can participate in the serious business of the cult.

The word serious bothered me a little. I've had nothing to do with the sort of thing he was talking about. What I've heard about cults here is that they do secret and scary stuff, and some people have been known to die as a result of cult activities. So I asked Awo Akinwunmi, What if I choose not to do the initiation, does that mean I can't do the dance? After all, I speak Yoruba well enough now to know and do what I'm required to do. Awo said, Well, that is true. But you remember what I told you before, don't you? It is not enough to speak our language to be a full citizen of our town. After all, some Europeans speak our language well. But there is more to it. You have to be fully involved in the life of the place and play a part recognized by tradition for a true native son. At any rate, your ancestor Akimbowale, who was taken away to America and whom you represent, was initiated in this cult. How can you be somebody you claim to be and refuse to play the part that that person played before he was recognized to be who he was? Well, he said, I am only delivering the message I was asked to deliver to you by *iya wa meji*. If you value their words, I think you should do what they have advised. So I said to him, What if something happens to me while going through the initiation? And he said, Now you are talking! Before anything can be done, he said, we have to consult Ifa to be sure that all will be well with the initiation. By now, I'm sure, you know what to do, he said. Let me not trouble you further. It's getting dark. I must go home. I expect to see you early in the morning on the day after tomorrow.

I'd arranged for one of the senior students on the basketball team to take charge of the free-throw practice scheduled for today. Early this morning, I went to Awo Akinwunmi's place with the coins needed for the divination. At the end of the divination, Awo told me that the signs were good for the initiation rituals; I had no reason to fear anything. I've been told the articles I should provide as sacrifice to Ifa and to the god Ogun, patron god of the cult I'm to be initiated into. I will do exactly as I have been told. I might as well go through with everything properly, the way it should be done. Why question forces I can't control, even if I may not claim to understand anything about them?

It has also become clear to me that I'm running out of time. The last bout of illness Iya Taiwo has just survived seems to indicate the clock is ticking fast. It makes a lot of sense for the women to recommend I prepare myself for the task I'm here to do. But something within me seems to say: Assuming you have been chosen by the ancestors to restore the broken line of our history, how right is it that you should also be the one to bring on the death of these women who have meant so much not just to your family but to this community as a whole? Perhaps these women are destined to die so our family may live again, and someone must be the instrument of this destiny. But I'm still struggling to resolve a question that refuses to go away: Why *me*? I don't want these ladies to die. Isn't there someone else in our family better qualified for the job, spiritually I mean?

I didn't go to school after the divination session. I've been home all day trying to figure out this whole business. Maybe somehow I'll come to some understanding.

Give my love to everyone.

Otis

February 16, 1965

Dear Mom and Dad,

If I'd written this letter some three or four days ago, I would have sounded very different. In fact, I'd started one that said I was making plans to return to the U.S. right away. Oddly enough, I didn't have the strength to continue writing it.

I was initiated into the cult of strong men five days ago. The day before, I had told Chip about it and asked him to come along with me to the enclave. When he came, he found a gentleman named Olu Adegboye waiting to take me there. Awo Akinwunmi had chosen him as my sponsor. However qualified you may be to belong to the club, you still have to be sponsored by someone who is already a member. Adegboye has a son in my basketball team, one of my favorite shooting guards. He himself is our school's food contractor and general supplier. According to Akinwunmi, Adegboye was acceptable to the twins as my sponsor for the initiation. He's known to be a good hunter and a man of honor.

At about 6 p.m., the three of us got into Chip's car. Chip listened carefully to Adegboye's instructions and stopped when we neared our destination. Adegboye had taken us to the northern end of the village, where a thick forest separates it from the village of Osubi. Then he told Chip to stop about fifty yards to the spot from which he and I were to enter into the cult enclave. Nothing could be weirder than that place. The trees were so tall they nearly touched the sky. The only sounds around were the hums of different kinds of insect. There was no footpath anywhere in sight, nothing to show the place was frequented by anyone. Adegboye probably knew his way in from sheer force of habit. He walked through the bush without watching his steps, but I was constantly afraid of stepping on a snake.

Adegboye finally led me into a clearing where some boys were sitting on the dirt floor. About seven or eight of them, mostly in their late teens. Some of them could have been students in my school. But they had their faces smeared with charcoal, so I couldn't recognize any of them. I asked Adegboye who they were. He said they were the age-set preceding mine in the village's social ranking. When we came into their midst, they quickly rose from the ground, without saying a word, and went into action. A couple of them came to me. Adegboye warned me to offer no resistance to anything they might ask or do. Another three walked to an edge of the bush where a dog stood tied to a wooden post. The poor animal was restless! Those first two boys suddenly gripped my shirt and ripped it off my body, leaving me naked to the waist. Next thing, they slapped my back and shouted *Oya, bata re!*—meaning I should take off my shoes at once. On that cue, the music of a *bata* drum and percussion sticks, accompanied by singing, erupted from another end of the clearing. I turned to see what the next demand would be. One boy came to me with a small calabash cup. Adegboye told me to drink up. I took one look at the greenish liquid inside and raised my eyes at Adegboye. The kids all shouted together, *Mu!* (Drink it up!). So I closed my eyes and drank the stuff. It smelled awful and had a strong alcoholic taste.

I can only vaguely recall the rest of what happened. I was so groggy from this point on, Adegboye had to act some of my roles for me. As the music rose steadily in pitch, I was guided into a dance by the boys who had stripped my shirt. I did my best to follow the complex steps: one foot before the other in alternating steps, a sideways kick of the right leg, a quick spin-around, a leap, and so on. My arms were working just as speedily around my body. Then the music and singing suddenly stopped. One boy shouted something I can't recall now. To this Adegboye replied, *Iro o!* (Not at all!). The boy shouted something else, and Adegboye shouted the same reply. To a third question from the boy, Adegboye shouted *Beeni!* (Yes!). The music and singing resumed. All at once someone handed me a machete and led me to the post where the dog was tied up. By now my head was spinning so wildly (it must be the alcohol in the drink) I could barely tell my bearings. One boy held the post to which the dog was tied, and two others held the struggling, screaming dog by the hind legs. Adegboye came close to me and said I should sever the dog's head with one stroke of the machete: if I missed, the ceremony would start all over again the next day, and I'd be responsible for providing a fresh dog. The music was pounding so loud, I was in no mood to argue with anyone. I may have held back for one brief moment. But I soon raised my arm and brought it down in a strong, clean stroke, separating the dog's head from its body. There was a loud ovation from Adegboye and the boys, and a lot of blood on the ground. The dog's head twitched briefly at the rope. One of the boys holding the legs spun the body round and round, and dropped it on the ground with a thud. Then the music and singing stopped.

The last thing I remember happening was when one of the boys snatched the machete from my hand: Adegboye led me through two wooden posts, both painted red, into a dark inner grove; then someone else shoved a piece of something into my mouth. At this point I'd begun to lose consciousness, so I wasn't sure what it was. But he shoved it in, then told me to chew it up and swallow it. Then there was silence, except for insects humming.

When I woke up, it was well past midnight. Chip was sitting on the bed beside me. I was confused and groggy. The scene was so different from what I remembered happening to me: cutting down a dog, going into a dark grove, something being shoved into my mouth. Chip said something like, How do you feel, man? Rather than respond, I raised my head from the pillow and looked around the lighted room, to see where I was. When I made to ask Chip something, I had the most terrible taste in my mouth and smelled the foulest odor. I dashed into the bathroom, drew some water in a cup, and tried cleaning my mouth. It did little to reduce the putrid smell. When I looked at my tongue, it was totally black, whether from the stuff I drank or ate I couldn't tell. I squirted some paste on my toothbrush and worked my whole mouth with it. That did some good, at least it wasn't as bad as before. My face looked so awful, I thought I was someone else.

I returned to the bedroom. Chip asked me if I was hungry, if I wanted to eat anything. But instead of hunger, I felt a dullness in the pit of my stomach. I shook my head and told Chip, No, I don't want to eat anything. Then maybe you should lie back down and sleep, he said, and I'll see you tomorrow. I tried to see him off to the door, but he indicated I shouldn't bother, he'd be fine.

I must have fallen asleep right after he left. When I woke up, it was past noon. There was no one in sight. It wasn't yet time for Mrs. Fagbenro to come from her shop and fix lunch for the kids and their father. I sat up on the bed and looked around for a while. The Fagbenros must have known what I'd been through and told their children not to bother me, because it was unusual for me not to see them in the morning before they went to school. I walked over to the kitchen and found Sumbo had swept it as clean as usual. There were chickens clucking in the Fagbenro backyard. Sounds of children from far off in the campus told me it was recess time. Soon after, I heard the school bell go for what must be the end of recess, about 1 p.m.

When I returned to bed, I felt some pain in both my wrists. Tiny cuts had been made on them with some sharp tool, though I hadn't been aware of this the day before. The wounds had sealed, but I could tell they had been smeared with a herbal mixture, possibly used in stanching them. I had no clue what the cuts were for. Nor did I have a clue what the other things I'd done in the enclave were for. I couldn't help feeling angry. I think that at some point I'd come to terms with the fact that I was going to play certain roles. But I'd expected at least to have those roles explained to me before I played them. Even if I had no choice in the matter, it would at least have helped to get myself gradually adjusted to something that was totally alien to my experience. How would Americans feel if I told them I severed the head of a dog in a ritual? They'd call me a crazy savage!

Did I remember anything that happened to me after I was led into the dark inner enclave of the cult? Frankly, no. I didn't, and I still don't. All I have in my mind, even as I write, is a blurry, abstract image, the meaning of which I don't in the least understand. I can only try to describe it as it presents itself to my senses. Now, picture yourself sitting in front of a mirror looking at your reflection. Suddenly your reflection, I mean the very image of yourself, begins to assume the shape of a bear. Or, better yet, picture yourself sitting face to face with a sitting bear. All of a sudden, the bear begins to change and become the image of yourself, and you in turn begin to change into a bear. Then the bear that has become you gets frightened and stands up. But you, the one who has turned into a bear, suddenly pull off the mask that made you look like a bear, and you become again the person you were. But the bear who has assumed your image remains you, so that now there are two yous staring at each other.

If you could imagine how confused you'd be to find you've ended up a double personality, due to forces you've never had to reckon with, then maybe you'll begin to understand the situation I'm in. I could dismiss the whole picture as some kind of irrational nonsense, which would be foolish, because I remember being there at the enclave and being put through certain rituals, some of them still quite vivid. Or I could try to accept that the picture is no more strange than the things that happened to me before I was brought to Africa to face whatever has been hidden for some three generations. Right now, I've had to concede that the best I can do is try to find out which of the two images of myself is the me before I came here and which is the me that I am now. If I cannot separate the two, then it means they were never meant to be separated, and I'll need to figure out how to reconcile the two images and be the person I'm supposed to be.

I finally got out of bed, had a bath, brushed my teeth, washed my mouth more thoroughly. The day began to look like any other day once again. By now it was time for the kids to come home from school. I had put on my shirt and was buttoning it as I strolled across the living room, when I noticed a tiny little face peering timidly from behind the back door of the kitchen. I shouted, Sumbo! and held out my arms towards her. She walked cautiously into them. I lifted her up and embraced her. My eyes were misty, but I laughed so she too could cheer up. I looked again, and there was Deji standing close to the door, his hands in the pockets of his brown shorts. Evidently, like the elder he is, he had asked Sumbo to check out the situation before he made *his* appearance. I laughed even more. I was so happy to see them again.

Mrs. Fagbenro had asked Deji to tell me that if I didn't come over right away, my *moinmoin* would get cold. She knows my weakness for that dish! Chip came to my place a couple of hours later. He was surprised to find me up and about, not slouching over my bed or maybe looking like a madman. He was pleased to see me in good spirits, and asked me to come out for a drive. I got in the car with him but asked to stop by to see the principal and explain my absence from school. When I walked into his office, Mr. Fagbenro greeted me with a short laugh, shaking his head. So they left you in one piece, he said. How do you mean, sir? I asked. Haven't you just been put through some pagan rites? he asked. And I said, Perhaps I needed it. If you think so, he said, then it's alright. Sorry I missed school today, I said. No problem at all, he said. In fact, I expected to hear you were still in bed.

Chip and I drove to Tim Dubitsky's place. His school is very new, so it has no housing on campus for the teachers. Only the principal's house is complete. Others are nearing completion. Tim lives in a house in Ikere town, not far from the school. He likes it a lot, says it puts him in touch with the local people much better than if he were to live on a secluded campus. When we got to his apartment, on the second floor of a duplex building, he was playing *ayo* (a game of checkers) with one of his students. He was relieved to see us, because he was getting clobbered by the kid, who couldn't be more than fifteen. He asked the boy if we could join, since the game could take as many as four players. I didn't know how to play, and it took me a while to recover my spirits fully.

Tim ordered some roast groundnuts and corn (called *epa* and *gugu-ru*, a very popular snack here) and some soda for the four of us. This kept us going for awhile. The game was quite exciting, and before we knew it the clock on Tim's wall said seven. Chip suggested we drive down to Akure for supper. I thought that was a good way to end the day, in the company of these two. It wouldn't be easy for me to forget I'm an American after all! While we were eating, Chip told Tim I'd been initiated into a local cult, and Tim went, You lucky son of a gun—how the hell did you swing that? I said I didn't have a choice, I was told I had to do it if I hoped to do the dance with the twins. He really thought it was such a big deal, and that surprised me. I'd expected him to feel sorry for me, or to think I'd gone completely out of my mind. I told myself that, if Tim really meant what he said about my initiation, then I ought to be careful how I judge people of a different race—they might have a healthy curiosity about other cultures. But I must be patient before drawing any conclusions. Awo often says to me, quoting Ifa, *Suuru ni baba iwa* (Patience is the father of character).

Yesterday evening, after sports practice, I walked over to Awo's place. I didn't mean to stay, and told him I just stopped by to say hello. He told me it wasn't polite to call on someone and remain standing. So I took a seat and asked for a glass of water. While one of his pupils went for it, Awo asked me if I'd seen the twins that day. I said, No, was anything wrong? He said, No, but he'd had a talk with them in the morning, and they'd decided it was time for me to start practicing with them for the dance. And who did they choose to play the music for the dance? Chip's drummer friend, who recently beat my praises at Chip's wedding. According to Awo, there is only one good drummer (*onilu*) in this village, but the sisters don't like him because he has a reputation for getting drunk and messing up the music. Since the business of our dance is a serious one, the twins feel we need someone who won't spoil a ceremony that's waited so long to be put right. We'll hold our first rehearsal next Monday, nine days from today.

Well, as they say in the States: It's on!

Love to everyone.

Otis

March 22, 1965

Dear Norma,

Your letter about the death of Malcolm X was very touching. Funny, but it seems I had to come to Africa to appreciate the importance of people like him and Dr. King in the fight for black liberation. Chip McAdoo, as you know, is a serious radical—he talks about it all the time. We'd read the news about Malcolm's death in the Nigerian press. Though we thought some of it slightly garbled, it seemed mostly to the point in terms of references to key figures among the Muslims. Chip expects to get his copy of *Newsweek* pretty soon. Maybe then we'll get the full analysis of the event. But your letter gave me a good sense of how grim it must have been.

What a waste! What a sad, stupid waste! It makes you wonder, what does it all add up to? You see all those policemen and their dogs beating up black men and women in the South, and you think that's not surprising: White people can't tolerate black folks speaking up for their rights. But, black people killing one another over the same issue? It doesn't make sense. Chip makes the same point you do, that there's a hidden hand in all of this. He thinks there were government agents working secretly with the Muslims who didn't like the fact that Malcolm broke away from Elijah Muhammad and has been attacking him. Besides, Malcolm angered a lot of white people when he said Kennedy's death was only a case of chickens coming home to roost! That could well be the case, and I said so to Chip. But why should black people allow themselves to be used against one another?

Not so long ago, Chip told me he didn't think Malcolm or even Dr. King would live long. He took Malcolm's death pretty hard. When Malcolm visited Nigeria last year and spoke at Ibadan University, Chip shook hands with him after the lecture and spoke with him. But all along he was convinced Malcolm's message was so heavy, there was no way his enemies would let him live. He thought Malcolm was bad news to so many people, they were bound to take him out soon. I doubt that killing him would stop anything. From what you wrote about the riots that broke out after his death, it's clear there's plenty of trouble to come. What can I say? God bless America!

You wanted to know how my preparations for the dance were coming along. Well, we held our first practice about three weeks ago: a little later than we had planned, but one of the twins had a fever on the day we'd arranged to do it. It was quite an experience. The first few moments were a little uncomfortable for me. Maybe the problem was within me. I had developed a reaction to the chant from the past, so any time it came up I cringed. But I felt a lot better as we moved along. On the whole, I thought the rehearsal went quite well.

Here's what happened. I have a copy of the text made from the one my dad had finalized with the twins. Also present at that time (when the text was finalized) was the man who is now part of our program: Chip's friend, the drummer. His name is Olumide Faboya. I remember dad telling me, before he and Fishbein returned to the U.S., that Olu (that's short for Olumide) already had a sense of the phrases that made up the chant. Obviously, he was an oral poet in the same tradition as the man who composed my family's *oriki* in the first place. When Olu played some of the phrases for me at Chip's wedding, I was a little shaken. But I soon pulled myself together when I realized what was happening. So I was pleased the twins appointed him as drummer for our performance.

The rehearsal took place at the home of the twins. First, I read out the full text. I was a little apprehensive at that initial reading. But gradually, my body survived the challenge and took control of the situation. Also, I must have been helped by what Olu and the twins did while I was reading. Although my Yoruba speech is quite good at this point, oriki poetry is framed in certain structures that require the right tonal control to do them justice. Once in a while, as I read, I looked up at Olu and the women and saw them nodding with appreciative smiles. Olu even struck the drum a couple of times to underline one phrase or the other in my reading.

Whether they were smiling at my crude handling of the poetry of the chant, or they were sympathizing with the tough job I was doing handling an unfamiliar tradition, I didn't try to find out. But it was clear that even Olu needed some practice himself. He had heard the text once or twice from the tape, and some of the phrases were obviously familiar to him from his experience as a drummer. But he hadn't composed the text, so he needed to hear it several times over in order to create the right music to accompany it. I had to read the text a few times before he could feel comfortable with its structure. At every reading, Olu struck his drum several times more, trying to match the pattern of his music to the tones of the text. And yet, he never followed any line through from the beginning to the end. I mean, he didn't match any one line of the text tone for tone, all the way through. He seemed to be spacing his drum strokes in such a way as to punctuate my reading. Even at those points where he struck his drum notes to follow my text, he didn't seem to be playing the same notes my text was saying.

I didn't really understand what was happening, until we did our second rehearsal last week. This time, Chip came along with us. I had asked the twins if it was alright for him to come along. They hesitated a little, but said he could.

Last week's practice was much better. By this time, I'd become more familiar with the text, and my reading was smoother. I could see a warmer smile on the women's faces. At one time, they even clapped their hands to commend my effort. And Olu had become sharper in supporting each line of my reading with one of his drum phrases. Something else happened that made me recall certain sensations I felt in the past when I chanted the text. At some points in my chanting, I would feel an impulse to jump or make some other strange movement. When Olu noticed that I twinged at those points, he seemed to know what was going on. He would stop his drumming and ask me to read the line again. If I repeated the movement I made before, he encouraged me to emphasize it, and showed me how to get it right. I realized that the movement was a flourish for responding to some word or phrase in the text, or the accompanying note in the drum music, or both. So Olu encouraged me to express myself fully and taught me how to make the right movement. By the end of that day's practice, I had mastered the subtle bodily movements needed at various points of the performance. Girl, you should see me *go*!

I talked about the relationship of Olu's drumming to my reading of the text (by the way, I'm near perfect at reciting the whole text by rote). The procedure is this. I would chant a line of text, and he would follow with a line of drumming, which is essentially a drum *reading* of the same line. Now, at the end of each line of text and music, I would look up at him with a silent question: I could sense *some* divergence between my sounds and his, and wondered if there wasn't something wrong somewhere. In fact, at the end of the day's practice, I did ask him, Why were you playing differently from what I was saying? And he said, It wasn't different. I was playing exactly what you were saying. And he would laugh at my concern. Mind you, I didn't think that practice had been a failure. In fact, for sheer warmth and impact, I thought we had done very well. I just had a nagging feeling that something had to be adjusted in order for us to achieve a perfect fit.

At the end of the evening, Chip and I dropped Olu off at his house. Then Chip took me to his place. Ireti had cooked us a meal of rice and tomato stew with *dodo* (fried slices of plantain). After we'd eaten, Chip said to me, You know, I thought you had a good point in the question you asked Olu during the practice. And I said, You mean about his music not matching my chanting note for note? Yes, Chip said, your question touches on an important issue in African music. How do you mean? I asked. He said, You must understand that African music is different from European or American music in quite a few respects, but especially in their *approach* to melody. The African musician, he said, always tries to adopt a glancing or indirect approach to the tune he has before him. When you accused Olu of playing different notes from the ones you sang, he told you, No, he wasn't. He said he was playing exactly the same notes you were singing. And you know what? You were both right. You *heard* different notes; your ears weren't playing tricks on you. But what Olu was playing were *corresponding* notes, or statements, to what you were singing.

Let me give you an example, Chip said. I've been listening very closely to things Olu has been playing and to things he's been telling me for some time now. In Yoruba instrumental music, it would be foolish for the drummer or hornblower to try to match the human voice tone for tone. I remember Olu telling me once that God created wood as wood and people as people: He never intended them to have the same voice. So wood has its own voice, and human beings have their own. If God wanted everything to be the same he would have made it so. When humans talk or sing in *their* kind of voice, the wood or skin responds in *its* own kind of voice. Even when they're supposed to be saying the same thing, the sounds come out differently. Besides, even if the wood or skin or horn *can* repeat the notes sung by a voice, the musician almost never tries to do that: he approaches the melody from a different angle. He takes it as a challenge to create something new yet related to the same melody he's given. That's what Olu meant when he told you he wasn't playing anything different from your singing. It's like jazz music. I'll show you what I mean.

He rose and pulled out a few of his LPs. Before he put one of them on the turntable he said to me, You've heard classical music, like an opera or a concert hall recital? I said, Well, I've never been to any of those kinds of concerts. But I know what you mean. Okay, he said, all I'm trying to say is, in European music, both the voice and the instrument, piano or violin or whatever, both voice and instrument generally express themselves in the same notes. The next time the same tune is played, you may be damn well certain they're going to do exactly the same thing. That's because the musicians think that, like scientists, they've achieved a system that should be capable of being reproduced again and again. The system has been established in the form of a musical score, with notes carefully written down, so anyone who wants to play the music can follow the notes faithfully. But African music is basically different. It relies on the principle of challenging one set of notes with a corresponding set of notes, without actually changing the structure of the music. Now listen to this.

He showed me an album by Count Basie, and said, I'm going to play you a tune from this album. It's called Cherokee, a Ray Noble composition, he said. Listen. He went ahead and played it. I didn't really understand what was going on, but I could see Chip smiling with his eyes closed. At the end of that tune, he got up to turn off the player before the next tune came on. Then he took up another LP and said to me, Here's an album by Charlie Parker, or Bird as most jazz lovers generally call him. Okay, he said, I'm going to play you a version of Cherokee as done by Bird—it's called Ko-Ko. He put it on, and again we listened.

What do you think? Chip asked me. I couldn't lie to him, so I told him right away, I don't think it's the same tune. Chip laughed and said, You bet it is! It's exactly the same tune we heard before, only it's been reconfigured. He tried to explain with some music notations—which made no sense to me—how Bird took the chord sequence, that's the progression of notes, and reordered it in a different direction, at a different pace. Jazz music is like African music generally, he said in operating on the basis of chords or a block of notes that can be lifted from one context and transferred to another context where it takes on a life of its own. I could play you a whole range of jazz tunes where you'd hear phrases quoted from different tunes, with little or no relation at all to their original sources. The challenge is to play the borrowed phrase in another song, like a quotation or something, he said. This way, the chord or block of notes becomes a *code* representing a unit or concept that could be used in a wide range of contexts where they would fit, without disrupting the even flow of sounds in the new context. In classical European music, Chip said, this would be unacceptable. But it is a key aspect of the creative nature of African music—blocks of notes as codes.

This brings me to drum sounds you've been rehearsing with Olu, Chip said. You know, he said, listening to him frequently, and following him to performances here and there, forced me to try and understand the nature of his art. Take some of the lines in your chant, the ones dealing with war or hunting or farming. I'm not saying I understand everything your chant says, but I think I have a sense of the principle that Olu's drum music operates on. Now, when you use the words for those things in your song, there's no way Olu will play exactly the same sounds you used in singing. Like I said earlier on, a drum skin is a drum skin and a human voice is a human voice; they're textured differently. There's a coded sound for the word war in drum music, and it can *not* play the same way your voice says war. I don't know what that way is. But its value is, it helps to differentiate the human sound for the word war from something else that sounds like it when reduced to drum sounds. You follow what I'm trying to say? I said, Yes. Now, suppose you use two notes for the word war. The drummer may use seven notes to represent the same idea, because if he should play the same notes you used it would mean something else to him. At any rate, his ears and the ears of drummers like him have been trained with a different way of playing war from the way the human voice says war. The coded language is extremely poetic, said Chip, much more so than ordinary language. I don't know the drum image for war, but let's just say it's something like— "the clash of blades and blood." So for the one or two notes you sing for war, the drummer plays about six, seven notes for the same idea, only his representation of that idea is more forceful than the one you did in words!

The result of using such coded notes in drumming, said Chip, is that when you hear a statement in words and the same statement in drum music, you think they're saying different things. Like you did with Olu. And I'll tell you another thing about coded sounds. Like I said, they come in blocks of notes—or what's called chords in jazz music. Any time one drummer hears another play the coded notes for war, he will know the player is talking about war. If it's a situation that's got nothing to do with war, then there's a good chance the player is an unskilled musician and doesn't know what he's playing. But these codes have a built-in risk of flying all over the place, because some players just strike a drum without knowing what they're saying with their sounds. A drum sequence of notes that goes like this—three high, two low, four high, in a combination with other sounds—may be saying something about sex, Chip said. If you struck the same sequence in front of certain people, you might be in a heap of trouble!

Believe me, girl, as the evening progressed, and Chip played me more jazz LPs, I was thoroughly enjoying the whole experience. Poor Ireti, after a while she started to fall asleep and excused herself from us to retire for the night. Chip's a very nice guy. I believe he loves Ireti very much. He smiled at her in such a way as to say, Sorry we excluded you from our conversation. Then he rose and walked with her into the bedroom, winking at me to indicate he'd be back in a minute. When he returned he had two books in his hand, which he offered to lend me. One was by a British scholar named Carrington and the other by a Ghanaian named Nketia, both dealing with the African art of drumming. You'll find these books extremely informative, Chip told me. They've helped me understand the complex nature of African music. They tell us it's primitive stuff. When you've read these books, you can decide for yourself who's the real primitive.

I haven't started reading the books, and may never find the time. That's because, by the time I'm through with the Yoruba story by J.F. Odunjo I'm reading now, I'll be moving on to Chinua Achebe's *Things Fall Apart*. Everyone's been talking about the book so much, it's like they're telling me I'm a fool if I don't read it. But after Chip took me home that night and I lay in bed trying to sleep, I started to think about the things he'd said. I was especially struck by how his description of African music related to sensations that had troubled me each time I heard certain sounds, especially drums. If what Chip says is true, that African music is made up of blocks of notes that could be transferred from one context to another, then the possibilities are endless, even frightening. From what I could gather, our drummer Olu found it fairly easy to master the text of our family's chant because some phrases in it are part of the standard idiom of Yoruba praises that drummers like him have often played with. Since these coded phrases are liable to move around from one place to another, there's a chance they're part of a peculiar texture of drum sounds.

In other words, since Africans moved from here to America, taking their drums along with them, some of these peculiar codes have a chance of cropping up whenever drums are played. If I am a reincarnation of my enslaved ancestor, as everyone seems convinced I am, I can see why some drum sounds, buried deep in memory since the traumatic moment of his capture, might excite certain sensations in me every time I heard drums play. And it may make no difference whether the music is from the U.S. or the Caribbean. After all, aren't the blacks who play them descendants of the old Africans? Be that as it may, whether or not the theory of African music as I understand it from Chip is right or wrong, it's clear that the sound of drum music provoking those sensations in me must be some spirit reminding me it's time for me to go and finish the job left undone when my ancestor was captured by slavers and taken to America.

I may be a little off the mark in these thoughts. Even Chip may have gotten a thing or two wrong. But in the last several months of being here, I have come much closer to understanding the character of African life and outlook than I was before I got here. I'm happy I took Akinwunmi's words to heart, that it takes a lot more than learning a language to become a native. Above all, I'm getting to *know* who I am and what's been happening to me. Though I have benefitted from guides given me by good people like Awo Akinwunmi and Chip McAdoo, I'm gradually charting the path of my re-creation of myself. I say this because, as I believe I mentioned in an earlier letter, it's quite easy in America to go sleepwalking through life and not know what you're doing. There's always somebody telling you who you are and where you're supposed to be or go. At least that's the way I feel right now. If I'm wrong, time will tell soon enough.

The twins tell me that since I've learned rather quickly, we need only a few more practice sessions before we fix a time for the ceremony. I'm glad to know it won't be long before I'll have paid my dues. Take good care of yourself, and my love to everyone. Mom, I think of you all the time. You too, dad. And Aunt Ella, be strong, okay?

Love, always,

Otis

April 8, 1965

Dear Norma,

We're on Easter break. There's a lot of political trouble in Nigeria now. Violence on the streets. Automobile tires hung around the neck of political enemies and set on fire. Lots of people thrown into jail. Such scary times! Sometime in March Chip, Tim, and I drove to Ibadan University to see a play, *Before the Blackout,* by Nigeria's foremost playwright Wole Soyinka. Some of the references were lost to me, but it was a truly moving event. It's about the present political crisis in the country: the corruption and criminal behavior of the leadership, etc. and seems to predict there's going to be an explosion soon. We met the playwright at the Mbari Center in town (where we heard the jazz concert last year). Mr. Soyinka is a most impressive and articulate man. Just from talking with him, you can tell he's been all over the world. His play really shocks with its harsh pictures of the country's plight.

We could see signs of trouble all along the way as we drove to and from Ibadan. Armed policemen at several check points—and they're not very pleasant. On our way home, there was an argument between Chip and Tim about the political situation—the first time I heard those guys going at each other. The argument was about the message of Soyinka's play. Tim thought the trouble in Nigeria was because the country obtained its independence from Britain before it was quite ready for it. Chip disagreed, saying that however long it took Nigeria to win its freedom from Britain, the British had made sure independence would amount to little. He stressed that the present crisis was because the British had planted the seeds of division in Nigeria by promoting the Muslims of the North over the better-educated Christians in the South. The British knew very well the southerners would not accept that at all. Tim argued, Well, if the southerners were so smart, how come they didn't see those tricks and prevent them from happening? Chip came back at him with something like, It's the same trick the white man has been playing all over the world, setting brother against brother. Things were getting ugly, so I stepped in and made some comments about actors in Soyinka's play. That diverted them from their argument. I didn't want them getting in a fight, at least not while I looked on. Things eased up, and there was no more arguing between them for the rest of our journey.

Here in the village, we don't see many signs of the political unrest. But one can't help reflecting on the implications of national politics even on our small village. Take my little friends, Sumbo and her brother Deji. I find it very interesting that, while black Americans are obsessed with African connections, Africans seem rather more interested in connections with the wider world. The kids are rehearsing for class performances, to be held just before school ends for summer vacation in the next couple of months. Deji is working on a song about some Grand Old Duke of York, while Sumbo is rehearsing a piece from the Cinderella story. And each of them plans to give the presentation fully outfitted in European garb! I thought to myself, How bizarre! They've got great songs, stories, dances, and a whole lot of beautiful things from their own Yoruba culture, and they want to play some crummy old British stuff? That's where, I'm afraid, I'm on Tim's side in that debate with Chip. I mean, if colonialism didn't succeed in robbing you of your culture, and you can still make use of it, then what stops you from using it, especially when it's so much more attractive than the foreign one?

That's not even half as troubling as what's going on in my school right now, which for me is just as bad as the crisis in the country at large. Our vice principal retired at the end of last year. The school has been asked to choose someone to succeed him. This means the teachers should look among themselves and submit someone's name to the authorities. The two strongest candidates are Mr. Bodunrin (the French teacher) and Mr. Siyanbola (the history teacher). They are both Yoruba men. Siyanbola is so popular in the school that if the students had a say in this, he'd win hands down. But he comes from Oyo, while Bodunrin is an Ekiti man from Iludun—Chip's town, just across the river. Most of our faculty are Ekiti people, and they think it's time a "son of the soil" (as they say) took over power here. They see that our principal Mr. Fagbenro is not himself an Ekiti man (he's from Ikorodu, near Lagos), and they can't stand the thought of yet another non-Ekiti person seated next to him in power. Deep down inside they love Siyanbola, but for reasons of tribal politics they'd rather have an Ekiti person positioned to succeed Fagbenro.

I might have guessed this sort of situation would arise any time, way back when I was learning to read and speak Yoruba. I used to help myself with Yoruba grammar books that Mrs. Fafunso recommended to me. But those books were all published in what is called standard Yoruba, which is really the Oyo dialect of the language. I would walk confidently into the staff room and brag about my Yoruba, making a few statements based on lessons out of those books. Some of my colleagues would laugh at me and say I was speaking Oyo Yoruba! They weren't being nasty to me; they were just making harmless fun, I thought. In time, I learnt a few differences between Yoruba dialects in some words. For instance, the common Yoruba word for the pineapple is *ope oyinbo*: it literally means, the white man's palm. Possibly the fruit was foreign to the Yoruba, so they didn't have a local name for it. But here in the backwoods of Yoruba-land the fruit has local names, which makes you wonder whether it's really foreign to this part of Africa. The Ekiti, my people, call it *ekikun*, while the Owo people, just next door to the Ekiti, call it *igogoyin*. The two words may be related linguistically, but they suggest differences of speech and maybe culture between the two groups.

You remember the experience I had last year, when I swam in the river? As I reported in that letter, the Ekiti would say, *O yaa we l'odo* (he went to swim in the river). But Mrs. Fafunso tells me that the Owo would say, *O gha gue l'odo*. According to her, that's more like the way the people of Benin, east of Owo, talk (the Owo had a long historical rela-tionship with Benin that has affected their language in certain ways).

There are many more such differences. But it boggles the mind to think that the situation would degenerate to a ridiculous extent in a small school like ours. If the competition for the vice principal job were between an Ekiti man and an Owo man, I'm convinced we'd have the same problem. Any wonder there's so much trouble in a country where many communities speak totally different languages, not just dialects of one language?

I'm supposed to be an Ekiti man and not say all this: I'm supposed to support Bodunrin! But this is simply ridiculous. In a meeting we held last week in the staff room to discuss this business, someone reported that Siyanbola's supporters had sworn they'd go to court if they found that their candidate was being unjustly denied the position he deserved. Bodunrin, incidentally, is rather old and should retire any time soon. I tried to reduce the tension by making a proposal I thought should be a fair compromise: Get the students to register their vote. Though the majority of our students are Ekiti, I was willing to bet their vote on the issue would be a disinterested one. But I miscalculated, and guess who shot me down? Crabs! No sooner had I made my proposal than he shouted from his seat, Is this a matter between Nigerians or what? That was the first time I was being put in my place in my own *home* town. And I thought America was the only place where they're always telling you where you belong!

I didn't respond to that remark. I decided not to let it bother me. Though I've done nothing to warrant the man's hostility towards me, I'm determined not to let myself be provoked by anything he does or says. In time, he will fall on his own face. As Ifa would say, *Sikasika fi idaji se 'ra re* (the evildoer does just as much harm to himself). I only hope he doesn't test me much further.

You'd have to decide whether or not my mom should read this letter. I know how she worries about things, and I don't want her thinking I'm in any trouble. But if you think she's read enough of my letters and is no longer afraid I'm surrounded by demons, then maybe she should read this one. Just let her know I'm okay and can take care of myself.

Love, always.

Otis

May 14, 1965

Dear Mom and Dad,

I'm not exaggerating when I say I had my first *real* sleep last night. After a whole year of being in this village I'm proud to say is the home of my fathers, I believe I deserve the exhilaration I feel now. It's been well worth the wait, and God be praised! We're getting set for the midyear vacation, so our sports practices have stepped up a bit. But let me describe, in some detail, how our great ceremony came to pass.

First, we had three or four more rehearsals—the twins, the drummer, and myself—just to assure ourselves that everything was perfect. In the final two sessions, the twins joined me in a full performance. They remembered everything as it should be: words, movement, everything. So they had little trouble coordinating with me as I sang and danced. As you would expect, they couldn't dance as strongly as they must had done in the past. But they were impressed with how well I did my own part, and they seemed satisfied with that.

The next thing they did, about two weeks ago, was to order the cloth we three would wear for the event. This was a job they gave to Madam Remilekun, their nurse: *asho oke* of alternating wine and silver stripes, the same design the twins had worn on the same occasion, over a century ago. We tried them on last week, and they fitted us perfectly. We also had a headpiece of the same material, and a horse-tail fly-whisk. Then there were beads and other kinds of ornaments, including Akimbowale's amulet. According to the twins, I had to wear it for the ceremony, since he had worn it for the same event.

216

Awo Akinwunmi played a prominent role in our final preparations. Once more, he consulted the oracles to ensure things would turn out right. The response was good, and we made the sacrifices Ifa recommended: one white yam, two white roosters, one white hen, two lengths of Nupe calico, ten shillings in brand new coins. Thanks, dad, for putting the $1000 into my Akure bank account for the event. It guaranteed I wouldn't starve to death after what turned out to be a more expensive ceremony than I'd anticipated. I had to provide a feast for the entire village—can you believe that? Though Chip and Tim threw in something, it still turned out to be a costly affair. When I complained about the expense to Awo Akinwunmi, he laughed and said, How often does anyone perform a ceremony that took a hundred years to complete? You're paying the accumulated interest, my friend!

Like I said, Awo had a lot of input in this event. In addition to consulting Ifa, he cleansed the site for the ceremony. As you know, the old town had been set on fire while the original ceremony was taking place. Everyone had fled to escape the enslavers and moved to the site where the town is presently located. The old town, called Ijoko-Oke, is now a thick bush—that's where I ran to embrace the ground the day we arrived here. On the day appointed for cleansing the spot, we all (the twins and myself) went with Awo to confirm the site. It was one of the most revealing experiences I've had since coming here. I think it's something you should report to Dr. Fishbein.

The twins live by the edge of the bush. Their hut sits on the same spot where Itayemi, the founder of our line, set up residence on arriving here as an Ondo exile. Since the day we arrived here, I had never had reason to enter the bush, though I'd come quite close to it every time I visited the twins. As we walked through the bush in search of the sacred ground, I felt very much at ease, as if the entire environment was familiar to me. I had to reduce my pace so as not to leave the old women behind. But something kept urging me forward. Every time I looked back to check, I could see an expression on the women's faces—not of amazement, but of restrained cheerfulness, more obvious on Taiwo than on Kehinde. They must have noticed how my neck strained to look at one tree or the other, how once in a while I stopped to feel the marks on this tree or that, or parted the shrubs on a spot in search of something. I was finally led, by impulse, to a huge iroko tree. When I got to it, I examined it thoroughly, as if looking for something I knew was there. Sure enough, high up on its trunk was a stout metal wedge that had been driven into it. When the twins and Awo Akinwunmi finally caught up with me, it was Kehinde who revealed the story behind the wedge.

According to local legend, the town once had a mighty giant who lived near the iroko tree. Being too tall to sleep in a normal house, he slept every night at the foot of the tree. With his bare hands he dug the earth for iron ore, from which he smelted metal bars that he fashioned into various items: cooking pots, a rod he used both as crutch and weapon, etc. He also drove a piece of metal into the tree as a wedge, from which he hung his bag of odds and ends. Long after the giant had passed away, the youths of the town used the peg for various exercises: swinging from it, or hanging an object as target for catapult or bow and arrow shots. Akimbowale had participated in these games in his youth. In time, the tree was used as a rallying point, especially for holding meetings on matters that affected the whole town and for periodic festivals.

I stood near that tree for some time, looking up at the wedge. After a while, I turned and walked straight to the spot where I embraced the ground the day we got here, a few steps from the iroko tree. This is all thick bush now. But it all felt like familiar stomping grounds to me. I felt some of the old tingling sensation, only by now I had acquired the strength to control it. But I sweated so profusely, it was clear that something was happening to me. Awo Akinwunmi couldn't believe his eyes. The twins must have known what it was. But they said nothing. I said nothing either. I remembered Dr. Fishbein had suggested I look out for things of this kind and make a mental note of them.

After I identified the spot of the old ceremony, Akinwunmi set down his ritual articles and began the process of cleansing the spot. Mainly, he chanted certain lines of prayer to which the twins and myself responded, *Ashe* (Amen). As he prayed, he sprayed dusts of white chalk over and around the spot. He had a ritual staff with a bunch of cowries around its head. This he jangled over and around the spot. Then he performed the same acts with the chalk and the staff over the heads of the two women and myself. Finally, he broke off a piece of the chalk, crushed it between his fingers, and rubbed the powder on our foreheads, all the time chanting a prayer to which we all responded *Ashe!* The prayers were to protect us against any evil forces that might try to stand in our way during the ceremony. We had made sacrifices to secure the protection of good spirits. But the evil ones are constantly at work to neutralize the influence of the good, so constant vigilance is always needed. The twins seemed so tired after the rituals were over, I wondered if they'd be strong enough for the coming dance. But then I thought, If they've lived for over one hundred years to do it, why can't they survive one day of even the most demanding steps?

Awo Akinwunmi next had to inform Baale Osunkunle of the date set for the ceremony. As head of the village, he has to be told of every major thing anyone plans to do. I didn't accompany Awo to the Baale's place. But he told me afterwards that the Baale received the news with some pleasure and summoned his advisers later in the day for a meeting to determine what should be done. It was decided that, this being such an important event for the town, everyone should rally round and give their support. A committee of able-bodied young men was set up to take charge of preparations for the ceremony.

A couple of days later, I was wakened by distant sounds from a crier. He was going round the village, beating a metal gong to inform the people of the day on which *iya wa meji* would complete the dance for their departed father. Nothing was said about me, but that's okay: I would have given the news the same way myself. Anyhow, in no time, the people swung into action to make the prescribed preparations. For the first time in the memory of the villagers, the huge bush that had covered the old site was invaded with machetes and hoes. Able-bodied men cut down trees and tore out roots and stumps to build a road leading to the large clearing where our ceremony was to be held.

I'll make this short—there's so much to tell, it might take forever! There was an incredible crowd at the ceremony. Before the twins and I arrived at the scene, the crowd was already being entertained by groups we had organized for the event. Madam Remilekun was there with her church group, all of them dressed in beautiful *asho ebi* and singing Christian songs, backed by percussionists and drummers. There was a band of young boys playing drum music and songs for a very colorful masquerade—masked as an ape, with a long tail, and cutting the most hilarious capers. I couldn't help laughing at the masquerade's antics!

Colored People's Time is alive and well here! After a truly long while, our turn came to do the long-awaited dance. The crowd shifted to enclose us in a ring at the center of the clearing. First, Olu the drummer struck some signature notes: our rehearsals had called for preliminary drumming, to which the twins and I were to dance briefly. After a few drum beats, I raised my right hand high and signaled Olu to stop. Then

I began chanting the text. The three of us danced to it, Olu playing a reprise to each line. I had a slight tremor at the beginning, just a little moment of panic. I survived it, and the rest of the performance went smoothly. Another tremor came towards the end, at the point where the old performance was disrupted by the slave raiders. In fact, I had some difficulty with that point in the text during our rehearsals, but thought I had mastered it. Here at the real event, it came up again. Olu noticed that I hesitated, and shouted to me in Yoruba to "hold it down." I closed my eyes and belted out the proper transitional line instead of the words I used to say, calling for help.

Here, at last, we have the final, *final* version of the chant that you, Dad, recorded before you left. It gives me deep personal satisfaction to set it down as the defining text of our family:

> *Akindiji! Akindiji! Akindiji o o o!*
> *Mo ke si o lere meta, omo Itayemi*
> *Okunrin ko ko 'kiti ofa meta lo s'ogun*
> *Balogun, ab' Akimbowale aba 'beji*
> *Alaya b'aya inaki, o fe gbaara, o sororo irun*
> *Okunrin ko yan tenkitenki sigberi ota*
> *Ko s'aya sile, pelu erin lerun*
> *Libi ko ti regberun apa*
> *Oko Asake, ab' Akimbowale aba 'beji*
> *Uku orun ian Tapa*
> *"Ma rin kangun aye ki mi yo p'eku uwoluwo re!"*
> *Omo Itayemi, usu po l'ogba*
> *Balogun alaya inaki kannti, okunrin ero, okunrin ogun*
> *Jagunjagun panranun luran aba re*
> *Agbe ayiye luran eye re*
> *Uku orun Tapa, omo Itayemi, okunrin ero, okunrin ogun.*
> > *Tapa Tapa, eji nana baabo*
> > *Taaapa, eji nana baabo*
> > *Tapa Tapa, eji nana baabo*
> > *Taaapa, eji nana baabo!*[13]

The twins surprised us greatly. While Olu played his reprise to each line, the women accompanied him with phrases of their own we hadn't practiced in our sessions. These turned out to be other praises apart from the original, which the twins had evolved over time in their uncommonly long life. They were clearly not in the script I had been carrying in my subdued memory. Olu and I looked at each other once: I think *he* wanted to be sure I was not rattled by this new material. I wasn't, thank goodness. And he's such an experienced drummer, he carried on as if there was no problem.

We were equally surprised at how vigorously the twins danced. Picture these women, over a hundred years old, dancing like ladies just past forty. Swinging their horse-tail whisks in robust rhythm. Enjoying every moment of their dance. It seemed as if they had spent every day of the past hundred years saving up their strength, just to balance an old account! The crowd was so energized seeing them, everyone joined us in the ring for the final chorus of *Tapa Tapa, eji nana baabo*. This went on so long it seemed it would never end, and the dust rose so high you barely saw anyone dancing close to you. After a while, the twins began to slow down. I motioned Olu to stop drumming. Holding each of the women by the hand, I led them to their seats. Everybody else knew it was time to stop.

Madam Remilekun came round with one of her friends to the twins. With handwoven fans, they whipped up some air to cool the twins down, all the while greeting them with praises I hadn't heard before. Olu played some strains to accompany the praises. There was no dancing. Everybody understood this was just an interlude to settle things down. Even I was so tired, I'd have raised a hell of a protest if anyone had asked me to do any more dancing!

The Baale wasn't there. Rulers don't go to funeral ceremonies; they're supposed to preside over life, not death, among their people. But he was represented by two councilors who also joined the crowd in dancing out the end of the song. Also among the dancers were Chip and Ireti, Tim, and even Phil Bigelow! So were Mr. and Mrs. Fagbenro, with Sumbo and Deji. I realized this when I felt Sumbo's little hand tugging at my *agbada* as I danced. Deji danced too, despite his smug little self. Some colleagues from the school also came, though I don't recall seeing Crabs anywhere. All in all, it was a *great* event, every bit worth the hundred years it's taken to bring it to a fitting end. At last, our family is as free and as strong as it once was. I'm grateful to have been the one chosen to restore its honor. The words of Ifa can hardly be more fitting here: *Ola silo n'ile, ola dehin s'ile* (Honor leaves the home, and honor returns to the home).

Madam Remilekun and her friend stopped fanning the twins, and

Olu his drumming, when Awo Akinwunmi stepped up to offer his final blessings. He thanked everyone for coming. He thanked *iya wa meji* for honoring us with their lives. And he thanked me for restoring their lost brother to the family and the community as a whole. He prayed the gods would guide us on our way from the ceremony to the homestead of the twins, where there was food and drink enough for anyone who had washed their stomachs clean! When he finished speaking, the twins rose from their seats. I rose too, holding them as we walked home. Olu and Awo came behind us. Someone raised the chorus *Tapa Tapa, eji nana baabo,* and the crowd took it up again. There was renewed singing and dancing following us, as a recessional, right to the home of the twins. Everybody had a great time and enjoyed the food and drinks.

So there—we did it like we had to! But while I rejoice, I cannot help wondering why in your last two letters there wasn't a word about Aunt Ella. Is there a problem you don't want to tell me about? I don't mean to spoil the triumph of the moment with fears I need not raise. But she was so instrumental to my making this trip, I can't help remembering her now her faith has been justified. If she is still there with you, please convey to her my warmest gratitude for bestowing her blessing on me. Tell her I know we've done the right thing by making the connection we needed to make, to know who we are and where we come from. Tell her I am not so naive as to think that, having fulfilled its duty, our family is at last free of whatever tests and trials God may have chosen to keep it strong. I think I am living proof that we can survive if we face these trials rather than run away from them. Whatever happens, tell her we deserve to celebrate this triumph God has given us. If there is one living person who may be judged responsible for guiding us to this triumph, tell her she is the one. Finally, tell her my share of the triumph will not be complete, until I can see her once more in full health and happiness.

My love to you all.

Otis

June 5, 1965

Dear Mom and Dad,

How devastating it was reading the news about Aunt Ella's death! I guess there was something all along telling me she didn't have long to live. My fears only got stronger as your silence about her condition grew. What makes her death so painful for me is that, although the spasms that brought me to Africa somehow indicated our ancestors were calling me, she gave the final jolt to my decision to come here. In a sense, she was the reserve umbilical chord that helped to link me with our people. So, sad as her death is to me, I take consolation in the news that she died on the very day of our ceremony. How can I doubt the meaning of the coincidence? Aunt Ella lived just long enough to nudge me home to the duty our ancestors had appointed for me, then she breathed her last when she was satisfied I had done that duty. If this sounds like superstition, remember that, as devout a Christian as she was, even Aunt Ella believed that our ancestors were beckoning me home to take care of some unfinished family business. Having played her part, she went up there to join them. That's not so bad now. We who mourn her should take solace in the words of Ifa: *Etutu kii tuka, ki o maa gbarajo* (Termites never scatter, without joining together again). Our world is whole again!

The twins settled one more piece of business for me last week. They'd sent for me, and when I got there, they asked me to sit down, they had something to tell me. First, they asked if they could fix me something to eat. I'd had lunch, so I said, No, I'd already eaten. Then they said they'd called for me because they thought it was time I assumed my Yoruba name. I told them, half in jest, that I already had a name given me by my students: Tokunbo. They laughed and said, Well, that's not wrong. After all, you were born overseas. But the name we have for you is the name you've always had, which is Akimbowale. That didn't come as a great surprise to me. Hadn't they always called me their *egbon*? Rather, I was filled with the deepest satisfaction and pride. I felt complete, in a way I never imagined possible. I heaved a sigh. Akimbowale!

Akimbowale.... The twins saw I was pleased. Next, Kehinde asked Taiwo to go into the room and bring "that thing." Taiwo did so and passed it on to Kehinde, who handed me the amulet I'd worn for the dance—Akimbowale's amulet, which he had thrown to the twins as he was being dragged away by the enslavers. It's a small bronze object: flat, square shaped, about an inch and a half and with two parallel lines etched on its smooth surface. I asked the twins what the marks stood for. They said they were not sure, but since Akimbowale made those marks I might be able to read them myself, or decide what they meant for me. The flat metal piece is suspended from a rusty iron ring, worn round the arm. I asked the twins if it *must* be worn round the arm, and they said I could wear it any place I chose. I liked that, because the ring was too small to go round my biceps. Later on, I cut myself a nice, fresh leather string and threaded it into the amulet. Now I wear it round my neck. It feels much better that way.

I hope you all can start getting used to these changes and not be alarmed when next you see me, wearing a shining bronze amulet round my neck! Now, it would be naive of me to expect you'll call me by any name but the one you gave me as a child. But if you can find it in you to call me by my new, ancestral name, it would be great. Akimbowale. If you find the full name too difficult for the American in you to deal with, you may just use a short form of it: Kimbo.

It's a pity Aunt Ella will not be around to see me in the shape she has helped to make possible. But I know she is smiling with joy now, wherever she may be. Love to you all.

Akimbowale

June 22, 1965

Dear Mom and Dad,

Something happened a few days ago you should know about. Mom, I'm counting on you to be strong now. Let me assure you that, whatever happens to me here, I can most certainly deal with it. Besides, I think I enjoy enough goodwill and support in this village to see me through whatever obstacles come my way.

Just when I am getting adjusted to my newly reclaimed identity, someone tries to throw a wrench into the whole process. You guessed right: Crabs! Ever since the U.S. got into the Vietnam War, he's been trying to draw me into an argument. He'd come into the staff room and make snide comments about American imperialism, big brother this and big brother that. Or he'd wave some newspaper or magazine where there was something published about the U.S. military. I'd done quite well in fending off any confrontation. Usually, I'd smile and say I wasn't really interested in politics. Or I'd simply agree that America had no business fighting in Vietnam. That's as far as things went most of the time, and everyone else in the room would sympathize with my peaceable attitude towards the guy.

But things took an ugly turn three days ago. There was a news item last week in the Nigerian *Times* about an American naval vessel docked off the coast of Lagos. A group of Nigerians started a riot there, and the government repressed it with the riot police, which is notorious for its brutal tactics. The U.S. ambassador came out with a statement clarifying the presence of the ship. There's been a rumor that the U.S. has been trying to set up a military base here. The ambassador assured the country that the ship was actually on its way to South Africa and had only stopped in Lagos for supplies; the ship would soon be on its way. Obviously the protesters weren't satisfied as long as the ship was still docked around Lagos. Four days ago, there was a picture in the *Times* showing Nigerian President Nnamdi Azikiwe smiling and shaking hands with the commander of the ship, with the U.S. ambassador standing next to the President.

That's the paper Crabs brought into the staff room. He made a big deal of the news, saying this was proof there was some shady deal going on between Nigeria and the U.S. I could have shruggled it all off. But he thrust the paper at my face and slammed it on my table, and said, Mr. Deputy Ambassador, what do you have to say to that? Your country is at its old game, wining and dining heads of state so they can sell their nation for a mess of potage. I smiled and said to him, What makes you think I'm here to defend whatever America does? And he said, There you go, just like the imperialist you are, lying through your teeth, pretending you don't know anything about what is going on. That's how your country has gone about lying to the Vietnamese that America is fighting to protect them against communism. Who says your capitalism is any better than communism? In any case, who are you to tell other people what is best for them?

Fancy that—me having to defend America's adventures all over the world! My temper was gradually rising. I had a mind to ask him, Would Nigeria *really* want to be a Communist country? But I'm glad I never did. Instead, I tried to make a joke out of the issue. I said, Why do you pick on me? After all, I'm Nigerian too, just like you. Everyone else in the room laughed. But Crabs didn't think it was funny, and said, That's what *you* tell me. That stung me, and I said to him, What do you mean? You do know my family in this town, don't you? And he said, I'm not going to stand here arguing with people who have questionable backgrounds! Then he walked over to his desk and sat down triumphantly. *Question-*

able backgrounds! Jesus—to think that, only a few days back, the whole village watched me perform rites that confirmed me as a native son. And here was a fellow citizen (if I may call him that) reminding me of my slave ancestry!

I decided I'd had enough. I took a deep breath, rose from my seat, and walked over to his desk. It was one of those table-seat combos donated in large quantities to the school by some American Baptist organization. The whole room was quiet as I walked towards Crabs. I did my best to control myself. Bending over him, my hands gripping the edges of his table, I looked him squarely in the eyes and said, Listen, man, I think you just stepped over the line. You know, I'm sick and tired of you throwing your weight around ever since I got here. I don't know what your problem is, but it's got to end right here and now. He started to rise from his seat and try to walk away. Sit down, I'm not finished talking to you! I roared at him. I was so angry when I said this, I lifted him and his desk clear off the ground and slammed him down. He was so frightened, his jaws dropped, and his lips shook. I heard someone run out of the room. I said, You have a nerve carrying on about America. But here you are, sitting your sorry ass on a seat given you by Americans. Did you ever think about that? I don't think so! Next time you open your big foul mouth to criticize Americans, maybe you'll have the pride to say no to their handouts, since you can't stand them. And let me tell you something else, I said. You talk about my *questionable background.* I know what you meant, you miserable slob, but you didn't have the guts to spell it out. Of course my ancestor was taken away to America as a slave. But who sold him off to the white man? It was exactly people like *you!* Again I lifted him off the floor, and slammed him down. Selling your own people off to the same white man, just so you can make a few lousy pennies. So what have you got out of it all? You won't hear it from me. But whatever you think, man, I'm home where I came from, and there's nothing you or any of your kind can do about it. Now, the next time you talk this way about me or my family, I won't just be lifting you up. You *got* that?! This time I took him up even higher than before and slammed him down with more resounding force.

He was so frightened, he was shaking like a chick in the cold rain. When I took my hands off his table, I heard the principal say to me, with a hand on my shoulder, Please Mr. Hampton, please control yourself. What is the problem? Someone must have run over to report there was trouble. Nothing sir, I told him, I was just about to leave. I picked up my things from my table and walked out of the room. On my way out, I saw a crowd of students outside the door. As I walked through them, they started chanting Toks! Toks! Toks!—which is short for the name they call me (Tokunbo). Word must have gone round about my standoff with Crabs, so there they were cheering me on—Crabs is extremely unpopular with the students. I went straight to my house.

I didn't feel right for the rest of the day. I never thought I'd get to a point where I had a fight with anyone here. After all, I'd come on a mission of peace. I had dinner with my usual company, Sumbo and Deji. The poor kids saw I was not my usual self, and they kept looking at me, not knowing what to say to cheer me up. I felt bad about that. After a while, I remembered the school competition they'd entered and won prizes the day before. I'd been at their school to watch them perform, and I was impressed though I didn't like the material—old British stuff. To lighten the atmosphere, I asked them to bring the certificates they'd been awarded. That cheered them up. They ran to their house to fetch them. I smiled the best I could and held Sumbo on my knee. Deji sat by himself, like the gentleman he thinks he is, but they were happy just the same. I made each of them perform a piece of their act for my benefit. They were pleased to do so, and that lifted up our spirits. I hadn't quite forgotten what had happened earlier that day. But my mood was brighter when we all retired to bed.

The next day I went over to Awo Akinwunmi. Perhaps because I disliked Crabs, I'd never quite taken the trouble to find out about him. I knew he came from this village, but that was about it. I knew nothing about his family, or anything else. I didn't want to bring up the matter with the twins. They might raise hell and make the place unliveable for Crabs and his family. So I went over to Awo and, after some hedging, I told him what was on my mind. He could see there was a problem. But, like the wise man he is, he wore a look on his face that said something like, If you have anything to say, I'm willing to hear it. So I told him what happened between me and Crabs. He said to me, Why didn't you tell me you had a problem with that man? And I said, Well, I didn't think there was anything to it. He shook his head and sighed. There was a knowing smile on his lips as he said to me, Be careful with that man. Be *very* careful with that man. When I pressed to know what he meant, he straightened up and said, That man does not mean you any good. What right does he have to talk about your background in that way? Perhaps you should have asked him, Was any of your family a slave in this town? Nobody in your family was ever a slave, and that is all that matters to us as far as anyone's identity is concerned. A man does not become a slave, just because some white man comes here and carries him away forcibly to work for him in another land. Our people who were carried away like that are not slaves in our eyes and will never be slaves in our eyes, whatever white people think of them!

And beware, Awo continued, that man is your enemy. Enemy? I asked. Yes, he said, enemy. Do you know what family he comes from? His father and Baale Osunkunle are one and the same family. I don't think he is on good terms with Baale Osunkunle, but that doesn't mean he is your friend either. I asked what all this had to do with me, and Awo said, Well, you don't know this town as well as I do. You see, there was a competition within their family long ago for the position of Baale. It was won by Osunkunle's branch of the family, and that has caused bad blood between the Osunkunles and the other branch from which your man comes. His name is Goke Dipeolu, isn't it? I said, Yes. That's right, Awo said. Their branch of the family is called Dipeolu. As you can see, he is a young man. He has been saying our village needs an enlightened leader. No doubt he thinks it is his turn to be the next Baale of Ijoko-Odo. I still don't see what all this has to do with me, I said. He looked at me and said, You don't? I said, No. Then he said, Alright, you think about it. You will find out that this has more to do with you than you realize.

I spent a good deal of that night thinking over Awo's words. All I could come up with was the ridiculous question, Does Crabs think I am here to compete for the position of Baale? I know our ancestor Akindiji was Baale before he died. But why on earth would anyone in Ijoko-Odo think I'd be interested in such a thing? I dismissed the whole idea—I thought I must be way out of my mind thinking like that. But the more I thought about Crabs, and how he nearly drove me to harm him, the more the scenario of my initiation started to unfold before my eyes. Had he, perhaps, been set up to test me?

I hadn't given much thought to my initiation since it happened. Now it was coming back to me in clearer outlines. I now recalled the questions the officiants had asked before I was handed a machete to behead the dog: Have you ever seen death? Have you ever inflicted death? If death stood face to face with you, would you confront it squarely? To the first two questions, my sponsor Adegboye said, No, but to the third he said, Yes. Fine—I could have said the same things myself, if I'd been conscious enough at the moment. But what continued to elude me was the meaning of that image of me and the bear exchanging identities, until we ended up as two images of myself facing one another. The more I thought about that picture, the more the meaning of the whole initiation resolved itself for me in light of my confrontation with Crabs. Violence, even bloodshed, is often necessary, whether for the defense of the community or, as with hunters, to provide meat for the table. But violence has its cost, and it is this the initiation may be intended to address: to disabuse those who shed blood, for whatever reason, of any illusion that shedding blood is a good thing in itself. Before you shed blood, put yourself in the position of the person or creature whose blood you're about to shed. If you still have to shed blood, though you may find you don't, let your intentions be right and your heart pure. Which is what Ifa says in the advice given to the bloodthirsty Ogun as he prepared to fight with Obara: Beware the man does not get killed in the fight!

I cannot swear I've totally forgiven Crabs for his hostility towards me. I will not be driven to violence against him. But now that I know what irks him, I'll do my best to put some distance between us. I don't want to be tempted into paths I've pledged myself to avoid. May God, and our ancestors, give us the strength to abide our reconstituted destiny, which has managed to bring us greater honor than we could have imagined.

Love to everyone.

Akimbowale

July 17, 1965

Dear Mom and Dad,

The sun did not stand still in the sky. Little babies born today did not stand up and walk before the startled gaze of their parents. Animals from the bush did not invade our homes or usurp our speech and demand to be served at our tables. Nor did men and women begin to walk on their heads, like a race of acrobats or like monsters we meet in grim fairytales. But, if they did, they would cause us no more alarm than our village is still struggling to survive. If you think I've lost my balance and hardly make sense, you are not far wrong. How could I or anyone else here for that matter? The world as we knew it has come to an end. The twins are dead.

For a week I couldn't bring myself to report the following account of what happened. I'd been over visiting at Chip's. Ireti had given birth to a baby boy, and Tim and I had put our hands together to organize an *idawo*, a child welcoming party. Women hate it, because the men are having a good time while the mother and the baby are still at the maternity clinic. But it's the tradition here. While the party was still on, I excused myself. I was feeling some discomfort: I thought I had a cold or something. So Tim took me home. I hadn't seen the twins for a few days, so I asked Tim to drop me off at their place. When I walked into their house, I thought it felt unusually cold. I called out to them. There was no answer, so I walked into their bedroom. Kehinde sat on the floor, looking at Taiwo, who lay flat on the bed, motionless. The room was dark, but for the faint light of a hurricane lamp sitting on a stool. I called again, Iya. Kehinde turned her head toward me, but did not look me full in the face. Though I'd been in this situation before, I didn't feel any easier this time. Iya, I said again. Still there was no word in response.

I got down on my knees beside Kehinde, and whispered to her, Is she ill again? It took a while before she said, No, she is not ill. She is dead. It did not hit me yet. For a while I was silent, waiting for Kehinde to retract her words. She must be joking, I thought. But she wasn't. When she still wouldn't say anything, I said, Dead? Kehinde neither spoke nor moved her head. I guess she felt she'd told me all there was to say. Dead, I muttered to myself. The reality of it was beginning to sink in. I wanted to raise a hand and touch Taiwo. But something told me there was no use. It would be foolish to doubt Kehinde, who had seen it all. I think she understood the shock I was in, and thought to put me at some ease. I heard her say, Toyosi Remilekun was here earlier this evening. I asked her to go home to her husband and family; I would take care of my sister myself. I did not want to tell her the truth. I wanted you to be the first to know. I was sure you would come. So I saved the news for you.

I was going to say, Iya, what do you want me to do? But, at this point, I saw Kehinde turn her face toward me in the eerie half-light of the hurricane lamp. *Egbon mi*, she said, there is nothing you can do. There is nothing anyone can do. Time has been kind to us. We would be foolish to ask more of it. That is why there should be no sadness, only joy: how many mortal men and women have known such good fortune as ours? And now, please go back to the living. I have turned my face toward you because I wanted the look of life to be the last thing you saw before you left us. Please, *egbon mi*, please listen to me. Do not turn your face any other way but toward the door that leads you to the company of the living. You came to touch our homestead with life. Though we who remained here are passing now, you have rekindled the fire that will bring new life. So go. Farewell, and our spirits go with you. When morning comes, be sure to tell Akinwunmi, son of Kujore, as much of what I have said as he needs to hear. He will know what to do.

I rose from the ground. It hurt me deeply not to look on *iya* Taiwo's face once more. But I knew better than to disobey Kehinde's advice. I'd reached the front door and was beginning to step into the darkness outside, when a voice came from behind me. I listened carefully. It was the voice of Kehinde, calling Taiwo three times. She reminded her that she, Taiwo, had once preceded her into the world to prepare the way for her; she should not forget to make the way just as good now they were rejoining their kin who had gone before. Then she called Taiwo thrice again and became silent. There was some ruffling from the bedroom. But that was all. I must have waited about five minutes longer. My eyes swelled with tears, and I yearned to run back in there. But a much stronger force held me to the spot, perhaps stopping me from doing anything stupid.

Whenever Sumbo and Deji don't see me in the evening, they assume something has kept me somewhere. So they eat dinner with their parents and spend the night there too. However, before I left my house earlier in the day, I'd told the Fagbenros where I was going and said I might not come home early. So I wasn't surprised the kids weren't at my place when I returned. Besides, I was in no mood to communicate with anyone when I got back. I hardly slept that night, and for the first time in my life, as far as I can remember, I let myself cry uninhibitedly.

It was barely daybreak when I left the house and walked quickly to Awo Akinwunmi's place. From the looks of me—bleary eyes, unwashed face, uncombed hair—he could tell something was wrong. He drew me quietly to his consultation room and said, *Alagba* (Big Man)—that's what he calls me. *Alagba,* he said, is anything wrong? I nodded, then put my hand to my face, thinking how to begin giving the message from Kehinde. Awo didn't have to be told. He put his hand on my shoulder and asked, Is it the twins? I nodded, raising my eyes gratefully to him. He lowered his head, shook it, and moaned deeply. So they are gone? he asked. I said, Well, I think so. Iya Kehinde said I should see you first thing today; you would know what to do. He thought silently for a while, then told me to go home and leave everything in his hands.

Yes, the world as we knew it—indeed, as we never really knew it—has passed. I know you'll be as sad as I've been. But, if we've read Iya Kehinde's last words right, we should celebrate the life we have rekindled, not mourn the death that put the light in our hands.

Love,
Akimbowale

July 24, 1965

Dear Mom and Dad,

Three days ago, Awo Akinwunmi gave me an update on the state of things. You must understand that, though I was family to the twins, they had achieved such a status in this community that they were more than just one family among others. They belonged to the people as a whole. Here's what Awo did after I left his house. There's an association of grand matrons in this village, headed by the Iyalode (Mother of the Town). In case of a great tragedy, as the death of the twins clearly is, these women are the first to be informed. When they've visited the scene of the tragedy and have done what should be done, they send one of their members to the Baale, asking him to summon his council to prepare a program of events. Once this has been agreed upon, the town crier is asked to announce to the whole village what has happened and what the leaders of the community have decided.

This morning, the crier broke the news of the twins' death with his gong. Many people had known of course. People here are not very good at keeping secrets, which is really a good thing. But part of the fault may be mine. The way I was carrying on, I must have drawn some attention to myself. Yesterday, I caught Mrs. Fagbenro looking at me in a curious way. She must have heard something, but didn't want to say anything to me—either because she knew that tradition demanded the news be withheld until the crier had broadcast it or because she wanted to respect my feelings. I hadn't told Chip or Tim anything, and I carried on with Sumbo and Deji as if nothing happened. We laughed as we shot hoops in my front yard or played other kinds of games. But no sooner was the news announced today than I got a few visits. Chip and Ireti have come by. A few other people too. Earlier in the afternoon, Mr. Fagbenro stopped by to offer a few words of sympathy, using the customary Christian language of course.

Also this morning, Awo accompanied me to the Baale's residence. There I was told the program of events for mourning the twins. By the way, their bodies have been laid in the earth within their own premises. Since I'm not a woman, and I'm too young to participate in traditional rites for women that old, I was kept out of the burial. It was carried out by the association of grand matrons, who kept the bodies emblamed for two days before laying them in the earth with the proper rituals. Here's the program the Baale and his council have announced. The village will observe a four week period of mourning. Every week, one prohibition will be imposed on the people. The first prohibition comes up three days from today. On that day, no marketing is permitted anywhere in the village, so families are advised to stock up on groceries and anything else they might need. In the week after that, there's prohibition against farming and hunting: for one whole day—no one is permitted to go into the bush for anything whatsoever. The third week, no one will be allowed in or out of this village for one whole day, which means there'll be no traveling across the boundaries of Ijoko-Odo. And finally on the fourth week, again for one whole day there's prohibition against playing music in any part of the village—no drumming, no singing or dancing, nothing at all in the form of music.

The rest of the program concerns our family. For a start, I have a couple my own prohibitions. First, on every one of those days when the village is under a prohibition, I'm forbidden to touch red (palm) oil or eat anything cooked with it. There's one other prohibition, if I may call it that. Earlier this evening, Madam Remilekun came to my house and tied a band of black cloth round my head. I am supposed to tie it on every morning, she said, and not remove it until I'm ready to retire for the night.

Finally, and this is where you all come in. On the last day of this month-long period, there will be a large festival of music, dancing, and other performances by various groups. These are intended to send the twins off fittingly as they join the ancestors. From the looks of it, this will be a more elaborate event than the song and dance ceremony we performed commemorating our ancestor Akindiji. This part is crucial. I've been told it's important for dad, as the oldest surviving member of our direct family, to head the final dance. Awo Akinwunmi adds that it's also fitting that dad should be accompanied by his wife for the dance; this would make it a truly dignified event. I hope by now mom has lost her fears about Africa. She definitely should come on this trip. I don't know what your time is like (my school closed for the midyear break ten days ago), but you should plan on spending about a week here. I think it's fitting that we end this segment of our family's history gloriously, as a properly reconstituted unit, in the eyes of everyone.

Dad, the Baale really looks forward to seeing you. He says he has a pleasant surprise waiting for you at the end of the ritual. Frankly, I have no clue what he has in mind. Awo Akinwunmi wouldn't tell me either. I've seen the Baale only twice since the incidents that happened during our first few days here. This being summer, I hope the trip will be convenient for you, so I look forward to seeing you all mid-August. Since Norma will be reading this, I need not tell her how much it would mean to me to see her here as well. By the way, none of you need worry about what to wear for the dance. Once you confirm you will come, I'll get Madam Remilekun or Mrs. Fagbenro to arrange the best possible outfit for mom and Norma. I'll take care of dad's.

Going by your last letter, I expect that by now Aunt Ella has been laid to rest in Augusta. May her soul rest in perfect peace. My eyes are starting to close. So, love to you all. Let me know your plans for the trip.

Akimbowale

P.S. It would be great for you to bring some presents for the Baale, Awo Akinwunmi, and my hosts the Fagbenros. I don't quite know what to suggest for the Baale. I know chiefs like something flamboyant, like a large embroidered robe. And some drinks, so he'll open one of them and bless you. Anything you can think of along those lines will be okay. I'm not sure about Awo Akinwunmi either. Though he occupies a specialized position here, he may not mind a couple of good looking shirts, since he has some Western education. Medium sized, please. I could have asked these men what they'd want, but I thought that would be awkward. And don't forget the Fagbenros. If you can throw in something for Chip's wife and child, that would be marvelous too. Just bring whatever you can..

ISIDORE OKPEWHO

September 5, 1965

Dear Norma,

Your letter arrived here in the fastest time I've known. Usually mail between the U.S. and Nigeria takes seven to ten days. But the stamp on your aerogramme shows it took barely five days to get here. I hadn't realized my dad was going to a conference in Brazil—thanks for telling me. I guess he'll read this when he returns.

You've all been gone only ten days, but this village is still abuzz about your visit. Your wonderful personalities, the funeral ceremony—especially the dance! Everyone of you gets glowing marks for the way you danced. Dad looked so much like a chief that nobody could have guessed he wasn't a native-born man of this village if they didn't already know who he was. And his dance was so graceful! But you and mom—wow! The women especially think you are *born* princesses. The way you danced, people thought you either had some practice before you got here, or dancing Yoruba music came naturally to you. I'd never been so proud of you all as I was on that day. Thanks for your kind words about my own dancing—you forget I was *once* born here!

It was great seeing Dr. Fishbein here again. People here still talk about his vigorous way of dancing. Never mind that he danced a little off-beat—his mere presence touched me very deeply. I greatly appreciate that he's moved beyond our patient-doctor relations and taken such a deep interest in this culture. He *is* a good man.

Our big dance was certainly the climax of the funeral rites. I'm glad we brought a fitting close to a program that began with those nightmarish spasms. I know I've said it to you before, here in this village, but I'll risk boring you by saying it again. I don't think I know how to define love. But if it's anything different from the way you've stood by me throughout these experiences, then there must be another meaning to it. I only hope that, in the years that we've been together, I haven't done anything that makes me less deserving of you than I should be.

The month-long mourning for the twins took a lot out of me. After it was over, and you all returned to the States, there were still things I needed to do. I had to do the rounds of the village, paying my respects to the major players in the whole event. Chip was great in offering his services and his car so we could easily visit a lot of people: the Iyalode (Mother of the Town); Madam Remilekun, the herbal nurse to the twins; the

235

Baale; and several others. We also hired trucks to return several articles we used for the festival dance, especially furniture. But the visits were the most important in terms of Yoruba cultural practices. Here, people get offended if you don't return to thank them for services they did for you, even if you *paid* them for these services. Money is fine, but people here place much greater value on personal contact.

Thank God the whole program happened during the midyear vacation. As soon as everything was settled, Chip, Tim, and I went out of town on a trip we'd been planning for some time. It's a pity your time here was so short. This was a visit you ought to have come along for, considering your deep interest in African culture. We went to Ile-Ife. In the Ifa tradition, Ife is called *Ondaye,* the cradle of the world. The Yoruba believe the world began at Ife. It was here that Olodumare (God) created the universe by tossing a few grains of sand on a large body of water. We visited the palace of the Ooni (King) of Ife. Though ours was an unscheduled visit, he graciously agreed to receive us into his presence when he was told some Americans would love to meet him. He's an old man who goes by the name Oba Aderemi, but he's a very enlightened man, very dignified. Ifa also says, *Elu k'elu kii t'Oni Ife* (No nobility can compare with the Oni of Ife). One of his officials showed us round the palace, giving us some background information on Ife's place in Yoruba cultural and political history. And the arts of the palace—girl, if they don't blow your mind, I don't know what will! And to think that a lot of those pieces were produced by native African artists at a time when few European nations had anything to show for their so-called civilization. You wonder, who's the real primitive?

Ife town itself is a big old sprawling city, much like Ibadan, which we've seen a few times. Unfortunately, Chip's car had a breakdown (it was the carburetor), so we had to wait while it was being fixed by a roadside mechanic. Chip is quite used to this sort of situation. We simply made ourselves comfortable on the wooden bench the mechanic placed for us in the shade of a nearby tree. Chip ordered *boli* (roast plantain) and *epa* (roast peanuts), which we chased down with Coke. The repair took all afternoon, a favorite trick by mechanics here to get as much money as possible from you. It left us too little time to see the rest of the place. So we had to rush our visit to the new University of Ife, which is still under construction. We returned home as nightfall was setting in.

School has resumed. But I'm hard at work with the construction company building the family memorial house my dad ordered. You recall he notified the Baale of this during the ceremony in which the Baale gave him a chieftaincy title. My dad left me a tidy sum to get the building under way. So I'm doing my best to make sure this project doesn't take any more time than it should. The foundations will be laid tomorrow. The building contractor (Philip Ashaolu) assures me construction will be completed by November.

We've read about trouble in the USA—civil rights riots, people burning their draft cards over the war in Vietnam, etc. Well, things are just as bad here in Nigeria. There are rumors of the military stepping in to take over power. The government's become quite incapable of controlling the violence by political rivals. In fact, the trouble is getting close even to the backwoods where we live. Just outside Akure, on our way back from Ife, we were stopped by two armed riot policemen. They asked to see our vehicle papers. Chip turned them over, but they went on to ask all kinds of questions: where we'd been, why we were returning so late, what we'd brought with us, etc.? They obviously wanted to get us upset or, as Chip suggested, to get a little something out of us. But Chip handled the situation well. So they got nothing but direct answers to their questions. Mind you, anything could have happened. People have been beaten up by these armed cops if they felt their answers weren't *respectful* enough. The atmosphere is getting really touchy.

You asked how much longer I plan to be here, now that my business appears to be over. My mom asked the same question. Right now my answer is, I'll wait to finish the family house, then I'll decide what my next agenda will be. After you all returned to the U.S., I started wondering: is my mission in this village finally over? I don't think I expect the spirits that brought me here to give me another sign telling me what to do next. It's my call now.

In the meantime, I see myself going to the States for Xmas. Beyond that, I haven't set myself a firm agenda. At least it won't be long before I see you again. I certainly don't intend to be separated from you for as long as I was the last time. Let's just leave it at that.

Love you, always.

Akimbowale

September 10, 1965

Norma,

I thought I'd keep this pain to myself. But I can't help getting it out of my system. This village has dealt me the hardest *personal* blow I've felt since I got here. You won't believe this.

A couple of weeks ago, Mrs. Fagbenro came to my place to say the family had made plans to circumcise Sumbo. The poor girl let them know she would submit to be cut only if I was there to hold her. Though I knew the custom still happened here, I never wanted to have anything to do with it. But, much as I felt strongly against it, how could I refuse Sumbo's call to me for help, at such a difficult moment?

The ritual was performed by Mrs. Adeloye, another female herbal expert here. She had objected to my presence, insisting that Sumbo must be treated like every other little girl in her situation. Sumbo, she said, should be allowed to feel the pain of the cut by herself, since it's part of a girl's growing up rites; these little concessions would only spoil her. But Sumbo's parents knew better than to stand against her. So there was I, a foreign body in female circumcision rites, but there only because Sumbo wanted me to. First the door was shut, then the window. Though it was daytime, the room would have been pitch dark but for the light of a candle lit for Mrs. Adeloye's use. And do you know what for? To heat the blade for making the cut!

As soon as the door and window were shut, Sumbo started to cry. That hurt me deeply. The last thing I ever wanted was to see anybody make Sumbo cry! With a heavy heart, I held her arms tightly round her body. Her mother and some other lady I'd never met held Sumbo down by her legs and hips. Mrs. Adeloye started her business by heating the blade—a pointed, triangularly shaped black piece of metal, with a short wooden handle. I wouldn't exactly call it a knife—it must be something specially designed for this purpose. She heated up this thing (to disinfect it, I guess), then held it up to the light. Her eyes closed, she mumbled some words to herself: I didn't bother to listen. Sumbo was already crying uncontrollably when Mrs. Adeloye brought the knife down to her tender parts. God, Norma: you don't want to hear the rest of it! One look, and my arms slackened a bit. I closed my eyes and looked away from the horror. Those women were saying consoling things to Sumbo, and I felt like screaming at them, Shut the fuck up, and stop brutalizing the poor child!

When she was done, Mrs. Adeloye rubbed some herbal cream between Sumbo's legs. Then she asked us to let go of her. I held on to Sumbo for a while longer, and kissed her cheek, to comfort her in her pain. Then I gently gave her to her mother.

I didn't stay in that room much longer. As soon as the door and window were thrown open, I excused myself. I didn't even look in Mrs. Fagbenro's direction when she thanked me for my help. *Help!* I had just helped them inflict untold pain on my little Sumbo, and I was being thanked for it? When I got outside, there was a film of water in my eyes and anger in my heart. I had taken the turn to my house, when I walked into Deji. He was pacing impatiently about, crying for his little sister. Seeing him hurt me even more. I'd never seen him cry before—he's the kind who'd never let you see him in such a state. I snatched him up and held him to my chest so he wouldn't notice the tears in my eyes. I took him into my house to let the pain, *our* pain subside. Poor Deji....To think that, behind all that smug posture, there's a tender little heart for his kid sister after all!

We've been back to school about three weeks. Though I've tried to put that experience behind me, I can't blot the picture of Sumbo's bleeding out of my mind. I vividly recall the initiation I was put through some months ago, which was designed, as I pointed out, to purify me against acts of blood and death. But I remember how I flinched, even in my dazed state, at being forced to kill a poor dog. I hope Ogun, the patron god of the cult and of the weapons used in drawing blood, will appreciate how much worse I felt when I had to participate against my will in the cutting of a little girl. Mind you, I'm not so arrogant as to condemn the practice of female circumcision outright. Though I can't defend the fear of female sexuality that might well be part of its logic, the Yoruba must have reasons other than sex for keeping the ritual alive as long as they've done. Still, growing up in a different culture makes it more difficult for me than for most home-grown Yoruba to accept this tradition without question.

You asked how much longer I'm going to be here. Taking part in the circumcision and seeing Sumbo bleed and cry makes me even less certain about it and more anxious to see you when I come home for Xmas.

Love,
Akimbowale

November 12, 1965

Dear Mom and Dad,

Welcome back from Brazil, dad. I find your report on the strong survival of Yoruba culture there very interesting. Forgive me if I don't greet it with the enthusiasm it would deserve under different circumstances. Here's what has happened.

Let me begin with the scenario of your visit some three months ago. Sure, you made a great impression here. After you got here, you paid the Baale a visit, greeted him with the honor his position deserved, then gave him the gifts you'd brought for him—one case of Johnny Walker whisky, and another of Gordon's Dry Gin, a large flowing silk robe with gold trimmings, with a hat to match, and other items that kept the smile on his face throughout our call. You also brought fine gifts for Awo Akinwunmi and, to my great delight, for the Fagbenros and their kids. Ireti still says to thank mom for the wonderful clothes she brought for her baby. You both, along with Norma and Dr. Fishbein, did a great job at the terminal dance for the twins. A few days later, the Baale made dad a chief with the title of *Atebishe* (recreator of his family). What a great tribute! In response, dad gave a short speech, which I translated to the Baale, saying how glad he was to be recognized as a son of Ijoko-Odo, what a great honor had been done to our family, etc. Dad promised that, in appreciation of the honor, we would build a house on our family's homestead to preserve its memory. Everybody applauded the gesture. So we could say that nearly everybody here loves us. Right? Sorry, *wrong!* We've been so busy trying to do what we judged to be our duty, we've overlooked the subtle politics of our presence here. Now it's all out in the open!

Five days ago, Pa Fadipe was found lying dead on the streets not far from his house. In the dim light before dawn, a palmwine tapper cycling to his trees braked suddenly to avoid running over a body lying by the roadside. On stepping down from his bicycle and turning over what he thought was a drunken man, he raised an alarm. Neighbors ran to the spot. People were still wondering what had happened to the poor old man when, the very next day, the attention shifted to me. Awo Akinwunmi paid me a surprise visit at our staff room. When I asked him what the matter was, he simply asked me to come along with him. He never said a word as we walked, he just kept shaking his head and moaning under his breath. We were just a few yards from the premises of the twins, only recently laid to earth there, when I was shocked to a standstill: our memorial building, which had been built up to its lintel, was no longer standing. When we finally got there—Jesus! The whole structure, blocks, bricks, doors, windows, every little thing was flat on the ground. I couldn't speak, my mouth was hanging open. I looked at Awo. He was still shaking his head and moaning, hand against cheek. A small crowd had formed at the scene before we got there. Some of them condemned the act as a desecration of the graves of *iya wa meji.*

Awo took me to his house. Here's how he broke it all down to me. He hadn't told me what happened earlier on to Pa Fadipe, because he feared I'd be worried. But he'd been told by one of the councillors who attended a meeting at the Baale's residence, some two weeks ago, that certain councillors had questioned our real intent in building a house here, especially so soon after the death of the twins. In the debate that followed, Pa Fadipe, who was resting as usual on the mud stoop, raised his voice and asked Baale Osunkunle, Since when has it become a crime for anyone to build a house in his family's compound? After all, doesn't the land belong to them? They said they were going to build a memorial house: Did they say they were going to live in it? Why don't you come out and tell us your real fear, Baale Osunkunle? The meeting didn't last much longer, Akinwunmi said. But the Baale did not forget the affront. Akinwunmi asked me, Do you still wonder what the connection is between Pa Fadipe's death and what happened to your house? Remember, Alagba, I did not say anything.

I was about to rise and bid him goodnight, but he motioned me to wait. He went into an inner chamber. After a long while, he returned to me in the consulting room. In his hand he had a calabash saucer containing a greenish paste he was stirring with a thin, flat blade. When he was through stirring, he said to me, Alagba, please listen to me. I am going to make some marks on your chest and rub this medicine into them. Before I could raise an objection, he said to me, Please, please! You don't know my people as much as I do. I am only doing this for your protection, you have nothing at all to be afraid of. I know how you feel about these things. Just let me do what I know is good for you. Please.

Taking off my dashiki, I bared my chest to him. The hairs made it difficult to locate a spot for his incisions. So he parted them each time he began to bring down his blade. He mumbled certain words as he made the incisions, but again I had no interest in listening. The marks *hurt!* I wondered if he'd taken time to disinfect the blade before making his cuts. But it was too late to ask, so I let him carry on. I didn't even look down to see the marks. I thought I'd seen enough bloodletting to last me a while. Honestly, I was *not* at all comfortable with this whole process. If anybody but Awo had offered to do it for me, I'd have said, No thank you, find someone else! But I respected and trusted Awo deeply. I was sure whatever he was doing was well intended. When he was done, he smeared the paste over the cuts. The paste didn't cause me any pain—perhaps my body had hurt all it could from the cutting. I thanked Awo and put my dashiki back on as he was seeing me to the door. He offered to walk me home, but I told him I'd be fine.

By the time I got home, news of the vandalism had gone round. People feared for my safety. Mr. Fagbenro offered to hire an armed night guard for my house, but I told him it wasn't necessary. Instead, I advised (and I did this reluctantly) that Sumbo and Deji sleep in their house for a while until the fears had died down. Later that evening, Chip's car pulled up in my front yard. He had a worried look on his face when he came in, saying the drummer (Olu) had just told him what happened. He wanted me to come right away and stay at his place, until the whole thing was over. Again, with apologies, I said, No. Since then, people have continued to stop me along the way and offer a kind word. Though I appreciate this, I'm getting quite tired of everyone feeling sorry for me. I've continued to sleep in my house, as I've always done, though my eyes are ever on the alert and I keep a machete by my side. So far, no one has made any moves against me. I hope I'll never have to use the machete. Two nights ago, I heard something fall outside my bedroom. I crouched quickly under the window, machete in hand. But nothing happened. Next morning, when I walked over to check for footmarks, I found the sound I'd heard was only a breadfruit dropping. There's been nothing else since then.

Your guess is as good as mine who's responsible for the damage to our house. Awo Akinwunmi suggested the Baale had a hand in it. He may be right, and I agree the death of Pa Fadipe is no mere coincidence. But I'm not ruling out Crabs. Since my last confrontation with him, he has been ignoring me, even when I look at him to say hello. He hasn't said one word to me (although nearly everyone else in the school has) about the damage to our house. His silence is probably part of his own general hostility toward me. But, considering what Awo told me about his political interest, I suspect he is as much to blame for the cowardly act as Baale Osunkunle may be. He *knows* my eyes are on him. That's good enough for me. Besides, I'm no longer as naive as I was when I first got here about the conditions that caused my ancestor to be taken to America. I'm angry, yes, but what's the point in being angry at little people like Crabs?

I'm preparing my teams for the year-end sports meet with Chip's school, so let me cut this short. First, I'll be meeting tomorrow with our building contractor, Philip Ashaolu, to decide what to do next, now that our building plans have been jinxed. I'm not sure what to propose to him, nor do I know how you would respond to my proposal. My off-the-cuff reaction is to pay him off for the work he's done so far, say 3,000 pounds. That's quite generous. I'll tell him we're suspending our plans until we can get to the bottom of this mess. The money should help him pay off his workers and give him a tidy margin of profit. Then we can give ourselves a breather and decide if this project makes any more sense. I can't see any other way out.

Here's what we need to do. We must take a close look at the political side of our commitment to this village, something we have taken too lightly thus far. I'm not saying this village is no longer the home of our ancestors. But we can no longer afford to be content with a romantic attachment to our *roots*, when some people here have shown, with very clear signs, that they have reservations about our presence. Again, I'm not certain what decisions we need to make. But we must open our eyes very wide and assess the evidence before us.

Mom, I know you're worried. But please trust me. I'm fine. And I'll *definitely* be home for Xmas.

Love,
Otis Akimbowale

December 16, 1965

Dear Mom, Dad, Norma,

I really don't have much time to write. But I thought I should do it before the Xmas mail congestion makes it hard for this letter to get to you. You'll be shocked to hear this from me, I know. But I'm sorry. I won't be home for Xmas after all.

Here's why, and I'll make it short. In the past few weeks, I've done some hard thinking about recent events and taken a decision. It's become absolutely clear to me that there's a strong connection between Pa Fadipe's death and the destruction of our house. So how would it look for me to simply pack up and return to America? Our family was dishonored by evil-doers a long time ago. By the grace and power of our ancestral spirits some members of the family were kept alive, well beyond the natural course of things, just so I could reconnect with them and restore the glory of the family. And now the same criminals who were responsible for dis-membering our family are up to their old game, making life impossible for everyone including ourselves, and all I do is run back to America? What good would it do that we have reconstituted our family and restored its honor, only to leave firmly in control forces that would ensure we never return to this village we call our home, even for a visit? And would it not be selfish on our part to take from this village the joy of our recovered roots, only to leave the people here, *our* people, in continued fear of their lives? After all, in returning to this village we set in motion a chain of events into which they've been drawn—and now we are leaving them to cope with it on their own?

Sorry, but I just couldn't deal with that. After I paid Philip Ashaolu for his work on the house, I sat down in my house to do a whole lot of thinking. Just before the end of November I paid Awo Akinwunmi a visit. Of course, he's a man who doesn't like any kind of trouble. So I was very careful in framing my questions to him regarding the feelings of our people about the present state of affairs, and especially toward Baale Oshunkunle and his administration. To cut a long story short, a lot of people are *very* angry now—not just with Oshunkunle but with his entire clan, including Crabs, that has dominated the lives of the village for too long. Again, to cut a long story short, I'm having a meeting early tomorrow morning in Akure—away from Ijoko-Odo, for obvious rea-sons—with those two councillors (Atilade and Kupoluyi) who took us to the home of *iya wa meji* the day we arrived in this village. They're now among the fiercest opponents to Oshunkunle's leadership. The mood in the village now is clearly for a new administration. I'll save you the details. But this village has done our family good. We should do it good in return.

Please have no fears about me. I enjoy considerable goodwill in this place, and I intend to use it wisely. I'll not be home for Xmas. But if things move at a pace that matches the mood of the people now, you may be seeing me not that long after Xmas.

Love,
Akimbowale

January 14, 1966

Dear Mom, Dad, Norma,

I've just had my flight to the U.S. confirmed: I'll be arriving in about two weeks, on the 29th. Things have moved pretty fast since just after the new year. I've settled my commitments with Bigelow's office and the high school, and I'm putting my things together in preparation for leaving. It's crazier than you can imagine.

Baale Oshunkunle is out of here. Not just him, but the entire Adebona clan, including Crabs. The Baale wouldn't open investigations on the death of Pa Fadipe and the destruction of our house. So his council, which had already too many scores to settle with him, demanded that he abdicate his post. He refused, and that sealed his fate. There's too much to tell, so I'll cut to the chase. A few meetings were held here and there. Early on the morning of January 3rd, a band of youths surged to the Baale's residence with clubs and fire-brands, and razed it to the ground. He'd gotten wind of the plot, so he and his household fled the village shortly before the youths descended on the palace. Some blood was shed, I'm sorry to say. A younger brother of Crabs's named Ajala—a dropout and thug popularly called "Ajasco"—was killed in a standoff with the rampaging youths. Crabs's house was also burnt down. He'd escaped with his family the night before. You'll hear *everything* from me when I return.

The village council has chosen a new Baale. Someone very much to my liking: Chief Olu Adegboye, the man who initiated me into the cult of strongmen in preparation for the ceremony I did with the twins. A man of unimpeachable reputation and good family, he was judged to be the best qualified (in the final list of candidates) for the task of putting the village on the right path after the long dark reign of the Adebona line. He'll be installed early in March. I think he'll do a good job. A week ago, when he heard I was making plans to return to the U.S., he visited me and pleaded that I stay—how could I afford to leave now, when the village needed me the most? I said I was sorry, I'd have to return to America first and gather my thoughts. But I certainly have no wish to remain here. I've paid my dues, and might be pushing my luck by staying here much longer. Chip thinks I'm copping out. I told him he was entitled to his opinion.

So I'll see you in two weeks. My only worry now is, how do I tear myself away from my most cherished company here—Sumbo and Deji, the Fagbenro kids?

Love
Akimbowale.

Boston
March 25, 1966

Dear Chip,

I feel like an idiot taking so long to drop you a line, and I'd perfectly understand if you thought of me as one. How could I forget all you and Ireti did to make my departure painless, especially driving me all the way to Lagos for my flight? How can I begin to thank you for that, and so much more?

Let me try to give you some sense of the situation here that has claimed much of my time. First of all, the welcome I received from friends and relatives, first at Logan airport and later at our home in Quincy, was especially touching. I guess they were happy to see me in one piece after what I wrote to them about the destruction of our Ijoko-Odo house. My plane touched down in Boston about 6 p.m. But it wasn't until about 2 a.m. the next morning that I was freed by my mom and Norma to sleep. *Eight* hours of welcome and some more for jetlag! Plus, discussions later in the day with my dad, who had wisely let the women take all of me the first day. I'll tell you some of the issues that came up during my talk with my dad. They bear on thoughts I want to share with you here.

I've spent some time with my shrink, Fishbein. We've had a couple of sessions so far, not on the couch any more, thank God. It seems my experience highlighted for him an area that has been of marginal interest in his profession. He is determined to pursue it. In fact, he's making plans, and he has asked my permission, to take me with him to a meeting of the American Psychological Association coming up soon. I'm not sure about that, because I have several other things on my mind right now. For instance, I took time to reactivate my student status at Bradley University and get my bearings back on the campus. What a difference a year and a half made! Besides, making the switch from my schooling in the oral culture of Ijoko-Odo back to regular Western education—it's a whole different scene here. It has certainly been a rewarding experience seeing education, culture, etc. from another perspective. More on this later.

Let me say a little more about the welcome I received, then I'll share my reflections with you on Ijoko-Odo and what it has meant to me. Just over a week after I returned here, my mom requested a special welcome home service for me at our church. We're Baptists, though I never took church that seriously. I didn't want it, but my mother insisted. Though she had a great time when they visited Ijoko-Odo, as you recall, she has not entirely abandoned her view of Africa as heathen land. So we had the service. My dad played the piano, while my mom sang a very moving rendition of *Balm in Gilead*. Even *I* was moved! I guess she used the service to thank God for delivering her only son safely from the blight of pagan spirits and back to the light of Xtian civilization. Well, bless *her* God. She's had the good sense not to ask me to any more services!

However—and here comes the interesting part—later in the evening, I was treated to more music. We've always had a piano in our house, but the music I'd always heard my father play on it occasionally wasn't really *music* to my ears: classical European music, spirituals once in a while. Never anything that people like me would appreciate. So it came as a surprise to me to hear my dad play (you guessed it) jazz! He played *In a Sentimental Mood*, which I'd heard in your place. When he noticed I showed interest, he asked me whose work it was. I'd forgotten, so he said it was Duke Ellington. He even went over and pulled out the same LP by Duke and Coltrane you'd played me in your house. He went on to play other tunes by Trane, Miles Davis, Thelonious Monk, and a few other pieces. My father has actually been buying jazz LPs in recent times: such an amazing change! I asked him when he started taking a liking to jazz, and he said, well, he'd always had *some* interest in jazz, but it was never a *compelling* one. That's the way he put it.

All this was significant for me, Chip, for two reasons. First, there was a pleasant coincidence because Coltrane was billed to play at a club in

Boston. I thought it a great opportunity for me to come face to face with a force in today's black music that was introduced to me first by you and then by my own father. I did go to the concert with Norma and boy, was Trane everything you said he was! Giant made quite an impression on me at the Mbari Center in Ibadan. But Trane—he nearly blew me out of my mind. Such intensity, such concentration, such racy command of the keys! And the way he compelled the same qualities from his men, especially the drummer Rashied Ali—I'd never seen anyone lay it on those skins the way the guy did!

The second reason my father's—shall I say, rediscovered—interest in jazz is important to me is that I think you've had as much to do with it as with my own new-found interest in the music. You must have noticed this, from the way I started getting closer to your LPs and helping myself to them. I had also reported your lectures on the relations between jazz and African music in one of my letters home. Apparently my dad—and I confess he *has* been a terrific one to me—has come to embrace something that has played an important part in my cultural and spiritual growth in the last couple of years. So I'd like to take this opportunity, Chip, not only to thank you for all you did in advancing my appreciation of our cultural heritage but also to tell you that, whenever you are able to retrace your way to this side of the world, you are sure to find kindred spirits (or shall I say, *soul brothers*) in our home.

One more thing. Norma and I got engaged last Saturday. That's right—our romance is now official! Her older sister Verene was down here for the event from Binghamton, N.Y. (know where that is?). My mom and dad were very happy about the engagement. You remember my telling you about my experience at a Caribbean restaurant in Boston? After the engagement, we all (Mom and Dad, Verene, Norma, and I) had dinner there. And Guinea Man himself, the wild man from the Caribbean, was there too. Norma remained in touch with him during my stay in Ijoko-Odo. We sent him a special invitation to the dinner and requested he come with the same music he played during our first encounter. Well, this time I enjoyed the music, maroon songs from Jamaica. So it seems my world has come full circle, after all. And I'm pleased about being engaged to Norma. I found a good woman, and I wanted her to know it. When do we take the next step? I don't really know. It certainly is on our mind. But right now, we've both got work to do.

One more thing occupying my attention I'm sure you'll want to know about. When I went to Ijoko-Odo in '64, I still had some of those crazy notions and fears that Americans generally have about Africa: Tarzan, people living on trees, etc. Besides, being raised in a black middle-class family, there was some embarrassment about identifying with Africa, for all sorts of silly reasons. In time, however, and I have you and Awo Akinwunmi to thank for this, I came to appreciate the amazing sophistication of African traditions in everything from the arts to philosophical thought to human relations. I had gone to find my family's roots in Africa. To do that successfully, I had to work my way through language and other activities into those deeply buried levels of culture that provide a basis for family as a unit of social relations. What I found there shook the very foundations on which my outlook as a child growing up in Western society had been built.

So it comes as a shock to me to return to my university and enroll in courses—and read text books—that describe Africa as a *primitive* society, a society said to be without history until Europeans got there! I'm not saying I find this in all the books we've read. But there's enough distortion to get one really worked up. Not only that. In all the course lists I've examined, there's not *one* devoted specifically to Africa, nor is there any book by an African scholar or writer. Yet there are many African scholars and writers today: at least I can speak of Nigeria, though I've come across some works from elsewhere on the continent. These people have written works that give us a better view of their societies than we've become accustomed to reading. You and I certainly met some of the writers at the Mbari Center—Soyinka, Clark, Okigbo, etc. And I remember what Jim Meredith told us about the new approach to writing African history at Ibadan University, where oral traditions were being used for reconstructing the African past. So, how come we hear so little about the work of these African intellectuals? It makes you wonder: Are their achievements being suppressed for the same reason the civilizations of old Africa were treated with scorn—to justify the domination and enslavement of black people?

There's a growing sense in campuses across the U.S. (and it's part of the civil rights revolution) that it's time to overhaul the American higher education system to reflect the history and culture of black peoples and the contributions they've made to the growth of American society in particular and mankind in general. There's a strong movement on at U-Mass, Amherst. In my college, I'm part of a caucus that's arranging a number of activities.

We've drawn up a list of black leaders and artists to be invited to speak here: Leroi Jones, Stokely Carmichael, Dick Gregory, etc. Also, the word is out about my African experience. So I'm scheduled to speak about Africa at a black student rally to be held in my university next week. If I've learned my lessons well, I must remember to see this as an opportunity to join my people in the search for truths that have been hidden from us too long.

Why have I written at length about our struggles here? I remember you telling me that your decision to make your home in Iludun was a result of choices you made because of the circumstances you found yourself in—or words to that effect. I believe the same could be said of the situation I found myself in at Ijoko-Odo, about which you know very well. You were there on our first day in the village, and you saw Baale Osunkunle's reluctance to welcome us and identify our family. You also know how hostile my fellow coach (Mr. Dipeolu) was toward me, and the subtle politics surrounding my presence in the village. When my house was destroyed by persons still unknown, you and I had our fears about what that meant both for my personal safety and for my family's commitment to our roots.

Well, we managed to take care of all this. I settled the family business that brought me to Ijoko-Odo in the first place. And though I'm not proud of the violence (especially the loss of life) that sent Baale Oshunkunle, "Crabs" Dipeolu, and the rest of their discredited clan into exile, I'm glad I played some role in the restoration of order and justice to the leadership of the village.

You thought I was copping out in not accepting the role offered me by the new Baale, our friend Olu Adegboye. But, given all the politics that surrounded my presence in the village, what good would my staying have done? Mind you, I will return sometime to rebuild our house there. We owe it to ourselves to keep our roots alive in Ijoko-Odo, even if only in the form of a hall we intend to donate to the new administration as a public memorial, to be called Itayemi Hall. But I have never desired a political role in the village, and I certainly have no wish to set us up as a target for future political antagonism. Let those who have spent all their lives in Ijoko-Odo take care of its political future. We are happy to identify ourselves with the history of the village, and to have made a contribution to its present welfare. But it's best for us to leave the administration of Baale Adegboye to organize the affairs of Ijoko-Odo without the presence of people like us who may send the wrong signals to certain political quarters.

Am I copping out? No, I don't think so. There's an Ifa line that says, *Ma ja, ma sa ni aimo akin* (Not knowing when to fight or run means not knowing the true meaning of courage). In other words, as we say in the West, discretion is the better part of valor. In thinking about the destruction of our house, I've come to the conclusion that there may be more than political interest behind that act. Think about it, Chip. What right did I really have to expect things to remain the same in the village after more than a hundred years? Times change. There's a new pattern of relations not only in Ijoko-Odo but in Nigeria as a whole. Though I had no political aspirations in the village, I needed to be careful about staking any claims my ancestors would scarcely have thought about twice. The burning may be not so much an affront to my person as a symbolic message aimed at the likes of me. The lesson I've come to learn from it is simply this: However sentimental our attachment to the concept of Africa, we blacks from this part of the world must learn to accept that the Africa of today is not exactly the same as the Africa of our ancestors. Sometimes when I listen to people in our movement talk about Africa, I just shake my head!

Far from copping out, I've chosen for now to divert whatever fight is in me to a different cause. Of course I'm home, where I should feel comfortable—among family, friends, and loved ones. But a lot has happened in the nearly two years I've been away, and I can't pretend I'm the same person I used to be. Before I went to Africa, I could have shrugged off the agitation for Black Studies as just another nuisance by troublemakers: I was so obsessed with my future in basketball, I couldn't look beyond my sporting nose! But I did go to Africa. What I learnt there has made it difficult for me to fold my arms while other people continue with the same tactics that caused our people to lose a sense of themselves. Mind you, I could make lots of money playing basketball. Oh yes, I saw my old coach recently. He wants me back in the team—Tiger, he called me, like they all used to! Well, I *have* grown, and I found my real name. There's a war on, and I've no illusions what side I'm on. We want nothing less than to establish a program on this campus that recognizes, respects, and projects the history and achievements of black people within the structure of American education. This is a fight I do not hesitate to join.

Speaking of fights, there's one that's been raging in my heart since I started making plans to return to the U.S. You know very well how much it hurt me to take leave of the Fagbenro children. I finally had the courage to write their parents three days ago. They were so instrumental to whatever comfort I enjoyed in Ijoko-Odo, it was hard to know where to begin thanking them. What you did not see, before you and Ireti came to pick me up, was how stubbornly Sumbo stuck to my side. She had long suspected there was something fishy going on: I just didn't know how to break the news of my leaving to her. She had to be literally pried from my leg by her mother (who herself had tears in her eyes) so she could go to school that morning. Even though I promised I'd come back soon, Sumbo was too upset by the mere thought of my going away to trust any promises. Deji took it hard too. But he didn't raise quite so much hell. Bless him and his gentlemanly ways!

The really tough part came when Sumbo told me she wanted to go with me to America. Of course I'd give anything to have Sumbo in my life forever—she's such a sweet kid. And it would cost me nothing to bring her here and have my mom raise her as her child. But two thoughts crossed my mind. First, if my own upbringing is any guide, every child should be raised by its own parents. Parents bring children into the world. Over time, they learn to strike the right balance between love and firmness; foster parenting should only be an unavoidable option. The second thought is closely tied to this. What if Sumbo found herself a victim of the racial prejudice that has ruined so many black children in America? What would happen to her, having been removed from an environment where she enjoyed every possible comfort, protection, self-assurance, *pride*? In one of the courses I'm taking right now to fulfill my humanities requirement, we read a poem by Ralph Waldo Emerson, where he laments taking a bird from the woods and putting it in a beautiful cage; he thinks it's a shame to remove the bird from a world in which it fitted so well. I felt much the same way about Sumbo, though I'm no happier now than if I'd acted differently. So, Chip, if there's anything you and Ireti could do to lessen the pain of my absence for her, I'd truly appreciate it.

I hear you asking, Will you ever return to Ijoko-Odo? Well, that depends on what happens here. First, I hope to finish college in the fall and that events don't intervene to mess up my schedule. Though I talk about *fighting* for Black Studies, I have no plans to use anything but peaceful means. My friends frequently invoke Malcolm X's phrase *by any means necessary*. I have reservations about that approach. But, of course, we know the forces we're dealing with, so we cannot rule out confrontation. So long as we recognize that our cause is just, we have no need of tactics that will reduce ours to a fight of dishonor. The second thing that might affect my decision to return to Ijoko-Odo is Norma's plans. As you know, she's all about Africa. Her visit to the village has fired her zeal to go to Africa for research; she has, in fact, made contact with Ibadan University. True, like me, she was hurt by the destruction of our house. But if things sort themselves out all around—the dust settles in Ijoko-Odo, we make progress in our fight for Black Studies, and (yes!) our relationship survives time and its stresses— you definitely will see us in the village again.

Excuse me if I've given you the impression I'm on the horns of a dilemma. But there must be some strength to be derived from balancing two types of commitment—to Africa on the one hand, to America on the other. You know, I've not stopped pondering the meaning of those double lines on the amulet I wear round my neck. If our people's metaphysical thought is anything to go by—and I don't for once doubt that it is—then Akimbowale's ori must have known, when he helped Olodumare design his destiny, that it was headed for a double path. What he would have done had he found out what that *other* path was, I have no way of knowing. Would he have sought a babalawo to help him reverse his destiny? Would he have continued with it, convinced that the future of the race would be larger than its past, and that someone in the family would help it brace up to the fortunes of history? I recently came across an essay by W.E.B. DuBois where he talks about the double consciousness of black people in America. If I'm truly on the horns of a dilemma, let's just say that my predicament has a respectable ancestry, at least in his thought!

Please give my warmest regards to the incomparable Ireti and to your son, Ben Omolere. I miss them a lot. I'll write Tim as soon as I can—he *is* a good man. And how can I forget our dear friend the drummer, Olu Faboya, who helped me realize a key component of my mission? By the way, you should have seen the look on my mother's face at Boston airport when I landed with the *dundun* drum hanging from my shoulder. She gave me a guardedly warm embrace! I struck the drum to assure her all was well now. I invited her to touch it, but she wouldn't. Only after my dad beat it with a confident hand did she come close enough to touch it with the tip of one finger. I suspect the church service might have been intended to expel once and for all whatever demons the drum brought with it!

Take care of yourself, Chip, and keep the faith! I'd like to think you let my team win that final game against yours—though my boys did put up a good fight, even if I say so myself. Finally, now you've drawn me into jazz, remember: If you ever want me to send you anything (LPs, jazz magazines, you name it), all you need do is ask.

Peace, my brother.

Otis Akimbowale

Boston
April 22, 1966

My dear Awo,

Omo Odudu! Omo Abebejoye! [14] I know you would want me to begin this letter by hailing some of your oriki. It is the proper thing to do. I hope you receive my salute in good health, and that your family enjoys good health with you.

If you are wondering why it took me so long to get in touch, you should remember how hard it was for me to say goodbye to you. Writing you would be accepting that you and I are now separated, which is also hard for me to do. I have other reasons related to problems of fitting into life here again, after being away for nearly two years. But none of these reasons is as painful as having to part from you and from Ijoko-Odo at all.

Let me say that, though I was sad about what happened to my house, you prepared me well for understanding the background to the incident. So I am not as angry now as I would have been if I didn't know anything. Also, because you prepared me so well, I avoided making the mistake of thinking the whole town was against me, when only a few people were to blame. At any rate, now that Alagba Adegboye has been unanimously chosen to replace Oshunkunle as Baale, I am happy that Ijoko-Odo has returned to the democratic system it had used to choose its head in the past.

Awo Akinwunmi, I suspect you will ask: Now that sanity is finally returning to our community, will you ever return here? I believe you would also be the first to advise me to follow the advice of Ifa and exercise patience over the whole matter, even if my own father were to be installed Baale of Ijoko-Odo. Whether I will return to Ijoko-Odo is not in doubt, the question is when. You can be sure that when the right time comes, I will not hesitate to revisit the land of my fathers. What is more important is that the village will no longer live in fear of a few men holding power that should never have fallen into their hands in the first place. When a community is happy as a whole, those of its members who happen to be living outside it should rejoice with it, and not lament that they are not physically present to share in its well-being. The village may, in fact, be the better for the fact that some of its citizens live outside. After all, it was you who taught me, in the words of Ifa, the value of gathering experience from as wide a field of life as possible: *Bi omo ko rin, omo naa kii gbon.*[15]

Awo Akinwunmi, I cannot end this letter without thanking you for the many gifts you gave me in Ijoko-Odo. It would be difficult to even begin to remember them, so I will try to mention just a few. By far the most precious of them is the gift of your friendship. I cannot imagine what a time I would have had in the village, if you had not taken me virtually by the hand from day one and led me through the steps I needed to follow to carry out my appointed tasks and be the person I am today. Without knowing me before, you made yourself available to me and took me as much into your trust as into your house, as a member of your household. So that, even though I had immediate family in *iya wa meji*, I considered you as much blood kin to me as they were. In every sense you were to me the kind of friend Ifa has spoken about:

B'ore ba ninurere l'a ninurere ju,
A da bi iyekan.[16]

In surveying the course of events that led me to Ijoko-Odo, it has become clear to me that I am a very lucky man. I was blessed with a good ori. That ori continued to press me to return to the home of my people. And it did not stop pressing me until it placed me safely in your hands. I don't think it was just an accident that you were the first citizen of Ijoko-Odo I saw on the day we arrived there *and* at the very place where I would perform the final rites for my ancestor! It must all have been prearranged by my ori, and you were there in its calculations. Can you see why I can never really be separated from you, no matter how far away from you I may live?

Awo Akinwunmi, in your company I learnt how important it is for one to pursue wisdom and to constantly seek to improve one's knowledge. Every day that I treaded in your footsteps brought me to appreciate the joy of expanding my store of knowledge. And yet it was not enough to accumulate knowledge, like one picking palm nuts from the ground. I also came to understand that life is all of a piece, that knowledge of one thing is not separate from knowledge of something else. The world did not come to us divided, and we have no right or power to make it so. For me this is a very valuable lesson, as I begin to live again in a country where many have sought to create divisions between our people.

Awo Akinwunmi, in the many conversations we held in our village, we touched very little on the condition of black people in America. This was because I was anxious to absorb as much of our people's culture as I could, considering the urgency of my mission. But you are surely aware that our people have been subjected to unimaginable injustices ever since they were forcibly brought here many centuries ago. Some changes have been made to the laws of this land, changes designed to guarantee that our people suffer no more of such injustices. Yet these changes are being rendered powerless by those who continue to treat us as both different from and inferior to themselves. But today, our people are determined to stand up and fight to ensure they have as much right as anyone else to live here, and to guarantee that the contributions they made to the growth of this nation and to the world are recognized. I am happy to count myself part of this struggle.

The provocations are many. Every day our leaders are thrown into jail; some are even killed. Only a week ago Norma and I were among a group of people arrested during a protest march and held in jail for a night. I have not fully recovered from the head wound inflicted by a policeman's club. I know that we are waging a fight of honor, and that you will join me in asking Ifa to give me the patience I need in my dealings with others, whoever they may be. But if the provocations I have spoken of mean I have no way of avoiding the dangers lying in my path, I am afraid I would be the last to refuse to answer the call of Ogun, whose patronage I have the honor of enjoying.

My dear Awo, I shall conclude by returning to the matter of my house and directly answering the question whether I will ever return to Ijoko-Odo. I went there because our ancestors summoned me to honor them and to repair the damage done to our family line by persons no longer known to us. On the death of the last of our direct line, *iya wa meji*, my father came over for rites ushering them into the company of our ancestors and offered to build a house on our land only as a memorial to our ancient line. Whatever the individuals who destroyed the house may have thought of our motives, for us the house was intended only as a symbol of our pride in a heritage that should never be erased. Should I fail to return and complete the house, it would mean that we have vainly answered the call of our ancestors and that the descendants of Akindiji, son of Itayemi, have spat on his grave. That, I know, you would not want me to do. So, look to see me some day in the falling dew.

Until then, my friend—

Emi ni yen

Otis Akimbowale Hampton

Omo jagunjagun alaya inaki.[17]

NOTES

[1]That leads the young hunter to ruin his gun

[2]Sir

[3]Please...wait, we'd like to ask you something.

[4]Isn't this Akin?

[5]Didn't I say so? It's Akin. This is Akin.

[6]Ah, come and look, Kehinde. This is him.

[7]Our (older) brother has come home!

[8] *The Evidence for Survival from Claimed Memories of Former Incarnations: The Winning Essay of the Contest in Honor of William James* (Tadworth, UK: Peto, 1964 [1961]).

[9]Orunmila says: However long it takes, the dispenser of justice will return yet again.

[10]Translation of the reconstructed chant is on page 259 below.

[11]Save me! O, save me!

[12]Whoever is in charge of affairs, should work for the good of all. Should the charge fall on you, bear it for the good of all.

[13]See page 259 for translation.

[14]Son of a stocky man! Son of a man who had to be begged to accept a chieftaincy title!

[15]If a child does not move around, it cannot become wise.

[16]If a friend shows extraordinary kindness, he is like one's sibling.

[17]It's me...Son of a warrior with the chest of a gorilla.

ISIDORE OKPEWHO

TRANSLATION OF *ORIKI* OF AKINDIJI

Akindiji! Akindiji! Akindiji o o o!
I hail you three times, son of Itayemi
He who bore three sheaves of arrows to war
Balogun, father of Akimbowale and the twins
Chest like a gorilla's, broad and bristling with hair
Who strode cheerily towards the enemy
With bare chest and grinning teeth
Whence to the end he sported a thousand welts
Husband of Ashake, father of Akimbowale and the twins
Scourge of the Tapa
"I will traverse the earth to snare the mole in his burrow!"
Son of Itayemi, barn sagging with yams
Balogun, chest like a gorilla's, man of peace and war
Paternally, he hailed from a long line of warriors
Maternally, he hailed from a long line of farmers
Scourge of the Tapa, son of Itayemi, man of peace and war.
Tapa Tapa, eji nana baabo
Taaapa, eji nana baabo
Tapa Tapa, eji nana baabo
Taapa, eji nana baabo!

Note: The last four lines are not Yoruba. They are ostensibly Tapa (Nupe) words and intended to mock the speech of the foreign invaders.

Acknowledgements

I would like to thank the following friends for their help in putting some flesh and form to this novel. Niyi Osundare has remained close to the story from its very conception at Ibadan University to its completion here in the U.S. Not only has he listened patiently to me talking about it again and again over the years, but he has graciously lent me a piece of his celebrated poetic genius by translating the *oriki* of Akindiji, the focal oral text of the narrative, into the appropriate Ekiti dialect of Yoruba. Niyi and I go so far back in our careers that he will probably consider this acknowledgment superfluous. But memories of old friendship are very much part of the fabric of the creative life. I'm certainly glad of this opportunity to record my appreciation of his enduring support of my efforts. Niyi, I told you I'd do something someday with those early forays into Yoruba oral poetry (*Oluyeyentuye...*)!

This novel represents my first effort in stepping outside my more familiar African terrain. I am especially grateful to two friends from the west-Atlantic side of the African world who read stages of the manuscript and offered invaluable comments on aspects of Afro-diasporic speech and behavior. Jay Wright, outstanding poet who has plumbed African mythology and cosmology in his work, was the first to read the original draft of the story and offer encouraging and helpful comments. Mike Thelwell of U-Mass Amherst has been extremely patient and helpful in reading successive drafts of the story. I am also grateful for his well-informed insights into the black revolutionary consciousness of the 1960s that forms part of the context of this story.

Other Yoruba friends have graciously answered questions I've asked them without knowing exactly why I've kept pestering them. Of these, I'm particularly grateful to Professors Jacob Olupona of UC-Davis, Roland Abiodun of Amherst College, and Oyekan Owomoyela of the University of Nebraska-Lincoln. If any errors of fact or interpretation are found in the story, it can only be because I failed to use their advice properly..

Finally, my family has given me the greatest possible moral and other support in this project. They read successive drafts of the manuscript and were more convinced than I was that this was a story that must be published. Bless their hearts!